BABY ON THE REBEL HEIR'S DOORSTEP

SOPHIE PEMBROKE

THE HEIR'S CINDERELLA BRIDE

DONNA ALWARD

MILLS & BOON

First published in Great Britain 2022
by Mills & Boon, an imprint of HarperCollins*Publishers* Ltd,
1 London Bridge Street, London, SE1 9GF

www.harpercollins.co.uk

HarperCollins*Publishers*
1st Floor, Watermarque Building,
Ringsend Road, Dublin 4, Ireland

Baby on the Rebel Heir's Doorstep © 2022 Sophie Pembroke

The Heir's Cinderella Bride © 2022 Donna Alward

ISBN: 978-0-263-30223-3

08/22

MIX
Paper from
responsible sources
FSC www.fsc.org **FSC™ C007454**

This book is produced from independently certified FSC™ paper
to ensure responsible forest management.
For more information visit www.harpercollins.co.uk/green.

Printed and Bound in Spain using 100% Renewable Electricity
at CPI Black Print, Barcelona

Sophie Pembroke has been dreaming, reading and writing romance ever since she read her first Mills & Boon as part of her English Literature degree at Lancaster University, so getting to write romantic fiction for a living really is a dream come true! Born in Abu Dhabi, Sophie grew up in Wales and now lives in a little Hertfordshire market town with her scientist husband, her incredibly imaginative and creative daughter and her adventurous, adorable little boy. In Sophie's world, happy *is* for ever after, everything stops for tea, and there's always time for one more page...

Donna Alward lives on Canada's east coast with her family, which includes a husband, a couple of kids, a senior dog and two zany cats. Her heart-warming stories of love, hope and homecoming have been translated into several languages, hit bestseller lists and won awards, but her favourite thing is hearing from readers! When she's not writing she enjoys reading—of course!—knitting, gardening, cooking...and she's a *Masterpiece* addict. You can visit her on the web at DonnaAlward.com, and join her mailing list at DonnaAlward.com/newsletter.

BABY ON THE REBEL HEIR'S DOORSTEP

SOPHIE PEMBROKE

MILLS & BOON

For everyone who has ever arrived home with a
new baby, then wondered what on earth you're
supposed to do next… (And for the next eighteen years!)

CHAPTER ONE

THE BALLROOM AT Clifford House was packed, wall to wall, with the great and good of local society. Lena Phillips glanced around the busy room and took in the familiar faces. Hmm. Also the less great and notoriously *not* so good, too, by her assessment. Although, in places as small as Wells-on-Water and Wishcliffe, she supposed hosts couldn't afford to be too stingy with the invitation list if they wanted a full house.

But it did mean her brothers were likely to be in attendance. Neither Gary nor Keith were ones to miss a free drink or a party, and she didn't believe for a moment that either of them would have been responsible enough to stay back and take care of The Fox, the family pub their father had left them when he died, two years ago.

She was almost surprised they hadn't asked her to cover for them. Perhaps after months of refusing to listen to any of her ideas on how to improve the place they'd assumed—correctly—that she'd turn them down flat. In the past, she wouldn't have. She'd never wanted to let her father down. But she had no such concerns about Gary and Keith. Well, hardly any.

She was worried about The Fox, though...

Helping herself to a glass of champagne from a passing waiter's tray—just one, she still had to drive home later—

Lena scanned the room again and began mentally cataloguing who she needed to speak to tonight, and in what order. She could see the Reverend Dominic Spade across the way by the terrace; she should collar him about holding the food bank at the church over the summer holidays, at least. But first she needed to speak to Trevor and Kathy about the news of the sale of the village hall and what it meant for their community hub. And she should probably try and find Paul Gardiner, the local estate agent, before that. See what information she could pry out of him…

Across the room she could see the party's hostess, Victoria Blythe—soon to be Clifford—mingling, a smile on her face, her hands resting on her pregnant belly. It was good to see; after the terrible loss of her husband and only son, Lena hadn't been sure that her friend would ever smile again. But it seemed that Finn Clifford had found a way to make her future bright.

She'd catch Victoria later, though. First she had village matters to attend to.

She couldn't spot Paul, and Rev Spade was standing a little too close to where Gary and Keith were holding court on the terrace for her liking, so Lena headed for the buffet table and Trevor and Kathy instead.

'Ah, Lena! Just the person I was looking for,' Trevor said as she joined them.

'You weren't looking for anything beyond the next of those mini sausage rolls.' Kathy snatched one of them from his plate and popped it in her mouth before he could object. 'You look lovely tonight, love.'

Lena glanced down at her shimmering blue dress, smoothing the fabric again over her hips, where it clung tight before falling all the way to the ground over her silver heels. 'Thanks.'

The mystery of Trevor and Kathy was one Lena had

never quite managed to solve, despite having known them both pretty much all her life. They weren't married, that much was certain—she'd checked the parish records to be sure—and they didn't live together, either. Instead, they occupied two adjoining terrace houses in a side street not far from the pub where Lena grew up, and were both regulars.

She'd never seen anything to suggest a romantic relationship between them, and they bickered far too much to be actual friends...and yet, they were nearly always seen together.

One day she'd figure it out. But today she had other priorities.

'I was looking for you two as well.' She eyed the buffet table. 'And maybe those duck spring rolls.'

Kathy grabbed her a plate, added several spring rolls, two sausage rolls, and a chicken satay skewer, then handed it over. 'Do you have news?'

Lena shook her head. 'I was sort of hoping you would. Nothing on the Save The Village Hall petition, then?'

'Apparently our "esteemed" local councillor has been telling everyone he speaks to that the hall was falling apart, and there was no money to repair the roof after it caved in, so selling it is the only option.' The expression on Trevor's face told Lena exactly what he thought of Councillor Morgan. She didn't entirely disagree.

'The biggest problem is that he's right.' Kathy sighed. 'The estimates on replacing the roof alone were astronomical, and it just wasn't getting enough use to warrant it. Even the local Brownies group decided to use the school hall instead, after the last storm. Brown Owl said there were more buckets than girls in there.'

'So they're just going to sell it for housing, like everything else around here.' The old cinema in Wishcliffe had been demolished and turned into flats five years ago, and even the Wells-on-Water Methodist chapel was now a *Grand Designs* transformation in progress.

'That's the talk,' Trevor confirmed, his voice glum.

'On the bright side, though, it looks like some of the money from the sale will go into the community funds account we set up as part of the charitable trust thing for the hall.' Kathy's face brightened as she spoke. 'So once it all goes through, we can start looking for a new location for the community hub project again.'

'That's good,' Lena said, although she couldn't quite find the same enthusiasm as Kathy. Whatever money they raised from the sale of the hall, it was unlikely to be enough to buy and pay for the upkeep of another property. Which meant renting, which would deplete funds even faster. She foresaw a lot of fundraising in her future.

Good thing that one of her main talents was sweet-talking the rich and privileged into supporting community projects. Well, that and running pubs. She was a woman of many talents, really—all of them unappreciated by her family.

But when something mattered to her, she didn't give up. And this village—and its people—mattered. So she'd find a way, as she always did.

'What we really need is a sponsor,' Trevor mused. 'Someone with the money and the inclination—or guilt… I'd take guilt—to make them want to do good deeds.'

'Guilt is very motivating,' Kathy agreed. Lena looked down at her plate and refused to think about her own motives. 'What about Finn Clifford, since we're here? Think we could hit him up for some contributions?'

'Probably,' Lena said, looking up to scan the room again in search of likely targets. 'But he's only just moved back here and he's got the baby on the way and the wedding to plan. We might get some money, but he's not going to be a figurehead or get properly involved or anything.'

'Besides, he's out here at Clifford House,' Trevor pointed out. 'Closer to Wishcliffe than Wells-on-Water. And for the community hub to be a success, we really do need someone connected to our community, don't we?'

Kathy hummed her agreement as, across the room, another figure caught Lena's eye, talking with their hostess. A tall, dark, brooding sort of a figure, he stuck out in the ballroom like a cactus in a rose garden. A large, prickly, unwelcome cactus.

He looks like...

The man turned, and Lena got a good look at his face, her eyes widening with recognition.

Never mind looked like. It *was*.

Even if she hadn't recognised his face, the way her heart suddenly beat double time would have given it away.

Quickly, she spun away, facing the buffet table again, suddenly very, very interested in the miniature Yorkshire puds with beef and horseradish.

But Kathy had already followed her gaze, it seemed. 'Now, there's a thought. Max Blythe. He's just inherited the Manor House, hasn't he? That's *definitely* Wells-on-Water territory, and by all accounts he's absolutely loaded. What do you think, Lena?'

I think if I never talk to Max Blythe again it'll be too soon.

'Perhaps,' Lena said, non-committally, trying to keep all the memories buried deep in her chest. 'What do you think about the halloumi fries? Too greasy?'

Kathy and Trevor ignored her attempts at canapé-based conversation.

'Heads up, ladies,' Trevor said. 'Victoria's got him in her grasp now. And they're heading this way.'

Max Blythe hated parties.

As a rule, he wasn't all that fond of gatherings, shin-

digs or social get-togethers in general. But he really didn't
like parties.

Even ones as deliciously catered and with such good li-
bations as the one Finn and Victoria were throwing tonight.

His problem wasn't with his hosts, who seemed like
perfectly nice and reasonable people. It wasn't even that
they'd invited him there tonight since it seemed they'd invited *everyone* in the vicinity and that now, rather unexpectedly, included him.

No, Max's issue with tonight's party in particular was
the Looks.

He didn't think there was a single attendee not guilty
of giving him one—unless, somehow, they hadn't spotted
him yet. A few people had tried to talk to him—or, more
likely, get some gossip out of him—but they'd all been
easily rebuffed. The rest…they just looked.

They said more with a Look than they could with words,
though. In every Look Max read a maelstrom of thoughts
and emotions.

Curiosity, of course, about why he'd returned to Wells-
on-Water after so many years, and about what his relationship with the Blythe family was now. Resentment or
disappointment from many who'd known him as a child.
Pity from some, probably those remembering his mother.
Anger from others, seeing where he'd managed to take his
life. Appreciation, from some female gazes—but that, at
least, was familiar from other settings, much as he tended
to ignore it. The fascination with his family, his history—
that was all particular to this area of the country. Wishcliffe and Wells-on-Water, the neighbouring small town
and village by the sea that had witnessed his miserable
childhood. The same place he'd vowed never to return to
after his mother's death.

Until Toby Blythe, Viscount Wishcliffe, had changed all that.

Max wasn't entirely sure how much his half-brother had made known to the general population of the area about his existence and why Toby had gifted him the Manor House at Wells-on-Water, but in his experience very little stayed secret in a place like Wishcliffe. And it wasn't as if anyone who'd lived in the area while he was growing up could have missed the pointed way his mother had named him Blythe, even if his father had never acknowledged him.

It was an open secret—and humiliation—in the community. Max was the illegitimate son of the old viscount, born between the two legitimate heirs, Barnaby and Toby. His mother had never tried to hide who he was, never denied it—in fact, she'd seemed to revel in forcing the uncomfortable truth on everyone.

You have to do what's right in this world, Max, even when it's hard, she'd always said. *And when it feels hardest, that's when it matters most.*

And it *had* been hard. His whole childhood, it had been unbearably hard. Dealing with all the sniggers behind his back that turned to all-out bullying as he grew older. The disapproving looks from the adults in the village, probably aimed more at his mother for 'flaunting her sin'—as one of them had put it once—than at him, but which still made him feel like a disappointment just for existing. And seeing, every single day, that huge house on the hill and knowing his father was up there with his two half-brothers, all pretending he didn't exist.

Was it any wonder he'd rebelled? Caused the kind of trouble that *made* people pay attention to him, rather than try to ignore his existence? That lived down to their every expectation of it?

Or that he'd run away as fast and as far as he could, as soon as sixth form was over?

He'd headed out into a world who didn't know or care who he was, and showed them who he could be without all that baggage hanging over him. He'd kept the surname—what else would he call himself after so long?—but outside Wishcliffe and Wells-on-Water the name Blythe didn't mean a damn thing to anyone. It was wonderfully freeing.

He'd made his fortune, made his own name, made his own life. And he'd been happy with it.

Until an email from Toby had turned everything upside down.

Now, here he was, back in the heart of Wishcliffe society, staring down all the looks and the disappointment again. Except, this time, he was there as Toby Blythe's brother. Rightful heir of the Manor House above Wells-on-Water village. His father might never have acknowledged him in his lifetime, but the old viscount's son had.

Max *belonged* now. Even if he still wasn't a hundred per cent sure he wanted to.

Not if it meant attending parties like this all the time, anyway.

'They'll get used to you soon enough,' Toby had said, when he and his new wife Autumn had invited Max to dinner the previous weekend. *'Forget you ever went away.'*

But Max didn't want them to forget. He wanted them to remember everything he'd achieved *in spite* of being the illegitimate son of Viscount Wishcliffe.

And more than anything, he didn't want anybody remembering the pathetic, lost and lonely boy he'd been before he moved away.

A movement across the room caught his eye—mostly because it was moving towards him. He steeled himself for another encounter with a local looking for gossip, before realising that it was actually his hostess approaching him.

Victoria Blythe made her way across the ballroom, her ever-growing belly clearing a path before her. Max couldn't help but smile; he'd met Victoria and her fiancé, Finn Clifford, at the Sunday dinner at Wishcliffe the weekend before and found his elder half-brother's widow to be both insightful and determined. Which was how she'd persuaded him to attend tonight in the first place.

'Max, they're going to talk about you whatever you do,' she'd said. *'At least if you're there it's harder for them to do it behind your back.'*

'Victoria,' Max said as she reached him. 'Thank you for inviting me tonight. You have a lovely home.' That sounded like the right sort of thing to say, didn't it?

She inclined her head to accept the compliment, so he assumed it was. 'Thank you for coming. I'm sorry my home is filled with such gossips.'

He chuckled at that, which made her smile.

'Why don't I find someone to introduce you to who probably won't ask you too many invasive questions?' she suggested.

'That would be nice,' Max replied cautiously, unsure that there *was* anyone in the room who wouldn't. But he couldn't exactly say, 'I'm happier standing here glaring at all your guests, thanks,' could he?

Victoria scanned the room for a moment, and then smiled in a way that made Max even more nervous.

'Perfect.' Taking Max's arm, she led him towards her target, as he wondered if there was still time to make a run for the door.

Then he realised exactly who Victoria was taking him to, and decided that diving out of the window would probably suffice. Anything except talking to—

But it was too late.

The blonde ahead of them, the one in the shimmering blue dress that clung to curves he remembered well, was already turning to face them. The older couple she was talking to began to fade backwards into the crowd around the buffet table, smiles on their lips.

'Max, let me introduce Lena Phillips. She's the manager of the King's Arms pub in Wishcliffe.'

Lena raised perfectly arched eyebrows in surprise, every inch the perfect class princess she'd been at school. 'Max Blythe. Really.'

Really what? Really there? Really daring to speak to her again? Really assuming she'd want to talk to him after their last…interaction, the night before he skipped town?

Max wasn't sure. So he just said, 'Apparently so. Hello, Lena.'

There wasn't much for it other than to brazen it out, Lena decided. Trevor and Kathy were already moving away towards the desserts table—traitors—and leaving her alone to face her doom. They probably assumed she'd be sweet-talking Max Blythe into donating squillions to set up some state-of-the-art community hub centre complete with computer access for those without it and a coffee shop with a ready supply of sausage rolls. When actually, she would just be trying to get the hell away from him as soon as possible.

Which would be easier if Victoria weren't standing right there watching them.

She needed to say something, Lena realised. Continue an actual normal conversation like normal people.

As if the last time she'd seen Max Blythe hadn't been minutes after he took her virginity in the back of his beaten-up car, then skipped town without looking back.

As if that one night hadn't changed the trajectory of her whole life.

At least he looked as shell-shocked at the unexpected reunion as she felt. He deserved to feel awkward and embarrassed. She didn't. *He* was the one who'd run out, after all. Well, run *first* anyway.

Victoria opened her mouth, obviously about to fill the uncomfortable silence, but before she could speak her fiancé, Finn, appeared at her side.

'Excuse me, Max, Lena, I just need to borrow my fiancée for a moment.'

'Borrow me?' Lena heard Victoria object as he steered her out of the ballroom. 'What am I? A phone charger?'

And then it was just her and Max. For the first time in sixteen years, since they were both eighteen and stupid.

'I didn't realise you'd be here tonight,' Lena said, not adding that she might not have attended herself if she had done. He'd guess that part, and it wasn't true, anyway. She'd have come—not to see him, but because of the networking opportunities Victoria's party offered. Because her life had nothing to do with him any more.

Lena hoped he got all that from her short, unimaginative statement.

Max gave her a crooked smile. 'You might be the only one here who didn't, then. Seems to me that the primary reason for attendance for most people was to stare awkwardly at me.'

'I think you'll find it was actually the sausage rolls,' Lena countered. 'They're surprisingly good.'

And you're not actually the centre of anyone's world, Max Blythe.

So many things she wanted to say to him. Curses and accusations and cutting remarks. Explanations and apologies, and the secrets she'd held tight to her chest for so long.

But she wasn't eighteen any more. At thirty-four, she'd learned to hold her tongue. To make nice, build bridges, charm people. Everything she needed to do for her business, and for her work in the community.

What she needed to do to make Wells-on-Water a better place. A place that eighteen-year-olds like they'd been didn't need to run away from in the first place.

But right now she wished she could be that young and careless again. A girl who hadn't learned to be so nice, yet. One who still said what she was really thinking.

Oh, who was she kidding? She'd never been that girl. Ever since her mother died when she was young, Lena had learned to say whatever she needed to say to keep everyone happy, to secure her place in the community, even if she was the daughter of a drunk and sister to two of the biggest troublemakers in the village.

'Sausage rolls?' Max looked hopefully over at the buffet table, just as Trevor popped the last one into his mouth.

Lena shrugged, feeling childishly pleased. 'You can't hang around at these things. You miss your chance and those sausage rolls are gone for ever.'

'I guess I'll have to wait for the next party,' Max replied, and Lena felt a jolt of uncertainty go through her.

'You're planning on staying around this time, then?' She cursed the words the moment they were out of her mouth. *Why* did she have to make reference to the *last* time they'd spoken? She'd wanted to pretend it had never happened at all. Or that if it had, she hadn't thought about it since. Now that was blown out of the water.

And she could tell from the surprise in Max's eyes, and the slow smile that followed, that he knew exactly what she'd been thinking about.

'Well,' he said, slowly, 'Toby did give me an entire house. Seems a shame to waste it.'

Since the house in question was closer to a mansion, Lena couldn't exactly disagree. Which didn't mean she wouldn't try.

'I'm just surprised you'd want it,' she said. 'I seem to remember you being quite adamant about getting the hell out of Wells-on-Water, and Wishcliffe, and never coming back.'

'That was a long time ago,' Max replied. 'I like to think I've grown up a bit since then.'

And boy, had he. The Max she remembered at eighteen had been darkly handsome, with the same dark brown eyes under his black hair, but he hadn't been *built* like the man in front of her was. At eighteen he'd been lanky and gorgeous, but Max Blythe at thirty-four looked…dangerous. From the broad, broad shoulders to the way his chest filled out his dinner jacket, and how those golden-brown eyes glittered with more than just a promise tonight. Tonight, they held knowledge of the world, and a cynicism that even Max at eighteen hadn't been able to match.

In short, he'd grown up. And he'd grown up *well*.

Of course, Lena liked to think she had, too. She might not be quite the perky blonde teenager he'd left behind, but she'd replaced that youthful enthusiasm with plenty of things she valued more. Self-knowledge, for one. And a daily yoga routine that kept her both toned *and* less stressed.

'We've all grown up,' she murmured, and watched as that dark gaze scanned the length of her, from her highlighted hair to the high heels on her feet, taking in the carefully chosen dress on the way. She looked good tonight and, seeing Max again, she was damn pleased she'd made the effort.

Except she always made the effort, and she made it for herself, not for him or anyone else.

She could feel the tension, the attraction, shimmering

between them, the same way it had that last night. Then, it had been a shock—something utterly unexpected. Now, it felt different. Part familiar, inevitable even. But part new, because they weren't eighteen-year-old innocents any longer.

Now, they both knew what the deal was. What they could have, if they wanted it.

She met his gaze, and knew that Max felt it too.

Then his attention jerked away, to something happening behind her. Lena glanced back over her shoulder and suppressed a groan at the sight of her two brothers trying to toss profiteroles into each other's mouths.

'Well, most of us have grown up,' Max amended, and with a wince, Lena nodded her agreement.

'I should probably…' She trailed off with a vague wave towards Gary and Kevin. Typical that they'd ruin the first interesting interaction she'd had with a man in years.

Max raised one eyebrow. 'Why? They're adults, aren't they? Not your responsibility.'

'Maybe not. But—' But what? He was right, damn him. They *weren't* her responsibility, even with both their parents gone. Hell, they were even older than she was. And yet, she knew that everyone in this room would expect her to step in, hand them both some coffee, and keep them out of trouble until they sobered up. Just as she had every other time in living memory.

God, she was sick of it.

Taking care of the community was one thing. Being responsible for her feckless, thoughtless and immature brothers was another.

'I say, leave them to it and come out onto the terrace with me, where we can have a proper catch-up. I mean, it's been a long time, Lena. I'd love to hear what you've been up to.'

Oh, this was exactly how he'd got her into that car sixteen years ago. That hint of a promise in his voice, the one that offered to take her away from all the things about her life that drove her crazy.

And she'd fallen for it, and then he'd left. And she'd been alone for everything that came next.

But this time…this time she was an adult. In charge of her own life. She could leave any time she wanted. And all he was suggesting was a conversation on the terrace, where she didn't have to watch her idiot brothers embarrass themselves—and, by proxy, her. If she wanted it to lead anywhere else…it would be up to her.

'Okay,' she said, and he smiled as she headed for the door, knowing he would follow.

Just a conversation. And this time, it would be Lena who walked away at the end of it. Or didn't.

CHAPTER TWO

OF ALL THE people Max had expected to reconnect with on his return home, Lena Phillips hadn't been one of them. Oh, not because he'd forgotten about her, or because he'd hoped to avoid her. He just simply hadn't imagined for a moment that she'd still be there.

She'd always claimed that she loved Wells-on-Water too much to leave, had told him so even that last night they'd spent together. But she'd also always shone so bright, so vibrant, he'd just assumed there would be some more exciting future out there for her somewhere.

And now he had an opportunity to find out why she'd never left, the way he had.

He pushed the terrace door shut behind them, hoping for a tiny bit of privacy, although glancing along the stone space outside the row of glass doors, all open to the ballroom, that seemed unlikely. The warm summer evening air had tempted plenty of other partygoers out onto the terrace, where they lingered by the sweet flowering roses that climbed the stone latticework between the gardens and the house. But there was enough clear space between their dark corner and the crowds that Max felt confident they should be able to speak in relative privacy.

But Lena was already looking back through the glass into the ballroom at the clownish antics of her brothers.

That wasn't what he wanted here at all, so Max slipped between her and the door to block her view.

She refocussed on him and smiled—but it was one of those smiles that didn't quite reach her eyes. A sharp, polite, society smile.

He didn't like it.

Lena's smile was something he remembered most from before. She was always smiling at someone or something, always keeping the peace and lightening difficult situations. Even those smiles had felt more real than this one.

But the smile he really wanted to see was one he'd only ever seen once before. That last night, at the party by the river to celebrate the end of sixth form, the end of their official school careers, before everyone left for university or work or whatever life held for them.

The secret smile she'd saved only for him, as they'd left their classmates getting drunk on the riverbank and escaped to the privacy of his new-to-him fourth-hand car...

He'd thought, when he'd spotted Lena across the room, that she was the last person he wanted to see in this place. But remembering that smile, he couldn't help but wonder if she was the *only* person he wanted to see.

'So,' Lena said, that sharp smile still in place. 'You wanted to talk about what's happened over the last sixteen years? Why don't you start? You were heading to London, I seem to recall, the last time we spoke?'

She didn't mention that she'd been half naked in the back seat of his car when he told her that. Curled up in his arms, a summer breeze floating in through the half-open window. The sex had been a little awkward—although still mind-blowing for him, as an eighteen-year-old virgin. But the conversation afterwards had been strangely comfortable, given how little the two of them had talked in the years before.

'London, yeah.' He shook the image of her eighteen-year-old self from his mind and focussed on the grown woman in front of him. 'I moved there, got a job, studied at night, that kind of thing.'

'And you did all right for yourself, by all accounts.'

'I did.' If becoming a millionaire before twenty-five and doubling it every year since counted as doing all right. 'I worked my way up to taking charge of the company I started at, then broke away and began my own firm. It's done well.'

'And now you're back here.' For the first time that evening, he saw genuine curiosity on her face. 'Why on earth would you want to do that? And don't give me that line about having grown up again. I don't believe that you suddenly got nostalgic for this place when you hit your thirties.'

Max barked a laugh at that. 'Maybe not. But…a lot does change in sixteen years.'

'Like your father died.' Had she always been this blunt? He couldn't remember. Maybe.

The Lena Phillips he'd known in school had been popular, pretty and friends with everyone. She'd been head girl, in charge of basically every student event they'd held, and the first on everyone's birthday invite list. And despite all the movie cliches, she'd actually been *liked*.

Even by him.

But she hadn't shied away from the difficult things, and she wasn't now, it seemed.

'Yes. He did,' Max said. 'And my half-brother, Barnaby, too.'

Lena's expression turned sombre. 'You have to know how sorry I was to hear about that.'

Max shrugged. 'It wasn't like I knew him.' The Blythe brothers—the official ones, anyway—hadn't gone to the local primary and secondary schools as he and Lena had. They'd been sent away to expensive, exclusive boarding schools, with the likes of Finn Clifford. They hadn't needed to make friends in the local area, although Toby had, a little, Max thought. But not with him. Whether that was because his father had warned him away, or just coincidence, because Max was a little older, he'd never quite found the courage to ask.

Still, it was a strange feeling, losing family he'd never really known.

When his mother had died, Max had lost a part of his heart, as if it had been ripped from his chest. And it had ended any real connection he'd had with Wells-on-Water, or Wishcliffe. He hadn't imagined ever finding a reason to return.

Until Toby got in touch.

But learning that his father had died had been different. More like missing a step on the staircase—a jolt, a brief moment where the world seemed to wobble, then snap back to normal as he found his footing again.

Barnaby's death, along with his young son, Harry, in a sailing accident at sea, had hit harder. Because even if his older half-brother had never acknowledged him, and his nephew hadn't known he existed at all, they were still too young. It was still a tragedy.

And a lost opportunity. Any chance that Max might have come to know them, one day, was gone.

Maybe that was why he'd answered Toby's email, when before then he'd have said for sure that he would ignore it.

'*Was* that what made you return?' Lena asked. 'Their deaths, I mean.'

Max knew that every person inside the ballroom tonight had wanted to ask the same question, but only Lena had the guts to actually do it. He wouldn't have answered the question from anybody else.

But Lena…

There was still a lingering guilt that hung over him at odd moments about the way he'd left her that last night. Maybe that was why he felt as if he owed her the truth.

'Partly. Toby…after he became the viscount, he found a letter our father wrote, before his death, telling them about me.' It was the only time, as far as Max was aware, that the old viscount had ever admitted that Max was his son. 'And he got in touch. Asked to meet me. Said he wanted to make things right.'

As if that were possible. As if it weren't all thirty-four years too bloody late.

But Toby had wanted to try. And that had meant something, despite it all.

Maybe it wasn't too late for other things to mean something, too. Like an apology for running out on Lena sixteen years earlier, without ever looking back.

He knew, instinctively, that they'd need to address that night at some point, if he wanted to continue any connection with Lena now he was back in town. And standing in the darkness with her, feeling the frisson of attraction that seemed to spark between them, Max knew he *did* want that. Even if it meant apologising, embarrassingly late after the fact.

He opened his mouth to say sorry, but Lena spoke first. 'So he gave you the Manor House at Wells-on-Water. And all the responsibility that goes with it. Interesting.'

Apologies flew from his mind. 'Responsibility?'

The terror in Max's eyes was honestly quite amusing— even if it had replaced the heat between them that had started to glow there. This party was definitely turning out to be more fun than she'd anticipated.

'Responsibility?' She could almost hear him gulp after the word. 'What responsibility?'

Lena gave a light shrug. 'Oh, you know. The owners of those old manor houses always have a certain sort of obligation to look after the village they're connected to, don't they?'

'Still?' Max asked. 'I thought that was one of those Middle Ages feudal-system things.'

'Oh, no.' Lena shook her head. Really, this was almost too easy. 'I mean, most of the cottages in Wells-on-Water *belonged* to the Manor House until surprisingly recently. We would all have been your tenants, not so long ago. And you know how our village feels about tradition.'

'Unfortunately.' Was he remembering all the summer fetes and traditional festivals of their youth, or—more likely—the disapproving glances his mother had earned from the more 'traditional' members of their society when he was growing up? Lena suspected the latter.

Really, she'd have thought there was hardly anything *more* traditional in British aristocracy than a son born, as her gran would have said, 'on the wrong side of the bed-sheets'.

But it was clearly a sore spot for Max, even now. She should probably stop tormenting him.

Only it was so much fun…

'What, exactly, will the village be expecting me to do, now I've moved in?'

Lena smothered a laugh at the apprehension in Max's voice. 'Oh, you know. Just the usual. There's the summer fete, to be held on the grounds, of course. A few open days through the year to let the locals poke around the Manor House. The harvest festival feast for the workers, of course, and the usual Yuletide celebrations—you have to kick off the carol singing, for definite. Oh, and the New Year's Eve ball, the Easter egg hunt—'

'Where I have to dress up as the Easter bunny?' Max asked, drily.

'Of course.' She looked up into his disbelieving eyes, and realised the jig was up. Oh, well, it had been fun while it lasted. 'What gave it away?'

'The carol singing,' he replied. 'No one who has ever heard me sing would even *think* of asking me to lead any carolling.'

Lena winced at the memory of music lessons at primary school. 'Good point.' She should have remembered that. 'But, you know, in years gone by you really *would* have been expected to do all those things.'

'Seriously?'

She nodded. 'Being Lord of the Manor isn't just lounging around while someone feeds you grapes, you know. It was a responsibility.' Even today, Toby and Autumn still held the Fire Festival up at Wishcliffe every autumn, and ran the Christmas celebrations at the house when December came. The church had taken over the Easter celebrations, and she'd never seen Toby or his brother or father in a rabbit costume, but the point still stood.

'Well, I'm not lord of anything,' Max said, uncomfortably. 'And I'm pretty sure no one around here ever wanted me to be. So that's the end of that.'

But it wasn't, Lena realised. It wasn't the end of anything.

Max had been an outcast in their village his whole life. And she'd spent forever trying to make Wells-on-Water the sort of place that didn't *have* outcasts. A place where everyone was welcome, and worthy of respect, kindness and support. A place where a person could ask for help—

and get it. The sort of place where Max, if he were growing up there now, wouldn't have been bullied or looked down on or treated as less.

His return, even as an adult, gave her the chance to prove her efforts had been worthwhile.

'No, it's not,' she said, with dawning enlightenment. 'It's the start.'

'What do you mean?' There was genuine curiosity in his eyes as Lena searched for the right words to explain.

'You coming back here at all. I mean, Max, when you left, you weren't looking back, right?' It felt odd, talking to a man who was practically a stranger to her so openly. Except he *wasn't* a stranger.

For one night, sixteen years ago, she'd seen inside the soul of this man. Oh, not because they'd had sex, but because of the way they'd talked after, in a way they never had before or since.

It might have only been one night, a long time ago, but Lena had the strangest feeling that they were just picking up where they'd left off. That his soul hadn't changed at all.

Had hers? She didn't know.

'I never planned to return to Wells-on-Water at all,' he said, so flatly that she guessed he was now wondering again why he had.

'So the fact you're here now…it has to be the start of something new,' she said. 'You're not the boy you were when you left. You're the brother of the Viscount of Wishcliffe.'

'Half-brother,' he corrected. 'And I was always that.'

'*Acknowledged* half-brother, then. The point is, this is your chance to start again here. To be the person you want to be, not the boy people always assumed you were.'

He looked at her then, but she couldn't read his eyes. 'You assumed I was him, whoever he was, too. Didn't you?'

She met his gaze without flinching. 'Not that last night, I didn't.'

Hadn't he felt it, too, that final night? The connection between them? It was sixteen years gone, and it wasn't as if she'd wasted a *lot* of time thinking about it in the interim. But now he was back... Lena could feel it tugging at her again.

Max looked away. 'Perhaps.'

'You have a fresh start,' she pushed again. 'Not many people get that in the place where they grew up.'

'All because of who my father was?' He shook his head. 'If that's the only thing that gives me value and respect in this place, then I don't want it.'

'Then you'll have to give them something else to value, won't you?' Looking through the glass doors into the ballroom, Lena could see Kathy and Trevor watching her excitedly. They obviously thought she was fleecing their latest resident for donations.

And she could, she realised. She could do exactly that, and he'd probably let her. He might even be relieved to be able to hand over some money and be done with any guilt or obligations. To buy his way into the community and call it done. To never really find a place or a home here.

But she wouldn't. Because she had a feeling that Max Blythe had a lot more to give to—and to gain from—Wells-on-Water. And if she had her way, she was going to make sure he did both.

She just needed to make sure she did it in a way that didn't involve giving up as much as she had last time they'd connected.

Or ever telling him how much that one night together had cost her.

Max wanted to ask Lena what she meant, about giving them something else to value, but before he could speak the doors crashed open and someone was tugging Lena's arm, demanding she come and deal with her brothers. So much for taking her away from *that* responsibility.

Max's memories of the Phillips brothers were far less fond than the ones he held of their sister, after all.

So he let her go, and enjoyed the solitude of the dark terrace a little longer, before venturing back inside and forcing himself to make polite conversation with people who had always disapproved of him.

Inside, the party continued. A band was playing at one end of the ballroom and people were even dancing—avoiding the spot where a waitress was on her hands and knees picking up what looked like a giant stack of squashed prof- iteroles.

But he couldn't stop Lena's words replaying in his head, even as he smiled politely and nodded at people who'd never given him the time of day before he had money and the right to use his father's name.

Give them something else to value.

Max had spent his childhood being shown through looks and whispers and pointed comments how little he mattered. How his mother's pretension—claiming her son, born out of wedlock, belonged to the most important man in the area—had only made him *less* important, not more. It was a strange existence—he'd somehow been both invis- ible and notorious at the same time. People hadn't liked to acknowledge him, not when he could see, but they'd talked about him endlessly behind his back.

Oh, at the local school the teachers had made an effort to treat him just like any other child sent to them for an edu- cation. Many of the staff drove in from surrounding towns and villages and probably genuinely hadn't cared whose son he was. But they couldn't influence what the parents told their kids, or the way those children had taunted or bullied him off the school grounds, especially once they'd moved up to the secondary school in Wishcliffe.

And the Phillips brothers had been the worst of the lot.

In fairness, it wasn't as if they'd *only* picked on him. Gary and Keith Phillips had been indiscriminate in their tormenting, he had to give them that.

And eventually he'd grown up enough to fight back. Which had just got him into another new world of trouble.

He looked up from a conversation with the vicar about the Sunday school to see if he could spot where Lena's brothers had got to. Just a hangover from the self-preservation tactics of his youth, he told himself, rather than a secret hope of seeing Lena again before she left. But there was no sign of any of them. Max suspected that Finn and Victoria would have had the Phillips brothers discreetly shown the door, so the party could continue more peaceably without them.

How much longer was it going to drag on for? And when could he reasonably make his excuses and head home? Even in London, parties like this really weren't his cup of tea. He preferred the intimacy of a private dinner, the chance to really talk around a subject and get down to what mattered. The surface chatter of these events grated on his nerves.

The vicar, clearly bored by Max's company, made his excuses and darted across the room to speak to someone else. *Anyone* else, Max suspected, and sighed.

It was just as well that no one really expected him to play Lord of the Manor here at Wells-on-Water. He was temperamentally unsuited for it.

'Those look like deep, dark thoughts,' Victoria said, appearing beside him, bump first. 'Penny for them?'

Max sighed again. Apparently it was becoming a habit. 'I was just thinking that it's probably for the best that the age of convivial lords of the manor who knew all their tenants by name and threw seasonal celebrations for them and so on is over. I don't think I'd be very good at it.'

Victoria laughed, high and bright, her eyes glinting in the candlelight. 'I think you're doing yourself down,' she said. 'But also, I think you'll find those times are not as dead and gone as you might think.'

He raised his eyebrows at that, and she continued to explain. 'Oh, I'm not saying you need to be the new best friend of everyone in Wells-on-Water. You're not running for Mayor—you don't need to win votes. But we're a *community* around here, Max. And the more you give to a community, the more you get out of it. You'll see.'

'Hopefully not,' he muttered, soft enough that she could pretend not to hear—even though her knowing smile suggested that she had. She thought she knew better. That now he had the authority of his father's name, even if the man had never acknowledged him in life, Max would find a place here. A home. Acceptance in a place that had kept him on the outskirts his entire childhood. That had ostracised his mother while she'd lived, and forgotten her in death.

As if he would *want* that kind of community at all.

Except Lena's words were still echoing through his head. *Give them something else to value.*

He pushed them away. He wasn't here to prove his worth to these people. He didn't need to. He knew his value, and that was enough.

'Did Lena leave with her brothers?' He regretted asking as he saw Victoria's gaze turn fiercely curious.

'You and Lena got along well, then?' she asked. 'I saw you heading outside together…'

'We're old friends. We went to school together.' *We lost our virginities together.* He didn't admit, even to himself, that he'd been almost hoping they might be heading for a recreation of that night. Somewhere more comfortable than the back seat of a battered old car.

'Right.' Victoria looked disbelieving. 'Well, she's still here somewhere.' She scanned the room, then pointed across at the desserts table, where Lena was now helping the waitress clear up the last of the squashed-profiterole mess her brothers had presumably left behind. 'There she is.'

Which meant he had to cross the room towards her, because otherwise his asking after her sounded creepy—as if he just wanted to stalk her from a distance. And since he wasn't really sure *what* he wanted to do now he'd found Lena, he couldn't even make a reasonable excuse to Victoria.

'Oh, good,' Lena said as he reached her and the waitress, both kneeling on the floor. 'Can you grab some more cloths, please? From the kitchen.'

So Max found himself running to the kitchen for cloths, and then helping to clear up fresh cream and choux pastry from the ballroom floor, and only realising afterwards that he had chocolate-sauce stains on his shirt. And it was still better than making small talk with the vicar.

By the time they were done, the party was mercifully winding down. Lena dabbed ineffectually at the stains on his shirt, and he tried to pretend that her closeness wasn't doing things to his body that were inappropriate for a public gathering. 'You need to soak this, and fast,' she said.

Max batted away her hands to try and hold onto his composure. Besides, if she planned to touch him tonight, he wasn't going to waste it on cleaning his clothes. 'It's done for. If my dry-cleaner can't fix it, I'll buy a new one.' Maybe she'd help him take it off…

She tutted at that. 'So quick to throw away something that could still be of use to you. Come on.'

He wasn't entirely sure where she expected him to go, but he found himself following her all the same. 'I need to call a taxi. The guy who brought me gave me his card…' He patted his pockets looking for it. Usually he'd have driven; he liked to be in control of when he arrived and, more importantly, when he left a gathering like this. But he'd had a feeling that he'd need more than one drink to survive the occasion, and he never drove after more than one glass.

'Eddie brought you? Yeah, he's going to be in bed by now—he never works after nine these days.'

Max looked down at the card he'd finally located in his jacket pocket. *Eddie's Taxis.*

'Is there another taxi firm… No. Of course there isn't.' Because this was Wells-on-Water, not the city. Not even a town. He'd been away so long he'd forgotten the impossibility of rural village life. 'Guess I'll have to walk.' It was only a couple of miles. The fresh air would probably be good for him.

Lena rolled her eyes and grabbed his arm. 'Come on. I'll give you a lift. And then I can show you how to soak that stain properly.'

She said it so matter-of-factly, it took Max a minute to realise that Lena had casually invited herself into his home. At night. Maybe she'd expect a nightcap. Or maybe even more…

Was he imagining the heat between them tonight? He didn't think so. But then she concentrated so hard on the road as they made their way from Clifford House to the Manor House that he started to doubt himself.

And either way, he couldn't make assumptions.

'You really don't have to come in,' he said as they

turned into the long driveway of the Manor House. 'Just giving me a lift is kind of you.'

'This village is good at kindness.' She shot him a sideways look. 'Well, usually.'

Kindness wasn't something Max really associated with the village. But he did associate it with Lena. Maybe this was just who she was, and he should say a polite goodnight and stop reading too much into it.

Her tiny, ancient yellow car juddered to a stop outside the Manor House, and she jumped out of the driver's seat before he could say anything at all and was already striding towards the front door. Max followed, still trying to persuade his body to stay calm and not get excited until Lena had told him exactly what she wanted. Maybe she just really had a thing about laundry…

Then she stopped, so suddenly he had to reach out and grab her arms to prevent himself from walking into the back of her. 'What is it?'

'You know we were talking about responsibility earlier?'

'Yeah?' What did that have to do with anything?

'Well, I think you just gained a new one.'

She stepped aside, but still it took him a long moment to see what she had obviously noticed the moment she approached.

The basket, sitting on the step outside his front door.

And even then, it wasn't until he heard the faint cry of a baby that he realised what she meant by 'responsibility'.

CHAPTER THREE

How DID SHE always end up in situations like this?

Okay, not *exactly* like this—Lena had never found a baby on the doorstep before—but situations where she couldn't do anything but help. It was past midnight, she was exhausted and wanted her bed, and yet here she was. Picking up a basket containing a squalling infant and carrying it over the threshold into the Manor House, while a shell-shocked Max Blythe followed behind.

She blamed her brothers, Lena decided. If not for their ridiculous antics at the party she wouldn't have been clearing up profiteroles and wouldn't have roped Max in to help. He wouldn't have got chocolate sauce on his shirt, and she wouldn't have been so irritated at his suggestion that he could just toss it away and buy a new one—had he never heard of the environment?—that she wouldn't have offered him a lift home, and she wouldn't have been there when he found the baby.

Although she knew that she wouldn't have left that party without saying goodnight to him. Without one last moment in his company, to see if she was imagining that the connection they'd forged sixteen years ago could still be hanging on by a thread, all this time later.

She knew herself well enough to know that the chances

were she'd have been giving Max a lift home, anyway. Maybe even more...

Besides, it was just as well for the baby that she *was* there. Max's wide and terrified eyes in the sudden light of the hallway as he flipped the switch suggested he wasn't dealing so well with the new arrival.

Lena placed the basket on the parquet flooring, and reached in to pick up the baby, carefully supporting its head. It was small, young, but not newborn, as far as she could tell. Dressed as it was in a simple white sleep suit with tiny giraffes on, there was no hint as to whether it was a boy or a girl, but Lena was sure it would need changing soon enough and they could check.

But first...

'Something you want to tell me, Daddy?' she asked, raising her eyebrows at Max as she held the baby out to him.

Max recoiled, horror in his eyes. 'You think it's *mine*?'

'No, I expect someone just left it on your doorstep because they thought you might be the parental sort. Of course it must be yours!' Why else would a mother abandon a baby here in the middle of the night, if not to reunite it with its father? 'I'd have thought you, of all people, would be more accepting of an unexpected child.' If his own mother had made different choices, this could have been him, couldn't it?

He flinched at that, but shook his head again. 'No, no. It can't be.'

His denial sounded more hopeful than as if he really believed it, Lena decided. But he still wouldn't take the baby.

'I should have known,' she muttered under her breath, feelings she'd buried sixteen long years ago starting to emerge once more.

'Known what?' he snapped back. 'That some crazy person would leave their baby here tonight?'

'That you wouldn't take any responsibility if they did! It's not like you called to check on me sixteen years ago, is it? For all you knew you could have come back to find a fully fledged teenager waiting for you.'

She hadn't meant to say it, but, Lena had to admit, seeing Max stagger backwards into the console table at the bottom of the stairs, horror clear on his face, it was kind of worth it. Actions had consequences, after all. She'd have thought *he'd* know that.

'I didn't…we used protection.'

'Because *that* always works.' The terror on his face hadn't dissipated. She almost didn't want it to. She wanted him to feel the same fear she had, back then, waiting for her period to come and knowing that if it didn't, her life as she knew it would be over. Protection or not, she'd been a teenage virgin who'd made a rash decision, and she'd known that if there *were* consequences, she'd be all on her own, with no way to contact him.

He was lucky it hadn't come to that. But a little terror wouldn't hurt him.

Eventually, too many years of making people feel better, of fixing situations, kicked in. 'Oh, relax. It was fine. But apparently you've never learned the lesson about follow-up. Assuming this little guy or gal is yours, I suggest you begin compiling a list of romantic partners who shared your bed around nine or ten months ago.'

The baby had fallen asleep in her arms, obviously soothed by the comfort of being held, and unbothered by their argument. Its tiny face was scrunched up inside the blanket, a small, knitted hat covering its head.

'I told you,' Max said, sounding desperate. 'It can't be mine.'

'Struggling to remember all the women's names, are you?' God, she'd actually thought he might be different. That night, sixteen years ago, she'd thought they'd had a connection—and he'd walked out without a backward glance. And then tonight, she'd honestly believed that his return to Wells-on-Water meant something. That he was ready to find his place in the community at last. Show them who he really was.

Apparently she'd misjudged him again.

'Quite the opposite.' Raking his hand through his hair, he moved closer, looking down at the baby in her arms with a softness she hadn't expected.

She tried to make sense of his words. 'What do you mean?'

'It's been a busy year.' He raised one shoulder in a half-shrug. 'I mean, first there was a big work contract, then Toby got in touch and since then... I guess it turns out that the baby really *can't* be mine. There hasn't been anyone in my bed in well over a year.'

Lena glanced down again at the bundle in her arms. Definitely *not* three months old.

'Well, you could have just said that.'

'Yeah. Sorry.'

For a long moment, they both just stared at the baby.

'So, what do we do now?' Lena asked.

Max huffed a laugh. 'You think I have any idea?'

The initial panic had faded from his face, but Lena could still see the fear in the shadows cast by the hall-way lighting.

She couldn't leave Max on his own with the baby. From the look of him, he wouldn't know where to start with changing a nappy, let alone food and care for the tiny thing. Capable and successful businessman he might be. Family man he was not.

Not that she believed that she was the best option. She was the youngest of three siblings, and there hadn't been that many babies in her family after her. She'd done some childcare training, and first aid courses, partly to help with running kids' events at the hub, though. And she had friends with kids, and she'd at least absorbed some of the basics. If all else failed she knew how to do an Internet search for information.

More than that, she knew people who *did* know babies. And they owed her enough favours to get them through this.

'Should we call the police?' Max asked, suddenly looking up from the baby to meet her gaze. 'That's what you're supposed to do in situations like this, right?'

A chill skittered down Lena's back as she realised. If this baby wasn't Max's, and hadn't been left here by a desperate ex-girlfriend, then the mother had to be someone local. Which, since she knew everyone in Wells-on-Water, meant someone that Lena knew.

How desperate must she have been to leave the baby here?

She must have felt she had no other options. *If the community hub had still been running, she would have.* They'd had family-planning advice, confidential counsellors, when she could sweet-talk professionals into giving up their free time for the good of the village. If nothing else, the mother could have come to Lena, or Kathy, or whoever was manning the hub at the time, and they'd have been able to put her in touch with someone who could help.

The mother could even be someone she'd helped through the community hub before. Someone who needed support and kindness, not the police.

She knew how it felt to be that girl.

This was why her 'pet project', as Councillor Morgan patronisingly called it, really mattered.

This could have been her, sixteen years ago, if things had gone differently.

'Let's not get onto the police and everything yet,' she said, quickly. 'Let's see if we can sort this out ourselves, first.'

'Sort it out? How?'

Lena motioned to the basket. 'Have a look in there, for a start. See if there's a note, or supplies, or *something.*'

Watching him rifle through the blankets, Lena thought, fast.

She'd been teasing Max at the party about the responsibility of occupying the Manor House, but it hadn't all been a joke. Around here, people *did* still expect some loyalty from the lord of the manor, even if he didn't own the village any more. The Viscount of Wishcliffe had fulfilled the role for years, but the older hands would still remember when the first son and heir used to live at Wells-on-Water Manor House, and look after the tenants there. A first step to learning to care for a community.

Had someone left the baby here because they believed Max could provide and care for it better than they could? Because they were desperate, and didn't know what else to do?

Lena knew her community well. In times of crisis, they turned to each other, not the outside authorities. Maybe it wasn't the best way, but it was the only way the village knew.

If Max called the police, social services would get involved, and whoever left that baby on the doorstep could be in a lot of trouble, very fast.

But if they could find the mother themselves, maybe they could help.

'There are some nappies, and a bottle of formula,' Max said, just as the baby woke up and started squawking. 'And this note. But it doesn't make any sense.'

He held the paper out to her, and she scanned it, quickly.

This is your responsibility. I know you'll look after her for me.

Looked as if the mother believed Max was the father, even if he claimed it was impossible.

'Right,' Lena said, decisively. Time to take charge. 'In that case, we are going to feed and change the baby. And then I'm going to make some phone calls. Okay?'

Max nodded mutely. Sensible man.

Lena left him holding the baby. Literally. Despite the fact that he'd managed a full thirty-four years on the planet without ever holding one.

'I don't know what to do with it,' he'd protested, after they'd managed to change the baby's nappy—and discovered it was a girl in the process—and failed mightily at the feeding aspect of things.

'Just sit there and try not to scowl at her,' Lena replied, rolling her eyes at him. 'I'll try her again with the formula in a minute, but there's a call I want to make first.'

She disappeared off into the hallway again, leaving him in the front room, sitting on the uncomfortable leather sofa that had come with the house, wondering what the hell had happened to his night.

He looked down at the sleeping baby, suddenly very conscious that at least one person in the room was having a far worse night than him. Even if she didn't know it yet.

'How could someone just leave you there?' he whispered. 'I don't get it.'

Max shifted position slightly, trying not to jostle and wake the child in his arms. He'd always known that there were plenty of things about the world, about people in particular, that he didn't understand. But this one...he had a feeling this would always be beyond him.

'Who in their right mind would think that *my* doorstep was a good place to leave a baby? I mean, have they not *met* me?'

Maybe they hadn't, he realised. But they'd probably know about him. About his parentage. His past. His story.

Maybe *that* was why. Maybe they thought he'd understand.

But he didn't.

He tried to imagine what he'd have done, sixteen years ago, if Lena had tracked him down in London to tell him she was pregnant. Or if he'd returned here to find her with a sixteen-year-old daughter with her hair and his eyes. But he couldn't. The whole idea was so outside his sphere of experience, he just had no frame of reference.

One thing he knew for sure, it would have damned him for ever in the eyes of the village, for defiling their favourite daughter.

Maybe someone was targeting him because of his past. For his audacity in claiming his family name, his birthright, this house even. Except who would use an innocent baby to make a point like that? Just to drag his reputation through more mud? Even he didn't think the people of Wells-on-Water capable of that.

The thought crossed his mind that perhaps the baby could be connected to him in another way, since she obviously wasn't his daughter. Could she be Toby's? Except Max was one hundred per cent certain that Toby hadn't looked at another woman since he'd met Autumn, a year ago.

Could his father have had another illegitimate child? One who'd found themselves desperate and alone and turned to him for help?

But why wouldn't his father have acknowledged them in the same letter he'd left for Toby, where he finally accepted that Max was his child?

'It just doesn't make any sense,' he muttered.

'Are you talking to the baby, or to yourself?' Lena stood in the doorway, her arms folded across her chest, her eyes tired but amused.

'Both. I just… I don't understand.' He met her gaze with his own, feeling the fire coursing through him as he spoke. 'What if I hadn't been here, Lena? I'm not living here full-time, and I don't ever plan to. I'm still in London most weeks. I'm supposed to be heading back there in the morning…if I hadn't been here tonight, how long might that poor thing have been out there? What would have happened to it? How could someone *do* that?'

Sighing, Lena dropped into the armchair opposite him. Her pale blonde hair was coming loose from the pins holding it up at the back of her head, and strands of it framed her exhausted face. For a moment, she looked almost eighteen again. 'I don't know, Max. Sometimes people do really stupid things.'

Like sleep with a boy who'll never call to check on you afterwards, he thought, but didn't say.

This wasn't about them, or their history together. It wasn't about his own past, his mistakes—even if almost everything since he'd returned to Wells-on-Water seemed determined to remind him of it.

'I still say we should call the police,' he said, instead.

'And I'm not saying you're wrong.' Lena's words sounded heavy, weighing down the air between them. 'Just asking that we wait.'

'Why?'

'Because… Damn it, Max, you know this place as well as I do. Or you used to.'

'Yeah, I do. Seems to me like an abandoned baby of questionable parentage is prime gossip fodder around here. Isn't it best to get her out of the way before people start talking?' What kind of childhood could the poor thing have, abandoned before she could even sit up on her own, let alone fight her own corner?

'You're worried that people will talk about you?' She flashed him an irritated look. 'Newsflash, Max, they already are. I'm not sure they ever stopped.'

'I'm not worried about my reputation.' Well, he was. But not as much as other things. 'I'm trying to think about what's best for the baby.'

'Max…' Lena's expression faded from annoyance back to tiredness. 'I'm not saying they're not gossips but…the people of Wells-on-Water stick together.'

'As long as you're on the approved list,' Max muttered.

She ignored him and ploughed on. 'Whoever left the baby here has to be a local, I reckon. Someone who believed that the big house and the rich guy who lives there would look after their child while they couldn't.'

'Their first mistake.'

'And who would make sure the baby was cared for.'

'By calling the proper authorities,' Max finished, triumphantly.

'Max!' God, how long had it been since a woman had sounded so thoroughly infuriated with him? Probably not since his mother died.

'What?' The baby in his arms started to squirm, and he attempted to rock her in the hope of fending off a meltdown.

The first cry told him he'd failed. He was not a baby

person, anyone could tell that—even this tiny scrap of a human that had been left on his doorstep.

He looked up at Lena to take the baby from him, but she just raised her eyebrows at him. 'I'd try her with the bottle again, if I were you.'

'Right. The bottle.' He reached for the small baby bottle that had been in the basket, along with a carton of formula milk. Lena had Googled temperatures, and they'd attempted some sort of sterilisation in the microwave, but the milk was cooling now. Was it still good? She'd rejected it the first time, when Lena had tried, but perhaps she was hungrier now.

Oh, I am really *not the right person to be doing this.*

As he tried to persuade the baby to take the teat between her lips and suckle, Lena began speaking again, softer this time, her frustration still evident but reined in.

'If we hand this baby straight to the authorities, that's it. It's done. There's no walking it back. But if we just give it a day or so to try and find the mother, see what the situation is there, and what we can do to help…'

Max sighed as it all started to make sense. 'You want to save them. Whoever left the baby. You want to save them.'

'I want to do the right thing,' Lena argued.

The words echoed in Max's head, as if they were doubled. As if he could hear his late mother saying the exact same thing, just as she had through his childhood.

Doing the right thing is more important than doing the easy *thing, Max Blythe.*

For his mother, the world had been black and white. There was the right thing and the easy thing. The easy thing—for both of them—would have been to lie about who his father was, to pretend. Especially when it had become clear that the old viscount was never going to acknowledge Max as his son. His mother could have made up a story about his parentage and people would have accepted it, even if the rumours still flew. And Max wouldn't have had to live with the public shame of a father who refused to admit he existed.

Maybe it wouldn't have made his childhood *easy*, exactly. But it would have been *easier*. And easier for the village to accept, too.

But it wasn't the *right* thing. And so his mother had vehemently stuck to her story in the face of all the arguments and the gossip. Max suspected that his father had even offered her money to make the rumours go away, but she hadn't taken that, either, however much easier *that* would have made their lives.

She'd done what was right, to her mind and her values, and damn the consequences.

Even today, Max wasn't sure if he admired her or hated her for it most.

He sighed. 'Who did you call, then?' he asked Lena, now.

'My friend, Janice. She's a GP. She's coming over now to check the baby over.'

'In the middle of the night?'

Lena shrugged. 'She's dedicated. And it's a baby, Max. Of course she's coming now.'

'Right.'

He half expected her to get up and leave, her work here done now she could hand over to the doctor. But instead, she leaned her head against the back of the armchair and let her eyes flutter closed.

'You're staying, then?' There was an unexpected bubble of hope in his chest at the idea. He didn't want to be alone with this—the baby, the responsibility, any of it.

And even if the evening hadn't gone at all the way he'd hoped…he didn't want Lena to leave. Not yet.

'Looks like it,' Lena said, without opening her eyes. 'For now, anyway.'

'That's…good.'

Maybe…maybe he just didn't want to be alone, at all. Which was a frightening proposition in itself.

In his arms, the tiny baby suckled another mouthful of milk, then pushed the teat away with her lips, her eyes closing too as she settled against him, apparently unaware that he was the least suitable person in the world for this job.

No, he definitely wasn't alone any more.

CHAPTER FOUR

LENA JERKED AWAKE, her neck aching from her awkward position in the chair, and her head fuzzy about what had woken her. Blinking, she sat forward, peering into the gloom of Max's sitting room. They'd left on only one small light, to try and help the baby sleep, and it seemed to have worked. On the sofa across from her, Max sat dozing, with the baby fast asleep in his arms.

It was almost…cute.

The baby was hidden from view mostly by blankets and the angle of Max's arm. But Max himself was perfectly visible—from the lock of dark hair that had fallen across his forehead, to the slight lines forming around his eyes. He looked younger in sleep, despite them—less weighed down by worry, or history, perhaps. And he looked far more comfortable holding the baby than he had when he was conscious.

In fact, if Lena had to find words to describe him right now, they would be 'adorably rumpled'.

Except she certainly wasn't supposed to be thinking of Max Blythe as adorably anything. And he'd probably glare lasers at her if she called him 'rumpled'.

Still. The point stood. And, in the dim light, Lena found she couldn't stop herself watching him sleep, the baby safe and secure in his embrace.

This really wasn't how she'd imagined this evening ending. And yet…

A knock at the front door reminded her that *something* had woken her—probably Janice arriving. Pushing herself up on the arms of the chair, she moved stiffly back into the hallway and pulled open the door.

On the doorstep, Janice looked her up and down, then gave a small smile. 'I have questions.'

'You're not the only one.' Lena stood aside to let her in, then shut the door behind her. 'The baby is sleeping, so if you want to ask them without a scream-along soundtrack, now is probably the time.'

'Okay. You said you found the baby on the doorstep?' Janice dropped her bag onto the floor then shrugged out of her coat.

Lena nodded. 'When we got back from the party at Clifford House there was a basket on the step. We looked inside and…baby.' Motioning with her left hand, she indicated the basket where it still sat on the hall table.

'No note or identifying details?' Janice poked around at the blankets in the basket.

'Nothing useful. Just a bottle, a carton of formula and a few nappies. And this note.' She handed it over.

Janice read it and grimaced. 'Max Blythe is the father, then?'

'Apparently not. According to him.' Lena believed him, but she could tell from Janice's expression that she wasn't convinced. Still, she let it pass, for now.

'And she seemed in good health?'

'I think so, but I'm no professional. That's why I called you.' Lena flashed her friend a grin. 'But she's had a little of the formula milk and we changed her nappy. She seems happy enough, considering.'

'Poor mite is too tiny to realise what's happening, I'd guess.' Janice tutted and shook her head.

'Any idea who the mother could be?' Lena asked. 'I mean, I know you can't tell me details, but you're GP to everyone in Wells-on-Water. If the mother is local she would have seen you for prenatal care…'

Janice looked thoughtful. 'Nobody springs to mind. But then…there's always the possibility that they didn't know—or didn't acknowledge—that they were pregnant at all.'

'And then panicked when the baby arrived,' Lena guessed.

'Exactly. Okay, next question—what were you doing here in the first place?'

'Are you asking that in your capacity as a doctor or my friend?'

'The latter,' Janice admitted, freely. 'I wasn't aware you were acquainted with Max Blythe. I mean, he's all anyone here has been talking about for weeks, and you never even let on that you knew him.'

That was the problem with having a best friend who'd only moved to Wells-on-Water for work, a few years before, when old Dr Mackay retired. As seamlessly as Janice had slotted into the tight-knit community, she didn't have the backstory of all the people there.

'I went to school with him; we're the same age,' Lena said. 'I guess I never mentioned it because everyone else around here already knew. Sorry.' She knew how Janice hated being reminded of her outsider status.

'So you were catching up on old times at the party, and came back here for a nightcap…?' Janice guessed.

'Not exactly.' Lena *really* didn't want to get into what sort of old times she and Max had to reminisce about, although she suspected Janice wouldn't let her get away with that for ever. 'He'd taken a taxi, and of course Eddie had already clocked off for the night by the time the party was over, so I offered Max a lift home. That was all.'

It was the complete truth. But Lena had to admit that a tiny part of her wondered what might have happened if there *hadn't* been a baby on the doorstep when they'd arrived. Would he have invited her in for a nightcap? Would they have started chatting more about old times? Would they have connected, the same way they had that last night before he left town—and would they have ended up sleeping together again?

If Janice had asked her yesterday, Lena would have said it was massively unlikely. Impossible even.

But here, at the Manor House, in the dark of the middle of the night, she wondered. And it didn't seem so completely impossible at all.

Still, she wasn't about to let on that, when she'd driven Max back to the Manor House, there had been…*possibilities*. Until they found the baby, anyway.

'Hmm. I'll believe you for now,' Janice said. 'But you better believe I'm going to have more questions later. *After* I've seen to my patient.'

'Of course you will.' Lena sighed. 'Come on, then. Let's wake up Sleeping Beauty.'

What mattered right now was the baby. *Not* whatever tonight's antics had stirred up inside her about the man she'd lost her virginity to, and the aftermath of that decision.

She'd deal with that later.

'Hmm? What? No. Don't send the giraffes in yet.' Max felt himself rising to consciousness, the concern about giraffes lingering from his dream into the waking world until he shook his head to rid himself of the last vestiges of sleep.

There was a weight in his arms. Something he needed to do something about. To protect. Probably not a giraffe.

'Giraffes?' an amused voice asked. 'Deal with a lot of them in your business, do you?'

Max blinked his eyes open, and found Lena standing over him, one hand on his shoulder.

Lena Phillips. What is Lena Phillips doing in my house, talking about giraffes?

He frowned, glanced down, and the evening's craziness settled back into his brain when he saw the baby sleeping on his lap.

Right. A baby on his doorstep, and his first lover in his home.

And an unknown redhead watching them from the doorway, with a very curious expression.

'Janice—Dr Graham—is here,' Lena explained. 'So if you're done with the giraffes for now, I'll take the baby for her to examine.'

The redhead must be the doctor; that made sense. His brain was coming to life again now, and he knew he needed to gather his wits to figure all this out for the best, despite the lack of sleep and the strangeness of the day.

But the first thing—the most important thing—they all had to do was make sure the baby was okay.

He handed the sleeping bundle over to Lena, then followed anxiously as the baby gave a tiny squawk at being moved across the room towards Janice.

'Sorry about this, sweetheart,' the doctor murmured as she laid the baby on a clean blanket on the floor and set about unfastening her sleep suit.

'So, what were you dreaming about?' Lena sidled closer to him to ask. 'Apart from the giraffes, I mean.'

'I don't remember,' Max replied. 'It was just one those dreams, you know? Lots of things I was supposed to be doing, lots of people looking to me, and everything going wrong.'

'Like the giraffes.'

He sighed. 'Apparently so.' Giraffes were new in his dreamscape, but he wasn't fastening any particular meaning to them, all the same. At least, until he looked over to check on Janice and the baby and spotted the tiny cartoon giraffes on the sleep suit.

Clearly his subconscious was still working on this looking after a newborn thing.

'Does everything look all right?' he asked the doctor, who had her stethoscope out and was listening to the baby's heart.

'She's hale and hearty, as my grandmother would say.' Janice put away her equipment and began fastening the baby back into her sleep suit again. 'Just a week or so old, I think, but thriving as far as I can tell. I doubt she could have been out there waiting for you very long. In fact, I imagine the mother was lingering somewhere nearby to check that you found her okay.'

'What makes you think that?' Lena asked.

Janice shrugged. 'It's what I would do. Wouldn't you?'

'I suppose so,' Lena admitted.

Annoyance coursed through Max's tired body and he shot a glare at Lena, even though he knew it was as much his fault as hers. 'If we'd thought about it when we found her, we could have searched for the mother then and there and ended this thing in time for me to get a decent night's sleep.'

'You did the right thing,' Janice reassured them. 'The most important thing was to make sure the baby was safe, and you did that. You called me.'

'The question is what we do now.' Max turned his attention back to the doctor. 'We should call the authorities, don't you agree?'

Janice and Lena exchanged a look he read all too clearly. *They don't think I understand. They think* I'm *the one being unreasonable here.*

And if the doctor was on Lena's side then he didn't stand a chance. His last hope for reason was gone.

'If we can't find the mother, we'll have to,' Janice admitted. 'I'm duty-bound as a doctor to do so.'

'But you can give us a day or so, right?' Lena pleaded. 'Just one day, to try and find her and sort all this out?'

'One day,' Janice conceded. 'And only because I know this village. The mother has to be one of us, right? And we look after our own.'

There it was again, that infuriating refrain. That holier-than-thou attitude of a village that had *never* looked after him—and now expected him to look after them. Heat rose inside him along with his temper, and Max bit down on the side of his cheek to keep it in check.

A cool hand on his arm calmed him, and he looked over to see Lena watching him under worried brows. 'It's just one day,' she said softly. 'Just to be sure. I know you don't owe anyone here anything, but…she could be scared, Max. She could be desperate and scared and need our help.'

His anger and frustration ebbed away at her touch, her gentle words, and Max couldn't help but remember another day, many years ago, when she'd done the same—stopping him from punching one of her brothers, the younger one, he thought. That was after he'd grown into his height, and his strength. Her brothers had never bothered him again after that day, though.

Strange how, for someone he'd never have claimed to know well, Lena had been there at so many important moments in his life. And here she was now, with this.

The curse of the small village, he supposed. That was all. *Someone* had to be there, after all, and there weren't that many people in Wells-on-Water of his age. It was nothing more than that.

He pulled his arm away from her hand. 'Fine. We'll look after her tonight, and try to find her mother in the morning. But after that we're calling the police.'

Lena's smile warmed him again, but in a very different way.

'In that case, you'd better come up with a name for her,' Janice said as she packed away her things. 'Even if she's only here for twenty-four hours, you can't keep calling her "the baby" the whole time.'

Max and Lena exchanged a look.

'I remember bringing a squirrel home once, and my mother wouldn't let me name it because then I'd think I could keep it,' he said. Was it totally crazy to worry the same thing about Lena in this situation? Not himself, though. Probably.

'Well, we're definitely not keeping her,' Lena said. 'But Janice is right. We can't keep calling her The Baby.'

Max stared at the tiny, scrunched-up, dozing face of the baby as she lay in Janice's arms. 'Willow. For the trees that grow down by the river, on the edge of the village.' It was only after he said it that he remembered that was the same spot he'd last seen Lena before leaving Wells-on-Water, after taking her back to the party.

Janice nodded. 'Good name.' She handed the baby back to him, and Max took her, almost without thinking, then panicked, juggling her slightly to try and hold her correctly.

'Willow it is, then,' Lena said, and smiled at him.

Janice left them with a bag full of newborn nappies, a microwave steriliser, formula and more bottles, along with baby wipes, changes of clothing, muslin cloths and other things Lena hadn't even had a chance to sort through yet. She'd never realised that a baby required quite so much *stuff.*

Their first priority, however, was sleep—for them, as well as Willow. 'We'll never be able to function tomorrow if we don't get *some* rest,' Max pointed out, perfectly logically.

Without a cot for Willow, they decided she'd have to sleep in the Moses basket she'd arrived in. Together, they shifted all the supplies—and the baby—upstairs, where Lena stopped on the landing and stared at the bedroom doors before her.

'You want me to stay the night?' She was almost certain he did, given his earlier words, but she'd never really envisioned actually sleeping in a bed in his home. Other things, perhaps. But not sleeping.

And *whose* bed?

'If you don't object,' Max replied. 'I figure we can take shifts, right? You get some sleep first—since I had a nap downstairs—then we'll swap after a few hours.'

'And you'll look after the baby while I sleep?'

'Of course.' Max frowned, suddenly looking uncertain. 'Well, once you show me what I need to do.'

Lena pulled a face. 'What makes you think I know?'

'Didn't Janice tell you?'

'No more than she told you.' In all honesty, she *did* have a pretty good idea, but it would do Max good to have to figure things out, too, rather than just assuming the woman would know all there was about childcare.

'Oh.' Max gave her a tired smile. 'Back to Google, then, huh?'

Between them, they got Willow changed and fed again—after finding instructions for the steriliser online.

While Max fed her—modifying his curse words to ones suitable for tender ears after her first glare—Lena read up on sleep for newborns in the book she found at the bottom of Janice's bag of tricks.

'It says here she'll probably only sleep for a few hours at a time at her age.'

'A few hours sounds positively blissful right now,' Max admitted, dribbling milk from the bottle all over Willow's clean sleep suit, then hurriedly getting the teat back between her lips at the first cry. 'What time is it, anyway?'

Lena checked the clock on her phone and winced. 'Just gone three-thirty in the morning. Urgh, I'm too old to stay up this late.'

Max chuckled at that. 'You're only thirty-four, the same as me.'

'Yeah, well, I feel older at three in the morning.' She yawned, her jaw cracking at the movement.

'Go to bed,' Max said. 'Really. I've got this now. Probably. Top of the stairs, second door on the left. It's the guest room.'

Oh, but that sounded tempting. 'What about you?'

He still looked uncertain, but the determined set of his jaw told Lena that Max wasn't going to let something as tiny as a baby break him.

'I told you. We'll take shifts. The basket is in my room so, once we're done here, I'll take her up and see if I can get her to sleep in it. If I can't, I'll sit up with her a while longer. Then I'll sleep once you take over.' That, she had to admit, sounded like the most likely outcome.

'Should I set an alarm on my phone?' Lena was already edging towards the door, the lure of a soft mattress and a warm duvet too much to resist.

Willow gave a sharp cry as the bottle slipped from between her lips again. Max gave Lena a tired smile. 'I don't think we'll really need it. Do you?'

Lena awoke some time later, cocooned in blankets in Max's spare room. It felt as if she'd only been asleep for moments, but the sunlight streaming through the open curtains said otherwise. Groping for her phone, her eyes barely open, she checked the time. Almost seven. It had to be her turn to take over with Willow by now.

A wail from somewhere nearby confirmed her conclusions. Stumbling out of the bed, she pulled her dress from the night before back over her head, then made her way towards the sound, pinning it down to the room next door. She contemplated knocking, but if Max was sleeping through Willow's cries a simple knock wouldn't wake him, and if he was already awake he probably wouldn't hear it over them.

She pushed the door open and peered inside. Max had obviously had the energy and foresight to actually close his curtains before bed, so the room was still dark. But she could hear the low rumble of Max's voice, and just make out his figure where he leaned over the Moses basket. As she watched, he picked the baby up and held her close to his chest, his shoulders slumped with obvious exhaustion. But the long night seemed to have at least made him more comfortable with the idea of holding the baby.

'Come on, Willow, just another half an hour, yeah? You've had your milk, your nappy is dry, I'm running out of ideas here, sweetheart. I mean, trust me, you don't want me to sing to you. Half an hour and we'll wake Lena up and see if she has any ideas.'

'I don't know about ideas, but I do have the energy that comes from three hours passed out in your spare room,' she said.

Max turned at the sound of her voice. 'Three hours doesn't really seem like enough.'

'Looks like three more than you got,' she pointed out.

He shrugged, but the movement seemed to exhaust him even more. 'I napped a bit here and there. Mostly by accident.'

Holding out her arms, Lena waited for him to place the baby in them. She'd stopped crying, at least. She seemed happier when she was being held. Lena supposed she could understand that.

'You're sure?' Max asked.

Lena rolled her eyes. 'You don't think I can cope?'

'I don't think *I* could. Or maybe that should be can.' With a tired smile, he settled Willow into her arms. 'Her milk and bottles are in the kitchen; steriliser is by the microwave. But she just had a bottle twenty minutes ago— well, some of it, anyway, most of it seemed to end up down me. And I've changed her nappy again—although you might want to check that, because I'm not sure I got it right—'

'Max. We'll be fine. Get some sleep.' Lena couldn't help but be a little amused at the way he'd flipped from wanting to make Willow someone else's problem to total concern for the tiny baby. They must have bonded overnight, she supposed.

'Yeah, okay. G'night.' He was collapsed on the bed, eyes closed, before she and Willow even left the room.

'Good morning,' she whispered to the baby as snores began to echo through Max's bedroom door.

Her head still spun a little from tiredness, so she took the stairs carefully, slowly making her way down to the kitchen. Once there, of course, she realised that without the basket she had nowhere to put the baby down while she made coffee, which was definitely going to be a prob-

lem sooner or later. She didn't want to risk scalding the
poor mite, but she also couldn't exactly put her down on
the cold stone floor of the kitchen.

Willow started to fuss again as she stared longingly
at the kettle, so Lena moved away from temptation and
stepped into the hall. She'd barely had a chance to explore
the ground floor of the Manor House the night before, and
now seemed like the perfect opportunity. If she was lucky,
she might even find a nice, thick blanket to use as a play
mat or something.

As she paced around the rooms of the Manor House,
however, the only thing Lena found was the reason why
Max had shepherded her into the small, front sitting room
he used as a study the night before: it was the only recep-
tion room with any furniture in it at all.

'He's been here on and off for weeks, Willow,' she murmured as she walked, gently jostling and rocking the baby,
since that seemed to make her happiest. 'Why hasn't he
bought any furniture yet? It's not as if he can't afford it.'

That was one point that the local rumour mill was all
agreed on, when it came to Max Blythe. Whatever he'd
been doing away from Wells-on-Water for the last sixteen
years, it had made him a very rich man.

The answer came to her as she wandered back towards
the kitchen, Willow content in her arms.

'He doesn't think he belongs here. Even now.'

Lena knew that Max's childhood hadn't been all fun and
games in the village. They might not have been friends,
exactly, but in a place as small as Wells-on-Water she'd had
a front-row seat to the way people treated him by default.

She'd told him the night before that coming back gave
him a chance to prove them all wrong. Maybe helping with
Willow was the first step to that. To finding his place here.

But they only had one day to make it count. Just twenty-four hours—less now she'd wasted some of it sleeping—to find Willow's mum *and* Max's place in the village.

'I'd better get to work, then, I suppose,' she whispered. Willow gurgled in agreement.

Taking a seat at the kitchen table, Lena stared at her phone and wondered how long she had before Max woke up. Long enough, she decided.

This was just like any other community project she'd taken on over the years, really. And if there was one thing Lena Phillips was *brilliant* at, it was bringing this community together.

And she knew just where to start.

CHAPTER FIVE

MAX CAME UP from sleep slowly, as if he were pushing his way through a vat of his mum's treacle pudding, sponge and syrup filling his ears. But even that sensation couldn't completely muffle the noises coming from downstairs.

Voices.

Laughter.

The scrape of furniture moving.

Since he had very little furniture here at the Manor House, that last was particularly worrying.

He blinked, and the night before came back to him, causing him to sit up so fast his head spun. Lena. The basket. *Willow.*

The Moses basket beside the bed sat empty, but since he vaguely remembered Lena coming and taking the baby before he passed out that wasn't too surprising. He was more concerned about whatever else Lena had seen fit to do with his home while he was asleep.

He washed quickly in the en-suite bathroom, running wet hands through his hair to try and tame it, and switched his clothes for cleaner non-black-tie ones. Then, he jogged down the main staircase—and stopped just before the turn in the stairs to stare down over the bannister at his hallway.

It was packed. As far as he could tell, half the village was in his home, and it looked as if they'd brought the contents of their own houses with them. He recognised a few faces from the party the night before—rather less dressed up than they had been then, of course. Others he picked out as familiar from his childhood. Older now, but still the same in his memories.

He turned away from those ones.

In the middle of it all stood Lena—still dressed in the sparkly, shimmery pale blue dress she'd worn for last night's party, although given the way it pooled around her feet he suspected she'd foregone the heels. Beside her, Janice held Willow, cooing down at the baby, while Lena directed villagers left and right into his main drawing room, or the kitchen, depending on what they were carrying.

And all the time they were talking. Every one of them chattered and gossiped away without ceasing. About the baby, the secret mother, the house…him.

He couldn't stand it any longer.

Treading heavily, he swung himself around the bannister to stand at the top of the final set of stairs, looming over the gathering in the hallway. It only took a moment for the house to fall silent.

From the centre, Lena smiled up at him, her eyes wide and guileless. 'Max! You're up. Great.'

At the sound of her voice, the tension in the hall dissipated. Conversations started up again, and people began moving around once more, shifting baby supplies and other such things from one room to another.

Robbed of a dramatic moment—or the chance to throw everyone out of his damn house—Max sighed and made his way down the rest of the stairs to where Lena was waiting for him.

'What, exactly, is going on here?' he asked, his voice tight. 'Why are all these people in my house?'

Lena's smile dimmed a little with uncertainty. 'Well,

I was thinking that if we only have twenty-four hours to find Willow's mum, we need to get moving, and we need some help. So I started calling around to see if anyone had any intel, or theories about who the mother might be. And then...' She trailed off, looking around her helplessly at the frenzied activity of the locals.

'And then?' Max pressed. 'Because I really don't see how information gathering led to whatever the hell this is.' How long had he been asleep, anyway? It couldn't have been more than a few hours.

How in the world had Lena managed all this in such a short space of time?

'I had to tell them what was going on, of course, to get their help,' Lena said slowly. 'And, well, when people heard that you were taking care of Willow—'

'*We're* taking care of Willow,' he corrected her. There was no damn way he was doing this alone.

'They wanted to help,' Lena finished.

'Help. How is invading my house and gossiping about me helping?'

'They didn't *invade*.' Exasperation leaked out of Lena's voice. 'They brought supplies—more nappies and formula, baby clothes, a bouncy chair for Willow, a proper play mat, that sort of thing.'

'Where do you want the coffee machine, Lena?' A guy Max didn't recognise walked past with a large box in his arms, shouting the question as he moved.

'Um, kitchen, please. It's that way—I think Kathy is setting things up in there,' Lena replied, pointing.

'And has Willow developed a sudden urge for caffeine since I fell asleep three hours ago?' Max folded his arms over his chest and raised his eyebrow in a way that past employees had told him was particularly intimidating.

Lena just rolled her eyes. 'The coffee is for us, idiot.

So are the meals Trevor is stocking the freezer with, and the spare furniture Janice's husband Tom is setting up in the drawing room, so Willow has a play space you won't mind getting covered in milk and baby sick.'

'They brought actual furniture?' Max was well aware that the furnishings of the Manor House were somewhat lacking. Beyond his bedroom, the spare bed, and the sitting room that also served as his study, he hadn't really thought about it. But after only a few hours in his home, most of them delirious with sleep deprivation, it seemed that Lena had.

Lena shrugged. 'Just spare stuff. You know, a sofa that was cluttering up someone's garage, someone else's old rocking chair—that'll be good for feeding her, or napping with her, come to that.'

'Seems like an awful lot of stuff for twenty-four hours' worth of babysitting,' Max pointed out.

She flashed him a smile that looked like trouble. 'Well, I guess we'll see how it goes, won't we?'

Before he could question her further on that, someone else was dragging her away to look at something, and he realised that Willow was crying in Janice's arms. Probably she hated this circus as much as he did.

He wanted to leave this whole mess to everyone else, to all the people who had taken over his home at a word from Lena. But he was *responsible* for the baby. That was what the note had said. And until he passed that responsibility on to someone else…well. He planned to live up to it.

He didn't believe in always doing the Right Thing with the sort of zeal his mother had, or even the way Lena seemed to—not least because he wasn't convinced there always was one right thing to do. But he sure as hell wasn't going to treat an innocent baby the way the haters in the village had treated him his whole life—as an outcast, a disgrace, just because of who her parents were or what they'd done.

They were helping now, but Max knew better than to believe that would last past this initial flurry of do-gooderness. If they didn't find Willow's mother, she'd always be the abandoned child, the one nobody wanted.

Max wanted better than that for her.

But for now, the least he could do was take her away from this circus.

'I'll take her,' he told the doctor. Janice beamed as she handed over the child. 'She probably needs a change and another bottle.'

He hoped so, anyway, since that was basically all he knew how to do with her. That and cuddle her to sleep. All of them imperfectly.

He'd leave Lena to the chaos out here and look after the baby. Something he'd never imagined he'd find himself doing out here in Wells-on-Water.

And then he was going to do something else he'd never imagined doing.

He was going to call his brother.

It took a while to clear out all her helpers once things were set up. Lena suspected that was because they'd all always wanted a glimpse inside the Manor House and this was the best opportunity they were likely to get.

Still, eventually it was clear that there was nothing left to do, and nothing left to be gained by lingering since Max had sequestered himself with Willow in his study. And so, slowly, the locals began to depart—still gossiping as they went.

Lena could understand why Max might feel uncomfortable amongst all the curious chatter. She knew how much of his childhood had been filled with people talking about him—about who his father really was, about his mother's words and actions, even about the trouble he'd himself got into and whether it was inevitable, given his background.

She'd been gossiped about enough herself through her life, too, even if it was more affectionately than Max had been subject to. She was a familiar and popular face around the village from her youth, given that her father ran the local pub. And she was a figure of pity or at least sympathy after her mother died.

The only girl in a family of men after that, she'd been sort of adopted by the older women of the village—all of whom seemed to have an opinion on what she wore, who she kissed, who she dated and what she did with her life. She'd be forever thankful that no one had seen her and Max together that last night, sixteen years ago, because if they had they'd still be gossiping about it now, she was sure.

Probably even more, now, given that she'd spent last night in Max's home.

She let out a sigh as the door swung behind the last visitor—or almost last, she realised, as Janice appeared from the drawing room they'd turned into a baby room.

'I brought you some clothes to change into, if you want to get out of that dress,' her friend said, holding out a bag.

Lena took it gratefully. 'Thanks. As much as I love this dress, it's hardly suitable for babysitting.'

Janice leant against the doorframe and looked her up and down. 'Could be perfect for seducing our new lord of the manor, though.'

'Do you really think that's what I'm doing here?' Lena asked incredulously.

'Nah. You're far too nice for that. But you could be,' Janice said. 'I mean, you have to have noticed the way he looks at you.'

'Mostly with annoyance,' Lena replied.

Shaking her head, Janice moved to perch on the stairs. 'I don't know the man, but annoyance was when he found his home full of people. When he showed up on the stairs I thought he was going to yell and toss us all out on our ears.'

'So did I,' Lena admitted.

'But then you whispered to him and he turned into a softie. He even volunteered to go change Willow's nappy and give her a bottle.'

'That was just because he wanted to escape being here,' Lena said. But she had to admit—to herself, if not to Janice—that she was surprised at how easily Max had taken to looking after the baby. She didn't get the impression that Max had much experience of looking after things— or being looked after, for that matter.

'So, did all this activity achieve anything more than access to the Morrisons' old coffee machine and other essential supplies?' Janice asked. 'Did you get any leads on Willow's mother?'

Because that was what it had all been about, really— even if Lena had to remind herself of that from time to time. 'Not much.' She hiked her dress above her knees and sat down beside Janice on the stairs. 'Oh, people had plenty to say, but you know what they're like. Not much of it had to be grounded in reality.'

'And they were all more excited about getting to poke around the Manor House and coo over the baby, anyway,' Janice guessed.

'Pretty much. What about you? Anything in your patient files that might give us a clue?'

Janice shook her head. 'Not really. I have a few people I want to follow up on at home, just in case. But only one of the pregnant women I've seen lately was due around now, and she was here today helping and still very pregnant.'

'Esther Jones,' Lena guessed. 'Right.'

'You really didn't hear anything from anybody?'

Lena leant back, her elbows resting on the stair above them. 'Plenty of theories but no evidence. Mrs Jenkins from the shop is adamant that it has to be the Havers's daughter, because she's been in buying ready salted crisps and Diet Coke, and that was all Mrs Jenkins's daughter could stomach when she was pregnant.'

'Never mind that Milly Havers was parading down the high street in what Hillary Jenkins deemed an "unacceptably cropped top" last weekend,' Janice said.

'She seemed to have forgotten that, yes.' Lena sighed. 'I don't know. I've got Terri Jacobs subtly raising it at the secondary school in Wishcliffe, since that's where most of our teenagers go, and Fiona is going to activate the parent phone tree, in case the mother *is* a scared teen who managed to hide her pregnancy. Dominic is going to speak about it in his sermon on Sunday—and he promises it will be all forgiveness and support and asking for help, not judgement. And I spoke off the record to Heather at the hospital, to see if she can find out anything. But I can't imagine I'm going to get many answers inside Max's twenty-four-hour deadline.'

'Then you'll have to convince him to extend it.' Janice got to her feet, brushing down her jeans as she stood. 'At least until we've had a chance to gather more answers.'

'And how, exactly, am I supposed to do that?'

Turning, Janice raised her eyebrows and flashed Lena a naughty smile. 'I'm sure you'll think of something.' Whatever reaction she saw in Lena's face made her laugh. 'Oh, I'm kidding. Like you'll have the chance with the baby here and everything. But I still reckon he wants you. Actually, you could probably seduce him without very much effort at all during one of Willow's naps...'

Lena bit her bottom lip, then said, 'What if I told you I already had?'

Janice's eyes flew open wide. 'What? When? Last night?'

'No, no. Years ago. Before he left Wells-on-Water after we finished school.'

'Wait, he was the guy you lost it to in the back of a car? The boy you shared a soulmate-like moment with?' Oh, Lena was regretting telling her that after too many glasses of wine one night. 'Why did you never tell me that?'

'Because he was gone. Because we were eighteen and stupid. Because it didn't really matter.' Except it had. It had mattered to her. Not just because it was her first time—although she'd tried to convince herself ever since that that was all it was.

But now he was here, and she was stuck playing house with him until they found Willow's mother, she had to admit the truth.

'Didn't matter?' Janice asked, eyebrows arched. 'And how is that argument holding up in the face of fully grown Max Blythe?'

'Badly,' Lena admitted. 'I don't know. He's not the boy I shared that night with. But I have to admit... I'm kind of intrigued by the man he's become.'

Janice glanced towards the closed study door. 'I can't say I blame you. So, go get yourself freshened up and changed, then go see if you can't reconnect enough to convince him to give you the time to find Willow's mum.'

Max felt far more relaxed with the study door shut on the mayhem outside, even if he wasn't actually alone. Willow lay peacefully in his arms and he wished he'd had the foresight to snag that bouncy chair Lena had mentioned so he could actually put her down.

As it was, he made do with the travel change mat and bag Janice had hung on his shoulder to lay her comfortably on the floor to replace her nappy—slightly more securely this time. Then, after using the anti-bac wipes on his hands, he settled onto the sofa to feed her while he rehearsed what he wanted to say to Toby in his head.

He waited until Willow had finished her bottle and was dozing, milk drunk, on his lap before actually reaching for the phone—cautiously, without sudden movements, in the hope that the baby might actually stay content long enough for him to have a conversation.

'Hello? Max?' Toby's voice sounded faintly panicked on the other end of the line. 'Is everything okay? What's happened?'

'Everything's fine,' Max replied, even though it wasn't strictly accurate. 'Why wouldn't it be?'

'Um, because you're calling me?' Toby said. 'That's not exactly an everyday occurrence. Or an ever occurrence.'

'I've called you before.' Surely he had to have phoned his half-brother at least once or twice since Toby got in touch. Hadn't he?

'You've *emailed* me before,' Toby corrected him. 'Even texted me, once. But call? Never.'

'Well, I'm calling now,' Max said grumpily. 'Because I need your…advice, I guess.'

'You are absolutely certain that the world isn't ending?' Toby joked.

'Mostly.' Although, given that he was sitting in his study with a baby in his lap and half of Wells-on-Water in his hallway, there was room for doubt.

'Sounds ominous. What's going on?'

It took surprisingly little time to recap the events of the previous twelve hours—returning to the Manor House with Lena to find Willow on the doorstep, and the subsequent home invasion by the locals. Toby didn't interrupt, although Max was sure he heard him smother a laugh when he got to the part about hiding in his study.

'Okay, so I have many questions,' Toby said, when he was finished. 'But my first one has to be: Why was Lena Phillips coming home with you at midnight?'

Max let his head fall back to stare at the ceiling. *Of course* that was what Toby would choose to focus on. He was all loved up with his new bride and a baby on the way, so he was seeing romance everywhere.

'She gave me a lift home from Finn and Victoria's party,' he said shortly. No way he planned to mention his and Lena's history together—or that he'd kind of been hoping that history might repeat itself, until Willow had appeared.

'Right,' Toby said disbelievingly. 'You know, I've always liked Lena…'

'Well, that's great for you. But since she's currently reconfiguring my entire house for a baby who doesn't belong to me, do you think we could maybe concentrate on what actually matters here?'

He hadn't meant to raise his voice, but the little cry Willow gave suggested that he had anyway.

'Is the baby there with you right now?' Toby asked, sounding amused.

'She didn't like all the chaos outside, either,' Max grumbled. 'And it was time for her bottle.'

Toby was unexpectedly silent at that revelation.

'So, are you going to tell me what to do?' Normally, Max hated being ordered around, in any circumstance. And Toby was technically his *little* brother, which made asking even worse. But he was so far out of his depth, and so damn tired, he'd take what he could get.

'Like you'd listen to me anyway,' Toby said, with a laugh. 'But honestly, Max, I don't see that you have very many options. You're right that you need to alert the proper authorities *and* Lena's right that the villages around here look after their own.'

'I told her I'd give her twenty-four hours to find the mother.'

'Do you think that'll be enough?'

'No.' He'd known it when he said it, and he suspected Lena had, too. 'So what's my next move?' he asked, after a long moment's silence.

'I'm thinking,' Toby replied. 'Okay, so the note you found with the baby—'

'Willow.'

'Right, Willow. The note hinted that she was your child?'

'Yes. Except she *can't* be.' And Max was just loving having to explain his lack of sex life to multiple people over the last twenty-four hours.

'But what if you thought there was a chance that she was?'

Max blinked. Either he was particularly slow this morning or Toby wasn't making any sense at all. 'What do you mean?'

'I mean, if Willow *was* your child, then you wouldn't have to hand her over to the authorities, right? You'd get to keep looking after her until Lena found the real parents.'

'So you're suggesting we contact the authorities…but claim she's *mine*?' That sounded even more crazy than anything his sleep-deprived mind had come up with.

'Just a thought,' Toby said. 'I mean, to be honest, you don't sound like you're all that keen to hand her over to social services.'

Of course he was. That was exactly what he wanted to do—hand her over to the proper authorities and get his life back to normal. Why wouldn't he?

'I'm sure Lena would stay on a little longer to help out, too,' Toby added slyly.

'She'd better.' Not that he was thinking too hard about why he wanted Lena to stick around. Not while he was holding an innocent child.

'Plus it sounds like all the locals are pitching in. You won't be short of babysitters, if I know the people of Wells-on-Water.'

Something else that was confusing the hell out of him. Because Max *did* know the locals, and this was not the sort of behaviour *he* expected from them at all. 'I just don't understand why everyone is here, helping.'

'That's what people do in times of need or crisis, isn't it?' Said with all the confidence of a man who had never been on the receiving end of that sort of kindness, because he'd never *had* that kind of need. Toby was the legitimate son, after all.

Not like Max.

'Not in my experience.' He knew the words sounded bitter, and, from the sudden silence on the other end of the line, he expected that Toby knew what he was referring to, as well.

The brothers had talked very little about their shared father, and the past hurt and betrayal between them. It had always seemed more important to focus on the future they could build together, instead. But now Max wondered if they'd ever really be free to be family, to be brothers, if they *didn't* address the elephant in the room.

The fact that their father's refusal to admit that Max was his son had made Max's childhood hellish.

'How do you mean?' Toby said, after a moment. Max wondered if he'd come to the same conclusion as he had and was facing it head-on.

But right now wasn't the time to get into the details, the bitter reminiscing. He had Willow to worry about, in the here and now, and that was more important than anything that had happened in the past.

He really hadn't expected the visceral connection he felt to the tiny child, especially since he *knew* she couldn't be his. But he had to admit, it was hard to imagine just handing her over to social services in—he checked his desk clock—fifteen hours.

'I just mean that, growing up here in the village, I remember people taking more of a judgemental line than a supportive one.' If people out there were slating Willow's mother for her actions, he hadn't heard it. Everything he'd overheard had been about helping the baby, and finding the mother to make sure *she* was all right.

He hadn't expected that. And he wasn't convinced it would last.

'Maybe they've all learned something, over the years,' Toby said mildly. 'If I were you, I'd ask Lena about that.'

'Lena?' he repeated in confusion. 'Why Lena?'

Toby chuckled. 'Because I think that for every community event, every campaign—from the hunt for Jayden's missing rabbit to the Teddy Bears' Picnic treasure hunt and party to raise money for the local community hub—Lena has been at the heart of it. Wells-on-Water *has* changed since you grew up there, Max. And a lot of that has to do with Lena.'

It shouldn't surprise him. In a way, it didn't. Even at school, she'd always been on the organising committee for school proms and fetes, or the one single-handedly running a campaign for recycling bins in the canteen.

Unbidden, a memory floated into his head. That last night before he'd left, he'd asked if she would go, too. Not with him, exactly, but at all. Even then he'd thought that a backwater village like Wells-on-Water was too small, too petty minded, for someone who shone as brightly as Lena Phillips.

'Maybe,' she'd said. *'But I think I'd always come back. I belong here. And there's too much that needs doing.'*

'Couldn't you do it somewhere else?' he'd asked.

'Why would I?' She'd turned then, he remembered, her golden hair spread out over his bare arm as she'd looked up at him with glittering eyes. *'Why try to fix the world without starting here in my own backyard?'*

'Of course it does,' he murmured.

Another reason to try to hold onto Willow a little longer so they could search for her mother floated into Max's mind. He'd run out on Lena sixteen years ago, and never even called her after to check in. She'd been right to call him out on that.

But maybe he could prove to her that he wasn't the immature boy he'd been then any longer, by sticking around and pitching in this time. By helping Willow, and hopefully her family, too.

Outside in the hallway, he heard the front door slam shut, and a single set of footsteps retreating upstairs. Craning to listen, he realised that the constant noise that had woken him that morning had faded.

'I think they've gone,' he told Toby, who laughed.

'Then it's safe for you to come out of hiding. And I'd better go, anyway. I think Mrs Heath has lunch ready for us, and Autumn really doesn't like waiting for food these days.'

Since Autumn was nearly nine months pregnant, Max wasn't surprised. 'Okay. Enjoy your lunch. And…thanks, Toby.'

'Any time,' his brother said easily, before he hung up.

And strangest of all, Max really believed he meant it.

CHAPTER SIX

LENA TOOK ADVANTAGE of the small en-suite bathroom attached to the room Max had shown her to the night before to shower quickly, before changing into jeans and a T-shirt. Janice hadn't packed much beyond the clothes, though, so she had to make do with the shower gel and deodorant she found in the bathroom, alongside the guest towels, which she guessed were spares Max had lying around, as they resulted in her smelling just like him.

Which wasn't distracting at all.

Still, she felt a dozen times better for being clean, and out of last night's underwear and party clothes. She bounced down the stairs to find Max, but the study he'd retreated to was empty.

Pausing, she sniffed the air.

Coffee.

Lena smiled, and headed for the kitchen, where she found Willow settled into the bouncy chair someone had brought, her eyes wide as she took in her surroundings. Or not. Lena had a feeling that babies couldn't see very far at all. But whatever Willow was looking at, she seemed content with it.

'You figured out the coffee maker, then?' Lena leaned against the kitchen table as Max handed her a steaming cup with frothy milk.

'It wasn't exactly rocket science. Not like this thing.' He motioned towards another machine on the counter. 'I think it's supposed to make her milk, or heat it, or something, but God only knows how.'

Lena laughed. 'Georgia Watkins brought that. Said it was a godsend when hers were babies, but she didn't need it any more. I think she left the instructions around here somewhere...'

She started to search the counter, but Max stopped her. 'We'll look after lunch. I'm starving.'

Luckily, amongst the many boxes, bags and dishes the locals had delivered was a plate of sandwiches and a few bags of crisps. Food that needed no preparation at all was definitely what Lena was looking for.

While Max fixed himself a coffee to replace the one he'd given her, Lena dropped the platter of sandwiches onto the kitchen table. 'Lunch is served!'

'Amazing.' He even sounded as if he meant it. Which, since she imagined that Max Blythe got to eat at the fanciest restaurants in London, was saying something.

Even Willow seemed to understand that food was vital to them all surviving the rest of the day, because she stayed happily staring around herself in her bouncy chair while Lena inhaled the first couple of sandwiches.

'So, along with the food, did we get any real leads on Willow's mother?' Max asked, after long minutes of nothing but the two of them chewing.

Lena recounted everything she'd told Janice, which felt even less optimistic than it had the first time around.

'Sounds like it might take a while, if she doesn't just come forward,' he observed. 'More than twenty-four hours, anyway.'

Lena winced. 'But that doesn't mean it isn't still worth doing. I mean, even if we'd gone straight to the police, do you really think they'd be doing anything more than we are?'

'Willow would be with people who actually know how to look after babies, though.'

'I know how to look after babies,' she snapped, then remembered she'd told him she didn't. Although that had only been because she hated the idea that she *should* know, because she was the woman. With a sigh, she explained. 'I actually took a fostering course last year, and am registered to offer emergency foster care. I haven't had a placement yet, but I know what I should be doing.'

Max surveyed her silently, and Lena tried desperately to figure out what was going on behind those clear, dark eyes. Was he thinking this explained everything? Lonely spinster whose biological clock was ticking tried to hang onto baby that didn't belong to her, that sort of thing?

Except it wasn't that. It wasn't that she wanted a baby of her own, exactly. She just wanted to help.

And she didn't want Willow's mother to go to prison, or have her life ruined, just because she was so scared she couldn't look after a baby on her own, or whatever else had driven her to leaving Willow on Max's doorstep.

After a moment, Max looked away, and reached for another sandwich. 'I called Toby.'

Lena blinked. 'Okay.' She didn't know what that had to do with looking after a baby, but she was hoping he'd explain if she gave him the opportunity.

'I didn't understand why everyone in Wells-on-Water seemed so eager to help a baby whose own mother didn't even want it.'

She sucked in a sharp breath. She hadn't thought of it from that point of view before. In her head, *of course* Willow's mother loved and wanted her baby, she just didn't think she could look after it. That was why Lena wanted to find and help her.

But in Max's head, Willow's mum had abandoned her because she didn't want her, and that was why she wouldn't come forward and claim her now. Just as his own father had never wanted—or claimed—him.

Why hadn't she seen that before?

'Toby told me that the community here has come a long way since I left,' he went on, still not looking directly at her. 'That it's more supportive, more inclusive now, I guess.'

'I hope so.' Lena's mouth felt dry. How had she not realised how personal this must feel for Max?

'He also told me a lot of that had to do with you.' Now, he looked up, and even if his dark brown eyes were still guarded, she could see the hints of turbulence behind them.

'I… I don't know about that. But I've always loved this village, and the people in it. I know not all of them treated you fairly, or kindly, but they looked after me after my mum died. They supported me. And I guess… I guess I tried to do something to pay that forward to the next generation that lived here.'

'Toby said you were behind basically every community venture of the last decade.'

Lena laughed. 'I don't know about that. But yeah, I've tried to keep involved. Find ways to bring people together.'

Leaning back in his chair, Max stretched his legs out under the kitchen table until they almost brushed against hers. She tucked her ankles under her chair to keep her distance, but she couldn't *quite* banish Janice's suggestions about seduction from her mind.

Serious conversation here, Lena. Not *the time to be playing footsie.*

'Is that why you feel so responsible for Willow? Why

you're so worried about the community, and her mother being out there somewhere?'

At least he didn't think she was a lonely spinster, Lena supposed. And it had to be better than telling him the *whole* truth. She wasn't ready for that. Not yet. Maybe not ever.

After all, they were getting along so well. Why ruin it?

'Maybe a bit,' she admitted. 'Mostly I tend to feel responsible for everything, so perhaps this is just a natural extension of that.'

She'd meant it as a joke, but Max's expression turned serious. 'Why do you feel responsible for everything?'

Why? Had she ever even asked *herself* that question? It was just the way it was.

No. That wasn't entirely true. She knew why.

It was just that if she delved *too* deep into the why… well, that way lay thoughts and conversations she really didn't want to have with him.

She shrugged, keen to move on, away from her own issues and onto Willow's. 'Guess that's just the way I am.'

He studied her for a moment, perhaps waiting for her to say something more. And when she didn't, he said, 'I remember back when we were in school, walking home one day, across the fields, and running into your brothers.'

Dread bubbled up inside her, the way it always did when someone mentioned an encounter with her brothers—even a decades-old one. The feeling that whispered, *What have they done now?*

'It was the same way I walked every day—we all did, remember?' he went on.

She nodded. The high school was over in Wishcliffe, so every day the kids from Wells-on-Water trudged along the muddy footpath over the fields to get there—rather than take the longer, cleaner route by road.

'And most days your brothers were waiting along the path, under the trees, ready to torment somebody. Sometimes me, but just as often some other poor kid.' There was no emotion in his words, almost as if he were describing something he'd seen in a film, rather than something that had happened to him.

'I'm sorry—' she started, but he cut her off.

'It's not your place to apologise for them. You're not responsible for their actions, not then and certainly not now.'

And Lena *knew* this was true. Intellectually, she knew it. But inside…her subconscious never seemed so sure. She *felt* responsible, even if she shouldn't.

'You were hardly ever on the walk home,' Max said, and she couldn't tell if this was more of the story, or a mitigation for her responsibility.

'Too many clubs at school, or committees for events,' she said, with a wry smile. 'I was always there late, sorting things out, so I'd walk home via the road if it was dark, so I'd have the streetlamps to see by, even though it took longer.'

He nodded. 'That's right. But I remember this one day, you *were* there. And you came across your brothers tormenting me and a friend. This must have been soon after we started at the high school, because it didn't take me too long into my teens to learn to fight back.'

'I remember that part, for sure.' He'd been in constant trouble for fighting at school. No wonder they'd never run in the same circles.

'Anyway, this one day, you stepped right up into the middle of everything. The crowds gathered around parted for you, and you stood between me and my friend and your brothers, and you told them *stop.*' Max met her gaze and held it. 'And, to everyone's amazement, they did.'

'The one time they ever listened to me, then,' she joked,

trying to dismiss the heavy atmosphere that seemed to have filled the kitchen like smoke.

Max shook his head. 'People always listened to you. They still do. You can make people do things they never thought they'd even consider—like taking in an abandoned baby, for instance.'

'You'd have done the same if I wasn't here.'

'I'd have called the police and washed my hands of the whole thing and you know it.'

She did know it. But she still wasn't sure what point Max was trying to make. 'Fine, you would. So?'

'I think that, because people have listened to you for so long, because you were the only person your brothers ever listened to, you feel responsible for them. For everyone in this damned village and probably beyond. But, Lena, the only person you can ever really be responsible for is yourself.'

Max watched as Lena absorbed the idea he'd put out there—that she couldn't be responsible for everything—and dismissed it with a small shake of the head.

'Maybe you're right,' she said, and he knew that there was a 'but' coming. 'But there are things that I *have* taken responsibility for, and gladly.'

'Like Willow.' He wished he understood why she felt so strongly that they should look after the baby. He knew why *he* had come around to that idea, but he couldn't help but feel there was some reason she wasn't telling him that made it matter so much to her.

'Yes, like Willow,' she said. 'But other things, too. Like the community hub.'

'The community hub? What's that?' He knew there hadn't been much time for conversation between looking after Willow and dealing with all the locals, but he was pretty sure she hadn't mentioned that before. Or if she had, he'd been too exhausted to retain the information.

Lena sighed, and looked over at Willow, who was now dozing in her bouncy chair.

No chance of an escape from this conversation there, he thought, mentally thanking whoever had donated the seat. It was definitely Willow's new favourite thing.

'About two years ago, I helped set up a community hub in the old village hall,' Lena explained. 'It was a place for people to come for help and advice, or just some company and a cup of tea. I nagged all sorts of local professionals into donating an hour or two a week there as well. Like, Mr McDonald, who is a retired family law solicitor, and Robbie Jenkins, who runs a home-maintenance firm in Wishcliffe. We had sessions on childcare and parenting, on looking after family finances, even cooking and healthy meal planning. And I got Janice and one of her nurses to run regular drop-in clinics there, including a private family-planning one.'

The sort of clinic that Willow's mum might have gone to for help, Max supposed, when she realised she was pregnant.

'It sounds amazing,' Max said. 'Who paid for it all?'

Lena shrugged. 'We did a lot of fundraising. But they let us use the hall for free, and most people donated their time, or other things. We had a mini-foodbank going at Christmas with another planned for the summer holidays, and a second-hand baby stuff bring and buy sale in the spring.'

'So what happened?' Because he could tell from her voice this story didn't have a happy ending.

'The village hall roof caved in. Right on top of one of our cooking demonstrations.'

Max winced. 'Is it being fixed?'

'I don't know. I guess that will be up to the new owners.' Getting to her feet, Lena paced across to the sink and began rinsing out their coffee cups and plates.

'The village is selling the hall?'

'It was deemed unsafe—which, I mean, nobody could really argue with that after the roof collapse. But it turned out that the roof was only the start of it. There was so much that needed fixing up…there was no way we could raise the money for it. So the village council decided to sell it, and put the proceeds aside for other community ventures.'

'Another hub?'

'Maybe. Except there's plenty of groups around here that deserve a share of that money, and whatever we get it won't be enough to buy or even rent another base of operations for the hub, not within the village anyway. We're a picturesque seaside village, Max. If you don't think half the buildings around here are holiday lets these days you haven't been paying attention.'

He hadn't, he realised. He'd been so busy thinking about what returning to Wells-on-Water meant to him, he hadn't even noticed all the changes within the village.

'That's why you started the hub,' he said, finally beginning to understand. 'To give the real locals a place that still felt like theirs.'

'In part,' Lena admitted. 'But also because…there aren't so many opportunities around here, you know that. People who choose to stay do it because they love this place more than the money they could earn elsewhere—or because they don't have many opportunities wherever they go.'

'And you brought both those sorts of people together, to see if they could help each other.'

'That's the idea. Or it was.' Lena's shoulders slumped over the sink as she stared out of the back window over the grounds of the Manor House.

Max had more questions he wanted to ask about the

hub, but he sensed that Lena's mood was diving fast just talking about it, so he decided to save them for later. Plus, he had an idea or two that he wanted to test out before he mentioned them to her. No point raising her hopes if he couldn't pull off what he wanted to promise.

'It really does seem like a different village from the one I left behind,' he said. 'And I think Toby's right. A lot of that has to do with you. You should be proud of everything you've done for this place. I have no idea where you even found the time, let alone the energy.'

She turned at that and gave him a tired smile. 'Well, when it's something worthwhile…' Her gaze slid away towards Willow. Another worthwhile project she'd taken on, he supposed.

'Toby had a suggestion about Willow, you know.' The words were out before he could decide if it was a good idea to say them. Until the moment he spoke he honestly hadn't been sure if he was going to share his half-brother's thoughts with Lena—let alone go along with them.

Now…now it felt almost inevitable.

She'd done so much for this place in the sixteen years since he ran away. Now he was back, the least he could do was back her up a bit. Wasn't it?

Even if the idea still scared him stupid.

'He had an idea who her mother might be?' Lena asked.

Max shook his head. 'No. No…it was something else. He agreed with me that we needed to contact the authorities.'

'Max—' she started to interrupt, but he held up a hand and, with a mutinous glare, she let him finish.

'But he pointed out that since the note Willow's mum left behind seems to hint that I am the father, and especially now you've told me you actually have foster-care training, perhaps those authorities—with a good word from

Janice, maybe—might be willing to leave Willow with us a little longer, under their supervision, while we try and sort all this out?'

Lena's brow creased into a confused frown. 'But you're *not* the father.'

'No.' That much, at least, he was sure of.

'And you'd let everyone around here believe that you might be—that you got some girl in trouble and abandoned her?'

He shrugged, as if that idea didn't bother him—even though the very thought made his chest tight. He wouldn't do that, and he knew it. That would have to be enough.

And maybe it was a little bit of punishment, for leaving Lena and never checking up after their first time together. If she *had* been pregnant...well, that was exactly what he would have done, even if it would have been unintentional.

'It's not like they don't all already think the worst of me. We can say we're waiting on a DNA test or something.'

'But this is your fresh start,' Lena argued. 'Your chance to show everyone around here who you really are. Who you can be.'

The idea of reclaiming his reputation, of proving all the gossips of Wells-on-Water wrong, still glittered in the corner of his mind. But Willow mattered more. And so did Lena. She deserved to not have *all* that responsibility on her shoulders for a change. He could share the load, couldn't he?

It's the right thing to do, his mother's voice whispered in his brain.

'I've still got the Manor House,' he said flippantly. 'And the rest of it? Who cares what they all think, anyway?'

'You do,' Lena said, more astutely than he liked.

'Not any more,' he lied, his voice firm.

She studied him carefully for a long moment, and he

schooled his expression to give no hint of his real thoughts. Finally, she nodded.

'Then we'll call Janice in the morning and see what she thinks.'

'You don't want to do it now?' he asked, surprised.

Lena shook her head. 'Let's wait out our twenty-four hours, first. Maybe some information will turn up on the mother before then, and you won't need to lie.'

'Maybe,' Max echoed. But he knew as well as she did that it was a long shot.

As she turned away to check on Willow, he realised what she was doing: giving him an out. Time to change his mind.

But he knew he wouldn't take it. He needed to do this. For Willow, for Lena—and for the boy he'd been, all those years ago.

He couldn't change his past in this village. But he could help Lena change its future.

Willow wouldn't stop crying.

Holding her against her shoulder, Lena crooned softly to the baby, hoping that a song might soothe her as it had earlier that day, but it didn't seem to be doing any good. She'd been wailing since dinner time, and she showed no sign of stopping any time soon.

After doing his own shift walking Willow up and down the length of the house trying to soothe her, Max had gone to deal with a few emails in his study. Leaving Lena to pace around the drawing room, dodging all the baby stuff that the village had donated to help with looking after Willow. None of which had seemed to be any help this evening.

She'd changed her nappy, fed her, winded her, checked her temperature was okay…and nothing seemed to be making a bit of difference. Lena had even flicked through the relevant chapters of the books Janice had left, and the on-line forums she'd bookmarked that morning, but none of them had any more useful advice than waiting it out.

Babies cry. It's what they do. It doesn't mean I'm doing this wrong.

It felt as if she was, though. God, how did new mothers cope with this? The complete helplessness in the face of a squalling infant who didn't seem to want anything but to cry?

'My turn.' Max's voice came from the doorway. 'You need some sleep.'

She shook her head. 'I can do a bit longer.'

'It's gone midnight, Lena.' He moved closer, holding out his arms for the baby. 'Let someone help you for a change, yeah?'

The thought was such a strange one, she stopped and stared. Oh, people helped her all the time—when she asked them for help. Like this morning with the stuff for Willow, or Janice bringing her clothes.

But the idea of someone else seeing what she needed and stepping in to give it to her without her having to ask? That one was new.

If she weren't so tired and her head weren't pounding from listening to Willow scream for the last hour, she might object to Max assuming he knew what she needed. Or she'd point out that the baby was every bit as much his responsibility as hers, if not more. As it was…

'Thank you,' she said, and placed Willow in his arms. Then, impulsively, she kissed him on the cheek and made a dash for the stairs.

She was still overthinking that kiss as she lay in bed in the guest room half an hour later, Willow's screams muf-fled but still clearly audible from below. It had just been a friendly thank-you kiss, nothing she wouldn't give to any other friend who helped her out.

Even if, being that close to him, the very scent of his skin had threatened to overpower her exhaustion and lead her thoughts down a path that had nothing to do with sleep or childcare...

Did he feel it, too, being close to her? That tug of a connection between them that had never quite disappeared, even after so many years? Maybe it was just because he'd been her first. Or because he'd grown up so damn well she couldn't help but wonder how it would be between them now. But whatever the reason, she had to admit that she wasn't only looking at Max as a carer for Willow.

She must have dozed off eventually, still wrestling with her thoughts about the man whose house she was staying in. But she jerked awake again not long after, Willow's cries suddenly nearer.

Swinging her legs slowly over the side of the bed, she padded to the door, and found Max in the hallway.

'Sorry,' he said. 'I thought I'd finally got her settled in her basket, so popped down to grab a glass of water.'

Lena shook her tired head. 'It's okay. She's really unsettled tonight, huh?'

'Seems so.' He gave her a weary smile. 'Go on, you head back to bed.'

But she didn't. Pushing gently past Max, she made her way into his room, and lifted Willow from her basket. The baby settled a little in her arms, at least.

'Worried I've done something stupid to upset her?' Max stood in the doorway, his arms folded across his broad chest.

'No.' Her exhausted legs were about to give way, so Lena dropped to sit on the edge of his bed. 'But we're in this together, right? And it looks like it's going to be a long night.'

'What do you suggest, then?' Max moved to sit beside her on the bed, and they both stared down at Willow's tiny face.

'She's happier being held,' Lena said, thinking back to everything she'd read in Janice's books. 'But I'm worried that if I try to sit up with her I'll fall asleep—and so would you,' she added before he could argue. 'And I don't want to be dashing back and forth between two rooms all night.'

'So we take turns?' Max suggested. 'Stay here while she settles, so we can both keep an eye on her and doze in between. And if we're lucky, maybe she'll fall deeply enough asleep to put her in the basket eventually.'

'Sounds like the best plan we've had so far,' Lena admitted. Holding Willow to her chest with one arm, she used the other to lever herself up the bed until her back rested against the headboard. She adjusted the baby in her arms, as Max manoeuvred the duvet from under her legs to cover her.

Then he settled himself on the other side of the bed. 'You okay with her for now?' he asked.

Lena nodded. 'Try and get a nap while she's quiet,' she suggested. 'Because when she starts crying again, it's your turn.'

'Fair enough.' Max's words were muffled against his pillow as he lay down on his side, facing them. 'Night, Lena. Night, Willow.'

She looked down at his dark hair against the white sheets, his face peaceful but exhausted, and grinned, despite her tiredness.

This really isn't how I imagined getting Max Blythe into bed again.

CHAPTER SEVEN

MAX WOKE TO SILENCE, which seemed unexpected, and a warm body in his arms, which was even more so. He opened his eyes slowly as he tried to make sense of the world.

He was lying down in bed, that much was clear, and he vaguely remembered Willow settling into a deep enough sleep that he'd risked putting her in her basket. That must have been—he squinted at the clock on his bedside table— two hours ago. He lifted his head a little more to check, and saw her small body still in there, the light blanket over her rising and falling with her tiny breaths. Still sleeping. Wow, that might be a record.

He turned his attention back to the bed.

Blonde hair over his pillow, and a pale arm thrown across his chest.

Lena Phillips is in my bed.

Oh, and didn't that just raise all sorts of interesting possibilities?

Now his brain had caught up with his body, he knew full well why she was there—and it hadn't had anything to do with a late-night seduction. But his body didn't seem to care. All it knew was that a beautiful woman was lying next to him. No, not just a beautiful woman. *Lena*.

Lena Phillips was in his bed, and that was taking his

brain—not just his body—down all sorts of interesting side paths.

Not that he intended to try and do anything about them. For one, Willow was still in the room, and bound to wake up at any moment. And for another…he and Lena had history. And they also had a future—at least for the next few days. They had to focus on Willow and finding her family.

Muddying the waters by doing anything about the sexual tension between them wouldn't help.

Right?

Max sighed. He was going to have to keep working on convincing himself of that, apparently.

Lena's eyelids fluttered, then opened, and she blinked up at him. As he watched, he saw the initial confusion in her eyes fade, replaced by something else. Heat. Want. The same things he'd felt on realising their position on waking.

Then she pulled away, an apologetic smile on her lips, and he knew that she'd just gone through the same mental gymnastics that he had, and apparently reached the same conclusion.

They couldn't take this any further while they had Willow to take care of.

The only problem with that logic, Max realised, was that once Willow was gone—hopefully safely back with her family—he'd be going back to London. And he really hadn't planned on spending much time in Wells-on-Water after that.

Lena belonged here, and he never had. And Max had enough trouble making time for girlfriends in the same city as him to believe that there was any hope of anything longer distance.

No, if they *did* try to make something of this, Max knew it would end the same way it had last time—with him driving away and leaving Lena to the life she deserved.

Except this time I'll leave a number, just in case.

On cue, Willow let out a small whimper, followed by a louder cry. Peace and rest were over.

Lena sat up against the headboard, and yawned. 'Well, at least we all got *some* sleep last night.'

Swinging his legs over the side of the bed, Max reached into Willow's basket and lifted her out. 'More than I'd dared hoped for at the start of the night.'

The baby settled against his chest as he sat back down on the bed, and he wondered when this had become natural to him. Not easy, for certain, and he was still sure he was going to mess it up every second of the day. But holding a baby, something he'd never done before this week, now felt perfectly normal.

As did having Lena in his home. In his bed.

'So, what's the plan for the day?' Lena asked.

Glancing over, he saw that she was worrying her lower lip with her teeth as she waited for his answer, and realised what she was really asking. Did he still want to go ahead with their plan from the day before: pretending he *could* be Willow's dad, so they could keep looking after her while they searched for her mum?

Did he?

He knew it was a risk. It could be a huge hit to his reputation here, which had always been a bit tattered to start with. If he *had* hoped to come back and make a life here in Wells-on-Water, people gossiping about how he'd knocked up some poor girl then abandoned her wouldn't make that easy. And if the truth came out, he knew people would find a way to doubt his motives, perhaps suggesting he was using Willow to get Lena into bed, or something. Which he wasn't, despite current evidence.

And if the police found out he'd lied about possibly

being the father, he didn't even know if there would be penalties for that.

But none of that changed a damn thing. He was doing it anyway.

'Well, I guess we'd better get things in motion with social services,' he said. 'And figure out what our story is going to be, if we want to keep this one with us a little longer.'

Lena's smile lit up the whole room, more so than the summer sun outside the window.

She jumped out of bed. 'In that case, you change Willow, and I'll go make up her bottle—and get the coffee machine going. And then we can call Janice and figure out how to do this.'

'Sounds good,' Max replied. 'Because this is definitely going to require coffee.'

Janice thought Max's—or Toby's—plan was a great idea. Lena knew her friend had been uncomfortable not notifying the proper people in the first place, and at least this way they were nominally following proper procedure.

'I'll make the calls,' Janice said eagerly, when she called. 'You guys sit tight.'

Which meant that, until Willow woke from her post-breakfast nap in what Lena was privately calling the Chair of Joy, there was nothing to do but sit around with Max, drinking coffee, and wondering how he felt about their... rather cuddly wake up that morning.

She knew how she had felt. She'd felt a little embarrassed, worried about her morning breath, guilty for forgetting about Willow for a long moment as she'd stared at him, and...

Well. Mostly she'd just wished that circumstances were different and she'd been able to take advantage of the situation. In fact, if Willow hadn't woken up just then, she couldn't say for sure that she wouldn't have.

There was just something magnetic about the way he looked at her. How he made her feel—as if her whole body had come alive despite its ongoing exhaustion.

Did he feel the same? What would have happened the other night when she'd brought him back to the Manor House if there *hadn't* been a baby on the doorstep…?

But there had been. And they still had to deal with that.

He'd been the one to insist she call Janice and go ahead with their plan.

Which brought her back to the question of why he was doing this.

He didn't want to be looking after Willow, she knew that. He'd admitted that if she weren't there, he would have handed her over to the police in a heartbeat.

So why? Had all that talk about responsibility shamed him into it?

Or was it something else…?

She'd been carefully ignoring the tiny corner of her mind that suggested he might be doing it to spend more time with her. Quite apart from the fact that he'd shown no indication that he was looking for a repeat of their last night together since the moment they'd found Willow on the doorstep—although before was up for debate—it was doing Max a disservice to think that way.

But that was before she'd woken up in his arms to find him watching her sleep, a heat she remembered well simmering behind his eyes. Maybe the chance to get her into bed wasn't *why* he was doing this—especially since so far sleep was far higher up the priority list than anything else they might be doing between the sheets—but she got the impression that it could be a pretty great added bonus.

For both of them.

She shook the thought away, forcing herself to face reality. If sex was really what he wanted, she was pretty sure he could find that anywhere he wanted. The fact that he hadn't sought it out in so long—long enough that he could be so sure that Willow wasn't his…well, she had to admit, that had come as a surprise.

But one they wouldn't be sharing with social services, if they wanted their plan to work.

They talked about it again, as they waited for Janice to arrive—over lunch, and into the afternoon, between taking care of Willow. They had a plan. They wouldn't mention Max's imaginary ex-partner if they could help it, just say that he wanted to preserve her privacy but, since he hadn't been aware she might be pregnant, wanted to alert the proper authorities in case this was some sort of scam.

Of course, that plan fell apart the moment the social worker Janice had called, accompanied by a representative from the local police force, finally arrived and started asking questions.

'Obviously our main concern is for the mother's safety,' Constable Robbins said, his bored tone suggesting that, actually, his main concern was getting all this sorted so he could forget about it. 'Normally with an abandoned baby we'd be doing appeals and all sorts. But you say the baby could be yours?' This last was added with a raise of the eyebrows that insinuated all sorts of things Lena didn't really like.

'The mother left a note suggesting that,' Lena said. 'That's one of the reasons we're so keen to keep Willow here with us until she's found.'

'Surely you must have some idea who she is, then?' Sarah, the social worker, asked Max. 'If you could give us her name, or, well, a list of names, I suppose, then perhaps we could track her down for you?' She was blushing now, poor thing. Lena supposed that Max's glower at the suggestion of his leaving a trail of pregnant women behind him was sort of intimidating if you didn't know how horribly embarrassed he must be by this whole thing.

'As I said at the start, I have not been contacted by any past…acquaintance to tell me of a pregnancy. And obviously, as this is a very sensitive matter, I would like to make contact personally to try and sort this out. Given my public standing, a DNA test will of course be required. Really, we were only alerting you as a courtesy in case it emerges that this is simply an attempt by a desperate woman to play off my wealth.' Hiding the lie within the truth, Lena thought. Of course he hadn't been contacted by anyone, because there was no one to contact him. Which meant those phone calls he was promising to try and track down Willow's mother were a blatant lie.

Lena watched Max's face as he spoke, the clipped, almost aristocratic tones clearly designed to end the discussion then and there. She could imagine him using such tactics and intimidation in the boardroom, negotiating deals and getting things done. And glancing over at Sarah and Constable Robbins, she could see that it was working. Sarah was already packing up her paperwork.

But underneath it, she could see the faint signs of stress in the lines around Max's mouth, the set of his jaw. He was hating this. Hating lying. Hating trashing his reputation this way.

And she started to wonder if he really was all that different from the boy she'd connected with on that last day of school, so long ago. If everything that had happened since—and maybe before, now she thought about it—had simply been a shield he'd built up. A mask made to help him survive in a world that had treated him unfairly for so long.

She'd seen the mask slip just once in all the years she'd known him.

She wondered now if she could make it slip again.

Janice, who'd accompanied them to ensure things went smoothly, hurried things along at that point, getting everything tied up for now and everyone who didn't belong there out of the house far faster than Lena thought she could have managed. In lots of ways the doctor had the same sort of authority Max exuded, except hers felt more natural, born out of years of study and more years of dealing with people every day, often when they needed someone to tell them what was wrong and what to do next.

And then, it was just Lena, Max and Willow at the Manor House again, left with nothing but a promise of a return visit from Sarah very soon to 'see how they were doing' and a reminder from Constable Robbins to get in touch if there were 'any developments'.

Lena sagged against the door as she closed it behind them. Max had Willow in his arms again, humming tunelessly to her as he paced the length of the large hallway, trying to soothe her. And suddenly it hit her, exactly what they'd agreed to here.

'What if we don't find the mother?' Her words seemed too loud in the almost empty house. 'What happens then?'

Max reached the end of the hall and turned to start back again, looking up from Willow's face to meet Lena's gaze with his dark, unreadable one. 'You'll find her. I have faith in you.'

Lena just wished she had the same faith in herself.

But faith counted for nothing if she didn't keep moving. Action was what mattered; she'd always known that. Ever since her mother died, and she became somehow responsible for a family of men, far too young.

'It's getting late already.' She pushed away from the

door and started towards the kitchen. 'We should eat. I think someone left some sort of pasta bake we can just shove in the oven for dinner.'

'Sounds perfect,' Max replied.

They tried to put Willow back in the Chair of Joy while they ate, but she was having none of it.

'I don't get it,' Max said, frustrated, as he picked her up again. 'She's clean, she's eaten, she's burped, she's slept… what else is there to want when you're this little?'

Lena gave a small smile. 'The same thing we all want. Connection.' Max looked puzzled, so she explained. 'Her eyesight is still very, very limited, remember. If she's over there and we're here, she can't see us. And right now, I guess she wants to know that she's not alone.'

Max looked back down at the baby in his arms with a softness Lena knew not many would expect from him. 'Well, okay, then,' he said, and proceeded to eat his entire meal one-handed, cuddling Willow throughout, even after she fell asleep in his arms.

'Do you want me to take the first shift with her tonight so you can get some sleep?' Lena asked as they loaded the dishwasher. Max had proved surprisingly adept at doing things one-handed, now he understood why it was necessary.

'No. You sleep,' he said. 'She's comfy enough here, anyway.'

'She certainly looks it.' Lena wondered what it said about her that she was almost jealous of Willow, who got to have Max's arms around her while Lena was going to bed alone.

Probably it said nothing more than, as she'd told Max, everyone wanted, needed connection. And it had been a long time since she'd had any. Max wasn't the only one who'd been through a bit of a dry spell lately.

She could always suggest they try the same tactic as last night, sharing the bed to share the load of looking after Willow…but she didn't want to sound needy. Or give him the idea that she was angling for more than just his help with the baby here. If he thought she was getting Ideas about them, he could call that social worker right back and tell her the truth—that Willow couldn't be his.

No. She should try to keep some sort of distance between them, at least for now. Until they got everything with Willow sorted out. She didn't want the heightened emotions of the situation to get them both tangled up in something neither of them had really planned for.

A second one-night stand, the night of the party, would have been one thing. But they were friends now, she hoped. And that meant anything that happened between them had consequences.

Like her having to tell him the truth about what happened sixteen years ago.

And she really wasn't ready for that.

Lena glanced at the clock on the wall: just gone nine o'clock. She'd never normally be in bed this early but right now she felt as if she could barely keep her eyes open.

'Go on,' Max said. 'You go up.'

'You'll come get me when you need to swap?'

'You bet I will,' he replied, with a smile. 'I'll see you in a few hours, yeah?'

Lena nodded, and turned to leave, before stopping suddenly and swinging back—something Max clearly hadn't anticipated, as he was right behind her, one arm raised to shut the door.

She managed to avoid crashing into him and the baby, but only just. And as it was, it put them closer than they'd been since they found Willow. Close enough that she could feel the warmth radiating from him and the bundle in his arms.

Willow was tucked in the crook of his left arm, his right resting against the doorframe above her head. And all Lena could think was that she was so close she could kiss him, if she wanted. If he wanted.

If he weren't holding a baby right now.

She blinked, and shook her head.

'Lena? You okay?' Max asked softly, and she nodded.

'Yeah. I just…' What was it she'd wanted to tell him? Why had she turned back?

The words came to her in a rush, and she looked up from his lips to meet his warm gaze instead.

'I just wanted to tell you that you're a really good man.'

She half expected him to laugh, to knock the compliment away with a joke about sleep deprivation or something. And she thought he almost expected that, too. But maybe they were both too tired to bother with that sort of thing any more.

Instead, his lips curved up into a slight smile, and he whispered, 'Thank you.'

And, God, she wanted to kiss him. But instead, she turned on her heel and ran for bed.

Max couldn't sleep. Which was ridiculous, because he was so far beyond exhausted. He'd finally given in and woken Lena up around three, when Willow had stirred for yet another feed. He'd moved the Moses basket into the guest room while Lena fed the baby, and refused to let himself dwell on how much easier this would be if they just shared his bed again tonight.

He needed actual sleep, and a wall between him and the crying baby. That was only sensible.

So he'd collapsed into bed in his blissfully silent bed-room certain that he'd be dead to the world until morning.

Except…

Except he couldn't get that moment out of his head. That brief few seconds when he'd honestly believed that Lena Phillips was about to kiss him. Again.

Instead, she'd told him he was a good man—which was absurd, because nobody had ever called him that before. A good negotiator, sure. A good businessman even. But he'd never been a good son, or a good friend, and certainly not a good boyfriend.

A good man?

It had to be the sleep deprivation talking.

But…he'd felt the truth of her words in his heart as she'd spoken, and known she believed them, even if he wasn't at all sure he did.

He told himself she was just grateful that he'd bought them more time to find Willow's mum. But that just brought him back to why he'd done that in the first place.

He wanted to pretend it was to keep Lena with him until they could finish what he'd hoped they'd been about to start the night of Finn and Victoria's party. But that would be a lie—especially since looking after a tiny baby who didn't sleep was objectively *not* conducive to seduction. If he'd tried to take Lena to bed tonight he was pretty sure that one of them would have fallen asleep before they'd even got their clothes off.

He'd done it because it was the right thing to do. Maybe his mother's ghost had been whispering in his ear—not that he believed in such things. But being back in Wells-on-Water, he had to admit that her memory felt closer than ever.

And more than anything, his mum had believed in doing the right thing, not the easy one.

Well, he hoped she'd be happy at his choices since he'd come back to the Manor House. Looking after Willow was not easy. And he had a feeling that resisting Lena's charms while the baby was in the house wouldn't be easy, either.

Finally, sleep must have claimed him because the next thing he knew it was morning, the sun was up, and he could hear Lena moving something heavy downstairs.

Bracing himself for another home invasion, he showered and dressed quickly before heading down, only to find the hallway empty except for an ancient-looking, huge-wheeled pram.

He peered into it and found Willow staring up at him. She didn't look any surer about this turn of events than he felt.

'Isn't it gorgeous?' Lena appeared from the kitchen, two travel coffee mugs in hand. 'I think Mrs Jenkins has been keeping it in her garage since her own kids were babies, hoping there'd be grandchildren one day who'd need it.'

'Are we sure it was just for her babies?' Max looked critically at the metal frame, but even he had to admit it was polished to perfection. 'Not, say, the last eight generations of her family? The thing looks positively Victorian.' If it had come from Mrs Hillary Jenkins, into his home, there was also the chance it could be booby-trapped to maim or injure him, although he didn't mention that to Lena. Mrs Jenkins had been…whatever the absolute opposite of his number one fan was, all through his youth.

'These prams are all the rage again these days, according to Victoria,' Lena replied. 'The originals go for silly money on Internet auction sites.'

'Maybe for social media photos,' Max allowed. 'But what are they like to actually push?'

'That's what we're going to find out,' Lena said brightly. 'We're going for a walk.'

'We as in…?'

'As in you, too. Come on.'

It seemed easier to go along with Lena's plans than argue, especially since she held the coffee hostage until they were outside. Together, they carefully manoeuvred the pram down the front steps and over the gravel until they hit the road into the village.

'Isn't it a beautiful day?' Lena took a deep breath of the summer air and beamed.

'How much coffee have you had already?' He knew she'd been up at least on and off since three, and yet she looked as fresh as the proverbial daisy.

'Lots,' she answered honestly. 'I'm scheduling in a crash mid-afternoon for a nap, so prepare to be on Willow duty then.'

'Fair enough.' At some point, he was going to have to get back to actual work, but it didn't look as though that was going to be today. He'd managed to respond to the odd urgent email, and send a message to his assistant to postpone meetings and take care of anything non-business-critical that came up, but that was about all. Besides, he wasn't sure he trusted his judgement when he was this tired.

It was ridiculous, really, he decided as they strolled down the hill towards the rooftops and warm stone buildings of Wells-on-Water. When he was working on a big project, or in time-sensitive negotiations, he frequently functioned on less sleep than he'd had over the last couple of days.

The difference, he supposed, was that time was then his own. Once the crisis was over, he could crash. He could hand over responsibility and sleep until he was refreshed. Or even take a weekend off to chill out at some resort somewhere, with or without company.

Here, with Lena and Willow, the sleep he did get was

broken by her cries and, more importantly, the constant need to try and interpret her desires. Even when she was with Lena, he never felt fully off duty. If she was in the house, he felt responsible for her.

That was the exhausting part. God, how did parents do it? He was in awe.

More and more, as the days went on, he was coming to understand how a scared, desperate, presumably single and maybe young mother could feel that her only option was to pass that responsibility on to an adult. One with resources she, perhaps, didn't have.

Money makes everything easier.

He'd known that since he was a child, watching his father's family living in a mansion in Wishcliffe, while his mother worked two jobs to keep them housed and fed. It was one of the reasons he'd left Wells-on-Water as a teen, determined to seek his fortune and build a different life for them.

That his mother hadn't lived long enough to really enjoy it still hurt.

But it hadn't occurred to him to use his money to try and fix this. Even Lena had called in favours and support rather than ordering new things, which he could easily have done. He could have called an agency, found a nanny, anything. But he hadn't.

Willow wasn't something he could throw money at to solve the problems that had brought her to his door. Not entirely, anyway.

Lena was right. The community was what mattered here.

If only it weren't one that had completely alienated him before he'd even turned eighteen.

The fields either side of the road gave way to houses, then shops, and then the familiar sight of the cross at the centre of the village, a memorial to those lost in the wars. Max had driven through the village since he'd arrived, but not spent much time looking around. Now, he took a moment to absorb the changes.

Some shops had changed hands, that was obvious, although Mrs Jenkins's corner shop still had pride of place by the cross. The church had new, more modern signs outside, which clashed with the ancient stones and the stained-glass windows. The pub opposite—the one Lena's dad had owned and operated—looked a little run-down around the edges, which surprised him. Maybe the family had sold it—hadn't Victoria mentioned something about Lena managing the King's Arms in Wishcliffe, now? He couldn't imagine Lena letting it get into such a state.

He turned his attention back to the streets around him. There were bins at regular intervals, which sorted recyclables from non-recyclables—something Max would bet large amounts of money Lena was behind. And there, at the far end of the village, he could just make out the village hall, the roof covered in scaffolding and canvas.

'Is it as you remember?' Lena asked softly.

'Mostly.' He turned his attention back to the pram he was pushing. For an antique, it moved surprisingly smoothly. Inside, Willow lay peacefully tucked up under a white crocheted blanket. 'She's asleep. Shall we see if anywhere will serve us breakfast?'

It was still early, but the cafe diagonally across from the corner shop was open, and the smell of frying bacon and freshly brewed coffee was enticing. Max wasn't at all surprised when, upon entering, Lena was greeted as an old friend by the girl behind the counter, and a man emerged from the kitchen in a greasy apron to hug her welcome.

'I wondered if we'd see you today, love,' he said, in a broad accent Max couldn't quite identify. 'I remember when my three were that age, some mornings all I needed was someone else to make me breakfast. No, don't bother with menus. I'll just bring you two of everything. That's what you need—a proper plateful.'

He disappeared back into the kitchen, and Lena guided them to a table in the corner where they could park the pram up against the wall without blocking any of the passageways between tables. The girl from the counter placed two giant mugs of tea on the table before they'd even sat down.

'You're a regular here, I take it?' Max asked Lena with raised eyebrows.

'Oh, everyone in the village knows Lena!' The girl flashed them both a grin. 'It just makes a change to be helping her out, that's all.'

She disappeared back to her post as the door opened and another customer came in. Max took a moment to savour his tea in silence—until a shadow covered their table, and he looked up to see one of the banes of his younger self's existence standing over him.

Mrs Hillary Jenkins herself.

CHAPTER EIGHT

EVERY VILLAGE HAD a Hillary Jenkins, Lena was sure of it.

Somewhere between her sixties and her eighties—Lena wouldn't dare try to guess which—Mrs Jenkins had steel-grey hair, tightly curled against her head, and wore the sort of dresses in thick floral material Lena didn't even know where to buy. She also had the biggest mouth of anyone Lena had ever met.

On her most charitable days, she reminded herself that while Mrs Jenkins's three children had left the village and not looked back, and her husband had run away to Southampton with a primary school teacher twenty years ago, Mrs Jenkins's devotion to Wells-on-Water and its community never wavered.

On her bad days, she muttered to herself that Hillary Jenkins was a gossiping busybody who cared more about catching someone doing something wrong than doing anything right herself.

Today was somewhere in the middle, but, since Willow was currently snoozing away in the pram that Mrs Jenkins herself had donated, Lena forced herself to smile and be charming—just in case Max went the other way. From what she remembered of their youth, and his comments earlier, she wasn't sure that Max and Mrs Jenkins had ever had the best relationship.

'Hillary! How lovely to see you.' Lena started to her feet, but Mrs Jenkins put a hand on her shoulder and pushed her back down.

'Don't you be standing on my account, Lena.' The glare she shot Max's way suggested that he should have considered it, though. 'You need to rest when you can, with a baby to look after.'

Another pointed look at Max. Lena suspected that the story about Max perhaps being Willow's father was fully doing the rounds, then. Well, he couldn't say she hadn't warned him.

'Honestly, Hillary, I'm just helping out. Max is doing all the really hard work.'

'Hmm.' Mrs Jenkins didn't look entirely convinced, but her demeanour softened ever so slightly, which Lena decided to call a victory. 'I've always said that men needed to help out more around here.'

'The beautiful pram you lent us has certainly helped with that,' Max said smoothly. 'Willow loves being taken for walks in it so much she's already fallen asleep. And it's in such good condition.'

'Well, I do believe in looking after things,' Mrs Jenkins admitted. 'And helping out where I can, of course. Speaking of which...'

She turned and motioned towards another woman by the counter, who'd presumably come in with her. It took Lena a moment to place her, only because she wasn't someone she was used to seeing hanging around with Hillary Jenkins.

'Hello, Margery,' Lena said, smiling as the woman approached. 'Max, this is Margery Griffiths. She moved here after your time, and she runs the craft shop down opposite the village hall.'

Margery, with her long boho dresses, brightly hennaed hair, and clinking silver jewellery, was often the subject of

Hillary's rants about the nature of the occupants of Wells-on-Water. Apparently, all that hippy-dippy home-made stuff could only be bad for the village. Lena suspected she was worried about her profits at the corner store if everyone started making their own jam.

But apparently the two of them had now teamed up together. Which made her nervous.

'Now. Lena. We know you're always doing a lot for this village, but taking on a baby single-handed goes above and beyond.' Hillary didn't even look at Max as she spoke, but Lena saw him roll his eyes at her exclusion of him from the narrative.

'Honestly, I wanted to do it,' Lena said. 'And Max has been doing most of it anyway. I'm just helping.'

'As he should,' Margery muttered under her breath. Yeah, the fake news that Max might be the father had definitely spread around the village. Lena didn't know *how* she was going to fix that.

'Well, there's no shame in asking for help,' Hillary went on. 'But since we know you never do, we're going to insist. Margery and I will be at the Manor House at seven o'clock this evening to babysit this little mite, while you two go out for dinner.'

'Roberto is already holding his best table for you,' Margery added. 'So you can't say no.'

Lena met Max's gaze across the table. He gave an almost imperceptible shrug, as if to say, *It's up to you.*

Dinner. With Max. Almost like…a date. Was this Hillary and Margery setting them up? Had they decided that seducing Max and looking after his possible baby was the only way Lena was ever going to get the happily ever after they'd decided she deserved?

Possibly. Or perhaps they were intending for her to rehabilitate him from his rakish ways, or something. That sounded more likely.

Did she even *want* to go out to dinner? Well, no. She wanted to curl up in her pyjamas and eat takeaway Chinese, as she always did.

But she *did* want to spend time with Max. Away from Willow, much as she adored the small girl. Time for just the two of them, to figure out where they might have ended up the other night if it hadn't been for a basket on the doorstep of the Manor House. Maybe even to talk about everything that had passed for the two of them since that night in the back of his old car, sixteen years ago.

Well, maybe not *everything*.

But a chance to figure out who they were now, and what that meant, now he was back.

Maybe nothing. But perhaps…

Lena smiled up at Hillary and Margery. 'That would be wonderful, and so very kind of you. Thank you for thinking of us.'

The two women beamed matching smiles. 'Then we'll leave you to your breakfast and see you at seven.'

As they headed for the door, Lena realised she was going to have to go home and find something suitable to wear for a date with Max Blythe.

Breakfast proved to be the biggest meal Max had ever eaten in his life—and he enjoyed every mouthful.

'You're always hungrier when you're tired,' Lena said, knowledgeably, when he commented on it.

'Guess we'd better skip lunch, if we're going out for dinner.' Two large meals in one day was plenty for a guy who often forgot to eat between meetings if his secretary wasn't nagging him. And really, he must call into work…later.

Max was sort of surprised that Lena had agreed to the

dinner in the first place, but not nearly as surprised as he was that Hillary Jenkins had offered, even when she clearly thought he was some feckless father who had abandoned a pregnant girl.

'Are we sure that going out for dinner is a good idea?' he asked. It seemed unlikely that Hillary Jenkins wouldn't have *some* sort of ulterior motive for the offer, even if he was finding it hard to imagine what it could be.

'Don't you want to?' Lena asked.

He swung his gaze to hers and saw the uncertainty there. Did she really think he was still the guy who ran out on her after their first time together?

'Of course I want to,' he said, with feeling. 'A whole evening with you, without the interruptions of nappy changes and feeds? It sounds brilliant.'

Lena's expression relaxed. 'Then you're worried about leaving Willow with Hillary and Margery?'

Yeah, that sounded better than 'I think this might all be a cunning ploy to destroy me somehow.' 'Something like that.'

'It's sweet that you're worrying.' Smiling, she reached across the table to place a hand on his, and Max felt electricity shoot up his arm at their connection. 'But I think they'll be okay. Hillary is one of the go-to babysitters for basically everybody in the village.'

'Poor kids,' Max muttered under his breath, making Lena laugh. 'Well, I guess we're going out to dinner, then.'

'I guess we are. But I need to go home first,' Lena said. 'Janice brought me some basics yesterday, but if I'm going to be staying with Willow and you at the Manor House any longer, I'm going to need my own stuff. Not to mention something suitable for Roberto's tonight.'

'Is it fancy there?' The poshest place to eat in Wells-on-Water when Max had lived there had been the sit-in fish and chip shop.

'Fancier than everywhere else,' Lena replied. 'It's a proper, family-run Italian restaurant. I think you'll like it.'

'I'm sure I will.' Especially if it meant spending an evening with Lena, with no distractions.

How could he not?

But by seven o'clock, the whole plan seemed in jeopardy.

Lena had left Max with Willow for an hour or so while she drove back to her cottage and packed, and after an initial existential panic about being left completely alone with a child, without supervision, Max had actually managed perfectly well for the first forty-five minutes. It was only the last quarter of an hour that went to hell.

First, he tried to give Willow her bottle, only for her to throw up the whole thing over herself, him and the donated sofa. Then she proceeded to have the sort of nappy explosion that he had never imagined outside horror movies. One that he proved inadequate to cleaning up with the usual array of wipes and cloths.

'This wasn't in any of the books,' he muttered to her. 'I'd definitely have noticed illustrations of *this*.'

Willow responded by screwing up her face in a sort of warning way. Eyes wide, Max grabbed for another nappy—but was too late.

Which was why he was standing in the bathroom in nothing but his boxer shorts, trying to clean them both off with tepid water, when Lena found them.

'Don't come in here,' Max told her as he heard her approach. 'Not unless you're wearing a hazmat suit, anyway.'

She giggled, and Max turned to look at her—finding her leaning in the doorway wearing a beautiful beaded

dress of coral-red, her hair pinned up except for one ten-
dril that curled down across her bare neck.

He swallowed. Hard. 'Definitely don't come in here
in that. I have no idea how you'd even begin to clean it if
Willow soiled it.'

'Carefully,' Lena said. 'And by hand. Are you all right
in there? I can go change and take over, if you need.'

Max shook his head. 'Willow and I have just been
reaching an understanding by which she never does this
to me again. But otherwise, we're almost clean. I'll get her
dressed in something not covered in sick or poo, and *then*
you can take her, while I take a shower.'

'Sounds like a plan.'

By the time he'd showered long enough to actually feel
clean, and dressed in a charcoal suit he hoped matched
Lena's levels of dressiness, Hillary Jenkins and Margery
had already arrived. He jogged down the stairs to find
them cooing over an angelic-looking Willow, in a pristine white sleep suit.

'She's just a little doll, isn't she?' Margery said.

Max didn't comment.

After Lena had left the two women comprehensive instructions, both their mobile numbers *and* the phone number of the restaurant that they themselves had booked, it
was too late for them to walk into the village. Not to mention that Max wasn't sure Lena *could* walk that far in the
tall, strappy shoes she was wearing. Even if they did do
amazing things to her legs…

Max pushed the thought away and concentrated on driving. Lena hadn't given any indication that she considered
this a date, and until she did he had to assume this was just
a dinner between old friends. Or sleep-deprived pseudo-
parents. One of those.

'Well, we made it,' Lena said as they settled into their table at Roberto's.

'I wasn't sure we would, for a while there,' Max admitted.

'Neither was I.' She raised the glass of champagne that Roberto himself had poured for her on arrival, and he picked up his to clink against it. 'Here's to escaping for a night.'

'To escape,' Max echoed.

Except escaping always made him think of *that* night. Of those unexpected hours spent in the back seat of his car with Lena, before he drove out of her life for ever.

Or so he'd thought.

Now he was back, what was it he wanted to escape?

He sipped his champagne anyway—just one glass, since he had to drive them home again, and the last thing he wanted was a hangover when Willow started wailing in the middle of the night.

The restaurant was much as he had expected—checked tablecloths, candles shoved into bottles, and intimate tables for two dotted around the low-beamed room of one of the older buildings on the high street. But the menu surprised him. Max had eaten Italian in some of London's best restaurants, not to mention Rome's, but this menu rivalled them all.

He studied it carefully as he dipped some truly delicious bread into olive oil and balsamic vinegar, then popped it in his mouth.

'I wouldn't bother looking at that too hard,' Lena said, sounding amused. 'Roberto will just bring us out whatever he thinks we'll enjoy anyway.'

'Does anybody in this village let you actually order or do what you want, or do they all think they know what's best for you?' Max asked.

Lena dropped her gaze to the table, a small smile on

her lips. 'I guess they all know me pretty well by now, and they like to surprise me. That's all.'

'Or we all know she's such a control freak in her everyday life that it does her good to give it up sometimes,' their waitress said, placing five small bowls on the table.

'That makes more sense,' Max admitted. 'Now, what do we have here?'

What they had, it turned out, was a sort of Italian tapas: five different sorts of pasta in five different sauces, to share. 'Roberto is deciding on your mains now,' the waitress said. 'But get started on these.'

'You first,' Max said to Lena as the waitress backed away.

Lena already had her fork in her hand. 'Mmm, you have to try this walnut one. It's delicious.'

She wasn't wrong. Each of the dishes seemed more delicious than the last—but Max's favourite thing about them was the look of pleasure on Lena's face as she tasted each of them in turn.

I want to make her look like that.

The thought came from nowhere, but Max knew it wouldn't be leaving his brain any time soon.

Last time, their only time, they'd both been young and inexperienced, but enthusiasm had made up for a lot. This time around…if there was a 'this time'… Max knew he could do a whole lot better. After all, not *all* of the past sixteen years had been as much of a drought as the last one. He'd learned things.

Like patience. And timing. And paying attention.

This time, Max knew he could do it right.

And he wouldn't want to escape afterwards, either.

Max was watching her across the table as if she were the most delicious thing on the menu they hadn't been allowed to order from.

Between them the candles flickered, and Lena felt a thrill of something almost forgotten shiver through her. He wanted her. She was sure of it—as sure as she'd been that night in the party. The two of them were unfinished business, in a way. Would tonight be the night they finally finished it?

Max pushed away his empty dessert bowl, just in time for Kelly, their waitress, to swipe it away and replace it with a large cup of coffee. Then she placed a mint tea in front of Lena, with a shrug. 'Roberto says it's better for helping you sleep.'

'Roberto doesn't think I need sleep?' Max asked, once Kelly had returned to the kitchen.

'Hard to say,' Lena admitted. Roberto was generally a law unto himself anyway. 'It's always possible he's given you decaf.'

Huffing a laugh, Max reached for his coffee cup. 'I think today, more than anything since I arrived, has definitely proved that Wells-on-Water has changed from the village I remember.'

'I'm glad you think so.' She felt a strange warmth at his admission. Almost as if she had fixed this place that had driven him away, which wasn't at all true.

Firstly, she could hardly claim responsibility for Roberto's family moving to the village and setting up a restaurant, or a hundred other changes.

Secondly, she still didn't know for sure if he'd be staying, once everything was settled with Willow. He still had next to no furniture in his house, and a life in London she couldn't imagine he was in a hurry to leave behind.

Still. She liked knowing that he'd recognised how Wells-on-Water had changed—for the better.

'The way people have treated Willow, and talked about her mother, despite everything…it says a lot,' Max went on. 'It makes me wonder what it would be like for me, and for my mum, if I'd grown up here now.'

'Different, I hope.' Lena met his gaze across the table and smiled. 'Mind you, you probably would still have got into trouble with Hillary Jenkins regularly, even now.'

Max laughed. 'Probably. God, if I could tell my twelve-year-old self that one day Mrs Jenkins from the corner shop would be offering to babysit for me so I could go out for dinner with Lena Phillips.' He shook his head. 'I'd never believe it. Especially the part about it being with you.'

Lena was pretty sure the heat that hit her cheeks at his words wasn't entirely due to the peppermint tea or the candlelight. Much more likely it had to do with the warmth in his eyes as he held her gaze, the slow smile that made her heartbeat kick up a notch. The reminder that this man had been the first to ever see her naked—and she wanted him to again.

Clearing her throat, she broke away from his gaze and cast about for a safer topic of conversation. One that definitely wouldn't lead to her trying to seduce him on top of Roberto's best table.

'Do you remember that bonfire night?' she asked, apropos of nothing, but Max seemed to know immediately what she was talking about.

'With the Catherine wheel that broke free from the fence and chased Mrs Jenkins around the village green?' He laughed, the sound ringing genuinely around the restaurant. 'Who could forget? I swear, at that moment, that was the best night of my life.'

'Others have surpassed it since, I imagine?'

Oh, but she wasn't imagining the fire in his eyes. 'One or two.'

She looked away. Again.

Would it always be like this? Leading him to the edge of a conversation about the two of them, about what it meant that they were there together, then losing her nerve? Probably, she admitted to herself. She was great at getting others to do what was needed, it seemed, but when it came to convincing herself to take action...well. There, she was a failure.

And it wasn't as if there weren't complicating factors between them. Willow, his life in London...and other things she wasn't ready to face yet, either.

Max seemed to recognise her need to change the subject.

'So, what happened to the pub?' he asked.

'Which pub?' Lena felt her brow furrow. 'The King's Arms in Wishcliffe?'

'No, The Fox. Your family pub.'

As if she could forget the pub her family had owned and run her entire life.

'Nothing happened to it,' she told him, baffled by the question. 'It's right where you left it.'

'But...your family don't own it any longer?' He sounded as confused as she felt. 'Victoria said you were managing the King's Arms instead.'

Oh. *Now* she understood.

Lena looked down at her mint tea, swirling the real mint leaves around with the silver teaspoon. 'No, we still own it. The boys run it, since Dad died.'

Max leaned back in his chair and gave her that look she was beginning to recognise all too well. The one that meant he was about to call her out on some aspect of her life, and Lena decided she'd rather not hear it right now, so she spoke again first.

'I went away to uni, you know, after you left. I'd planned to stay close by, so I could live at home and commute in for lectures.' She chose her words carefully, picking her way between the things she was willing to tell, and the secrets she still wanted to keep.

'I remember,' Max said softly, not interrupting, just confirming that he was paying attention.

'But after...well, after that night, with you. When you talked about getting out and seeing the world... I guess I wanted a slice of that, too. I always knew I'd end up back here—Wells-on-Water is just where I belong. But I decided that didn't mean I couldn't see a bit of the world outside first. So I went through clearing and got a place at a university up in the north, to study hospitality and marketing.' All true. Just not the whole truth.

Lies of omission are still lies, Lena...

'What did your father and brothers think about that?' That one question told her that he really *did* remember everything she'd said that night. About how she was tied to home, and family, and the pub, since her mother's death. That they needed her.

'They...weren't pleased.' Understatement of the century. 'I tried to convince them that me studying these things would help us build up business at the pub, but they weren't buying it. There was a bit of a scene.' She hadn't told them the truth, either, about why she'd needed to leave. Her father would never have understood, and her brothers...

Well. She knew full well what they thought.

'I can imagine. But you went anyway.' His smile looked almost proud. He wouldn't smile like that if he knew the truth, she was sure.

He probably thought this was all because of him. Which, well, maybe it was, but she wasn't going to let him be smug about it.

'I am capable of making my own decisions,' she said. And she had, until that had been taken away from her, too.

'I never, for a single moment, doubted that.'

Her heart felt too tight at all the memories she'd tried so hard to forget. She pushed on, eager to reach the end of this story. 'Anyway, I studied and I learned and I came home in the holidays and worked in the pub like always, and then when I graduated…nothing changed.'

'How do you mean?' Max asked.

'I had all these ideas and dreams for The Fox—I mean, it was my home, and I remembered how it used to be when Mum was alive. Full of families and good food, a real social hub of the community. But after she was gone…well, you know.'

'It went downhill,' Max said, which Lena thought was generous.

'The majority of people who went there were old men who were already too drunk to care about the sticky floor and the truly grim bathrooms,' she said. 'I did my best, but the changes it needed were huge, and they wouldn't let me make any of them.'

'So you left.'

'Not immediately.' Lena gave a small half-shrug. 'But eventually I got sick of drunk old men trying to feel me up. I applied for a job at the King's Arms instead and got it. The manager there liked my ideas, and actually implemented a lot of them. The pub got more popular as word got around and, well, when the manager left they promoted me to his job.'

'And the place went from strength to strength, from what I've heard.' Max smiled at her. 'Although, I have to admit, it was a bit of a shock to see Wishcliffe featured in a "Britain's Best Hidden Pubs" feature in a London paper last month. If it had said that you were behind it, maybe I wouldn't have been so surprised.'

That feature had been the pinnacle of her career so far;

she couldn't quite believe he'd actually read it. And suddenly she didn't mind so much if Max felt a bit responsible for her achievements. Because, in a way, he was.

Before she could stop herself, she met his gaze across the table, and told him the truth. Maybe not all of it, but enough, for now.

'You were my first rebellion, you know. Without you... I don't know if I'd have done any of it.'

CHAPTER NINE

MAX BLINKED, her words echoing in his head but still making no sense.

'I don't think I can take any credit for that,' he said. 'Everything you've done, you've done it yourself, Lena.'

She smiled. 'Yes, I have. But it's true. That night with you… You know, my whole life until then I'd done the Right Thing. What people expected from me. I didn't cause trouble—because I knew that wouldn't be fair to my dad with my mum gone, and three kids and a pub to look after. I did all the right things in school, partly to try and make up for the hell my brothers had put all the teachers through before me. I was polite to everyone, helped everyone, dressed in a way even Mrs Jenkins couldn't object to…because this village had saved us, after Mum died. They'd looked after Dad, even the people who didn't like him or his pub. They'd even given the boys more chances than they deserved. And they took care of me, a poor, motherless girl. All because they'd all loved Mum.'

'From what I remember, she was a very loveable woman,' Max said. 'I never heard anyone say a bad word against her. Much like you.' He didn't tell her how many people had stopped him over the past day or so, when they were out and about or when people brought things to the house, to tell him to look after Lena. To protect her.

She mattered to everyone in the village, because she'd given everything she had to them.

He hadn't known how to tell them how much she mattered to him, too.

And he *really* hated to think how fast they'd kick him back out of Wells-on-Water if they ever learned that he'd taken teenage Lena's virginity and then run out on her.

'The point is, I never thought about what *I* wanted. I only considered what was the right thing to do. Until that night with you.'

Max barked a laugh at that. 'Because I was definitely *not* the right thing to do.'

The smile that spread across Lena's face at that warmed something deep inside him. 'Oh, I don't know. There are definitely worse choices for a girl's first time,' she said. 'But, no. I don't think anyone in the village would have approved of me seducing you in the back seat of your car on the last day of sixth form.'

'And here I was thinking that I seduced you.'

The look she gave him completely dispelled that idea.

'But I wanted you, just for myself,' Lena went on quietly. 'That night, the way we talked, the things I learned about you… I'd lived side by side with you my whole life, and never seen inside your heart and soul that way before. Never really known you. And when I did…'

'I left,' Max reminded her bluntly. Right now, it was hard to remember why, or even how, he'd walked away from her. Except leaving Wells-on-Water had been his ambition for so much of his life, perhaps it was always going to take more than one night to overturn it.

But she hadn't been the only one who felt as if they'd got to know a whole new person that night.

'You did,' Lena allowed. 'But before you went, you showed me it was okay to want things beyond the village.

To want something just for me, not for anyone else. Like I say, you were my first rebellion. The ones that came after were all the easier because I'd already done it before.'

He wasn't sure what to say to that. On the one hand, it didn't seem to him that Lena had lived a particularly rebellious life. But by her own standards, she had. She'd left home. She'd found another job when her family wouldn't let her grow where she was. She had turned Wells-on-Water into the kind of community she always knew it could be, but that it wasn't always—not to him, for starters—without her influence.

Max thought that maybe more rebellions should be like Lena's. Quiet, determined—and world-changing, for the people living in that world.

'If I have played any small part in helping you become the woman you are today, then I'm proud of that,' he said. 'And just grateful to have been there.'

He held her gaze for a long moment, watching her cheeks turn pink in the candlelight, and hoping she felt the truth in every word.

'We should get back to Willow,' she said, after a long moment.

'And Mrs Jenkins,' Max agreed. 'Who knows what she'll have done to my house in my absence otherwise?'

'You know that she's going to have gone through all your drawers, right?' Lena teased.

Max nodded. 'That's why I hid the really scandalous stuff in your room.'

Roberto wouldn't accept payment for the meal, but Max managed to slip a couple of notes into the tip jar for Kelly, the waitress, at least.

They drove home in silence and found the lights of the Manor House still blazing against the fallen twilight on their arrival. It looked almost welcoming, lit up like that, Max thought, staring up at it as he exited the car.

'What?' Lena asked as he paused. 'What's the matter?'

'Nothing. I just…it's always dark when I arrive,' he explained. 'I've never seen it like this before. It looks…'

'Like a home?' she finished for him.

'Yeah,' Max breathed. 'I guess it does.'

But he knew in his heart it wasn't just a few lamps that made it feel that way. And he had a terrible feeling that Lena's ongoing rebellion might have stretched as far as his house, too.

Worse still, it might have infected his heart.

Hillary and Margery were pleased that they'd had a good time and swore that Willow hadn't been a bother at all, but the speed at which they left suggested they might have been stretching the truth a little on that point.

Still, she'd had a bottle recently, and was contentedly sleeping in her Moses basket, so Max carried her carefully up the stairs, as Lena ran ahead to open doors and clear the way.

'Want me to take first shift tonight?' she asked as they reached the hallway.

Max shook his head, then winced as the basket shook, too. 'You sleep. You've been up for hours, and I'm better at late nights, anyway.'

'If you're sure.' As tired as she was, there was a part of Lena that just didn't want the night to end. Not yet.

Something still felt…unfinished.

'Just wait here a second.' Max disappeared into his bedroom, and through the open door she watched him place the basket carefully on the stand someone had donated, peering in at Willow and straightening her blankets.

He was good with her, in a way Lena really hadn't expected. If he hadn't been so certain that she *couldn't* be his, she'd have suspected some sort of paternal instinct.

Finally satisfied with the blanket arrangement, he re-emerged, pulling the door almost closed behind him, but open enough that they'd still hear Willow easily if she woke.

'Everything okay?' Lena whispered.

'She's fine,' Max replied. 'I just wanted to...'

She thought he'd stumble for the right words. Maybe try to thank her for staying and helping with the baby, or something.

Instead, he leaned in and cupped a hand against the back of her neck.

'I've wanted to kiss you all night,' he murmured, so close she could feel the words against her skin. 'May I?'

All the reasons she'd been telling herself why this was a bad idea flew from her head. Swallowing, she nodded, and tilted her lips up to meet his.

She'd thought she remembered his kiss well. Thought she remembered everything about the night they'd spent together.

But this kiss was nothing like their teenage fumblings, so either she was remembering wrong, or Max had learned a *lot* in the intervening years.

He teased her mouth open with his tongue, his lips always moving over hers, caressing and warming her mouth, sending shots of sheer lust shooting through her body. Apart from his hand at her neck they weren't touching at all, Max keeping just enough distance between them that, if she wanted it closed, it would have to be her choice.

And, oh, she *did* want to close that gap. But given how Max was setting her whole body on fire with just a kiss, she wasn't sure she could risk it.

'Lena…' He breathed her name against her mouth. 'God, Lena.'

'I know,' she whispered back. 'I know.'

Exactly what she knew, she wasn't sure. But whatever it was he was right there with her.

Maybe this was one of those times where she just had to throw caution to the wind. Forget the past, forget tomorrow, and just enjoy the now.

Closing her eyes, she shifted her whole body towards him, sinking into his kiss as she brought her hands up to press against his back and keep him close. Max made a sound somewhere in the back of his throat that didn't even sound like a word, and deepened the kiss beyond the mind-bending experience it already was.

God, she could feel him hard against her, pressing into her stomach, showing her exactly how much he wanted her. And she remembered that, too. How desperate he'd been to touch her, to kiss her, to be inside her…

But in other ways this was *nothing* like their first time together. They were grown-ups now. There was no taboo here, no rebellion—no real reason at all she couldn't spend the night with this single, devastatingly attractive man if she wanted, without having to believe it would lead anywhere. He could leave again tomorrow and it wouldn't break her heart, or her spirit, just as it hadn't last time.

Max's hands had wandered to her back now, one roaming down to cup her backside and hold her against him, the other splayed across her spine. She felt a sudden jolt against her back and realised he'd spun them—away from the risk of the stairs, so her back was against the wall between their two bedroom doors.

Another reason it could be so much better than their first time: they had access to an actual bed this time.

'Max,' she said, the word swallowed into his desperate kisses. 'We should—'

He stopped, pulling back just enough to meet her gaze, and she could see his chest heaving with the effort. 'Stop?' There was actual pain in the word, she could hear it.

She smiled. 'Find a bed.'

'Oh, thank God.' He kissed her again, then grabbed her hand. 'Your room?'

She hesitated, just for a moment. 'We'll still hear Willow?'

As if in answer, a cry went up from inside Max's room, a thin, little wail that spoke of hunger, or the need for a cuddle or a dry nappy.

Max's forehead hit the wall beside her head. 'Apparently so.'

'I'll go.' She began to wiggle her way out of his arms, but Max shook his head.

'No. It's my turn. You go get some rest.'

'You'll find me after?' She wasn't ready to give up this moment, this opportunity, just yet.

Max gave her a small smile. 'I most definitely will.'

Willow cried out again, and Max pushed away from the wall, turning to head into his room. Lena watched him go, admiring the way his shirt stretched across his back— who even knew what had happened to his jacket?—and the perfect fit of his trousers...

She shook her head, as all those reasons she'd forgotten came rushing back. Willow was what mattered most right now. Max was right; she needed to go rest.

After all, if she and Max ever got the chance to follow through on what they'd started tonight, she was going to need all her energy.

Two hours later, Max was starting to wonder if Willow had a personal objection to her two current carers finding any sort of pleasure or happiness in each other's arms, or if it was just a coincidence that nothing in the world seemed to settle her tonight.

He'd tried changing her, feeding her, winding her, rocking her, re-wrapping her blankets in the special way Janice had taught them…everything. In the end, he resorted to pacing around the house with Willow in his arms, humming low in his chest the way she seemed to like. It stopped the screaming—at least, as long as he didn't try to put her down.

Eventually, though, even Willow's tenacious desire to stay awake gave way and, not long before the sun started rising, she finally fell properly asleep again. Gingerly, Max laid her back in her Moses basket, and considered what to do next.

Lena had to be asleep by now. And as much as he wanted to go and wake her, he knew he was on the edge of exhaustion, too. Even if they were both able to stay awake long enough to make love, he didn't kid himself for a second that he'd be able to perform at his best.

Surely it must be better to both get some sleep, and hope they got a better opportunity later.

It was just that he'd never been a very patient man.

And what if she *wasn't* asleep? What if she was lying awake and waiting for him? He at least owed it to her to check, right?

But when he peered around her bedroom door, the room was in darkness, and he could just make out the gentle rise and fall of the duvet wrapped around her as Lena breathed the slow, regular breaths of a deep sleep.

No, he couldn't wake her up. He'd just have to hope that she was still willing to revisit this development of their relationship again tomorrow.

Max padded back to his bedroom, checked on Willow

one last time, then slipped gratefully between the sheets on his bed and let his body relax.

For now, he'd just rest up in readiness.

Willow was gone from her basket when Max awoke the next morning, but he could hear Lena singing sweetly to her downstairs, so he allowed himself a moment to wake up properly and take a shower before heading down to join them.

By the time he got there, though, the singing had ended and Lena was frowning at her phone, while Willow bounced in her fabric chair on the floor.

'Everything okay?' He dropped a kiss onto Willow's forehead, then moved towards the coffee machine. God bless whoever had upgraded theirs and donated this one to the Manor House; Max really wasn't sure he'd have made it through this week so far without it.

'Hmm,' Lena replied, which told him nothing.

Max checked her coffee mug and, finding it empty, re-filled it for her. Maybe that would help.

'Thanks.' She gave him a tight smile as she took it from him.

Rocking back on his heels as he waited for his own coffee to brew, he watched as her attention returned to her phone. 'Everything okay?' he asked again.

'Just a message from work. They've been great about me having time off to help with Willow this week, but I think I'm going to have to go in today. I can probably take Willow with me...'

But she wouldn't be able to concentrate on whatever had her frowning like that, Max was sure.

'Leave her here,' Max said. 'I've got to do some work today, too, but I reckon she'll be a dab hand at filing in no time.' He'd managed a full hour alone with her yesterday.

And yes, it had ended with them both covered in bodily waste and in desperate need of a shower, but nothing really terrible had happened. A little longer alone with her today couldn't be any worse, right?

'Are you sure?' Lena worried her bottom lip with her teeth. 'If you got video calls or meetings...'

'She'll be fine,' Max assured her. 'Besides, I'm the boss. If she acts up, they'll just have to deal with it.'

'If you're absolutely certain...'

'I am.' He wasn't, not really, but he could tell from Lena's nervous tapping of her coffee cup, the way she was still biting down on her lip, that whatever was going on at work was important, and she needed to focus on it.

This might not be the conversation he'd *wanted* to be having with her this morning, but there was no point trying to discuss what had almost happened between them the night before while she was worried about work stuff.

Lena nodded, decision made. 'Okay, then. I mean, you know where everything is, it's your house, and you've spent as much time looking after Willow as I have, so I guess I'll...go.'

'I'll see you later,' he said, with a warm smile. 'In fact, I'll even root around in the freezer, see what delicious delights the neighbours have left us for dinner.'

'Perfect little house husband, huh?' Lena joked, then her eyes widened. 'Not that I'm saying... I mean, I'm not assuming...last night...'

'Lena,' he interrupted. 'I have just enough social skills to understand when something is a joke, rumours notwithstanding. Go sort out whatever it is you need to sort out, and we'll talk later. Okay?'

'Later. Right.' With a swift smile, Lena downed the rest of her coffee, then moved from the table to kneel on the stone floor beside Willow to kiss her goodbye. 'You be good for Max today, you hear?'

'Oh, we'll get along famously, I'm sure.' Max was under no illusions after the past few days; he fully expected his day to be interrupted by cries for milk and hideous nappies. But, to his immense surprise, he found that he was okay with that.

Lena stood up and, after a moment of obvious deliberation, bent to press a quick kiss to Max's lips, too. 'Later,' she said, and Max heard it for what it was.

A promise.

The hardest part, Max found, was trying to type, or hold a phone, with Willow in his arms. While she'd be happy in the Chair of Joy for short periods—he really must stop calling it that—inevitably she wanted to be held or fed or changed just when he needed to do something that required both arms.

He was wrestling with a spreadsheet with one hand, while rocking Willow in the other arm, when Toby called.

'So, this talking on the phone thing is something we do now?' Max asked, in lieu of a greeting.

'Apparently,' Toby replied, nonplussed. 'I just thought I'd check in and see how things are going. I understand from Autumn, who had it from Victoria, who heard it from God knows who in the village, that Willow is still with you?'

'She is.'

'And that you even had Hillary Jenkins babysitting for you last night.' The awe in Toby's voice suggested to Max that his half-brother's history with the formidable Mrs Jenkins might not be miles away from his own, albeit for different reasons.

'I think that was probably for Lena's benefit.'

'Ah. That makes sense,' Toby said. 'So, how *is* it going?'

I can't decide which is distracting me from work most: the baby, or thinking about Lena and last night...

'I'm trying to type up some figures while also persuading Willow to go to sleep. Basically, I need an extra arm. Maybe two.' Octopuses had the right idea, he decided, when it came to juggling childcare and work.

Toby laughed. 'Lena isn't there?'

'She had to go into work.' And that was distracting him, too. She'd looked worried this morning—not just 'someone screwed up the order of scallops' worried, or 'someone called in sick' worried. Genuinely concerned about something that mattered.

He wondered if she'd tell him what it was, later.

If he survived until later without his arm falling off.

Holding the phone between his ear and shoulder, he switched Willow to his other arm.

'Have you got one of those sling things?' Toby asked vaguely.

'I have literally no idea what you're talking about,' Max replied.

'Autumn brought one home from her baby shower. Actually, she brought two, for some ungodly reason, and insisted on demonstrating both of them with some doll that someone had given her. They're for holding the baby against your chest, so they feel like they're being held but you can actually get on with doing things. Apparently babies love it.'

A sling. Part of his brain rebelled against the idea of being some sort of yummy daddy with a baby strapped to his chest. But another, larger part countered that this was a way that both arms could be his own again *and* he could still hold Willow to stop her crying. It didn't have to mean anything about his personality, or that this situation was going to go on much longer.

Practicality won out. 'Do you think Autumn would mind if I borrowed one?'

CHAPTER TEN

LENA CUT THE ENGINE, parked her little yellow car neatly outside the Manor House, but made no move to get out. She needed just a moment to process the day before she re-entered the cosy world she'd created with Max and Willow. Before she tried to have that *later* conversation that Max had put off that morning.

Why was it that, whenever something was finally going well in the world, something else had to get screwed up to balance it out?

The late-afternoon air was still warm with summer sun, and she had the window open to let in a breeze. Outside, she could hear the contented buzz of insects, the drone of a plane overhead—probably a vintage one from the local airfield, by the sound of it—and the wind as it rustled the leaves of the trees that edged the property.

And above it all, she could hear Max. Yelling.

She frowned. No, not quite *yelling*, but certainly talking forcefully at somebody.

Unbuckling her seat belt, she climbed out of the car and headed around the side of the Manor House, towards the sound.

As she turned the corner onto the back lawn, she spotted him, pacing away towards the trees at the far end, one hand holding his mobile phone to his ear, the other gesticulating wildly. Clearly this was a work call, from the snatches of words that reached her on the breeze—*targets, projections, stakeholders*...

So where was Willow? Panicked, Lena glanced around the terrace at the back of the house, looking for the Chair of Joy, but there was no sign. And the back doors were closed, and Max wouldn't have shut her in the house on her own, Lena was sure of it.

Then Max turned to begin pacing back towards the Manor House, and Lena noticed the baby sling strapped to his chest, her breath whooshing out of her chest in relief.

Spotting her, Max ended his call and shoved his phone into his pocket, picking up his pace to almost a jog as he headed towards her. 'You're back.'

'I am,' she said, with a smile she didn't quite feel. 'And I see you've found a new way to manage babysitting and working at the same time.'

'It was Toby's idea,' Max admitted, looking mildly uncomfortable at being caught in such a domesticated set-up. 'Autumn had two, so he brought one over and, countless YouTube tutorials later, here we are.'

'It's a good idea. So, your day has been okay?' She should be grateful that at least one of them had had a good day, she supposed. Even if it wasn't her.

'It's been fine.' Max frowned. Possibly her smile wasn't as convincing as she'd hoped. 'What went wrong with yours?'

Lena sighed. 'Basically? Everything.'

He put an arm around her shoulder and guided her towards the door. 'Come on. If you promise not to laugh at me for going full-on stay-at-home dad, there's some sort of chicken casserole thing in the oven, and a bottle of wine chilling in the fridge for you.'

'If those are the conditions, I think I can manage.' It

wouldn't do to tell him how adorable she found his descent into domesticity.

'Good. Then I'll get Willow out of this thing, pour you a glass of wine, and you can tell me all about it.'

Lena let herself be led, and tried not to think about how easy it would be to get used to all of this.

'So, they're selling the King's Arms,' Max said some time later, when Willow was back in her Chair of Joy, full of milk and ready to sleep, and the two of them were sitting at the kitchen table sharing out someone's family recipe for chicken casserole. 'Why?'

Lena shrugged, and snagged another potato from the pot. 'Because they can, I guess. There's a buzz around the place and a good offer came in, from some celebrity chef who wants to build on what we've already done with the place.'

'And will they keep you on as manager?' Max topped up her glass, and she realised she'd already drunk half of it. She'd have to slow down, or getting up at four in the morning with Willow would be unbearable.

'They might.' Harold, the current owner, hadn't been completely clear on that point. 'Or they might have their own people they want to bring in. And even if they do want me to stay...'

'You're not sure if you want to,' Max guessed, and Lena nodded. It was nice to have someone to talk this through with, she realised. Someone who understood, if not the specifics, at least the feeling she had about her career, and wanting to take charge of it.

'Part of the fun of working there for me has always been the freedom to do things my own way. And I can already tell from everything Harold has said that wouldn't be the case with the new owners.'

'Maybe it's time to start looking for a new challenge, then?' Max suggested.

'Perhaps.' Lena sighed. 'But there's only so many pubs in this neck of the woods left that haven't been turned into houses. And of them, there aren't many that would be suitable, and I don't know that any of them would take me.' Especially not her brothers, still running The Fox into the ground in the village.

'They'd all be lucky to have you.' Max reached across the table and took her hand in his. 'But there are other things you could do—other challenges you could turn your many talents to.'

'Maybe.' It was just hard to see forward to any of them, when she was still mourning the hard work she'd put in that would now be lost. Not just the King's Arms, but the community hub as well.

Perhaps the universe was trying to send her a message. Time to move on with her life.

Except Wells-on-Water *was* her life, it always had been. And she wasn't sure she was ready to give any of it up without a fight.

She looked up at Max and wondered, just for a flicker of a second, what it would be like to seek that next step on her ladder in London, with him. Then she shook the thought away again.

This week, here at the Manor House with him and Willow, was a moment out of time, that was all. As the night they'd lost their virginities together had been. It wasn't what real life, or a real relationship between them, would be like.

She couldn't afford to let herself get swept up in that

fairy tale. Not when she was already worrying about how bruised her heart might be when this moment ended.

Not when the memories of the aftermath last time still haunted her.

Max supposed he should be grateful that Willow had managed to stay peaceful and content while Lena had told him about everything that was happening at the King's Arms. But the fact she started wailing the moment dinner was over, and didn't stop for well over an hour and a half, wore away a lot of that gratitude. Eventually, once she'd taken her bottle, he put her back in the sling and paced around the garden in the cooling night air, where she acted like his own little hot-water bottle.

He'd sent Lena upstairs for a bath, and an early night, sensing that, with everything that had gone on today, this wasn't the *later* they were waiting for to continue last night's…conversation. But that didn't stop him wondering what she might have said, if they *had* had the opportunity.

Or imagining a different universe where he might join her in that bath, instead of pacing up and down with a fractious baby.

Thinking about Lena was a bad road to head down, especially alone in the night—well, alone except for a dozing Willow pressed against his chest.

Maybe it was just as well that Willow had interrupted them the night before, because Max really wasn't sure where they'd have been heading. Except for bed, that much seemed clear. But what then?

He sighed, and looked down at the downy hair on Willow's head, pressing a kiss against it as his thoughts swirled.

Sixteen years ago, he'd seduced Lena—or she'd seduced him, depending on who you asked—and run out on her hours later. He'd left her without a backward thought. Well, not many, anyway. And never enough to make him turn around and return to Wells-on-Water.

Since then, they'd both forged their own lives—and it was only a coincidence that had brought them back together again.

If Victoria hadn't reintroduced them at the party. If Lena's idiot brothers hadn't knocked dessert all over the floor. If he hadn't stained his shirt. If the village taxis ran past nine o'clock. If not for all those things, Lena would never have been with him when he'd found Willow on his doorstep.

He'd have handed the baby over to the proper authorities, and gone about his life again, whatever that damned note said. He'd have stayed holed up at the Manor House until it was set up, then headed back to London and work, as had been his plan. He'd have used the house for the odd party, or a getaway, or to visit Toby and Autumn, occasionally, but that was all. And his path might never have crossed Lena Phillips's again.

It had been the same sixteen years ago, he remembered suddenly.

If he hadn't had a fight with his mum and walked out, he never would have joined the usual crowd of cooler kids hanging out down by the river. If she hadn't had a fight with her brothers that evening, she wouldn't have been feeling so edgy and out of sorts that she'd drifted away from her friends towards him. If he hadn't been for a drive to check the car was running okay before he left for London the next day, he'd have walked, and they'd have had nowhere to go. If her friends hadn't been stupid and drunk, they'd have noticed she was missing sooner. If they hadn't both been feeling so out of place that night, they never would have started talking.

And if they hadn't talked that night—really talked, for the first time ever, even after years of growing up in the same village, being in the same class, and knowing all the same people—they definitely would not have ended up naked in the back of his car, parked up behind some of the abandoned sheds on the edge of the Wishcliffe estate.

The talking, he thought, had surprised him even more than the sex. To discover there was so much more to Lena Phillips—so much under that surface of good girl, popular girl, nice girl, and every other label people gave her. Or perhaps she gave herself.

And now, here at the Manor House with Willow, it was the talking that had undone him again.

Last night, hearing her talk about her rebellions, had been one such moment. But it was so much more than that. Chatting with her over coffee, discussing Willow's little ways. Watching her talk to the people of the village. Hearing her speak about the community hub she'd worked so hard for, and lost through no fault of her own. How much she'd given to the King's Arms only to have it snatched away.

Every moment he spent with Lena seemed to drag him deeper.

Had he known this would happen, sixteen years ago? Was that why he'd run so far and so fast after their night together?

No.

He'd run because he was eighteen and stupid and hadn't even realised what was in front of him.

What worried him now was that he wasn't sure he wouldn't run again.

He stopped at the edge of the trees and turned to look back at the shadow of the Manor House against the night sky. He'd left one small light burning in the kitchen, but the rest of the house was in darkness. Abandoned. If he didn't know Lena was sleeping inside, he'd assume he and Willow were alone.

Soon, Willow would go—back to her mother or family, if they could find them, or to social services if not. Because, as much as he might have not hated playing house with Lena, it wasn't real. It wasn't even *right*, by anyone's standards. He could hear his mother nagging about doing the right thing, even now, across years and years and the divide of death.

The right thing would be to admit that Willow *couldn't* be his daughter, and let her find a real home. One with loving parents who knew what they were doing, and didn't take two hours of YouTube videos to figure out how to use a sling. With a loving couple who adored each other, as well as Willow, perhaps, rather than two people wanting to recreate a one-night stand. Or at least a single parent who was ready to fight and strive for their child the way his own mother had.

The right thing would be to set Lena free to find her own future again, wherever that might be.

Max wasn't under any illusions that whatever had caught fire between them last night would last, any more than it had sixteen years ago. Lena had only stayed at all because of Willow, and once she was gone, Lena would be, too.

Lena was a good person. A loving, honest, kind person. And Max had never been any of those things.

He was a troublemaker. A grumpy, single-minded, oblivious fool, according to more than one of his ex-girlfriends. He wasn't good at relationships, or people, and if Lena truly believed that the people of Wells-on-Water might change their mind about him after all these years... well, she always had been an incurable optimist.

He knew that he'd only been tolerated here this week because of Lena, and because he was helping Willow—even if the locals did believe he might be responsible for fathering her. Once this was over, they'd all remember why they despised him again.

And then it would be time for him to leave, whatever Toby said.

Whatever he was starting to think he might want.

The next day went more smoothly than the day before had, in some ways. Lena woke late, but found Willow and Max both asleep in his room. Their *later* conversation still hadn't occurred, but she had hope that it might today. Now she was over the initial shock of yesterday's news, she felt almost ready to face the future. Especially if it had more of Max's kisses in it.

When Willow stirred, Lena took her downstairs and started their day together with a clean nappy and milk for the baby, and coffee for her.

A little while later, she was surprised by a knock on the door—and even more surprised to find Kathy and Trevor on the doorstep when she answered it.

'We thought you might like some company,' Kathy said, eyeing the bundle of baby in Lena's arms. 'You know, of the not-infant variety.'

'Thought we could take a walk down to the cafe or something,' Trevor added. 'We'd offer to take the baby for you but—'

'We really wouldn't know what to do with one,' Kathy admitted. 'So you'd probably better come, too.'

Lena beamed at her friends. 'That would lovely. Hang on.'

Letting Kathy and Trevor inside, she popped Willow in the Chair of Joy and set about getting things together to leave the house—which always took far longer than seemed reasonable.

She'd planned to leave Max a note but, hearing movement from his room—and realising that Willow's best blanket was in there, too—she headed up to tell him herself, leaving a nervous Kathy and Trevor to watch the baby for a moment.

'Max?' Lena pushed open his bedroom door when there was no response, but found the room empty. Frowning, she hunted for the blanket and, having found it, was about to turn and leave when the door to the en-suite bathroom opened. And out stepped Max.

He wasn't naked, at least. Lena was almost certain that was a good thing. But the low-slung towel around his waist left very little to the imagination all the same.

She swallowed, her mouth suddenly very dry, and realised she was staring.

'Lena?' Max paused in rubbing a second towel over his hair. 'Is everything okay?'

Unable to find words just then, Lena nodded, and held up the blanket as evidence.

Max lowered the towel in his hands and watched her, a slow smile spreading across his face. 'You're sure? You look somewhat…distracted.'

She shook her head. 'I'm fine. Just came to tell you…' Damn it, what had she come to tell him?

'To tell me…?' He took a step closer, and she could feel the warmth radiating from his skin after his shower. He rested a hand at her waist, and she looked up into his eyes to see an even greater heat building there.

God, what if she'd come up here a minute or two earlier? What if she'd stepped into the bathroom and found him, naked in the shower?

What if she'd joined him…?

'Lena? Are you ready?' Trevor's booming voice echoed up the stairs and shook Lena out of her daze.

Without stepping back, she glanced over her shoulder, hoping her friends wouldn't come up to find her. 'Trevor and Kathy are here. We're going to take Willow for a walk down to the cafe and get a coffee.'

'Right.' Max's voice sounded husky, and he cleared his throat before continuing. 'I'll…uh…get some work done this morning, then. So I can take over with her when you get back.'

Lena nodded. 'That would be good. I need to head down to the King's Arms after lunch.'

'Of course.'

But neither of them moved. They just kept staring, letting the crackle of tension and want between them grow.

Maybe they didn't need to have that *later* conversation. Maybe they just needed to jump each other's bones and have done with it. Like last time…

'Lena?' Kathy's voice had joined Trevor's now, and she sounded closer. As if she was climbing the stairs…

'Coming!' Lena yelled. Clearly Trevor and Kathy were getting antsy alone with the baby. 'I'd better…'

'Yeah. Okay.'

Turning, Lena moved towards the door, but paused, one hand on the frame, to look back at him. 'Later, though?'

'Definitely later,' Max said, adjusting his towel.

Lena grinned, and headed downstairs to rescue Trevor and Kathy.

After coffee and cake with her friends, Lena returned to the Manor House with just enough time to hand Willow over to Max so she could spend the afternoon at work at the King's Arms. The atmosphere in the pub was tense and frosty, despite the sun beating down on the beer garden, and full tables all along the riverbank. It was almost enough to dampen Lena's enthusiasm about the evening ahead with Max—but not quite. Every time she felt it slipping, she remembered him in that towel, and smiled.

She rushed back after work, and found Max still on a work call, with Willow asleep in her Chair of Joy. Flashing him a quick smile, she went to pour herself a glass of wine and bung another freezer meal in the oven.

It was done just in time for Max to join her, and they settled at the table together. Lena's pulse kicked up again just at the sight of him, and she hoped that Willow would sleep tonight, for once.

She was so tired of waiting for *later*.

But for now, everything felt perfectly domestic, and happy and easy.

Until Max said, 'Janice called earlier. She wants to stop by with that social worker this evening.'

Lena froze with a mouthful of food halfway between her plate and her lips. 'Did she say what about?'

Max, chewing, shook his head, even as he loaded up another forkful. He swallowed, and said, 'No. But I imagine it's to do with Willow, don't you?'

'Yes, but what about her?' Lena dropped her fork to her plate. Her heart pounded against her ribcage, a reminder that everything could change in just one of those beats, and life would never be the same again.

She'd experienced it the day her mother died, and again when her father passed on. It had been there that night with Max and again when she told her family she was going away for university. And that awful day that September, when her whole world had felt as if it were ending.

She'd felt it when her father's will had left the pub to her brothers, and her only her mother's jewellery. It had happened the day the roof had caved in on the community hub. And she'd felt it as recently as yesterday, as Harold had told her he was selling the King's Arms.

What would it be this time? That they'd found the mother, or another relative? That they were taking her into care? That Max had to take a DNA test they knew would be negative? What?

Lena pushed her plate away, her appetite gone.

'I don't know exactly what Janice is going to tell us,' Max said, watching her cautiously. 'But we both knew that this situation wasn't going to go on for ever.'

Lena stared at him. It was funny. Two days she'd been waiting for their *later* conversation, and now they were there and it was nothing like she'd expected.

'No, of course not,' she said faintly. Because she *had* known that.

She had known, intellectually, that Willow would be leaving soon. That *she* would be leaving. Hell, she'd been the one fighting for more time to find Willow's mum so they could reunite them without Willow being whisked off into care.

But in her heart… Well. Her heart had got used to being here at the Manor House with Max and Willow. It had got used to being needed and having a place. It had got used to late-night conversations with Max and early-morning grunts over coffee. It had got used to the tired way he smiled at her and told her to sleep. The way he reminded her who she was—for herself, not for what she could do for others.

It had even got used to the lack of sleep and a whiny baby who wouldn't take a bottle and the terrible nappies and the ridiculously huge and old-fashioned pram.

She'd known this couldn't last for ever—or even for more than a week or so. So how had her heart grown so attached in so little time?

Was it just that this—this life with Willow and Max—
was another thing she was being told she had to walk away
from? Was that why it hurt so much?

'Wait and see what Janice has to say,' Max said gently.
'My mother always used to say there was no point borrow-
ing trouble—not when I already caused so much anyway.'

He'd said it to make her laugh, she knew, but all she
could manage was a small smile.

Would he go back to London when Willow was gone?
He'd hinted as much on several occasions. She'd hoped she
would be able to help him integrate into the community
here, in a way he never had as a child, but now it seemed
as if she was out of time. He'd go, and visit for holidays or
parties or whatever, and the Manor House would be just
another holiday home—albeit a huge one—like so many
of the picturesque cottages around the village.

It all seemed such a waste.

'Hopefully it's good news,' she said, forcing some cheer
into her voice. 'If they've found Willow's family, and social services are happy to work with them, it could be a
happy ending for everybody.'

'Just like you wanted,' Max reminded her.

'Just like I wanted.'

So why did she feel as if it was going to break her heart?

CHAPTER ELEVEN

'It was actually Terri Jacobs at the school who found her.' Janice was settled on the sofa in the study, with Lena beside her, while Max sat in his desk chair. The social worker, Sarah, was on a kitchen chair Lena had dragged in for her, and Willow bobbed happily in the Chair of Joy on the floor beside them.

He'd thought that the study sitting room would be cosier, more friendly than the larger drawing room with its borrowed furniture and baby equipment. But now it just felt as if the walls were closing in.

'She was a student, then?' Lena asked.

Max watched her as she spoke, noting the tension lines around her eyes, the way her hands were clasped tight in her lap. And, most of all, the way her gaze kept darting to Willow, then back to Janice.

It never landed on him, so she couldn't know how closely he was observing her. Checking for cracks in the calm, smiling, sensible exterior she always showed to people of the village.

There weren't any. Not that anyone else would notice. But Max had got very good at watching Lena Phillips over the last week.

'A fifteen-year-old,' Janice confirmed. 'She was terrified. She hid the pregnancy for the whole nine months, then went to stay with an older cousin a few towns away for the first couple of weeks of the summer holidays. Had the baby there, and didn't know what to do. When she came back…she was too scared to tell her parents, and she panicked.'

'But why leave Willow on *my* doorstep. And with that note?' It was the note, more than anything, that made no sense to Max. Why try to claim he was the father?

Sarah gave him a sympathetic smile. 'It appears that people around here have been talking a lot about you since word came you were moving into the Manor House.'

'So?' Max still didn't understand.

Lena made a small noise in the back of her throat, and shifted beside him on the sofa. 'I think I get it.'

He turned to look at her. 'Care to explain it to the idiot at the back of the class?'

She gave him a fond smile. 'For months, people have been talking about how rich you are, how handsome, your reputation with women.' She waggled her eyebrows at that. 'Honestly, they were mostly making it all up, I'm sure, but by the time you arrived half the village was convinced you were some rich playboy who slept with a dozen different women a week.'

'She thought I was promiscuous enough that I might believe I actually *was* the father?'

'Didn't you?' Sarah asked, eyebrows raised, and Max remembered, too late, their little white lie.

'I thought it was unlikely,' he said diplomatically. 'But of course I wanted to check with any women I might have been involved with before I could say definitively.'

Sarah looked amused, if disbelieving, so at least it didn't seem as if she was about to try and get him arrested for something.

'It wasn't just that, though,' Janice put in. 'I mean, look at this place.'

Max eyed the dark, gloomy study, and totally failed to see her point.

'Nobody who lived here could be short of money,' Lena explained. 'I imagine that Willow's mother hoped that you would be able to give her daughter a better life than she could hope to.'

'Not to mention the whole "lord of the manor" thing,' Sarah added. 'I mean, I grew up in Wishcliffe, and I know that whenever a family is in trouble there the first place they go is still Wishcliffe House, even in these modern times.'

'And Toby always helps,' Max said. It wasn't a guess, so much as a certainty he felt, deep inside. 'Willow's mother hoped I'd do the same.' Sarah nodded.

It all made a peculiar kind of sense, viewed through the lens of the village of Wells-on-Water. And it made him think of the place, and Lena's part in it, differently, too.

'Are you going to take her home now?' Lena asked.

'Willow's grandmother and grandfather have been told everything—by their daughter—and are, well, a bit shocked, I think, but determined to help. Willow's mother won't be alone with her baby any more; she has her family on her side and I think, between them and some help and support from us and the community, they're going to do okay.' Sarah smiled as she said it. Max supposed this had to be the best possible outcome for her.

'And Willow's mother won't be in any trouble?' He wasn't completely sure how he felt about that.

'She's going to get the help and support she needs for herself, as well as the baby,' Janice said. 'I don't think it's in anyone's interest—least of all Willow's—to punish her. Do you?'

'No,' Max said. 'No, of course not.'

'Can we…will we get to meet her?' Lena's voice wavered just a little and Max knew what she was really asking was 'will we see Willow again?' Because that was what his heart was asking, too.

'Right now the focus is just on helping them adjust,' Sarah said kindly. 'They did ask us to thank you, though. And to say sorry.'

'We didn't do it for the thanks.' Max got to his feet. If they were going, they might as well get moving now. No point in drawing out the goodbyes.

It didn't take long to put together the essentials Willow needed.

'There's a lot of stuff here people lent us to get started,' Lena said. 'I'm sure most of them would be happy to pass it on to Willow's family to help them, too. I'll check, and maybe you can arrange to get it to them?'

'I'm sure they'd be very grateful,' Sarah said.

'But she has to take the Chair of Joy now,' Max put in. 'It's her favourite. And Toby lent me a sling she really likes…'

Strange how his whole life had been taken over by such a small person. One who could change everything in just one short week.

Even stranger to imagine things going back to normal again tomorrow. To an empty house, and an empty heart.

Finally, it was time to say goodbye. He gave Willow a last cuddle, pressed a kiss against her downy hair, and made a promise he hoped nobody else could hear. He passed the baby to Lena, and purposefully didn't listen to whatever it was she whispered to her. Those words were private, like his.

And then they were gone, and the house echoed with the final closing of the door.

But Lena was still there, amazingly.

He looked at her, forced a smile. 'Do you want, I don't know, wine? Supper? Something?'

She gazed back at him for a long moment. Then she said, 'You,' and kissed him.

What am I doing?

Lena wasn't sure she knew the answer to her own question, but she did know she didn't want to stop. Kissing Max, touching Max, feeling his arms come up around her and hold her close…she didn't want the feelings that brought out in her to end.

She didn't want to stop and think. She just wanted to feel, for a change.

And it wasn't as if Max were complaining. He'd hauled her so tight against his body that she could feel *exactly* how much he didn't mind, and he groaned into her mouth as he deepened the kiss, turning them so he could press her up against the door Willow had just left through.

Not thinking about that.

'Are you sure?' He broke the kiss for a moment to ask, pulling back to gaze into her eyes. She wondered if her pupils were as blown with want as his were. 'We never got to that "later" talk.'

She shook her head and reached for him again. 'We don't need it. Not for this.'

Maybe later never needed to come. Maybe she could just have this, have him, for tonight.

Lose herself in him and worry about all the rest tomorrow.

That was all she wanted for now.

And it seemed Max was happy to go along with it.

They couldn't bring themselves to break apart as they headed for the stairs, which made navigating them a little tricky. Lena bashed her hip against the banister as they went, but she refused to stop and let Max check it. 'Upstairs,' she told him. 'Now.'

His room looked empty without the Moses basket in the corner, so she shut her eyes and pulled him down on top of her on the bed. When she opened them again, all she could see was him—and that was all she wanted to see.

Smiling at last, she began unbuttoning his shirt, stripping it from his shoulders even as he reached down to pull her top up over her breasts, then off completely.

Lena ran her hands down the firm planes of his chest. 'I was right. You did grow up well.'

Max gave a low chuckle in return. 'I'm not the only one,' he told her, then dropped his mouth to her breast, suckling the nipple through the fabric of her bra. 'I'm thinking this will all be a bit different from last time.'

'I should hope so.' She arched her back, her body desperate for more of his touch. 'We've had sixteen years to get better at it.'

'That's not what I meant.'

But before she could ask what he *did* mean, he had slid her skirt over her hips and down her thighs, following its path with his lips. Then, as she kicked the fabric away, he settled between her legs, shot her a knowing smile, and got to work.

It didn't take Lena very long to decide that this was *much* better than last time.

Max woke, stretched out an arm, and realised he was alone in the room.

The bed was cold. No Lena.

And no Moses basket in the corner. No Willow.

He sat up slowly, processing all the events of the night before. From the unexpected ache at handing Willow over to be returned to her family, to the even less expected bliss he'd found in Lena's arms.

They'd needed each other last night. He'd known they should talk first, but in the moment…they'd needed each other, and that was enough. Touch, affection, distraction, pleasure…maybe it wasn't the best way for them to deal with their shared loss, but it had felt right in the moment.

Now, though, he wondered. As pleasurable as last night had been, had it been the wrong move? Otherwise, why wasn't he waking up with Lena beside him for another round?

Maybe she'd just gone to get coffee, he thought, but his optimistic side was still a work in progress, so he didn't really believe it. He listened out all the same for the sound of her footsteps on the stairs, or her singing in the kitchen.

He frowned. There were voices downstairs, but they weren't Lena's. And the footsteps he heard were too heavy to be hers.

Swinging his legs out of bed, he began to hunt for his clothes, pulling them on quickly before going to investigate.

Downstairs, it was a reversal of the first night Lena had stayed over, the morning after they found Willow. Once again, half of the village seemed to be in his home—but rather than bringing furniture and baby stuff, this time they were taking it away.

'What's happening?' he asked Janice, sleepily, when he found her directing operations at the bottom of the stairs.

'Lena called around first thing, asked people to either come and collect their stuff, or donate it to Willow's family,' she explained. 'Hugh Francis, the plumber, brought his van so we can drive things around. Most people are loading their stuff directly into it to donate.'

Of course Lena had found a way to keep helping Willow, even after she was gone from their lives; Max wasn't even surprised.

But he did want to talk to her. One topic of their 'later' discussion really did need to become more of a 'now' talk, he felt.

'Where *is* Lena?'

Janice's smile turned a little awkward, and he instantly began to worry how much Lena had said to her friend about what had happened after she left the night before.

'She had to go,' the doctor said. 'One of her brothers called from The Fox. Said they needed her for a family meeting.'

Because that didn't sound ominous or anything.

'Do you think you can handle everything here?' he asked.

Janice nodded. 'Yeah. No problems. Anything you want me to make sure they don't take?'

'The coffee maker,' Max called back over his shoulder, already halfway out of the door.

He needed to talk to Lena. And if she was at The Fox with her brothers…well, that was where he was going, too.

CHAPTER TWELVE

LENA SIGHED AS she stared down at the paperwork her brothers had laid out for her along the bar.

'I just don't understand how you let things get this bad.'

'Right, because this is all *our* fault,' Gary said over the top of his pint glass. 'Where were *you* when the bank started demanding money?'

Earning a living somewhere else because you wouldn't let me do it here.

She sighed again. Reason had no hope with Gary and Keith. But something in her told her she had to try anyway. 'Dad left the pub to the two of you,' she pointed out. 'Not me.'

'So you punished us by not helping.' Keith tossed another dart at the board on the far wall. 'Just like you always managed to blame us for everything, so you could swoop in and save the day.'

'Saviour complex, that's what Daisy says you have,' Gary added.

Daisy, as far as Lena was aware, got all of her psychological insights from other people's social media rants, rather than any sort of formal training. Lena had also never seen her less than tipsy, and usually a lot further into drunk. She'd been a great drinking pal of her father in his later years, but never much of a fan of Lena.

'And does Daisy also have any suggestions of how to get you out of this mess?' Lena asked, gesturing towards the stacks of paper that all told the same story. Gary and Keith both looked away without answering, which Lena supposed was answer enough.

The Fox had never been a massively lucrative business, but it did well enough to keep going, and, since they all lived on site in the sizeable flat above the bar, they hadn't needed much more than that.

But in the two years since their father had passed away, it seemed that the boys' needs had become greater—or perhaps just that the time dedicated to the pub had dipped even lower. Because they weren't even breaking even now. They were haemorrhaging money every month, and it was fair to say that the bank had noticed. They needed to fix things—fast—if they wanted to hold onto the pub at all.

So of course they had called her for help. Because this was what she did, wasn't it?

All their lives she'd fixed their mistakes, she'd cleaned up after them, made apologies on their behalf, and stopped them doing some truly stupid things.

Maybe Daisy was right. Maybe she *did* have a saviour complex. What else explained moving in with Max Blythe for a whole week, giving her heart to a baby she *knew* wouldn't be staying and—worse—to a man she knew wouldn't, either.

Max had all but said the same when they went out for dinner, that she did everything for others, but never stopped to think about what she needed to do, or wanted to do, for herself. The last time she had…it had been the day after she lost her virginity to Max.

And here she was, with history repeating itself.

What was she going to choose? To help save her family pub—and her brothers—from ruin, or to walk away and seek her own path? It frightened her to realise that she really wasn't sure.

Before she had to make a decision, though, the pub door opened—and Max Blythe strolled in.

'Well, if it isn't the prodigal son returned,' Gary said, with a snide smile. 'I heard they killed the fatted calf for you.'

'*I* heard they gave up their firstborn,' Keith countered. 'Or was it *your* firstborn? Depends who you listen to, I guess.'

Lena's chest tightened at her brother's words, but Max ignored them both, heading straight for her. Frowning down at her with concern, he took her hands in his. 'Everything okay here? Janice said there was some sort of emergency.'

Lena tugged her hands from his grip and stepped back. Max had been gone a long time, but the village had long memories—and he'd humiliated her brothers, once, before leaving. They wouldn't have forgotten.

Not to mention all the rumours swirling around the village about him—not just about him being Willow's father, but about the fortune he'd made before he came home. The last thing she needed was her brothers deciding that she was a way into Max's money, if they realised how close they were.

But she was too slow, or her brothers were too quick. They'd never been stupid men, just lazy ones, and they'd seen whatever flickered between her and Max and the possibilities it held instantly.

'So now you're back, I imagine you're looking to right past wrongs, huh, Max? Or do we have to call you "Milord" now?' Gary stepped out from behind the bar, closer towards them.

Lena wrapped her arms around her middle and tried to

think of a way out of this. She could see the whole scene unfolding before her, and she just couldn't see a way to stop it.

'I don't have a title,' Max replied, his voice tight. 'Nor any past wrongs to make up for, as far as I'm aware.'

Gary and Keith shared a look at that. 'Really? I imagine our little Lena feels differently, don't you?'

'Keith, stop it.' They ignored her, as always.

'What do you mean?' Max asked, his eyes on her, not her brothers.

'Why, leaving her here. Alone. Pregnant.' Gary articulated the word so clearly it hung in the air between them, a ghost of a time she'd hoped she'd left behind.

And there it was. The memory she'd been trying her hardest to suppress since he'd returned.

They'd been there, that night, at the river. It wasn't as if there was much else to do in a village like Wells-on-Water. And even if no one else had noticed her sloping off with Max, her brothers had.

Max's face had drained of colour, his eyes heavy with confusion. 'You said—' He broke off, obviously remembering what she *had* said.

That he'd never called to check. That he'd left without thinking about it. Leaving any consequences for her to deal with. She'd said it was fine.

That bit had been a lie.

And okay, she'd lied a little bit more when they'd gone out for dinner and she'd told him that it was just spending that one night talking with him that had changed her mind about leaving the village. The positive pregnancy test had had a lot to do with it, too. She hadn't had a clue what to do, but she'd known she couldn't do it in Wells-on-Water.

This was the conversation she'd known they had to have

later. The one she'd been hoping she could postpone as long as possible.

'So you can see why we think you might have some reparations to pay, mate,' Keith said. 'And as it happens, the pub here could do with a little help. I'm sure Lena would consider the debt paid if—'

That was the breaking point. The one she'd felt coming—felt her whole existence starting to crack—but not quite known when it would hit.

With a last look at Max, Lena turned and walked out.

She couldn't take it a moment longer. She'd dealt with this her whole life. She'd been the convenient, reliable sister who took care of trouble, who fixed problems—first for her family, and now for the whole damn village.

And when she'd had a problem…a real one, a baby growing inside her, a family who'd shun her rather than support her, and no way to contact the father…she'd run, because she'd known she'd be on her own.

Now, she hoped, things would be different. But back then, it had seemed like the only choice.

She hadn't even known that her brothers had found out, until she'd come home for Christmas, months later. Gary had looked her up and down, taken in her flat belly, and shared one of those horrible, knowing looks with Keith.

'Took care of it, did you?' he'd said. *'Good girl. Last thing we need around here is another mouth to feed.'*

She supposed they'd found the test in her bedroom bin, and cursed herself for not being more careful. But it wasn't as if anyone else ever *emptied* the bins, so she'd assumed she'd be safe.

But her brothers loved knowledge that they could hold over others. She shouldn't have been surprised that they'd searched her room. And at least it had explained why they hadn't kicked up as much of a fuss as Dad about her leaving; they'd known why she had to go.

Heaving deep breaths, she stopped, just a short walk away, opposite the crumpled shell of the village hall. She leaned against the low stone wall outside the shops, gripping the cold stone so tightly her hands felt numb, and stared at the collapse of her best efforts to help this damn village.

She'd never wanted another girl to feel the way she had felt, staring at that pregnancy test. As if there was nowhere to turn, and nowhere to go. She'd worked her whole adult life, since returning to Wells-on-Water, to try and make it the sort of place where people supported each other, no matter what they were going through. Somewhere where *everyone* had a place to go, when they needed it.

But she'd failed. Otherwise Willow's mother would never have felt as if she had to abandon her baby on the doorstep of a man temperamentally unsuited to taking her in. The fact that Lena had been there had been pure chance, a fluke.

One last chance for her to try and do good.

And maybe she had, for that one baby. But what had really changed?

The next time some poor girl felt that desperate, Lena might not be there. And what then?

She couldn't fix every problem on her own, and, to be honest, she didn't even want to.

Max would be leaving for London again soon—maybe he'd already gone, now her brothers had outed her secret. He wasn't likely to forgive her for keeping that from him in a hurry. She'd screwed up, and that wasn't allowed. Growing up in Wells-on-Water had made that very clear to her.

She'd lost Willow, Max, the comfortable familiarity

of the Manor House—not to mention her job, and now it looked like the family pub, too.

Where did she go from here?

Lena had no idea. So she just started walking, and hoped she'd figure it out.

Max looked up at the facade of Wishcliffe House and, not for the first time, imagined what it might have been like to grow up there, with his half-brothers. A pointless fantasy, especially after so many years, but one he'd never quite been able to shake.

And now, it was coloured by another daydream. What might have been if Lena had found him, sixteen years ago, and told him the truth.

Had she terminated the pregnancy? Or given the baby up for adoption? Perhaps even left it on a doorstep somewhere, like Willow. Her brothers hadn't known—or seemed to much care, beyond the fact that it hadn't been a drain on their finances.

But Max cared.

He'd searched for Lena, once he'd escaped her brothers' grasping clutches, but she was nowhere to be seen. By the time he'd made it back to the Manor House Janice was just finishing packing up, and confirmed that Lena hadn't been back there, either.

They needed to talk. But as the man who'd walked away from her when it turned out she had really needed him, even if he hadn't known that, he didn't feel as if he could chase or hound her now. She'd come to him when she was ready, he hoped.

And finally they'd have that 'later' talk, even if it wouldn't look anything like the one he'd imagined a day ago.

Climbing the front steps to Wishcliffe House, Max prepared to knock—only for the door to swing open before he even reached it.

'You're here!' Toby beamed at him with a manic gleam in his eyes, somewhere between utter joy and pride, and the complete devastation that came from not sleeping in a few days. 'Come and meet your nephew.'

His nephew. Not his half-nephew, or sort of relation. Toby had embraced him as a new brother whether Max liked it or not—and to his surprise, Max found that he did.

He couldn't go back to London until he'd met his new baby nephew, and so Max had stayed a few more days. He kidded himself that the delay had nothing to do with hoping that Lena might show up.

Toby ushered him through the house, the rooms dimmed by half-closed shades, through to a cosy sitting room where Autumn was installed on a padded rocking chair, a tiny bundle in her arms. She smiled tiredly as Max approached.

'Benjy's first visitor,' she said. 'I'm so glad it's you.'

'Finn and Victoria will be by later, too,' Toby added. 'Then he'll have met the whole family.'

'You called him Benjamin?' Max reached out a finger into the bundle, crouching beside the chair. A tiny hand wrapped around it, and he felt his heart melt.

'Benjamin Harry Blythe,' Toby said. 'We were hoping you might agree to stand up as his godfather?'

'I'd be honoured.' He already knew he'd do anything for this tiny scrap of a human, the same way he would have for Willow, if needed.

As he hoped he would have for his and Lena's child, if he'd known.

A week ago, he'd arrived in Wells-on-Water with no interest in babies, or family, or settling down—and certainly not looking for love. The kind of domesticity Autumn and Toby had here—the kind he'd shared with Lena and Willow—would have made him shudder and step away in disgust.

Or maybe in fear. Because he hadn't known how this sort of life was supposed to work. It wasn't something he'd had before, or even really seen modelled for him.

But now he'd experienced it, even by accident… Max knew he couldn't be fully happy in this world without having it again. It might not have been what he'd ever have thought he wanted, but it turned out it *was* what he needed.

He just had to hope he might find it again. One day. The real thing, rather than a sham of a family set-up as he'd been acting out with Lena this week.

And maybe this time, he'd get to keep it.

The housekeeper, Mrs Heath, brought tea and biscuits, and Max settled down on the sofa to share all the small tricks he'd learned for coping with life with a newborn over the last week. Autumn and Toby soaked them all up, which surprised him.

'You probably know all this already from the books,' he said, after a while, embarrassed to have been going on so long. He knew Autumn had put together a veritable library of baby books over the last six months.

'You'd be surprised,' she said wryly. 'So many of them focus on what happens during pregnancy, or birth—but not so much on what happens afterwards.'

'And even the ones that do aren't much help,' Toby added. 'Benjy doesn't seem to be the sort to conform to what a book says he should be doing.'

'I wonder where he gets that from,' Max said mildly, pointedly not looking directly at either of Benjamin's parents.

'But what about you?' Autumn asked. 'We heard that they found Willow's mother, and her family are supporting her. That's good news, isn't it?'

Max nodded. 'The best we could have hoped for, really.' Even if it had bruised his heart a little. And losing Willow *and* Lena in the same twenty-four hours…

He reached for another biscuit.

'I bet the Manor House feels kind of quiet and empty now,' Autumn said. 'Unless Lena is still staying with you…'

Toby laughed. 'You don't have to answer that, Max. My wife has a terrible habit of fishing for gossip—even, it seems, after a very long couple of days here.'

Autumn rolled her eyes. 'Like you weren't wondering the exact same thing.'

'But *I* didn't ask it.'

'Because you knew that I would.'

Max decided to stop this argument in its tracks before what would usually be flirtatious banter between the two of them became something serious through sleep deprivation.

'Lena isn't there. I don't know where she is, actually,' he admitted. 'She…left. The day after Willow went home. Janice says she's not at her cottage, and she hasn't been back to The Fox, either.' He'd checked, reluctantly, when there'd been no sign of her for a full twenty-four hours.

Toby and Autumn exchanged a look.

'Tell us what happened,' Toby said.

'We can help,' Autumn added. 'And you can have a cuddle with Benjy. That will help.'

Max had never been one for sharing his feelings, let alone airing his relationship problems. But somehow, with his brother and sister-in-law listening with concerned faces, and the warmth of a newborn baby in his arms, telling them everything seemed like the most natural thing in the world.

So he did.

Everything. Starting sixteen years ago and bringing them right up to the moment that Lena slammed out of the pub without looking back.

He looked up at the end to find them both watching him with wide eyes, and all the biscuits gone.

'So?' he asked. 'What do I do now?'

They exchanged another one of those wordless looks that seemed to contain whole paragraphs.

'Just to be clear,' Autumn said. 'You do realise that you're in love with Lena, right?'

Max blinked. Love? He hadn't thought about love. Because everything they'd shared that week had only been pretend. A convenience, for Willow and her mother's sake, rather than theirs.

Not love. He just…needed to know she was okay. To help her. To be with her and support her in whatever she wanted to do next. To come home to her every night and talk about their days. To have her support in chasing his dreams, too. To work together towards shared dreams, come to that. To kiss her and hold her and make love to her again as they had that last night. And maybe to one day share again what they'd had with Willow with their own baby…

Oh.

Right.

'Of course I realise that,' he said, not feeling it was necessary to point out that the revelation was only a few seconds old. 'The question is, what do I do about it?'

Lena hadn't told anyone that she was coming back to Wells-on-Water to clear out her cottage and hand the keys back to the landlord. She hadn't wanted a welcoming committee on the doorstep, or even her brothers coming to hound her for money, or anything else. She'd known that her return—and her absence, for that matter—probably wouldn't have gone unnoticed. But still, she'd hoped she'd be able to get in and out in the minimal possible time, and without any drama.

Her hopes started to fade when she drove past Mrs Jenkins, standing outside her shop with her hands on her hips, watching her. Lena raised a hand to wave, but Hillary had already turned and gone back inside.

Lena sighed. Looked as if people were mad with her for leaving. She could understand that. They'd got used to having her around, fixing problems, getting involved. Keeping the wheels of the village turning.

She'd got used to it, too. She missed it. But she knew she had to think about what *she* wanted from life, as well as what others needed. It had taken her a lot of years to learn the lesson, but now she was there, she couldn't risk backsliding.

She still wanted to help, though. That was why she'd been applying for a different sort of job, from her room in her temporary rental in the capital. Fund-raising jobs, assistant roles at charities, that sort of thing. She'd hoped that her experience in hospitality would help her get a foot in the door, but it seemed that these roles were harder fought for than she'd expected—and she was older than the average candidate, straight out of university.

One recruitment agency she'd spoken to had told her, rather bluntly, that she was the worst of both worlds. Overqualified and under-experienced for the roles she was applying for.

But Lena had faith that she'd find the right thing. An opening where she could, finally, really make the difference she'd been craving in the world, without the possibility of having it snatched away from her again at any moment. *That*, she'd decided, was what mattered most to her.

And if she was focussing her search in London, well, that was just common sense. Lots of charitable organisations headquartered there, after all. The chance that she might bump into Max again—by accident or design—when she was ready, and prepared to face what had gone between them in the past and perhaps move on to something that could be between them in the future, total coincidence.

That was what she told herself, anyway.

The only problem was, she admitted to herself as she drove through the village towards her cottage, she missed Wells-on-Water. She missed the community, the people, the shops, the sea nearby and the big skies above. She missed making a visible difference, rather than an anonymous one. She missed even the chance of seeing Willow thriving with her real family.

And she missed Max, most of all. Much as her brain tried to deny it, her heart was very clear on the matter.

She passed the church, Roberto's restaurant, the craft shop, The Fox. And at each location, anyone outside enjoying the sunshine disappeared inside the moment she appeared.

Clearly she really was persona non grata. The thought hurt, but at least it would make it easier to leave again.

Her cottage was much as she had left it, when she reached it. Although she'd been renting it for several years now, it had never *quite* felt like home, not least because the landlord wouldn't let her decorate or do anything to soften the edges of the stark, clean white look he'd gone for.

Lena pulled two large suitcases from under her bed, and set about packing up her worldly belongings, ready for her next adventure, wishing she could feel a little more excited about it.

Maybe a cup of tea would help with that.

She'd just made her way downstairs to click on the kettle, when the front door crashed open behind her, and Lena spun to find Max standing in the doorway, his face shadowed by the sun from behind him, but his chest moving with deep, heaving breaths.

She blinked. 'How did you know I was here?'

'Are you kidding?' Max gave a low laugh. 'Every single person you drove past on your way into the village called me to tell me.' The phone in his hand began to buzz, and he checked the screen. 'That's your brothers, about fifteen minutes behind the curve, as usual.' He declined the call.

'Gary and Keith phoned you?' This made no sense at all. 'Why would *anyone* call you? And why are you even still here in Wells-on-Water? Weren't you going back to London?'

And why was he just standing there? Had he really waited here for her to yell at her for lying about the baby, all those years ago? Could he be that furious, still? Oh, she'd really wanted to put a bit of distance between them and that awful last scene at The Fox before she saw him again. She'd wanted to be a success, as he'd become, to meet him as an equal this time.

But here he was. And God help her, Lena wasn't going to send him away. And she wasn't going to run, either. Not this time.

It was time to face this—face him, face her future—head-on. And she was ready.

'Max,' she said, when he just stared at her rather than answering any of her very reasonable questions. 'Why are you here?'

CHAPTER THIRTEEN

MAX SHOOK HIMSELF out of the trance that seemed to have come over him on seeing her again, and searched for the right answer. The one that would make things right between them. That would explain to her how much this meant to him—but not scare her away at the same time. The one that would get him the answers *he* needed, too.

'Can I come in?' he asked. 'This might take a bit of explaining, and I'm half expecting an audience of locals out there at any minute.'

'It wouldn't surprise me.' Lena watched him, warily. 'Okay, since you don't seem about to yell at me, you can come in.'

Max shut the door quietly behind him. 'Why would I yell at you?'

'For lying about the consequences of what happened sixteen years ago.' She dropped down to sit on the edge of the white sofa, looking uncomfortable. 'For running away when you found out.'

He glanced around the strangely white and impersonal lounge, and took a seat on the chair opposite her, deciding quickly it was the most uncomfortable chair he'd ever sat on.

'I ran away first,' he said carefully. 'Do I wish I'd known the truth? Yes. But I wasn't there, and I hadn't left you any way to find me. And while I hope you will tell me what happened, it's your story to share when you're ready.'

'I lost the baby.' The words blurted out of her, and Max felt his heart break and mend at the same time. Break, because it had been his child, and because she'd had to go through that all alone. Mend, because she'd trusted him enough to tell him the truth.

'I'm so sorry.' He wanted to reach out and take her hand. No, he wanted to fold her into his arms and keep her there. But he couldn't push her. He needed to listen, first.

'It was my first week at university. Everyone else was out partying for Freshers' Week, and I...well. Wasn't.' She'd been dealing with a miscarriage instead. Alone.

'I wish I'd known. I wish I'd been there with you.' He looked down at his hands, shaking his head. 'I wish I hadn't been such an idiot eighteen-year-old to walk out on you as if there was no chance of consequences.'

'I wished that, too.' Lena gave him a lopsided smile. 'But now...these are the experiences that made us who we are. There's no going backwards.'

'Was that why... I mean, part of it anyway...why you were so determined to find Willow's mum and help her? To look after Willow until she was found?'

Lena nodded. 'I think so. I just kept imagining if it had been me, if I'd been the one stuck in this village, scared and alone. I'd worked so hard for years to help the people around here, to give them a place to go when they had nowhere else, to help and support them. And a lot of that was because *I* didn't have that, when I needed it. When my mum died, people had rallied around—because that wasn't her fault, and I was young and alone, and I apologised for my brothers and my father and I tried hard. Because I was a good girl, and I did what they thought were the right things. But they wouldn't think that any more.

I'd seen how they treated you…because of something that wasn't even your fault. Nobody shamed your father for sleeping with your mum and getting her pregnant. They shamed her for telling the truth about it.'

He wished he could tell her she was wrong, but he knew she wasn't. 'So you left. And then you came back and *changed things*. Lena, do you even know how amazing that is?'

She shook her head. 'I tried. I don't know if I succeeded.'

'I do. Willow and her mum and her family do. Everyone you've helped does.' He reached out now, and she met him halfway, her fingers intertwining with his in a way that made his heart leap with hope. 'Wells-on-Water isn't the place it was when I grew up, and that's thanks to you. Now, if someone needs help, they're not shamed for it. They *get* it. That's incredible.' And he wanted to help her keep doing that work. But only if that was what she wanted, too.

Lena pulled her hands from his. 'I went to London, you know.'

'London? Why?' It was hard to imagine her so far from home, alone. Wells-on-Water had always been part of who Lena was. He hated to think that anything he had done could have taken that from her.

But as he listened to her explaining about her job search in the capital, what she was trying to do there, he knew that nothing had really changed, not at heart.

As she finished he took a breath, and tried to figure out his next move.

'What?' she asked, frowning. 'What's the matter?'

'I'm trying to figure out how to say something.'

She rolled her eyes. 'Then just say it, idiot. Do you really think there's *anything* we can't admit to each other at this point? You've known me since birth; we watched each other grow up. You've seen me naked—at eighteen and thirty-four. We've discussed our mistakes, our pasts—hell, we've even co-parented for a week. What can you possibly need to say to me that's so scary compared to all of that?'

'I'm in love with you.'

Lena stared at him, her mind a sudden and complete blank. 'What?'

She could see him swallow before he responded. 'You asked me why I came here. Why I'm still in Wells-on-Water. Why everyone called me to tell me you were here. And you asked me what was so scary I almost couldn't say it. And the answer to all of those questions is the same thing: I'm in love with you.'

She needed to reply. She needed to say something, but there were no words left in Lena's head.

'I knew it the moment you left,' Max went on, then winced. 'Okay, not quite the same moment. But it didn't take me long. I realised that, while I missed Willow, what was really breaking my heart was not seeing you every day. Not coming home to you. Not talking about our days. Not being able to help you in your non-stop campaign to make the world a better, kinder place. And I didn't know where you'd gone, but I knew you'd have to come back here eventually. So I went around the village and I told everyone.'

'You told them you were in love with me?'

He smiled. 'No. I wanted to save that for you. But to be honest, I think they probably all knew before I did. I just told them that I needed to talk to you, and if they saw you they should ring me.'

'And they did. All of them.' All those friends and acquaintances who'd disappeared inside when they saw her.

They hadn't been shunning her. They'd been calling Max, so he could come here and tell her he loved her.

All those people who'd made life difficult for Max his whole childhood. He'd gone to them for help, and they'd given it.

Maybe she really had changed something, after all. And maybe part of that something was Max.

'All of them,' he echoed. 'Even Mrs Jenkins, who it seems loves you more than she hates me. Even your brothers. Who, by the way, have a new manager at the pub.'

'You gave them money?' she asked incredulously.

'No, I gave *your* family pub the expertise it needed to get it back on its feet. Her wages come out of the profits, and your brothers have to do what she says or she walks. I think they hate it.'

'I think I love it.' She frowned. 'You didn't think I might want to do that job?'

'Not really.'

'Because I was gone?'

'Because your heart wouldn't be in it.' Max tilted his head as he looked at her, a fond smile on his lips, and Lena felt her heart contract. 'You're a great manager, I have absolutely no doubt about that. But you studied hospitality because you wanted to help your family, not because it was what *you* wanted to do. And more than anything I want you to be able to choose what you *want* to do, not what you think others need, for once.'

'And you know what I want?' Because that was kind of presumptive.

He laughed. 'Hell, no. I mean, I have some ideas, but I'm waiting for you to tell me. And then I'll help you make it happen.'

'What?' None of this was making any sense.

Max shifted to the edge of his seat, reaching out to

take her hands again. He gazed into her eyes, holding her attention completely as he spoke. 'I told you I love you. And that's new for me—loving someone else. But since I came home to Wells-on-Water, I think I've learned a bit about what it means. I've seen it with Toby and Autumn, with Finn and Victoria. And I've seen it most with Willow, and with you. The way you loved that baby and helped me love her, too. And the way you love this village, and all the people in it who adore you back, even if they're not great at showing it. You've all taught me. And this is what I've learned:

'Loving someone means supporting them, helping them towards their best lives, and their best selves. It means letting them go if that's what's best for them, and holding on tight if that's what they need. So I let you go when you needed to, and now you're back… I had to tell you I love you. And I'll do anything I can to support you, to help you do whatever it is you think you need to do next. It doesn't matter if you feel the same. Because my love for you? It's not about me. It's all about the incredible woman you are.'

Lena swallowed around the lump that had taken root in her throat and blinked her burning eyes. 'You have that much faith in me? Even if you don't think I love you back?'

'Yes,' he said simply. Then he dropped her hands and got to his feet. 'Which is why I'm going to go back to the Manor House now, and I'll be there when you figure out what you want your next move to be. You decide you want to save an endangered dung beetle in Outer Mongolia, I'll help you plan how and fund the expedition. You want to tell me I'm wrong about you wanting to run The Fox, I'll fire the new manager and put you in charge—hell, I'll buy the place from your brothers if that's what you need to feel fulfilled. Whatever it is, you know where I am.'

Lena jumped up as he turned and moved towards the

door. 'And what if…?' She swallowed again as he paused, his back towards her. 'And what if what I need is you?'

Max felt his heart soar at her words, and he spun to face her so fast that the whole world seemed to tilt.

'What if what I need most in the world is to love you back?' Lena asked.

'Is it?' he whispered, barely daring to believe it.

She gave him a lopsided smile in return. 'Well, I could go for some of Roberto's chocolate pudding, too, but…yes. Max, why do you think I went to London?'

'For a job?'

'For *you*. Because I thought, after a while, maybe we could try again. Third time's the charm and all that. I figured you'd be going back there for work and, well, maybe we'd have a chance, away from all the history here.'

'But you *like* the history here. It's our history.'

'It is.' Stepping forward, she took his hand and tugged him closer, and he wrapped his other arm around her waist. 'I love this village.'

'I know,' Max said. 'And, actually, I've grown weirdly fond of it, too.'

'Good. Because I love you, too.'

His heart lightened at the words, as if the weight of years and years had just lifted away, and the world had opened up to another chance.

'So, you'll stay here? With me?'

'I already gave my landlord notice…'

'That works out nicely, then, because by "here" I meant the Manor House,' Max admitted, and she laughed.

'That could work,' Lena said. 'I will still need a job, though. I'm not good at sitting around doing nothing.'

'I'd never noticed,' he said drily, and she stuck her

tongue out at him. 'I already told you. Name it, and I'll be here to support you.'

She bit down on her lower lip, chewing it as she thought. 'I think… I think I want what I've always wanted,' she said finally. 'To make this village the best it can be. So that nobody here ever needs to go hungry, or feel lonely, or be afraid and feel like they have nowhere to turn. People like Willow's mum, or you when you were a kid. I want them all to feel welcome. And I want to help them all.'

'You want to build a new community hub,' he guessed.

'A better one,' she corrected. 'With proper therapists and training courses and baby groups and a food bank and a creche and—'

'Everything Wells-on-Water needs,' he summarised, before she could get too carried away.

'Exactly.'

'Then that's what we'll do,' he promised. 'Together.'

'Together,' she echoed. 'I think that's my favourite part.'

'Mine, too,' he admitted as he kissed her.

She broke away suddenly. 'What about what you need?'

'If I've got you, that's all I need,' he said.

Lena rolled her eyes. 'That's marvellously romantic, but not true. What is it that *you* want to do with your life?'

Sensing she was serious, Max stepped back and thought. 'Well, I genuinely believe in what you want to do here, and I want to help you with it. I've already built my own business, had wild success…and I want to keep my hand in there, too, but I have good people on staff, so a lot of it I can do from here, most of the time. But I guess the one thing I really want is something I've never had.' Swallowing, he met her gaze. 'A family. With you.'

Her eyes widened.

'I know, it's too much, too fast,' he hurried on. 'And I'm not saying now. But one day, when you're ready. That's what I want—what I dream of. Marrying you and having a family together. If that's what you want, too.'

Reaching up, she placed a hand on the side of his face and pressed a soft kiss to his lips. 'One day, probably not very long from now, knowing us, that's exactly what we'll have.'

And this time, when she kissed him, Max saw their whole lives together stretching out ahead of them. Filled with laughter and love, happiness and hard work, dreams and determination.

He couldn't wait for any of it.

EPILOGUE

THIS YEAR'S FIRE FESTIVAL seemed to burn brighter and more joyous than any previous year, Lena thought. Or perhaps that was just because she was happier than she'd been, ever before.

She tucked her arm through Max's and huddled against his side as they made their way around the field, checking out all the delights on offer.

At the sweet stall, there was a long queue of school children growing. Beside it, she saw that the mulled-wine tent was also doing a roaring trade—in fact, she could see Finn and Victoria sharing a mug beside their new daughter's pram.

Up on the stage, a folk duo was performing—a fast and fun tune that had people on their feet dancing. Lena squinted up at the stage, sure she recognised one of them, but unable to place him.

Amongst the dancers was Autumn, holding Benjy in her arms as she moved to the music, a swirl of colour in the firelight.

Lena glanced around for Max's brother, and found him holding court a little way away. Sitting on a wooden toadstool, Toby was surrounded by a group of entranced kids as he told them stories Lena suspected were rather more spooky than their parents would necessarily like.

'Ah, there they are,' Max said, and Lena glanced over to where he was pointing. Behind another stall, lit with fairy lights showing off the Wells-on-Water Community Hub logo, Kathy and Trevor were dealing with a small throng of people, all picking up leaflets and asking questions. 'Shall we say hi?'

As Lena watched, Kathy took down the details of a woman she recognised as a local businesswoman, hopefully volunteering, and Trevor handed one of their new fundraising packs to Dominic, the vicar.

'I think they've got things covered for now,' she said. 'And I want to go and get some of that hog roast before it's our turn to take a shift on the stall. Come on.'

They made their way around the huge bonfire at the centre of the field, heading for the hog roast.

There were plenty of families at the festival this year, Lena was pleased to see. But every buggy that went past, she still couldn't help but check if it might be Willow inside. Janice said she and her family were doing well, and that was all she could really hope for.

That and, maybe, a chance to do it all again with her own baby in the future.

She brought her hands together and twisted her engagement ring under her gloves. Maybe that future wouldn't be too far away.

And she couldn't wait to live every moment of it, here in her home village, with Max at her side.

* * * * *

THE HEIR'S CINDERELLA BRIDE

DONNA ALWARD

MILLS & BOON

It might sound strange to dedicate a book to my deck,
but I'm doing it.

Dear deck, thank you for providing me
with my "summer office."

Sitting in the sunshine with my laptop,
a cold drink, and the sound of the birds
are the best working conditions I could ask for.

CHAPTER ONE

THERE WAS NOTHING worse for Stephen Pemberton, Earl of Chatsworth, than feeling as if he'd just been *handled*.

Not like he really stood a chance when his sisters and mother ganged up on him. And it wasn't as if his brother, William, or cousin, Christophe, had taken his side. They'd been conspicuously silent when Aurora had issued the edict that he was the one who must return to Chatsworth Manor to oversee the construction of the new garden, which was to be a memorial to his father, Cedric Pemberton, the late earl. Two weeks, his mother had said. Time to approve the plans and be there to oversee breaking ground and the initial installations. Oh, and there was the local gooseberry festival in the village. Wouldn't it be lovely to have a member of the family in attendance again?

No, it would not. Be lovely, that is. But he would go, because for years his father had gone and good-naturedly judged the contests for best preserves, pies and puddings made with the abundant fruit. And since Stephen was the current earl, he would carry on the tradition, paste on a smile, and then when the garden was well begun. Then he'd head back to Paris and his office at Aurora, Inc.'s headquarters where he was COO of the family empire of fashion, cosmetics, and jewelry.

The supervision of the memorial garden was nothing

but a ruse. This was the family's way of "suggesting" he take a vacation. At first, he'd balked. But then Aurora had looked at him over the top of her Chanel reading glasses, and he'd reconsidered. Not for her sake, but for his.

Peace was in short supply within his family. For the past few years, he had been managing one crisis after another. Now that everyone was romantically paired up, it seemed all eyes were on him as the sole single sibling. And frankly, it was a relief to leave Paris and the meddling members of his family behind for a bit. Not that he would let them know that. They might think they'd "handled" him, but Stephen didn't do anything he didn't want to. He fully intended to spend the next several days in solitude, attending to Chatsworth estate business and avoiding whatever new drama the rest of the family cooked up.

Which was why he was now exiting the car in front of the manor house while the driver retrieved his bags.

Stephen let out a deep breath, and a measure of calm filled his body.

Home. Resentful, reluctant…whatever his feelings, he couldn't deny that out of all the family properties around the world, this was home to him. It always would be.

He shouldered one of the bags and the driver followed him up the cobbled walk to the massive oak door. Which remained firmly closed, instead of opening at his arrival.

He frowned. His appearance could hardly have gone unnoticed. With a sigh he lifted a hand, reaching for the knocker, then hesitated.

It was his own bloody house. Why did he have to knock?

Instead, he turned the heavy knob and opened it himself, stepping inside the foyer with his garment bag over his arm and tugging his suitcase along behind him as the driver departed.

He was greeted by heavy dark woodwork, polished floors, and unusual silence.

Where was everyone? And what exactly did the staff get up to when the family wasn't in residence? The last thing he wanted was to have a "conversation" with Mrs. Flanagan, the housekeeper. Something niggled at the edge of his brain. Mrs. Flanagan...she was ill, wasn't she? Maman had mentioned something about it when she'd given him the details about the festival and the landscape architect. Alarm skittered down his limbs. What if something had happened to Mrs. F? Was that why there was no sign of any staff? Lord, he hoped not. Mrs. F had been the housekeeper at Chatsworth Manor ever since he was a boy. His fondest memories were of her, and of her daughter—

"Stephen?"

Stephen turned toward the sound and his eyebrows immediately lifted in surprise. The woman before him was definitely not the russet-haired housekeeper he'd known since he'd been a child. But she was familiar. She'd barely changed at all. "Esme?"

"Good afternoon, my lord."

She'd recovered somewhat, and he watched with fascination as she schooled her features into a polite mask and carefully modulated her voice. It annoyed him. There was only one other time she'd ever called him "my lord," and it was branded on his brain as if it had just happened yesterday, instead of when he was thirteen. It had been their one and only fight, and it had been a big one.

He let go of the handle of his suitcase. "What are you doing here?" Her eyebrows lifted just the tiniest bit, and his cheeks heated as he realized he'd sounded less than polite. "I mean, I wasn't expecting to see you."

"I'm overseeing the household."

Stephen stared at Esme. The last time he'd seen her,

he'd been barely a teenager and she'd been all of twelve. Her mother, Mrs. Flanagan, had been the housekeeper here since he'd turned four. She'd had a three-year-old daughter who had become his best playmate. Esme, with her dancing green eyes and red hair and sense of adventure.

But more than twenty years had passed. He'd gone away to school. She'd gone on to…what? He was ashamed to admit he didn't know. Regardless, she was far more subdued than that precocious child now, standing before him in black trousers and a black shirt, comfortable shoes on her feet. Even though years had passed, though, there was no mistaking her. Her coppery hair was pulled back in a utilitarian twist and her clothing was plain, but she was just as beautiful as he remembered, with soft, mossy green eyes and a dusting of freckles over her nose.

"Are you done staring, sir?"

He frowned. "First of all, don't call me sir. Or my lord. Or Lord Pemberton."

"Then what should I call you?" She stepped forward now, that implacable mask still in place. "You *are* Lord Pemberton. And I am a member of your staff."

She wasn't wrong, but the knowledge—and her uptight tone—grated. "I know it's been a while, but we've made mud pies together. Surely we're beyond that kind of formality."

She sighed, but her voice warmed slightly. "That was a long time ago."

His brows pulled together. "Where is everyone else? Why is there no one at the door, or…" He looked around. "It's like you're the only one here."

She sighed again. "That's because I *am* the only one here. With no family in residence, nearly all the staff is on holidays."

"Except you, apparently."

"And the gardener, and the grooms at the stables. But I'm the only one in the house for the next ten days."

Which was damned inconvenient, since that was pretty much how long he would be here at Chatsworth. How could Maman have suggested a thing if she'd known? And she must have authorized it. The urge to rub his hand over his eyes was overwhelming. Hopefully it had just slipped Maman's mind, and she wasn't having her own crisis. Keeping his brothers and sisters in line was a full-time job, it seemed. Adding worry about Maman gave him a headache.

"Honestly, I feel the need to be more formal than I would normally be in order for the staff to take me seriously. I'm not my mother, you know?" She turned those lovely green eyes up to his and he was speechless for a moment.

The red-haired, impish girl had grown into an incredibly alluring woman.

"Speaking of, where is your mother? I wasn't aware she'd left. Did she retire?" He hoped his slight recollection about her health was wrong.

Esme shook her head. "No, she's been ill. Look, why don't I get you some coffee, and I can give you the details in the library? Marjorie left a Victoria Sponge in the kitchen before she left yesterday."

It was a favorite, and his stomach growled. "I didn't have lunch, so a sandwich before sponge would be appreciated as well, if you don't mind."

"I'll see to it right away."

"Thank you, Esme."

She turned to walk away, and his mind raced back to how many times they'd gotten into mischief together as children, how she'd never cared a bit that he was in line for the title. An ache settled in his chest. It might as well be a century ago. He certainly didn't resemble that fun-loving boy any longer.

"Esme?"

She turned around with a questioning expression, as if wondering if there was something else he needed. It was so odd, thinking of her waiting on him. That he was essentially her...boss.

"It's awfully good to see you."

She smiled then, and it lit up the room. "It's good to see you, too, Stephen."

Then she turned to the right and disappeared through a doorway, leading to the downstairs and the kitchens.

He turned left toward the library. Esme as the housekeeper. But how ill was Mrs. Flanagan, and why had Esme been the one to take over for her?

And why hadn't anyone told him?

Esme put together a full tray for Stephen's lunch, the weight of it heavy in her hands as she went back up the steps from the kitchens and to the library. She hadn't known he was coming, and it left her feeling totally off balance. The family always let the staff know when someone was going to be in residence. Now here she was, the interim housekeeper, and all the staff on holidays precisely because no one from the family was supposed to be here.

She'd manage. There was no way she was going to call anyone back from a well-deserved break. Unless, of course, she was ordered to. She was staff, after all. Not like she could forget. Stephen was ensconced in the library while she was the one holding the tray.

The library was her favorite room in the house. Always had been, with its delightfully rich furniture in dark wood and brocade fabrics, a massive fireplace, and walls covered with books from antique and rare titles to recent bestsellers. There was even a smaller bookcase in a corner that housed children's titles, along with pint-sized chairs for wee ones to curl up in. She'd spent a number of afternoons in that corner after school, either doing the meagre bit of homework she'd brought home or reading one of the titles that the earl had allowed her to borrow whenever she wanted.

Cedric Pemberton had been a good man. Certainly, he had been good to her mother and herself, providing the single mum with a reliable job and allowing Esme to tag along with his other children.

Now they were all grown up, and there was no disputing the evidence of that fact as she entered the library and saw Stephen sitting at the large desk—Cedric's old desk. Heavens, he was handsome—all dark looks, chiseled jaw, and broad shoulders. He was in the news occasionally, so it wasn't like his appearance was a shock, necessarily. But seeing him in person…hearing his voice…it set off a flood of happy memories. She doubted he knew how much his friendship had meant to her as a child, or how much she'd missed him when he'd turned thirteen and suddenly wasn't around anymore. The Pembertons had done the proper thing and sent him off to school.

"Your lunch," she said, approaching the desk, biting off the "sir" that threatened to escape her lips.

"Oh, thank you." He looked up from his laptop and offered a small smile, which was so tight it actually seemed to pain him. He looked at the assortment, then up at her. "You should have brought a cup for yourself."

"This isn't the old days," she chided gently. "I'm staff."

"I meant so we could talk about what will be happening this week."

That was her put in her place, then.

"Besides," he added, "having a conversation with you hovering above me feels weird."

Esme sighed. "I'm fine." She pulled up a nearby chair, so she was closer to the desk. "I suppose this does provide an opportunity for us to talk about what your needs are for the next few weeks while you are home. Do you expect anyone from the rest of the family to be joining you?"

He added sugar to his coffee—no cream, she noted for future reference—and stirred it. "Doubtful. Charlotte is in Richmond while Jacob is working an assignment in Turkey. Bella and Burke are just back from their honeymoon, and Sophie is still apparently trying to catch up on sleep since the baby was born." He shuddered. "Everyone is getting married and having babies. Next I expect Will and Gabi will be adding to the grandchild list."

Stephen reached for his napkin and sandwich.

"I take it you're not into marriage and babies."

"Not exactly." He took a bite of his sandwich.

"That must be interesting, considering you're the heir."

His dark eyes hardened, almost imperceptibly, but Esme caught the coolness and wondered what was behind it.

"With my siblings procreating, it does take some of the pressure off." He dabbed his lips with his napkin and sent her a look that she could only describe as cynical. "After being burned twice, I'm content with my life as it is."

Ah, yes. The broken engagements. Once, three years ago, maybe four, if her memory served correctly, he'd been set to marry Bridget Enys but the engagement had been broken off only a few months before the wedding, though no one seemed to know why. The more recent event, and far more scandalous, was Gabriella Baresi leaving him at the altar...and then marrying his brother, William. It certainly looked like there were no hard feelings now, but her mum had told her that Stephen had been livid when

Gabi had disappeared on the day of the wedding, and a bear to live with for months, storming around, barking orders. Looking at his imperious expression now, she didn't find it a stretch to imagine. It might be best to leave that topic alone.

"So," Stephen said, breaking into her thoughts, "what's going on with your mum? Is she very ill?"

Esme nodded, worry churning in her stomach. Sometimes she nearly forgot as she went about her work, but the anxiety was always there, waiting for her when she took a moment to pause. "Ill enough. She has breast cancer. She had surgery and then radiation, but now she's starting chemotherapy. She's found her recovery from surgery more difficult than she expected, as she developed a post-op chest infection." Esme swallowed around the lump that seemed to form in her throat every time she thought of her mother in hospital, hooked to IVs and drainage tubes, so pale and tired. "She was so worried about her job—"

"She shouldn't be." He frowned and tilted his head a little. "My mother must know all of this. Odd she didn't tell me." He put down his sandwich and met her gaze directly. "Please tell me we are giving Mrs. Flanagan paid sick leave."

She smiled, relaxing a little. "Oh, yes. Lady Pemberton has been wonderful that way. She offered to pay Mum's wages while she's sick so she won't have financial struggles."

"Good." He gave a satisfied nod and took another bite of the sandwich. She softened just a little, too. In many ways, the man before her now was a cold stranger, but he'd immediately shifted into making sure her mother was cared for. It made her glad to see there was a good man beneath the cool exterior.

"What I meant before was...well, Mum was worried

about who would look after the house." She grinned before she could stop herself. "I think Chatsworth Manor is her other child."

He smiled back. "And that's where you came in."

Heavens, when he smiled his whole face changed, morphing into something familiar that sent a pang through her chest. She nodded, pushing the feeling away. "I cleared it with my boss and took a leave of absence from my job at the inn. Goodness knows I've spent enough time here, working odd jobs, helping Mum out from time to time. With the family not in residence, it's a small staff to oversee." A smile flirted with her lips. "And now they're on holiday for a week. Cushiest job I've ever had."

It wasn't a lie. She'd worked as a housemaid, as hotel housekeeping, as a waitress, a bartender, front desk…there wasn't much in the service industry she hadn't done. It wasn't the tasks at Chatsworth Manor that she found difficult, not at all. It was feeling like she was "Mary's daughter" rather than simple Esme Flanagan. Not everyone took her seriously.

"But your mum…she's going to be okay?"

Esme smiled, though it felt wobbly. There was real concern in Stephen's voice, which she appreciated. She liked to think her mum was more than just a housekeeper to him. Esme and Stephen had scampered into the kitchen often enough after school, looking for snacks. Her mum had always been around, and while it hadn't been her place to discipline Stephen, exactly, the two of them had known without question that any bad behavior would result in Esme being in trouble with her mum and Stephen would have to pay the piper with Aurora.

"I hope she will be," she whispered, then cleared her throat. "There are no guarantees, of course. The survival

rate for her type of cancer is good, though, over eighty percent. There was some lymph node involvement."

Stephen reached for the plate of cake, then frowned.
He took the unused knife on the tray and cut the generous
slice down the middle. "Let's share," he said. "Marjorie's
sponge is perfection."

She was tempted because he was right. No one did a
Victoria Sponge like the cook. But it wouldn't be right. She
couldn't sit in the library and share cake off a plate with
the Earl of Chatsworth, no matter how long they'd known
each other. Her mother would have a fit if she knew they
were even chatting in such a casual way. As much as Mary
Flanagan adored the Pemberton family, the line between
staff and employer was one that she simply did not cross.
It had been fine when they'd been kids, but Esme and Stephen were not children any longer. She watched his long
fingers as he replaced the knife on the tray. No, indeed.
They were not children.

"I should get back to work. While the rest of the family
is out of residence, we've been turning out the bedrooms.
I've been carrying on while the maids are off."

"It's just cake, Esme."

"And you're the earl, Stephen. We're not eight years old
any longer and climbing apple trees after school."

His relaxed expression turned to one of annoyance, as
if he wasn't used to being contradicted or turned down
for anything. "You were always better at climbing than I
was," he admitted.

She half laughed, half snorted, then straightened her
face. "I was nimble. But you were always faster on your
bicycle."

"Longer legs," he replied, cutting into the cake with
the side of his fork.

Not that she'd ever breathe a word of it, but she found

his height quite attractive. There was something about a tall man that was so alluring. At five-eight, she appreciated a man who would still be a little taller than her, even if she were in heels.

Which was altogether silly as she wore very practical black shoes at work, and they would not be seeing each other anywhere other than in the house. And the conversation had taken a turn into a trip down memory lane, which was even more inappropriate. She stood, knowing she needed to go. Get back to her job…the one he was paying her to do.

"Mmm. I have missed this." He closed his eyes as he chewed and swallowed the first bite of cake. He speared a piece on his fork and held it out. "Come on, Esme. One bite won't kill you."

One bite, from the fork that had just been in his mouth. Something delicious swirled in her stomach at the thought. He was acting as if it was nothing at all, but to her it felt intimate. She absolutely shouldn't. But he gave the fork a small wiggle and she gave in, leaned forward, and closed her lips around the tines.

The soft sponge and sweet jam mingled in her mouth, and she closed her eyes for a moment. She didn't eat cake anymore. Didn't eat a lot of things, and for a lot of reasons. But the single bite was heaven, and she let herself enjoy it and the moment, as neither could happen again.

"See? Delicious. You should have brought two forks."

She swallowed and forced a smile. "It is delicious. And now I really do need to get back to work. First of all, I need to ensure your room is ready for you, since you weren't expected."

His smile faded and was replaced by a look she interpreted as annoyed. Well, one of them had to be sensible. One bite of cake off his fork and her heart was hammering.

He was the stereotypical tall, dark, and handsome man, and he had a title. That would have been enough to make her a little awestruck. But having history with him? That just made things worse. And she would absolutely not be foolish during the next two weeks.

"Of course." He took his cue from her and the officious-looking mask fell over his face again, almost as if the little moment of familiarity had never happened. "I will be working in here for the remainder of the afternoon. I'll expect dinner at seven and tomorrow morning I'll have breakfast at eight. The garden designer will be here at nine to go over the plans."

"Of course. I'll make sure to have everything on time. Will you be wanting a coffee service for the meeting?"

"That would be really nice, actually. Thank you."

"It's my job," she said simply. Only right now she was looking at being housekeeper, housemaid, and cook all in one.

It took all she had not to affect a little curtsy before leaving as she knew he'd hate it. Actually, knowing that tempted her a little more, but she showed restraint. "I'll come back for your tray shortly. Enjoy your cake. And just ring if you need more coffee."

She turned to leave the room and made herself drop her shoulders and try to relax. What was it about Stephen Pemberton that both put her on edge but also made her feel so at home?

As she pulled the door shut behind her with a solid click, she sighed. Her role here at the manor had always been a bit of a paradox. Daughter of staff, but friend of the eldest child. And right now, that made her feel as if she really didn't belong anywhere.

CHAPTER TWO

IT WAS TEN o'clock before the garden designer left Stephen in the library, now the recipient of sets of plans for the rather ambitious "traditional English garden" that Aurora had commissioned. The designer came highly recommended and was one of the best in the country, having recently worked on the team that had created the sunken garden at Kensington Palace. As far as Stephen knew, he was just there to approve things and make sure everyone got paid. Both things he could have accomplished from Paris, but it was becoming increasingly clear that his mother—and perhaps the rest of the family—had wanted him out of their hair for a while.

Not that he didn't care about the garden…he did. It was in honor of his father and since his death, the family had come close to falling apart more than once. And it had been up to Stephen to lead them through it.

Stephen's hands stilled on the plans as he considered the last few months. He was so weary of carrying the load of being earl and eldest son. Just when everything had started to come together—Bella and Burke, and then Christophe marrying Sophie, and everyone adjusting to new roles at Aurora, Inc., drama and scandal had struck yet again. He was still trying to work through his feelings about having a half-sister only six months younger than William and

Charlotte. He tried and tried to reconcile the man he'd known as his father with the man who had stepped out on his wife, fathered a child, and kept it all secret for nearly thirty years. Who was Cedric Pemberton? Stephen felt he needed to know, because until their half-sister, Anemone, had arrived in their lives, Stephen had made it his mission to emulate his father's perfection. With that image shattered, he felt rather adrift—particularly in his role as the current earl. It was hard to know what to do next.

He certainly didn't think his father's mistake should erase all the other wonderful memories or deeds, though. It only proved Cedric had been human. But Stephen was torn about his father's hypocrisy. The man had instilled the importance of honesty and integrity in his children from the time they were walking. Knowing he hadn't followed those same principles left Stephen with unanswered questions and a hefty amount of resentment.

"You look as if you're carrying the weight of the world on your shoulders."

He looked up from the plans and saw Esme standing just inside the door, carrying a tray with the ubiquitous coffeepot, freshly filled.

"Not the world." The words came out clipped, and he let out a sigh. "Sorry. Maybe I'm carrying a small part of it, though."

She came forward and put down the tray. "I won't disturb you," she said. "Ring if you need anything else."

Stephen lifted his hand and ran it along the back of his neck. "Actually, there is something you could do for me."

Esme turned back to him, her green eyes alight with curiosity. "Yes?"

"Come for a ride with me." The moment the words were out of his mouth, he knew a ride throughout the estate was just what he needed. "It's been months since I was on horseback. I've been cooped up in an office."

"I have a job to do. If you don't want to go out alone, maybe one of the grooms would go with you."

He knew it wasn't right to put a staff member in this position. But this was Esme. She was different. It surprised him to realize he'd been longing for a friendly face. One with no agenda and no complications.

"You used to go out riding with me all the time."

"When we were ten. It isn't exactly the same, sir—I mean, Stephen." She lifted her chin. "My mother would have a canary if I did such a thing."

"Why?" he asked, truly curious about her answer. But she remained silent, her mouth set in a stubborn line. It annoyed him. Not because he was used to having his orders followed, but because she seemed so determined to make a lot out of their differences. He frowned. Goodness, she didn't think he was a snob, did she?

"You know why," she replied quietly. "I'm sorry, Stephen. I can't go riding with you today. But I will send word to the stables to have one of the horses tacked for you."

"It would be nicer with company."

"I'm sure all you'd have to do is pick up the phone and you could have all the company you would ever want."

Was that a hint of jealousy in her voice? Or just disdain? Either way, he liked it. Not because he enjoyed winding her up, necessarily, or arguing. But because despite the power differential between them, which she annoyingly kept bringing up, she was not afraid to voice an opinion. It would be no fun at all if she simply answered everything with "yes, sir, right away, sir" which was what he often got in Paris at Aurora headquarters.

"I could," he admitted, replying to her last statement.

"But it would be tiresome and…work. Being social, I mean. And worse, someone might read something into it."

She laughed then, a light, surprised sound. "So I'm not tiresome? Or work?" She lifted an eyebrow. "And you don't think people would read something into it if I spent an afternoon out riding with you?"

God, he loved how she challenged him. It was invigorating. "Who would? There's no one here. And if I must be here, doing all the earl-like things, it might be nice to know I have a friend nearby."

Her face softened as she came a little closer, peering up at him with her startling green eyes. "Are you lonely, Stephen?"

He made a sound that came out like "Pssht."

"Of course not. I'm just looking for something low-key and comfortable." But her question came a little too close to the mark. Lonely wasn't quite the right word, but he wasn't sure what was. He just knew that this bit of banter with her made him forget all his other worries for half a minute.

"Well, you'll have to be low-key by yourself. I have work to do. Since you're paying me to do it and all."

"I could command you to go. As your employer." The moment the words left his mouth he regretted them.

"But you won't," she said easily. "It's not your style. Oh, I think some people think it is, but it's not, not really. Go. Have your ride. It'll be good for thinking."

"I shall." He wouldn't let her refusal deter him, even as he mentally thought backward to the last time someone had refused him anything.

It was quite possibly his non-wedding to Gabi. Was he really that intimidating?

She left then, and he went to the coffee tray and poured himself a cup. There was a little plate with biscuits, too, and he smiled to himself. The biscuits on the plate weren't from the Pemberton kitchen. They were a particular favorite of his that came out of a package. Hobnobs, Esme had called them when she'd once packed a basket for the two of them. He had been seven, she six, and they were planning to run away from home because Mrs. Flanagan and his mother had said that Esme could not take music lessons with him. They'd both been livid at the injustice of it all, particularly Stephen who did not want music lessons to begin with. He had come up with the plan to run away and Esme had said she would provide the food, and so the basket had contained her favorite foods: peanut butter sandwiches, a thermos of chocolate milk, and a sleeve of chocolate- covered Hobnobs.

They'd made it all the way into the village when Cedric had finally found them. Stephen had been afraid he was going to get into huge trouble, but Cedric sat beside them at the town square, thoughtfully ate a peanut butter sandwich, and said he expected they should get home as Mrs. Flanagan was bound to be worried about Esme.

Stephen wondered now if his father hadn't understood that urge to run away from all the rules and expectations. Now he could never ask him. Or ask him if his affair had been the result of rebelling against his restrictive life.

All Stephen knew was that he wouldn't make the same mistake.

The August day was hot but not overly so; the sunshine felt glorious on his face and soaked through the fabric of his shirt while the muscles of the animal beneath him shifted rhythmically in an easy gallop. The saddle was familiar and yet not; it had been too long since he'd taken an afternoon to go riding. He eased his seat a little, slowing his mount until they reached a walk, and then reached down and gave the gelding's neck a pat. No sense overheating the animal just because he was feeling the need to blow off some steam.

The park surrounding Chatsworth Manor was nothing short of splendid, consisting of rolling green hills, leafy trees and a brook leading to a pond where he now took his horse for a drink. He dismounted and hooked the reins around his hand, walking forward, breathing in the rarefied air and marveling at the quiet surrounding him. There was nothing but the whisper of wind in the trees and the sweet chirping of birdsong in the bushes. No traffic. No chatter or phones ringing. Occasionally the odd sound of an airplane overhead. But mostly…peace. Tranquility.

He wished Esme had come with him, but thinking about it now, he knew she was right in that it had probably been wrong to ask. They weren't children anymore. And it wasn't that she was an employee, either, though she was correct that it could make things awkward. It was more this moment, and the solitude, and realizing how intimate it would be with two people, far away from the house or any other eyes. She inspired a comfort in him that was highly unusual at this point in his life, simply because she'd known him as a child. But what did that mean, really? He would be foolish to trust her—to let her in—based solely on their past association as children. Besides, was that what he really wanted? It wouldn't be fair to use her as a diversion.

Now that he was here at the manor house, he was beginning to realize he needed to face some things head-on. And as a man who'd made an art form of controlling his feelings, the thought of giving his emotions some control was terrifying. He didn't trust it. Come to think of it, he didn't trust anyone or anything these days. He suspected that was a great deal of the problem.

As his horse dipped his head to the pond, Stephen rolled his shoulders. Ah yes, trust. It apparently worked for some people, but it certainly never had for him. He'd trusted Bridget—he'd loved her, for God's sake—but she'd betrayed him horribly. And he'd trusted his friendship with Gabi, even if their engagement had been a sham, and she'd left him at the altar. Even family…look at Anemone. Her whole arrival at Aurora in Paris had been based on false pretenses, not to mention the greatest lie of all—her paternity, which his parents had both known about and never revealed.

People let people down. That was all there was to it.

Now he was supposed to be thrilled to be supervising this massive undertaking for a garden and fountain to honor his father when he had so many conflicting feelings he wanted to wash his hands of the whole responsibility.

Maybe Esme was right. Maybe he was lonely.

He tilted his neck to either side, trying to release the tension there. His mother had "suggested" the trip as a way to relax. But all the relaxing was doing was making him think too much. And the thinking made him feel things—uncomfortable things. Like anger and frustration.

As the sun soaked into his skin, he let out a gigantic sigh. What he really wanted to do was escape this life for a day. No, more like a week. Pretend he wasn't an earl, wasn't the COO at Aurora, Inc., pretend he was an ordinary bloke with ordinary responsibilities.

Except…he wasn't ordinary, and never would be. From the time he'd turned thirteen and he'd been sent off to school, he'd been groomed for this life. He'd never had a choice. And it had never bothered him very much… until now.

His horse was sufficiently rested, so he swung back up into the saddle again and adjusted the reins in his hands.

His afternoon pity party was at an end. Because back at the house all his responsibilities waited, and he felt the burden of them as he spurred his mount and moved forward.

Esme watched Stephen lead his horse back to the stables and held back a sigh of appreciation.

His long legs, his great butt... Buff-colored riding breeches disappeared into riding boots, and he wore a white polo shirt, which contrasted with his muscled, tanned arms. His stride was long and easy, and her mouth went dry as he walked through the garden. She'd stepped outside to check the moisture levels in the herb pots when he'd returned from his ride. She was sorry now that she'd refused his invitation, no matter how improper it would have been. Oh, it wasn't even the impropriety. She wasn't *that* stiff. It was the shocking discovery that the silly schoolgirl crush she'd started developing just before he'd gone away hadn't been as silly as she'd once thought. It had flickered to life again on his arrival, and with every encounter it flared just a little bit brighter. How embarrassing. How...

Well. If she were being honest—only with herself—it was rather surprising and not entirely unwelcome. Her ability to feel attraction had been rather dead for quite some time, and she was only thirty-four. It came as something of a relief to realize that part of her still worked. For a very long time, she'd thought her marriage and subsequent divorce from Evan had killed it stone dead.

But Stephen? Ridiculous. For one thing, he was the earl. He was stupid rich, and lived in Paris most of the year, and ran in the same circles as celebrities and VIPs.

That didn't mean she couldn't admire the package, however. And it was a very fine package.

She went back inside, knowing she needed to get back

to work. There was an evening meal to plan—that she had to cook—and other duties on her list that needed checking off. Esme had planned to take this week to catch up on random tasks that were done on more of a quarterly or annual basis.

She was counting linens when Stephen's voice interrupted her.

"You're still here."

She jumped, losing count. Her pulse thrummed at the sound of his voice, especially since she'd been thinking about him. This was a big house, but perhaps it wasn't going to be big enough for the next few weeks.

But she schooled her features and nodded. "I am. I'll be here until after dinner." She'd set some short ribs to braise an hour ago and intended to make garlic mash and glazed vegetables to go with it. Thankfully last night Stephen had mentioned that he didn't normally eat pudding so there was no need for desserts while he was home. Esme was a decent cook, but there was no way she could bake like Marjorie.

"After dinner…" He frowned, and then his eyebrows shot up as if he'd just come to the correct conclusion. "No other staff. You're doing it all. Including the cooking?"

She nodded. "It's no trouble. I like to cook. Though I can't compare to Marjorie."

"Last night's roast chicken was delicious."

"Well, thank you. Anyway yes, I'll head home after the tidying up." And then worry about her own dinner, and washing dishes, and getting up in time to be back here to start his breakfast. Oh, and checking in on Mum. Because now that she was doing chemo, the side effects were more worrisome.

"My being here has definitely caused an imposition," he said, his voice low. "I'm sorry."

"How can it be an imposition if it's my job?" she asked. "You're paying me to do it."

She realized how sharp she sounded, and it wasn't what she intended at all. Here she was trying to not be overly friendly—to maintain the boundaries that needed to be maintained—and instead she just sounded…crabby.

"It's a very long day for you, that's all." He pursed his lips. "Esme, at home I fend for myself quite often. I can do so here, as well. Especially for breakfast." He shrugged. "I can make coffee. And toast. And even fry an egg."

"It's not necessary…" She looked away, feeling oddly embarrassed. Would he give someone else the same consideration? Or was it just because it was…her? There was no way she would ask. She felt strange about it already.

"Suit yourself." He took a step back, his face closed off again. "However, I can certainly eat earlier than seven. So you're not so late getting home."

He was being kind, making adjustments, and she was being…not herself. She didn't know how to act around him anymore, and that made her sad. She thought back to all the years as children when they'd actually finished each other's sentences. This was what they'd become. But what if it could be different? What if they could be…friends? Did she even want that?

"I'm sorry," she offered, softening her voice. "I've been short with you, putting boundaries in place because of, well, who we grew up to be. I don't mean to be off-putting."

"Maybe it would be better if we just said what we mean," he replied, shoving his hands in his pockets. It made him look a little bit boyish, and she responded to that.

That was the problem. She responded to him, and she didn't want to, and there was no way in the world she could say it to his face.

Then he surprised her.

"Would it help if I said that I am absolutely not looking for any big complication, that I remember our time as children fondly, and I would like to spend my time here relaxed around each other?"

Could she manage "relaxed"?

She lifted her chin. "Actually, that helps a great deal, because I feel exactly the same way."

He let out a breath. "Good. Then let's agree to call each other by first names, and perhaps in the days ahead I'll do my work and you can do yours, but we might actually be able to hold a conversation without tensing up and wondering if being friendly crosses some sort of invisible line."

Esme met his gaze, ignoring the jolt that went right to her toes with the eye contact. "As a friend, I'd appreciate moving the dinner time by an hour. That means I can check on Mum on my way home."

"And if you need time for any reason, to take your mum to appointments or anything, please take it. I know I'm... authoritative. But I'm not an ogre." A smile ghosted his lips. "Despite what my siblings might say."

"Surely they don't—"

"Oh, they do," he said, cutting off her protest. "And if I'm honest, I deserve the criticism. At least some of it."

She wondered why. Wondered what had changed, where the fun-loving boy had gone. Though she rather suspected that beneath that cool veneer was a man who cared about things very deeply. What she didn't understand was why he kept that side of himself under lock and key.

And that thought took her way past "friendly" yet again. That simple request was going to be the hardest to follow.

Stephen tapped a long finger against his top lip. Esme couldn't help but follow the path of it. The shadow of the day's stubble already darkened his jaw, even though he'd been clean-shaven for his meeting this morning. She wondered if it was prickly or soft.

"I suppose it would cross a line to ask you to join me for dinner tonight?"

Both responses—*it would* and *of course not*—flitted through her brain. As if sensing her hesitation, he lifted a shoulder in a shrug. "It's a bit lonely, sitting in the dining room all by myself. And you have to eat, too. There's no reason why you shouldn't fix a plate and join me."

She gave up. While she had her reasons for putting space between them that went beyond the simple employer/employee relationship, she couldn't deny he was making sense and she was creating friction where there didn't need to be any.

"Fine, I will," she answered. "But before I can do that, I need to finish counting these linens."

He nodded. "And I have some estate things to go over in the library."

"Then I guess I'll see you in the dining room at…six?" It sounded ridiculously early, considering the family usually ate at seven thirty or eight. But he nodded and offered a small smile.

"Six is perfect," he said, and before she could catch her breath, he turned on his heel and disappeared.

CHAPTER THREE

STEPHEN PULLED OPEN the heavy wood door that marked the entrance to The Tilted Lizard. He was immediately treated to the sound of fiddly folk music and the smell of chips and beer. Inside the door, behind the hostess lectern, was a carving of a gecko, leaning sideways on a cattail and wearing a broad grin. Stephen laughed. It was ridiculous and perfect all at once.

He scanned the pub for a seat but instead of an empty table, he saw Esme.

Lord, she was beautiful. It hit him like a ton of bricks every time he saw her. Last night, sitting with her in the dining room over a delicious meal, he'd loosened up and actually smiled and joked a little. It was impossible to remain immune to her easy charm and smile. The way her face lit up seemed to warm him from the inside out. And sure, it had been a little awkward at first, but they'd relaxed over a single glass of wine with their food. It had only lasted thirty minutes, but she'd opened up a bit about her mother's illness, and he'd responded with similar worries after Maman's heart scare at Gabi and Will's wedding, the parental worry providing common ground between them.

One of the staff had stopped by her table. Esme said something and gestured with her hands while the other woman nodded enthusiastically, and then they both laughed. He swore he could hear the lilting sound through the rest of the din, and his heart gave a solid thump in response. She was so animated, so utterly lovely with her easy smile. It was a revelation. Since he'd arrived only a few days ago, and with the exception of dinner last night, she'd been so uptight, so reserved. It had worried him, wondering why she'd changed so much from the girl he remembered. Clearly she was at home here in the pub, as her face was relaxed and her smile easy—in a way it wasn't with him.

He wondered why.

Regardless, he certainly didn't want to encroach on her evening. He'd find somewhere else to have a pint. Maybe. He wasn't exactly spoiled for choice in the village. He was about to turn back to the door when her gaze lifted, and she saw him there. Immediately heat rose to his cheeks. To leave now without at least saying hello would be rude, and he'd been surly enough over the past few days. So he gave a little wave and started forward, pretending that he hadn't just got caught staring at her.

He reached her table and offered a smile, though his usual protocol of social greeting made him nearly lean forward to kiss her cheek. Totally not appropriate in this situation, so instead he offered a hello to the waitress as he pulled out a chair.

"Sandy, this is Stephen. Stephen, Sandy. Sandy and I used to work together."

"And get into trouble together," Sandy offered, sending a wink in their general direction. Stephen liked her already.

"Interesting. Same here. Getting into trouble, I mean."

Sandy hadn't put together who he was, for which he was grateful. "Oh?"

"I've known Stephen since I was a kid."

"And when we got in trouble, I always took the blame."

"You always offered," Esme retorted, but her eyes twinkled in a way they hadn't since he'd shown up at the manor.

"It was the gentlemanly thing to do," he replied.

Sandy was chuckling. "Es has already ordered her drink, but what can I get you?"

He would have taken a whiskey, but he wondered if that would be too...well, predictable. "What do you recommend that's on tap?"

"Depends on what you like."

"I'll have a pint of an IPA...surprise me, Sandy."

"Ooh, an adventurous type." She waggled her eyebrows at Esme as she smiled. Esme just rolled her eyes. "Back in a flash," Sandy said, spinning about and walking away with an extra jut of her hip.

"That girl..." Esme shook her head and laughed. "We've had some good times together."

"She seems fun."

"She is. Young yet. Though her latest boyfriend might just make her want to settle down." The words were infused with skepticism, and Stephen had the fleeting thought that Esme soured on romance. He certainly understood that.

"That's not for you, though?" Stephen found himself curious to learn a little more about Esme's past. It wasn't like any details ever got filtered from the household staff to the family. He hadn't even known Mrs. Flanagan was ill, and the last he'd heard mention of Esme... He wracked his brain. He seemed to remember Mrs. Flanagan saying something in passing a few years ago about a divorce. Had Esme been married? And what fool had been stupid enough to let her go?

She shrugged. "I thought it was, once."

He snorted. "Yeah, me too. Not anymore, though."

His reply caused an awkward silence, which Esme

thankfully covered. "So," Esme said, "what brings you to The Tilted Lizard?"

"I came in search of a pint and some noise. The house is very quiet when you're in it all alone."

"You don't strike me as the social type."

He chuckled a little. "To be honest, I like the background noise. I don't need to be social."

Her cheeks colored a little and he hurriedly covered his gaffe. "Present company doesn't count. I don't mean to intrude on your evening."

"You're not. My best friend is supposed to be joining me for a few drinks, but she's running late. But I understand if you'd rather be alone. You won't hurt my feelings if you want to sit at the bar."

Now he felt like an ass. "I don't mind keeping you company for a while if you don't. I mean, until your friend gets here."

"I don't mind." She smiled a little, almost shyly, which did a strange little something to his chest.

Her gaze swept over him, and her eyes lit with approval as she nodded at his jeans and casual button-down. "No Savile Row in sight."

"No, not tonight." Tonight he'd dressed far more casual than normal.

She leaned over and looked under the table, then back up at him. "Well, except the Italian leather. Those give you away."

"They're my favorite shoes," he explained.

"Don't you have trainers? Something that at least looks a little scuffed?"

"Trainers are for the gym." He sat back as Sandy returned with their drinks. "Thank you, Sandy."

"Shall I start a tab? Do you know what you'd like for dinner?"

"You know what I'm having," Esme said.

"Two pieces cod and chips, hold the tartar, extra vinegar," Sandy supplied.

Esme beamed.

Sandy looked at Stephen. "We've got a steak sandwich on special tonight, served with chips or mash. Also our signature dish, Bangers and Smashed. Two sausages, garlic mash, veg of the day and a glass of beer."

Heart attack on a plate, both of them. He looked at Esme and back at Sandy. "As much as Bangers and Smashed sounds amazing, it's just the beer for me, thanks. I ate earlier." Esme had been off the hook for cooking tonight, as he'd set up meetings in London and he'd grabbed something before driving back.

Sandy looked at Esme and grinned, hooking a thumb in Stephen's direction. "He's all right," she said, and then scooted away again.

Esme put down her glass and looked up at him. "Did you really come here for background noise?"

He took another drink of beer before putting down his glass. Esme was staring at him expectantly, and all he could do was think about how pretty she was in her faded jeans and cute top. It was tomato-red with a scoop neck and a little tie at the throat that she'd left undone. The color should have clashed with her hair, but it didn't. Hoop earrings were in her ears, too—the kind that she apparently didn't wear to work at the estate.

"I did. I've been thinking about what you said the other day, about the possibility that I'm lonely. It's entirely possible. Though perhaps instead of lonely, solitary is a better word."

She smiled softly. "You aren't comfortable in your own company, but you don't want anything intimate, either.

Don't let anyone close, but don't spend so much time by yourself that you overthink everything."

He stared at her.

"What?" she asked. "Did you think you were the only one in the world to feel that way?"

He bristled a little on the inside, both because she'd verbalized exactly how he was feeling and because she'd accurately pointed out that this was not his unique circumstance, and he felt a bit embarrassed.

"Listen, I'm not trying to elicit any sympathy, but the life I lead…it's one of expectations."

"As the Earl of Chatsworth."

"Yes, as the earl. And in my position as COO. And the eldest child. And the one to follow in my father's footsteps. My father who—"

He stopped himself before he got carried away and said too much. He'd been trying to carry the load of, well, everything for months now, living up to an ideal he no longer believed in. It surprised him to realize he was actually quite angry about that. "Anyway, seeing you the last few days reminded me what it was like when I was younger. Before expectations and obligations and, well, consequences. At least big consequences. Esme, I don't actually remember the last time I had fun."

She took a drink of beer. "That's pathetic. What happened, you inherited the title and automatically got a stick up your butt?"

He burst out laughing and oh, it felt good. She'd surprised him but there was joy in the feeling that expanded his chest and sent the laugh out of his mouth. This was the Esme he remembered. The one who said exactly what she thought and called him out on his bull. Yes, it had been strained around the house, but tonight he loved that she was treating him as no one special. "Oh, Esme. I haven't laughed like that in a long time."

"You really are in need of an intervention. I think it's going to take more than a pint and some footy on the telly."

"You might be right. Maman sent me back here, ostensibly to oversee the garden plans, but I could have done that from Paris. She really sent me to take a vacation and get out of everyone's hair. I've become a bit of a grump."

"I believe you used the word *ogre*."

"You certainly express your opinion much more freely here than at the manor," he observed. It wasn't a criticism. He was rather enjoying her teasing. Most people just stared at him and avoided eye contact.

Her face flattened, though. "Oh, I'm sorry. Truly. I was teasing but not if it cuts a little too close."

"It doesn't. It's refreshing. Besides, Maman is right, though I won't admit it to her face. I needed to get away. I need to…figure a few things out." And he hated it. Navel-gazing and sorting through feelings was so not his thing.

Her face softened and she reached out and touched his hand. "What is it? Is it work? Or is it the estate? It must be so hard without your father. I know how you idolized him."

"I suppose it's all of that." He considered telling her about Anemone, but that *trust* word popped up again, and he avoided the subject. "It's like running two businesses, really. The estate interests and Aurora's, as well. And while I was a part of both for the past several years—"

"It's different when you're the one everyone looks to. When it's your signature on the bottom line."

He nodded. They both sat back as a different server brought Esme's food and set it before her, as well as another beer for Stephen. "Sandy says she thinks you'll like this brew." The young woman smiled as she put down the glass.

"Thanks, Sarah." Esme smiled up at the server. "And another for me, please." She gestured at the near-empty glass.

She looked up at Stephen. "I live just down the road. No need for me to drive."

She reached for the cruet and drizzled her fish with the tangy vinegar. "So," she said, reaching for a bottle of brown sauce and putting some on her plate. "What I'm hearing is the Pemberton version of *'Heavy lies the head that wears the crown'*."

She wasn't wrong. "It's that predictable, is it?"

Esme shook her head. "No, I suppose not. But I know firsthand that trying to live up to someone else's expectations is a sure way to set yourself up for failure."

He stared at her as she dipped a chip in the sauce and popped it into her mouth.

Esme couldn't believe she'd actually said that out loud. The last thing she needed was for Stephen to start asking questions. He certainly didn't need to hear about her crash-and-burn marriage to Evan, and how she'd turned herself inside out trying to be what he wanted. And yeah, maybe she'd known Stephen longer, but the simple fact remained: he, and Evan, too, lived in a different world from her. The piece of fish she'd stabbed with her fork fell off the tines and back onto the plate. "Sorry," she offered weakly. "I might have been projecting a bit there."

Stephen put down his beer. "You're right, though. I have never not been either the earl or the heir or the first-born or part of the business. The time we had as kids… that was as close to normal as my childhood ever got." He sat back in his chair and met her gaze. "My upbringing was ridiculously privileged. And I'm lucky, I know that. But I'm afraid it's also turned me into someone who isn't

much fun and lives in a constant state of stress so perva-
sive that I don't know what it would feel like to not have it."

"So…you going off to school. Is that why you never…?"
She hesitated. "Why you disappeared?"

"I came home for holidays. But suddenly I was no longer a child—I was the future heir training to take my place.
I don't know how else to explain it."

She knew she shouldn't say it, but she couldn't help
herself. "And a friendship with me didn't fit in that place."

His cheeks pinkened a little bit. "It's not…well, maybe
it is. I was thirteen. You were twelve. Us running wild
over the estate was suddenly not the done thing." He put
air quotes around the last, as if someone had said those
exact words to him. "And I think it had nothing to do with
you or where you come from and everything to do with me
leaving childish things behind and growing up."

While she understood the sentiment, she balked at the
words "childish things." Their friendship had been her
mainstay. Cedric Pemberton had been the closest thing
to a father she'd ever had, and Stephen her best friend.

"I understand," she said, picking at her battered cod.
"But I was horribly adrift after you left. Nothing was the
same."

She probably shouldn't have admitted that, and she
couldn't make herself look at him. She was too embarrassed. But then his hand was warm on hers, sending tingles to her fingertips and a fluttering sensation to her belly.

She should not be this aware of Stephen Pemberton.

"I'm sorry," he said softly, just loud enough that she
could hear it over the sound of the other patrons. "If it
helps, I missed our friendship, too."

There was that word again. *Friends.* She regained her
composure and slid her hand away from his, then picked
up her fork again, taking a bite of the fish. The golden bat-

ter was perfection, the fish fresh, the vinegar adding just
the right tang. When she'd finished her mouthful, she was
steady enough to look at him again.

He looked absolutely contrite, the hard lines of his face
softened as he looked at her. "I should have made more
of an effort."

She tried a smile. "We were kids. It's all right. I just
didn't have a lot of friends. I'd always had you. And the
house wasn't the same without you in it, either. Bella was
nice to me, but it wasn't the same."

She pushed away her plate, no longer hungry. Where the
heck was Phoebe, anyway? She should have been here an
hour ago. A quick check of her phone showed she'd missed
a text. "Looks like my friend got held up. She should be
here soon, though."

What she didn't say was how she'd really felt when he'd
been sent away. She'd felt invisible, like she wasn't important, and that she wasn't good enough to be his friend. And
she deeply regretted the argument they'd had just before
he'd gone off to school, where she'd thrown his title in his
face. It didn't matter that she'd been twelve. She'd been
hurt and she'd lashed out, and so who could blame him
for not coming back?

At least with Evan it had been different. She'd had the
same feelings—of not being good enough, and often invisible. Definitely criticized. But she'd been the one to do the
walking. And she had no regrets except that it had taken
her so long to get up the gumption to go.

"But you finished school here. And then?" he asked,
prompting her.

"Nothing so glamorous as Aurora or aristocracy. I didn't
know what I wanted to do in school, so I started working. And then…well, the pay is terrible, but I actually love
my job. I manage housekeeping at the inn. I've worked in

just about every position there, and hospitality suits me. I love welcoming people and making sure their experience is special."

"And is there a husband? A boyfriend?" He looked at her more closely. "Girlfriend? I don't want to presume."

"No boyfriend, no girlfriend, and a *was*-band." She rolled her eyes. "We divorced four years ago."

"And no kids."

"No."

"Well, I suppose that makes cutting ties slightly easier. I'm sorry, though."

She shook her head. "Don't be. I'm far happier now." She took a sip of her beer. "And I know you're single. Unless you have a girlfriend hiding away from the paparazzi."

Stephen made a noise that was somewhere between a scoff and a snort. "No girlfriend. Two failed attempts at the altar means I'm not in any sort of rush to try again."

There was an awkward silence, and then Esme bravely held up her glass. "A toast then, to Evan and Bridget and Gabi. Their loss."

He stared at her, a stunned expression in his eyes. "You know their names."

"One word, Stephen. Tabloids."

He muttered something incomprehensible, but she caught his meaning and grinned, then waited for him to tap his glass to hers. He did, they drank, and she settled back in her chair, feeling better somehow. Talking to him tonight had been good, and perhaps easier because they were on neutral territory.

"I should be on my way," Stephen said, interrupting her thoughts. "There are still some aspects of the estate that aren't settled. The solicitor is coming tomorrow. I do have to prepare a few things."

It was a paltry excuse and they both knew it. It was

unlikely he'd go back home now and stay up to do paperwork. Perhaps the conversation that made her feel better had been more uncomfortable for him.

"Let me know what time, and I'll make sure to have a coffee service for you."

"Thank you, Esme." He got up from his chair, but suddenly crouched down, one hand braced on the table and the other touching her knee with the barest of touches. "Esme, I am sorry about your divorce, and I'm sorry that our friendship was a casualty of my… I don't even know what to call it. It sounds horrible to complain when I have everything a person could ever want, but good friends are a rare find. We should never be careless with them."

She swallowed and nodded, touched, unsure of what to say, feeling the ridiculous urge to tip just a little bit forward and kiss him. Kiss him! What a foolish idea. Especially since that *friend* word just kept cropping up over and over again. He couldn't be more clear about where he stood.

"I'll see you at the house tomorrow," she said instead, and he gave her a brief nod.

"Yes, tomorrow."

"Thank you for the company," she offered, feeling both relief and sadness that he was leaving.

"Thank you," he replied, and bestowed a rare smile on her. "You're much nicer than background noise from the telly."

And then he was gone.

CHAPTER FOUR

ESME REFILLED THE coffeepot and prepared to take it to the library, where Stephen was meeting with his solicitor. She'd baked some sugar biscuits this morning and added them to the tray, making sure they were arranged prettily on the plate. Then she lifted it all, took a breath, and stepped out of the kitchen.

She'd already seen Stephen after his breakfast. She'd arrived promptly at eight, planning to fix him something to eat, only to find he'd already made himself scrambled eggs and toast. The jeans and button-down from the night before were nowhere to be seen. Instead, he was in one of his pristine suits, this time in a charcoal grey with a blue shirt and striped tie.

Every inch the earl, even if he had fried his own eggs.

The end result had Esme feeling off balance. Last night she'd thought more about Evan than she had in months. And it wasn't that she was bitter; it was more that she didn't like who she'd become during the years she'd spent with him. At first, she'd been taken in by his charms. His family had taken a house nearby for a year while his father commuted to London. He'd been home from university for an extended vacation and he and some of his mates had booked into the inn for a week, using it as a base while they got up to…well, all sorts of things. She'd been clean-

ing rooms at the time, and there were always bottles to pick
up the morning after, but Evan had been a great tipper and
had a way of smiling at her whenever they crossed paths.
His friends had departed, but Evan still found reasons to
pop round the hotel. And Esme had been swept off her
feet, like Cinderella at a ball.

He'd finished university, proposed, and after the wedding they'd moved to the city for four long years. Four
years in which Esme didn't work. Evan didn't want his
wife doing menial labor. She was better than that, he said.

And so her years of being isolated had begun.

She shook her head, trying to rid herself of the memories and the heavy feeling they evoked, and approached
the library door. She heard Stephen's voice, and another
man's answering it. Granted, Stephen didn't seem to look
down his nose at what she did for a living, but the fact
that they were from two very different worlds was pain-
fully obvious.

She entered the library on soft feet and left the tray on
a side table.

"Thank you, Esme." Stephen halted his conversation to
acknowledge her, and her cheeks heated.

"Let me know if you need anything else, sir." She added
the *sir* simply because he was with someone. It felt odd,
though. This was his fourth day here and already they were
being consistently familiar with each other.

He found her later, still in the kitchen. She was rolling out
pastry for this evening's beef Wellington when he entered.
His hair looked as if he'd run his fingers through it several
times, and his movements seemed slightly agitated—stiff
and uncomfortable.

"Is something wrong?" she asked.

He rolled his shoulders. "Too much coffee, maybe? I

don't know." He sighed. "I hate dealing with the will and estate, and it winds me up a bit, I suppose."

She stopped rolling and looked up. "You're still dealing with that? But your father…" She let the sentence trail off. Cedric had been gone for over two years. She'd naturally assumed the terms of the will had been settled long ago.

"With Anemone's appearance, we decided as a family to have another look at Dad's will, find a way for Anemone to get a share. The decision was a family one. The execution of it is up to me and the legal firm to sort through."

Anemone. Ah, yes. The illegitimate daughter. Esme still had a difficult time wrapping her head around the fact that the man she remembered so fondly had had an affair. If she found it difficult to believe, Stephen—and the rest of the family—must have been floored by the revelation.

"It must have been tough for you to learn that about Cedric," she said softly, taking the pâté-topped tenderloin and encasing it in the pastry.

Stephen took a bottle of sparkling water out of the fridge and twisted off the cap. "More than tough. It wasn't just the affair, either." He hesitated, then met her gaze. "It feels strange talking about this outside the family."

"You know nothing goes further than these four walls," Esme assured him. "But if you don't want to talk about it, I understand."

"Actually, no. Maybe it's good that I do."

She stayed silent, waiting.

He pulled up a stool and perched on it, took a drink of the water. "I was the first to find out, you know. Me and the accountant. Dad had been sending her mother money twice a year. I scheduled an audit of the books when I took over the estate and there it was. Then I had to tell the rest of the family."

Esme could only imagine how awful that must have been. "Ouch."

He sighed again. "You know, I guess I felt that it was my responsibility to look out for everyone's interests. To be the steady, objective one. But I had my own feelings to deal with. The man I loved…idolized…and whose footsteps I had to fill, had cheated on my mother and had another child."

"It hurts when our heroes let us down," she whispered.

His gaze held hers. "It does. And I thought I was coming to terms with it all when we found out that Maman knew about Anemone all along. It was like the ground was ripped from beneath my feet."

She slid the Wellington into the refrigerator and washed her hands, then fetched him a glass with some ice for his water, all while absorbing the new information that Lady Pemberton had known of this girl's existence. "But I bet the whole time you told yourself you had to be the steady one. The one who had to look out for the Pemberton best interests."

He nodded. "Apparently I'm a quick study."

"I've known you a long time. As much as we got into scrapes and had fun, you were always looking out for your brother and sisters. Especially Christophe, when he arrived." Christophe was technically Stephen's cousin, though he'd been raised like a brother. More than once, Stephen had stood up for the younger boy at school. He'd stood up for her, too.

He didn't answer, just poured his drink over into the glass.

"So you've been bottling up your feelings about it all this time?"

"Bull's-eye again. And I wasn't very nice to Anemone, who was more of a victim of all this secrecy than anyone."

Esme started picking up her dirty dishes. "Yes, but you couldn't know that."

He was quiet for so long that she stopped and looked up. He was staring at her quite intently, his dark eyes curious. "What?"

"It's just nice that you understand that."

"Listen, I'm a pro at bottling up my feelings and redirecting them elsewhere. The big question is, where has this left you, and why do you walk around with a pained expression on your face all the time that only disappears when you forget it's supposed to be there? Is it guilt? Or stress? Or all of it together?"

He let out a breath with a whoosh. "You know, your mum was always great to talk to when I snuck to the kitchen, but I never felt like I was in a therapy session."

Esme chuckled. "Maybe you should try therapy. It can be quite helpful."

"Personal experience?"

"I walked away from my marriage. It was the first strong thing I'd done in the six years since I met Evan. I had a lot of stuff to unlearn." She could say it matter-of-factly now. But it had been so hard at first. "And," she added, "I wanted to protect Mum from any nastiness, so she really doesn't know about the therapy."

"Maybe you should talk to her about it."

Esme laughed. "She still thinks I was crazy to leave him. And I don't want to argue with her while she's fighting cancer. It's all right."

But she could still relate to how he felt, handling things alone.

He tapped his fingers on the countertop and frowned. "Do I really walk around with a pained expression?"

Esme poured herself her own glass of water and took

a sip as she considered him. "Yes. Sometimes your face could frighten small children."

That, at least, made a tiny smile curve the corners of his lips.

"You're unhappy," she said plainly. "And feel as if you don't have a right to be. How close am I?"

"Pretty close."

"And you're soured on love and relationships, because you've crashed and burned, and you probably don't want to a) go through that again, and b) have another Pemberton scandal in the papers."

"Do you charge an hourly rate, doc?"

She laughed again. "Oh, Stephen, it makes so much sense. But heck, understanding the why is the easy part. The healing and moving past it? That's where all the work is. And I can't help you with that. You have to do it yourself. You could maybe start by smiling once in a while and doing something fun."

The way his eyebrow lifted in a skeptical quirk that clearly communicated, "Fun?" made her want to laugh.

"I'm not sure I know where I'd start. Especially here."

"Well, first of all, solitary rides through the countryside and an evening game of billiards in the games room is not fun. You came close last night, though, by popping into the pub. I don't know, go to the gym? Pop into a few shops? There's always a game of something on at the park, either footy or cricket. You might actually meet some people."

He looked so horrified at the idea she cracked up. "Come on, Stephen, I dare you to do something normal."

His jaw tightened and she knew he would agree to something because he couldn't resist a challenge. It was lovely to discover he really hadn't changed all that much. As kids, all she'd had to do was issue a dare, and he'd instantly reacted. If she'd said "Oh, don't go up there, the apples are fine on this branch anyway," he'd taken the bait and climbed to the highest branch. Or if they'd been out on their bicycles, and she'd poked at him with "oh, that hill's too big to bike up anyway," they'd be off to find out what wonders were on the other side. Looking back, it was a wonder they hadn't broken their necks. But it brought back good memories, too. At one time, the memories had been painful, especially when Stephen had gone off to school and she had become a teenager—redheaded, freckled, and awkward. She'd missed those early days horribly, but eventually she'd started to look back on her childhood as a little bit magical. Not every little girl could say they had the run of an English country home when they were small.

Now Stephen was back, too, and knowing that the precocious little boy was still somewhere inside the tall, serious man warmed her heart, made her feel like she hadn't warped the memories over the years.

"So what do you suggest for fun? Shopping and a pickup game of footy isn't really my thing."

She shrugged. "For starters, you could un-starch yourself and dress more casually. Maybe Friday night darts at the pub? There's always a tournament on. And the gooseberry festival is coming up as part of the fair next weekend. There'll be rides and games."

He grimaced. "I have to go anyway. I'm judging some entries or something. My father used to years ago. Apparently this falls under 'duties of the current earl'."

"Oh, darling. That is going to be precious. You, handing out ribbons for gooseberry tarts and jams." She couldn't stop the wide smile that came over her face.

She didn't tell him that her mother entered every year, and this year would be no different, despite Mary's health and cancer treatments. Esme wasn't about to deny her mum the simple pleasure, even if it meant Esme had to help out on top of work.

"Thanks. You're having a little too much fun with this idea."

She got serious again, then, and went to him. She stood on the other side of the counter, facing him, and took one of his hands in hers. It was possibly too familiar a touch, but he'd shared things this morning that had been personal. And he did want to be friends...even if the casual touch of his hand beneath her fingers sent all her senses into overdrive. He didn't need to know that.

"Stephen, my memories of you when we were kids are filled with smiles and laughter and challenges. Where did that boy go?"

"Es..."

The soft way he said the shortened version of her name reached right into her heart and held on.

"You deserve good things too, you know," she continued. "We all do. Loosen up for the next week and leave some of your troubles behind. The world won't end, I promise."

He nodded and cleared his throat, as if he didn't trust himself to speak.

"Now." She brightened her voice, let go of his hand, and broke the moment before it could become uncomfortable. "I have a mess to clean up. And you've spent enough time lollygagging in my kitchen."

"You sound just like your mum when you say that. All right, point taken. I'll get out of your kitchen. Oh, and Esme?"

She'd started running water in the sink for the stack of bowls beside her. "Yes?"

"If I have to ditch the suits, you can ditch the uniform.

It's only the two of us here. No more black. Dress in what makes you comfortable."

Her cheeks pinkened. "Oh. Well." She gave a little laugh. "I've been in hotel uniform or black tops and bottoms since I was eighteen, I think."

"Then this will be a change for you, too."

Esme wasn't sure she needed change. After all, she was quite happy with her life as it was. But if she wanted Stephen to step out of his comfort zone, it wasn't unreasonable that he'd request the same. "I'll be sure to dress differently tomorrow, then," she replied.

Stephen left the kitchen and went to the library. He sat at the desk, thinking about his conversation with Esme, then picked up the phone. This was his fourth day here and he hadn't yet touched base with his mother. He knew she was especially invested in the memorial and since they were breaking ground tomorrow, he knew he should call.

The phone rang in his ear and on the third ring she answered. "*Bonjour*, my darling."

"*Bonjour*, Maman," Stephen answered, resting an elbow on his desk. "How are you?"

"Hot." It was August and Aurora had decided to spend the bulk of the summer at the château, traveling to Paris occasionally to see family and pop into Aurora, Inc. headquarters. "It is cool inside, but I cannot seem to get enough of the garden. The lavender is blooming, and the air is gorgeous."

He could picture it and almost wished he were there. There was nothing in the world like Provence.

"Are you expecting company for the weekend?" Often his brothers or sisters would pop down with their significant others or, in Christophe and Charlotte's cases, with grandchildren. He knew Aurora loved that and was adoring being semi-retired.

"Yes. Anemone and Phillipe are visiting. They are planning an October wedding here at the château. Isn't that lovely?"

"It is," he said, his throat tight. He was still getting used to the fact that he had a half-sister. It was…an adjustment.

"I hope they're very happy," he said sincerely. "I know I wasn't necessarily fair to her in the beginning."

"Oh, darling, it is understandable. I wasn't as open as I should have been with you all, either. It brought back some painful memories for me. But she is here, and she is lovely. At some point I think we must let go of the past."

Something he'd never found easy, and he acknowledged his own resentment that everyone seemed to be able to move beyond it faster than he could. After talking with Esme this morning, he understood it had little to do with Anemone and far more to do with his parents' secrets that he'd inherited along with the title.

"Maman, you were right about me taking a break. I'm still checking on things a little, and keeping an eye on the memorial project, but I've decided to actually use the time here to relax." It was a big thing to admit.

Aurora's rusty laugh, so much like his own, came across the line. "Do you know how, my love?"

He grinned in response, because her laugh could always make him smile. "No. But I've enlisted some help. Esme is caring for the house while Mrs. Flanagan is recuperating. I wish you'd mentioned that, by the way. She didn't even know I was coming."

"She didn't? Oh, *mon Dieu*. I'm sorry. You two used to get into some scrapes as children. I think Mrs. Flanagan ended up using as many plasters on your knees as Esme's." Again came the rusty laugh.

"A lot has changed, Maman. But I'm overdue for some downtime. I don't think I knew how much. I went for a ride and then to a pub for a pint. It felt nice to not be on a tight schedule." Even admitting this felt strange, but necessary. Now that he'd stopped to pause and catch his breath, he realized how he'd buried himself in work to keep from dealing with his personal life.

"Is this my Stephen talking? I don't believe it." After the bit of teasing, Aurora added, "You should enjoy it. You know, I stayed on as CEO for a long time, thinking no one could run Aurora like I could. But when I had my health scare at William's wedding, I realized that I had to step back at some point. And guess what? The company is doing even better. It won't fall apart if you look after yourself from time to time, *mon petit*. I would rather you recognize when you need a break now, rather than when you are my age. It shouldn't take a cardiac episode to make us pay attention."

"Yes, Maman." He smiled fondly to himself. "And Esme said the same thing. That the world wouldn't end if I relaxed once in a while."

"She's right." There was a pause, then she added, "Are you spending a lot of time together?"

There was a tone of innocent speculation in her voice that sent alarm bells ringing in Stephen's head. There was absolutely no way that his mother could be matchmaking. Digging into his personal life, though? Certainly. "Not really," he answered. "We've talked a few times."

And sat at the pub. And held hands…no, not really holding hands. Not that way. And just because they shared a few long gazes and he was aware of her every time she entered a room…

Oh, no. No. Last night he'd said friends and he'd meant

it. Being attracted to Esme would be a disaster in the making.

Moreover, he wouldn't hurt her for the world. And he was certain he couldn't offer her a happy ending.

He deftly changed the subject. "Maman, I also called to let you know that I have seen the plans for the garden, and I think you're going to love it. We should be able to dedicate it next spring, on Father's birthday."

"That sounds lovely. Thank you for handling this, Stephen."

"I'm the earl. I'm his son. It's not just my responsibility, it's my honor, Maman." He meant it, too—despite his conflicted feelings about his father.

Was that a sniff he heard on the other end? But Maman never let emotion get the best of her, least of all tears. Stephen felt a corresponding stinging at the back of his eyes as well.

What on earth was wrong with him? It had to be exhaustion. Perhaps the conversation this morning on top of the meeting with the solicitor had left him a tad vulnerable.

"I should go now," he said, clearing his throat for the third time that morning. "But enjoy the garden and put on your sunscreen."

She laughed then. "I will. And please send my best wishes to Mrs. Flanagan."

"I will, of course."

They said their goodbyes and Stephen hung up, then sat back in his chair. He'd nearly misted up just now, which wasn't like him at all.

Perhaps he was more stressed than he realized. It was starting to dawn on him that this break was probably long overdue. A man couldn't go on as he had been forever. But darts at the pub? There had to be a better way to unwind.

An idea popped into his head that had no place being there, involving a redhead with mossy eyes and a sweet smile.

Esme was not for him. And he needed to put her out of his mind before someone got hurt.

CHAPTER FIVE

ESME SHUT DOWN the computer in her mother's office and went off to the kitchen to find some lunch. Stephen would be looking to eat shortly.

"Hi," came his voice from behind her.

She spun around and pressed her hand to her chest. "I didn't hear you come in. I was making a list in my head."

"I thought I might get some lunch. I'm hopeful I can put together a sandwich for myself."

"Of course! I'm sure the makings are all here, including the last of the leftover roast chicken. Take a look in the fridge for what you'd like. I'll get the bread."

She retrieved a cutting board and a bread knife and then put a lovely loaf of Marjorie's harvest bread on the surface. While Stephen retrieved condiments, meat, and cheese from the fridge, she set out two plates and put the bread on each. "Butter?" she asked.

"No, thank you." He met her gaze. "I'm supposed to be making my own, remember?"

"Oh, right." She shouldn't be so flustered, but it felt different, being here alone with him now. Making a sandwich was not an intimate act and yet it felt as though it was.

She watched Stephen out of the corner of her eye, smiling a little to herself as he precisely layered on his chicken and then cut the tomato into ridiculously even slices. Not a huge surprise that he was a bit of a perfectionist, and she debated cutting a crooked slice just to see what he'd do. But he looked so pleased with himself when he finished his mammoth sandwich that she couldn't do anything but grin. She dipped a fork into the pickle jar and stabbed a thick spear, then plopped it onto his plate.

"So," she said, once they'd got themselves glasses of water and had settled at the kitchen table to eat, "what's on your agenda for the rest of the day?"

He shrugged. "Just…details. Things that would likely bore you."

"Or that I wouldn't understand?" she asked.

"Maybe, but I didn't mean it that way." His brow wrinkled.

"It's no secret I'm not a businesswoman. Though I sometimes think I'd like to be. I've kind of always dreamed of having my own little inn or B&B."

"You didn't want to go back to school?"

"I considered it. I thought I'd do business or maybe hospitality management, since I like the industry so much. But…" She halted, then lifted her chin. "Let's just say my husband wasn't overly supportive. Of either school or me working."

Stephen's mouth dropped open as he stared at her. "What do you mean?"

"Evan's lifestyle is…well, you could probably relate more than I. He liked me to be…available, I guess is the best word. In case he needed to entertain, or if there was a company function. I was there to support his career, not the other way around."

Stephen snorted. "That's such an antiquated notion."

"Thank you! That's what I said. He didn't like it much." There were lots of things he'd criticized, too, but she wasn't about to give Stephen a laundry list of all the ways Evan had found her wanting. "But I guess your family is different. You might have grown up with that old school aristocracy and wealth thing, but you also had a strong, independent mother who ran her own business…and a massively successful one." It still blew her away when she saw the family in the tabloids or on the entertainment shows, mixing with movie stars and other celebrities.

"We did. And my father was always supportive of Maman's ambitions. I guess, at least in that way, I had strong role models."

She nodded. "And to be honest, my mum was a good role model for me. After my dad died when I was a baby, she picked herself up, found this job and made a career out of it, raising me alone."

"She's a strong woman," Stephen said.

"She is. And yet…"

She hesitated again, until Stephen leaned forward and peered into her face. "And yet what?"

"She never understood why I was unhappy with Evan. I think because she'd had to work and raise me alone, she thought I'd landed in clover when I married him. I didn't have to work, I had a gorgeous house and lovely things… I suppose, all the things she wanted for me. But" —her throat tightened— "I didn't have room to be myself, and I wasn't happy."

"Wealth and privilege can be its own cage."

"I guess you probably thought I've always been the girl in the poky flat having a pint at the pub, but I had a taste of a different life once. I didn't like it."

The air between them became awkward after those last words. She'd be a liar to say that there hadn't been a little bit of tension, even attraction on a low simmer between them the past few days. But this was the truth, though, wasn't it? Not a thing could come of it, because it wasn't just that she was of a different class. It was that she'd tried living up in that stratosphere and it wasn't for her.

Stephen's mood darkened during the rest of the day. The conversation over lunch had unsettled him, not so much from what Esme said, but what she didn't say as well. What kind of man would take a woman like Esme—gorgeous, smart, energetic—and make her into a trophy wife?

And yet…he recalled Bridget's ambitions and realized that some people aspired to that life. She'd wanted to marry an earl. She'd wanted to have the life that being the wife of the COO of Aurora could provide. A flat in Paris, country home outside London, a château in Provence. Chartered planes and champagne and designer everything. But she hadn't wanted him. It occurred to him that Bridget and this Evan guy would likely have made the perfect pair.

He'd told his mother that he needed the downtime, and it wasn't a lie, but he also needed to be…vital. What was he supposed to do, wander through the house? Watch television? Go for a stroll in the village? Two hours of that and he'd be stark raving mad. He needed to be doing something, and so he pulled up reports and started looking at proposals to expand Aurora assets into the North American market outside of New York. Several scenarios were unsustainable, especially with the current global financial market. Expansion was great but only if it worked with their overall strategy. And since one of the proposals was Bella's, it meant a difficult conversation ahead since she was the CEO.

Normally this was all in a day's work for him. But something was niggling at him. Something that he couldn't put his finger on.

He opened a drawer in the desk and pulled out a velvet box, putting it on the desk in front of him. Maybe it wasn't his job at Aurora that was causing him to be unsettled. He dealt with acquisitions, proposals, projections every day. But this… He opened the box with a slight creak of the hinge and stared at the pocket watch inside.

It had been his great-grandfather's, passed down to each earl on his twenty-fifth birthday. Twenty-five, because the story went that he'd commented to his eldest son that at twenty-one a man hadn't yet acquired a brain. Stephen remembered laughing over this with his father. By twenty-five, Stephen had his MBA and was working his way up within the company, but, as Cedric had rightfully joked, he was still clueless about women…and the kind of woman who could be a countess.

He reached out and touched the gold case, the metal cool beneath his fingertips. Being titled in this day and age was very different from his great-grandfather's time. The challenge now was stewardship of history, maintaining that history without going bankrupt.

And if Stephen had his way, the estate would be self-sustaining, without needing any sort of infusion from Aurora's coffers.

He took the watch out of the velvet. "Why?" he whispered. "Why did you cheat on Maman? How could she take you back? How could you not acknowledge, not know, your own flesh and blood?" His jaw tightened. "How could you teach me to be a good man when you were so flawed?"

And that was just it, he realized. The memorial garden was a fine idea, he supposed. But his father was gone. Stephen was tired of being in his shadow when his actions betrayed the man he'd pretended to be. And Maman… he loved her, of course he did, but on some level, he was angry at her, too.

It was time for him to stop following in his father's footsteps, and instead start making his own path.

He lifted his head when a knock sounded at the door-jamb. "I hope I'm not disturbing you."

Esme stood in the doorway, a hesitant smile on her face. He realized he was scowling and softened his expression. "Not at all. What can I do for you?"

"Your dinner is ready," she said. "I figured you'd lost track of time."

He had. She stepped into the room as he moved to put the pocket watch back in the box. "What's that?"

He held out his hand. "It belonged to my great-grand-father. It's been passed down to every earl since."

She took it, turned the weight of it over in her hands. "It's lovely. Such a piece of history."

"I suppose it is."

"You're not fond of it?"

He sighed, taking it back from her and slipping it into the case, then tucking it in his drawer. "I am, I suppose. I've just been thinking about what it means to be the Earl of Chatsworth today. I don't know if I like the answer."

"Then change the answer," she suggested. "You are the earl. You can make of that whatever you want."

Could he, though?

"I just realized a few minutes ago that I don't want to look backward. I don't want to be the earl my father was. But I don't quite know what that means."

And Stephen was used to being on solid ground. Not knowing put him off balance, made him unsure…something he often felt but never let anyone see.

Except Esme seemed to notice everything.

She was looking at him now with a broad smile. "Con-gratulations," she said, her eyes lighting up. "You're about to begin what will be *your* legacy to the title. It's incredibly freeing when you finally take charge of your life and de-cide to make your own way…with your own boundaries."

"Like you did with your divorce?"

"Exactly," she answered. "Stephen, you can take the earldom and put your own stamp on it. You're a smart, hardworking man. You care. Those three things together mean you're going to get this right."

It was true his father had done a fine job with the actual estate. It was his personal life that he'd messed up—and covered up. Stephen's track record was nothing to celebrate, either. But he could do better now. He had no desire to marry, but if he ever did, it would be the right woman, for the right reasons. And no secrets.

Not that it was going to be an issue anyway.

"Now," she said, in her ever-cheerful voice, "I've made a chicken curry that you're going to love. Come eat and tell me your plans."

He followed her out, leaving the pocket watch—and his introspective mood—behind.

The activity of eating dinner did little to ease the ache in Esme's chest every time she got near Stephen.

She couldn't resist sneaking glimpses at his taut backside and broad shoulders. Esme was truly doomed. She was physically attracted to present-day Stephen and emotionally connected to childhood Stephen and unsure what to do with all of it. And the longer she was here, the more involved she became. She could see beneath the cool exterior and realized he was really struggling with his father's infidelity and what it all meant for him as the man stepping into the title. She thought she could understand. As a child he'd idolized his dad. Everyone had liked Cedric Pemberton and in Stephen's eyes, Cedric could do no wrong. She could only imagine what it had felt like, learning about Anemone. *Let down* didn't quite cover it.

What she really wanted to do was go to him and give

him a hug. Wrap her arms around him and squeeze, as if to tell him it would be all right. The Stephen of their childhood would have welcomed it. The man before her now, with his deep frown and stiff posture, would shun such an overture of affection. Besides, just because they were talking about stuff didn't mean they were suddenly best friends again.

He was an earl. She managed a staff of six housekeepers at the local inn. He got his clothes tailor-made in Paris and London, and she popped into the chain stores on the high street to scan the sale racks. He ate at Michelin-starred restaurants, and she headed to the local where everyone knew her standing order. Moreover, these were the lives they had—for the most part—chosen.

She had no business thinking of him romantically. Especially since the last thing she would ever do is put herself in a position to be looked down upon again. To be criticized and found lacking. To be "too" anything. As she surely would be. She did not belong in his world.

And he certainly didn't belong in hers. They were eating in the kitchen again, but he looked out of place in his fine trousers, crisp shirt, and silk tie. He'd removed his suit jacket from his meeting, but that made little difference. It was in the way he carried himself, too. With breeding and confidence.

"It feels odd without the kitchen staff here," she admitted, putting down her bowl and going to fill water glasses. When she put his down in front of him, he looked up.

"Thanks."

"Of course."

She waited for him to take the first bite. This curry recipe was a particular favorite, and one she made nearly every week. When a smile broke over his face, she thought again how ridiculously handsome he was when he wasn't looking so severe.

"It's good. Really good."

"This is one of my go-tos for when I get home and I'm tired and want something I can put together easily. I try to keep things simple and nutritious."

She didn't mention that she had to work really hard not to overanalyze all her eating choices. Obsessing about what went in her mouth, feeling guilty, stepping on the scale every day…those were things she tried to keep in the past, but it was hard. Not that she'd breathe a word of it to Stephen. She'd already said too much about her marriage. Besides, his company was in fashion, for heaven's sake. Pressure to be thin and perfect had to be part of the environment, like the air that they breathed.

"What's wrong?" he asked, putting down his fork. "You've barely touched it."

"Oh! Nothing's wrong." She pasted on a smile and scooped up some basmati and chicken. "I just got lost in my thoughts for a moment."

"Anything you'd like to share?"

She looked at him and lifted an eyebrow. "Not exactly. Not unless you want to hear about my flaws, neuroses, and hang-ups."

He laughed. "I wasn't aware you had any flaws."

"We all have flaws." She rolled her eyes and took a bite of the meal.

"Sorry, I don't see any from where I'm sitting."

She looked up and met his gaze. He was watching her steadily.

"Esme, you're gorgeous. You've got the most glorious hair, and a cheeky smile and your eyes…they're full of devilment, just like they used to be. You're funny and smart." He affected his scowl again. "Evan was a damned fool."

"None of us are perfect," she whispered, touched by his words, but not quite believing him.

"Of course not. But the girl I knew was fun and clever and had a good heart. I wish I had grown to be half as good as you."

She lifted her head sharply. "Don't say that. You're a good man."

"Am I, though?" He put down his fork. "Most people go through hard times, and they learn from it, and it makes them more understanding and compassionate. Not me. I became a bit of a git."

She snorted; she couldn't help it. "I'm guessing that's the exact term your sisters used."

He nodded. "They're right, though. Since my dad died, I've been so overwhelmed that I might have taken this 'head of the family' thing a little too much to heart. I ordered Will about when it came to dealing with Gabi... and for heaven's sake, I was going to marry her for all the wrong reasons. When it came to Charlotte, I arrived here and had a sit-down with Jacob. Charlotte was joking about pistols at dawn, but my behavior warranted it. And Anemone..." He sighed. "The circumstances weren't her fault, but I treated her horribly."

"Stephen, you ended up with a crazy amount of responsibility in a short amount of time. I'm sure you're being too hard on yourself."

"I'm not." He took a bite, chewed, swallowed, and then looked up at her again. "I was unhappy, and I took it out on those closest to me and justified it by telling myself I was looking out for them."

She didn't know what to say. She wasn't going to argue, because it was clear that he'd done a lot of thinking today.

Instead, she reached out and touched his hand with her fingers. "I'm sorry you were unhappy."

He swallowed and pulled his hand away. "It doesn't matter now. It's moving forward that matters, right?" Then he shook his head. "I think I've talked more in the last eight hours than I have in the last eight months. Sorry about that."

"Don't be." She smiled. "I'm glad you feel comfortable enough with me to share what's going on. I'm glad I can be someone for you to talk to when you need. It makes me feel…"

She broke off. She'd been going to say needed. Important. *Seen.*

And not just seen, but seen by him.

"Makes you feel what?" His voice was husky, soft, sending ripples of awareness along her nerve endings.

"Useful," she croaked, gathering up her bowl. She moved to the sink to get ready to wash the dishes.

He scooped up his last bite and then joined her at the sink, putting his hand over hers as she turned on the faucet. "Let me help with the dishes," he said quietly. "Your workday ended a while ago."

"I don't mind, really."

"If I were on my own, I'd have to do the washing up. This won't take any time at all. I'm sure I can handle washing and drying some dishes." He looked around, then back at her with a small smile. "If you can show me where the towels are."

The simple request broke the tension and they both relaxed a little, working companionably in the quiet kitchen until the last pot was washed. He held out his towel for her to dry her hands, and when she reached for it, their fingers touched, sending a jolt right to her feet at the innocent contact. Their gazes touched, held, and Esme couldn't breathe.

Oh, no.

The moment lengthened, and her pulse ratcheted up as his gaze dropped briefly to her lips and back up again. Not just her, then. He was feeling it, too. This pull that happened at the oddest times, taking them from old friends to something new and exciting…something that could never be,

Despite all her self-assurances about not wanting to be a part of his kind of life, she did want *him*. And right now he was leaning closer, closer…

The sound of the *Bridgerton* theme blared through the kitchen: Esme's mobile. As her cheeks flushed, she stepped away and hurried to the counter, where she'd left it charging. She answered while Stephen calmly folded the dish towel, and she wondered how he could be so damned calm when she was struggling to breathe normally and answer the phone as if nothing had happened.

"Hello, Mum."

Stephen's gaze slid to hers again, concern in the dark depths, and she liked him all the more for it. Esme gave a nearly imperceptible shake of her head—nothing was wrong—and so he went about looking in cabinets and cupboards to put things away. When she hung up a few moments later, he stopped what he was doing and faced her. "Everything all right?"

She nodded. "Mum just asked if I could pick up her new anti-nausea medication on the way home. The chemo plays havoc with her tummy." She pushed down the worry—these were expected side effects, after all—and tried a smile. "Would it be all right if I took some of the leftover curry? If she's not feeling well, she probably didn't make any dinner."

"Of course you can, don't be silly." He turned in a circle, then faced her again and held out his hands. "I would get you a dish to put it in, but I have no idea where anything is."

She laughed a little, trying to get them back to a "normal" vibe…whatever that was. "They're in here." She went to a cabinet where a selection of covered dishes was organized precisely by size.

She went to the counter where the larger dish was cooling and scooped some out. "Is there anything you need before I go?" she asked, and chanced a look up at him. If he mentioned the almost-kiss, she was sure she'd die of both embarrassment and want. But he shook his head, obviously recovering better than she was able to as he acted as if nothing had happened.

"Go look after your mum and tell her I said hello and to follow doctor's orders," he said softly.

It was easier to dismiss him when his voice was hard and impatient, like it had been when he first arrived. But these moments, when the caring man beneath the hard exterior shone through? In these moments, he was hard to resist. If he took two steps toward her and gave her any encouragement at all, she rather suspected she'd find herself in his arms.

How was it possible to want something so much and be so afraid of it at the same time?

"I will." She took a step back and inhaled deeply. His words about following doctor's orders prompted the fear that she tried to prevent taking over, but sometimes the thoughts snuck in. Her mum was her only family. What if she lost her, too?

"What is it?" Stephen asked.

"It's nothing. I just worry about her. About…losing her."

Understanding warmed his eyes and his mouth. "Of course you do. I wish I could offer you guarantees."

"No one can," she replied, her voice shaking a little.

"But your mum is a strong woman, and she's getting good care, yes?" His gaze sharpened. "Esme, if anything's been lacking, please tell me. If there's anything I can do to help…"

"No! I mean, she's had very good care, the best. And the family has already been so generous and understanding. I'm sorry I said anything. I try not to bring my personal problems to work."

"But we're friends, too, aren't we?" He stepped closer, his gaze never leaving hers.

"I suppose," she answered, biting down on her lip. Complicated friends.

His gaze followed the action and her breath caught. It was torture when he looked at her lips that way, as if he wanted to kiss them, taste them…

She stepped back, knowing she couldn't allow herself to get sucked into whatever silly attraction she was feeling. Hadn't he just said *friends*? Being foolish would only break the tentative relationship they'd forged over the past few days.

"I—I should get going. I'll see you in the morning." Because she still had to be here to do her job, even though the rest of the staff was gone, and she was in this house with him, *alone*.

He stayed where he was, thankfully, and she turned to head toward the kitchen door.

"Es?"

He used the shortened version of her name again, and oh, the memories that single syllable brought back. It stopped her in her tracks and made her turn, though she was now several feet away from him.

"You will let me know if there's anything I can do for Mrs. F, won't you?" he asked.

She nodded, too touched at his caring tone to risk answering. And then she turned around and got out of there as fast as she could without running.

Stephen Pemberton might think himself a git and think he'd let down his family, but all she could see was the concern in his eyes and the flash of vulnerability anytime he spoke of his family and his recent actions. He was a good man who had suffered his own pain, a man who appeared strong and formidable but had a heart that could easily be wounded. It had always been so, but perhaps no one got to see that side of him. Perhaps he took great care to keep it hidden.

But she knew. And because she knew, she also knew she was in grave danger of getting in over her head.

CHAPTER SIX

MARY FLANAGAN WAS too determined to let anything get her down for long, which was why Esme was so shocked to find her mum sitting in a chair with her feet up and a blanket over her lap. Esme covered her alarm and pasted on a smile. "Hello, Mum."

"Hello, darling."

"Feeling all right, then?" Esme went to the kitchen and automatically filled a glass with some water and took it to her mother's side.

"Tired today. And a little cold, though I don't know why."

Esme peered into her face. "Chills?"

Mary flapped a hand. "Don't fuss. I'm fine."

"I'm going to take your temperature just in case." The chemo meant that Mary was particularly susceptible to infections. If she were running a fever, she should see a doctor.

She grabbed the digital thermometer and took a reading from her mum's ear. Her temperature was slightly elevated, which gave Esme some concern. "We'll call the doctor in the morning," she advised. "And I'm staying here tonight to keep an eye on you."

"Oh, for heaven's sake—"

"I don't want to hear it. Have you eaten any dinner?"

Mary's mouth took on a stubborn set.

"I figured as much. I brought you some curry." She put the thermometer away and headed toward the small kitchen. "Stubborn old cow," she muttered.

There was a bark of laughter from behind her and a sharp, "I heard that, brat."

Esme smiled. Their banter was a form of affection between them, and when her mum talked back Esme knew nothing was super serious. Still, she didn't want to take any chances. "Drink your water and I'll heat this up in a jiffy," she called.

She put the dish in the microwave and started tea. Before long it was all heated up, the tea was steeping, and she carried the simple meal to her mum on a tray.

"Oh, Esme. You didn't have to go to that bother."

Esme put down the tray. "Leftover curry is hardly a bother. Tomorrow I'll make sure you have something, too. You just tell me what seems appetizing, and I'll see to it."

"Thank you. And for picking up my medication." There was always a period of nausea and vomiting after a round of chemo, and ensuring Mary got nutrition during those days was a challenge.

"I'll be back with the tea."

She poured them each a cup and took it to the living room, placing her mum's on her tray but holding hers in her hand as she sat on the edge of the sofa. She sipped her tea and let her mother eat, all the while thinking about Stephen's parting words. His offer to help was sweet. More so because she knew he'd been absolutely sincere.

"You're quiet, Es."

She looked up. "Oh, just stuck in my thoughts, I guess."

"How are things going with Stephen?"

She hadn't told her mum that she was the only household staff working right now, and that she and Stephen were alone in the house. For some reason, she wanted to keep that knowledge to herself, even though it was hardly a secret. But her mum would ask questions—questions Esme didn't want to answer.

"Fine," she answered, making her voice bright. "He's overseeing the plans for the memorial garden. I believe they're breaking ground tomorrow."

Mary nodded. "It's a lovely idea. Cedric was a good man."

Esme had always thought so, too, but the news of Anemone's parentage had changed her view of the man who'd been a part of their lives for so long. "It's been hard on Stephen since his father's death," she said. "And finding out about his half-sister. Those kids worshiped their father. News like that is a blow."

"Surprised me, too," Mary mused. "But people make mistakes. The worst thing we can ever do is expect someone to be perfect, and then act surprised when they're not."

When her mum said things like that she often wondered if it was just her folksy wisdom or if there was a little dig about Esme's marriage to Evan hidden in the words. Mary had liked Evan a lot, but she hadn't had to live with him. Certainly hadn't had to deal with his nitpicking and putdowns.

"It does set people up for failure, doesn't it?" Esme asked, her voice a little pointed. For all her mum's talk, Esme had always rather felt like she never quite measured up to her mum's expectations.

They loved each other dearly. But their relationship, like any other mother-daughter relationship, had its foibles. "Anyway, Stephen is well."

Mary smiled. "You spent a lot of time together as children."

"Until it got to be too inappropriate."

Mary nodded. "Well, yes. He went away to school, after all. But until then, you were like peas in a pod." She scooped up a spoonful of curry and popped it into her mouth.

"I'm not sure anyone realized how much I missed him after he was gone." Esme met her mum's gaze. "He was my best friend. And the girls at school..."

Mary's eyes softened. "I know, darling. Those years are always awkward..."

"But up until then I had Stephen after school. We did homework together. Climbed trees."

"Got into trouble," Mary added, chuckling. "And don't tell me it was all Stephen's fault. He covered for you."

Esme grinned. "A time or two." She hesitated and then added, "It's been good to see him, though. We've had a few laughs about those years."

Mary Flanagan had always been close with her employers, but her gaze sharpened now, and Esme felt as if her mum could see right past the deliberate "catching up" vibe she was projecting and into her heart, which was a lot more attached.

"As long as there's nothing improper," Mary cautioned.

"Give me some credit, Mum." Esme took a sip of tea. "We were childhood friends. But he's the Earl of Chatsworth, and what am I? I know better."

Mary put down her knife and fork. "That is not what I meant, Esme. You're just as good as any of the Pembertons, and just you mind that."

Esme stared.

"It's got nothing to do with good people. Heavens, having money and a title doesn't make someone virtuous. If only. And I'm not saying the Pembertons aren't good people. They are. Some of the finest I've ever met. Maybe improper was the wrong word. It's just that you work for him right now. What's that line from the movie we watch all the time?"

Esme knew exactly what she was referring to. "Don't dip your nib in the office ink."

Mary chuckled. "That's the one." Her green gaze held Esme's. "The Pembertons live in a very different world, pet. People like us…we don't belong there."

A part of Esme wanted to dispute it. It was a classist statement and she wanted to say that the "people like us" could belong wherever they wanted. But she also understood what her mum was saying. After all, Evan had been upper-class and that had been a disaster. She was tempted to remind her mum of that fact but didn't want to get into the subject of her failed marriage.

Besides, if she flipped it around, she could just as easily say that Stephen didn't belong in a world like hers. The physical attraction she felt was nothing more than an inconvenience and the result of a romantic and sexual dry spell. And it was a stupid thing to be thinking about, anyway. Nothing had happened with Stephen. Nothing *would* happen with Stephen.

"Nothing to fear there, Mum. It's been a fun little trip down memory lane, but that's all there is to it. Besides, I quite like the life I've built for myself here. I have a job I like. Friends. You're here. I have my own little flat… I'm contented. And before you say it, yes, it sucks to be single at thirty-four, but better that than be with the wrong person, which I was." She lifted her chin. "And while I've enjoyed this little conversational detour, we really should be talking about how you're feeling. Better since having something to eat?"

"Fine as a flea," Mary said, making her laugh. "But I know you're going to stay, anyway, so let's break out a movie and make a night of it."

Esme was glad her mum wasn't going to make a big time about her staying over. She found a movie for them to watch and then pulled out her phone to send a quick message.

Mum's a little under the weather. Spending the night so I can call the doctor in the morning. Will you be all right for breakfast?

It wasn't long and a reply came back.

Of course! I'll be fine. Let me know if you need anything.

She put the phone away, thinking about how kind and generous Stephen was, when everyone thought he was stern and formidable and...cold.

He was anything but. And maybe she was the only one who knew it. That, more than anything else, made him so very dangerous to her heart.

Stephen was in the kitchen making coffee when Esme came in, her black uniform replaced by faded jeans and a cute, flowered top in light blue. With her coppery hair tumbling over her shoulders, she took his breath away.

"Good morning," he said, and she smiled at him, sending a warmth straight into his heart. She was like a ray of sunshine.

"Good morning to you, too. You made out okay with breakfast?"

"Just fine. I need another caffeine infusion, though."

She went to the cupboard to get a second mug; apparently she was joining him. "I see you left your suit in your closet. Denim suits you."

He'd put on a pair of jeans and a short-sleeved button-down, and it felt strange but also comfortable. "We have an agreement," he reminded her.

"Indeed. Do you have enough water in the press for two cups?"

"I do. How's your mum?"

Esme went to the fridge for milk. "I just took her home from the doctor's. Her fever was still up a little this morning. He's not overly worried. It could be nothing, but it's worth watching. Besides, if she gets sick, she might have to delay her next chemo treatment. So I'll be keeping an eye on her, looking for any additional symptoms. Her test results will be back later."

"I'm sorry, but glad you were able to go with her."

"Thank you for that. Mum tends to downplay things, but she can't get away with that if I go with her."

Stephen smiled. Esme and Mrs. F were clearly still very close. He was glad of it. Esme stood beside him as he poured, and the light fragrance of her perfume wrapped around him, fresh and floral and clean. His jaw tightened and he stirred the sugar into his coffee a little aggressively. He thought about Esme far too often. He thought about her gorgeous hair and her sparkling eyes and wide smile. The touch of her cool fingers on his hand, the sound of her laugh.

At first it had been memories of their childhoods together, rainy days in the library, hot chocolate in the kitchen, summer days at the pond or climbing trees in the orchard. But he'd be a big fat liar if he didn't admit—at least to himself—that he was attracted to Esme for the woman she was now. Kind. Independent. Forgiving.

Which was completely impossible. Wasn't it?

Why did it matter that they came from different economic situations? He didn't give a damn about that kind of thing.

He stood there, his coffee growing cold, and stared at Esme for several moments.

"Are you okay?" she asked, lifting her cup to sip. "You seem out of sorts." Then she waited patiently for him to answer, as if sensing he was trying to sort it out. How was it she knew that about him so easily?

"Yes, I'm fine." The response came out sharpish, and he sighed. "Sorry. I didn't mean to snap."

"I don't care about that. But I'm concerned about you, Stephen. About why you're so tightly wound. Oh, you forget now and again and loosen up, but you're still…" She sighed. "You're unhappy. I can tell. You used to get the same look on your face when you were frustrated at something."

He ran his hand over his face. "I think it just takes practice to let things go. And it's something I haven't had much practice at…ever." He stopped, unsure how to articulate what he was feeling. "Yesterday I was all set to carve out my own path. Today… I have no idea what that looks like."

Esme came forward and put her hand on his arm. "As my nan used to say, you're all sixes and sevens. But you'll figure it out. Don't be so hard on yourself, and give it time."

He nodded, all too aware of her fingers on his arm, how cool and soft and reassuring they were. And he wanted to talk to her about the bubble of discontent that had been sitting on his chest for so long, but it was hard. Of all the people in the world, he should be able to trust Esme, but trusting was difficult. He'd thought he could trust lots of people before and look where that had got him.

A broken engagement.

Left at the altar.

She took a step back. "You should finish your coffee. Didn't you say the team was breaking ground today?"

He nodded and reached for his cup. "They are. Scheduled to be here in about an hour. Esme, I—" But he stopped, not knowing what to say next.

She let out a sigh and smiled. "It's okay. Stephen, you've always been one to hold your emotions inside. You're a man of action instead. I know talking about your feelings is probably way down on your list of desired activities, and that's okay. I just know that you're struggling. You need to find a way to put down the burden you're carrying, and then sort out what parts of it you're willing to pick up again." Her green eyes were soft with compassion. "And I know because I've been there. So if you need a friend, I'm here. Your secrets are as safe with me as they always were, I promise."

She had no idea that part of his problem was her...or at least the attraction that kept getting in the way every time they were in a room together. What scared him the most was that he did want to open up and let her in, tell her everything. He wanted to pull her into his arms and hold on, and last night... God, last night he'd taken one look at her soft, pink lips and wanted to kiss the daylights out of her. Out of Esme, the girl who'd once dared him to eat a worm. The girl who had angrily cried the day he told her he was going away to school and how he was going to be a great earl like his father and be rich and powerful. That girl had said hurtful things and then affected a perfect, deep curtsy before spitting the words, "Goodbye, my lord," in his direction, a mockery of everything he'd thought was important.

He'd hurt her. And to indulge in this little fantasy of them being together would hurt her in the end, so he shoved his feelings down with all his other ones and locked them away.

"I'm fine, but I appreciate the offer." He knew his tone

was back to being cool again, saw the rebuff in her eyes
as hurt crossed her face. She was right. He did have a hard
time letting go, and he didn't know how to stop hurting
people because of it.

"I'd better get to work," she said softly. "Before my boss
finds out I've been slacking in the kitchen."

He appreciated her attempt at lightening the mood, but
it was spoiled, nonetheless. She slid past him and out the
door, presumably to her office to start her day, or at least
away from him. Stephen sighed, took a drink of his cooling coffee, and forced himself to swallow. As far as secrets,
she didn't know the half of it. And sharing his vulnerabilities had never gotten him anywhere.

CHAPTER SEVEN

ESME RESTED HER head on her hand and let out a long, slow breath.

It was a blessing and a curse, her tender heart. It made her empathetic—a good quality, surely—but it also meant she sometimes took on more than she needed to when it came to other people's struggles. First her mum, and now Stephen.

It was more than that with Stephen, though. The wounded boy in him called to her heart. But the man he'd become…she responded to him like a woman. Last night sleep had been a long time coming because she'd been imagining what it might have been like had her mum not phoned and they'd actually kissed.

Not that she'd admit it to anyone other than herself, but she couldn't stop thinking about Stephen as a lover. And every time she put on that bright smile and pretended to be perky and friendly and helpful, it cost her just a little bit.

This morning it had taken all she had not to go over to him and put her arms around him. But then what would have happened? She was sure he didn't feel the same way about her, even if he was feeling the tiniest bit of attraction. Not once since he'd arrived home had he even suggested he was interested in her in that way. They were friends, and he made sure to repeat it at regular intervals.

Sure, he cared, but that wasn't the same thing. He cared about his sisters, too, and his horses, and probably puppies and kittens.

Besides, her tender heart had got her into tons of trouble before. She had a disturbing tendency to look for the best in people and then ended up disappointed.

She let out a little growl and decided to check on the progress in the garden. The sound of heavy equipment had filtered through to her little office and she'd found herself curious as to what was being dug up. The fact that Stephen was probably watching didn't matter; she could stay out of sight and at least get an idea of how it would all take shape. All she knew right now was that the area just above a little copse of trees was going to become the memorial garden, and that the current rose garden would lead to its entrance.

She grabbed her sunglasses and headed outside. The day was another sunny one, though showers were likely to sweep through later in the evening. The rose garden was past its prime now, with only a few straggling blooms giving a wisp of sweet scent, but Esme took her time walking the stone path past the different varieties. The noise from the equipment ground through the air, so foreign to her ears when the estate was generally so quiet and peaceful.

At the edge of the rose garden, she stopped and stared at the chaos before her.

There was a reason they called it "breaking ground." A large backhoe was scooping up dirt and putting it in a huge pile, while stakes outlined the perimeter of the proposed garden. It was a large space, but other than that, there was no clear clue as to what the finished installation would look like. A few workmen stood to the side, pointing and talking while the equipment operator went on digging, digging.

Digging into the green space where Esme and Stephen had once run free, heading for the grove of ash and beech trees. Stephen had wanted to build a treehouse, but Cedric had said no. Instead, the two of them had cobbled together a fort on the ground. Esme had taken out a large plastic storage tub, which held a couple of old cushions and a blanket so they had something to sit on and Stephen had been in charge of snacks, since he could always sweet-talk Marjorie into something delicious after school. There had always been lots of biscuits and a bottle of something to drink that they'd shared.

It had been such a good childhood, until he'd been sent away.

She could still see the shady trees and wondered why she hadn't yet wandered through the field to visit their old haunts. Probably because she'd only come back to work, not play, and to indulge in a walk down memory lane meant she wasn't doing her job—the job that was her mum's livelihood and life. Ever since coming to the manor, Esme felt such pressure to do everything right, as her mum would.

It dawned on her that Stephen must feel the same way about his title, only magnified by about a hundred. After all, he'd been training for this moment since before his voice had even changed.

He wasn't anywhere to be found at the moment, and the pull to the grove was strong. It wouldn't hurt to take a peek, would it? See if that fort was still there somehow? She doubted it, but she wanted to see anyway. Wanted to go back to those idyllic days before she'd found herself without her best friend, before she'd gone on to school without him, teased by girls and boys alike, before she'd found herself growing breasts and getting curves and attracting unwanted attention. Her stomach clenched, but she let out a deep breath. She'd hated her teen years.

She skirted the construction zone and waded through the grass toward the wilder parts of the property—the grove and the field beyond that was bisected by a brook. The summer air was fragrant with the scent of grass and flowers and the redolent aroma of warm and fertile earth. Esme breathed deeply, soaking it all in, heading for the trees and the shade she would find within.

The path was still there, which surprised her. Perhaps a bit narrower than it had been, but there nonetheless, leading into the leafy canopy of beech and ash. The tension Esme had felt in her muscles earlier eased; her breath came out in a glorious sigh. Being here was a happy place. Why hadn't she come before?

The fort would be just around the bend in the path, if she remembered correctly. Her stride quickened as she got closer, hoping it was still standing though it was doubtful after over twenty years. A few more steps…

She halted, shocked at the scene before her.

It was as if nothing had changed at all! A closer glance showed her the exact opposite of what she'd expected had happened. It hadn't fallen into disrepair, hadn't been blown down during a winter gale. It had been reinforced. Perhaps made a little bigger. Someone was still using this fort.

She stepped forward carefully, curious. A branch snapped under her feet, the sound sharp in the quiet. Even the birds had gone surprisingly silent. Esme bit down on her lip and took another two steps closer to the opening that was the door.

"I brought the biscuits. Do you have anything to sit on?"

She gasped and pressed a hand to her heart at the sound. "Stephen! What on earth are you doing here?"

He poked his head out so she could see him, a small smile on his face. "I could ask you the same thing."

He was here. In their fort. They were in their mid-thirties, for heaven's sake. "I was wondering if this still existed. Clearly it does." She waved a finger at the structure. "Is this you? I mean…did you do all this?"

He nodded. "I did. Came back on summer hols one year and fixed it up. Whenever I wanted to disappear, it was here for me. You'd think there'd be lots of room at the house to find privacy. Not so much, as it happens. But some of Marjorie's biscuits and a book did the trick. When I got older, I'd grab a Pimm's and hide out."

He leaned back so she couldn't see him anymore. "Are you coming in?"

She shouldn't. Heavens. The two of them sitting in some tree fort like children…but excitement rushed through her veins. How many people got a chance to recapture their childhood? "What kind of biscuits are we talking about?"

He laughed, and she delighted in the rare sound. "Hobnobs, of course. I found them in a tin in the kitchen this morning."

She went to the opening and looked inside. There was an old plaid blanket on the ground, and Stephen sat there with his long legs crossed. He swept his arm wide, inviting her in, and his sleeve rode up his arm a little, revealing a partial tattoo. She blinked. The Earl of Chatsworth—the uptight, autocratic eldest child of this blue-blooded family—had a tat. Nothing could have surprised her more.

She wondered if they should compare. The thought of showing him the tattoo just above her tailbone sent heat rushing to her cheeks, so she dipped her head and stepped inside the structure.

She sat down immediately; the fort was far too short for either of them to stand. Stephen's grin widened, transforming his face, and he held out the tin as she crossed her legs. "Biscuit?"

She reached in, took a Hobnob, and nibbled on the edge. So delicious. A few crumbs landed on her shirt, and she brushed them off. "I haven't been here since you left years ago. There wasn't any reason for me to visit the manor much, and when I did, I…well, I didn't have the same liberties. I ended up staying in the kitchen or in Mum's office. I certainly wasn't in a position to have run of the place."

"But you've been back here for weeks now." Stephen reached for another cookie. "Why wait until today?"

She shrugged, trying to rid herself of the surreal feeling of being in a childhood fort with him after all these years. "I went to see the garden site. Then I saw the grove, and, well, curiosity got the best of me." She finished her cookie and looked up at him. "When the entire household staff was on, I couldn't just disappear. My mum…well, those are big shoes to fill. Especially as her daughter. I think everyone expects me to do things exactly the same way."

"But you don't?"

"No one does. Your father was the earl, and so are you, but there are differences between you. You probably feel pressured to carry on the same legacy, but you shouldn't. You should be able to make your own."

He stared at her for a long moment. "Not a single person has understood that in the last two years," he said quietly. "The great Cedric Pemberton. And now the scandalous Cedric Pemberton. To be honest, I don't think I'll ever be as great as he was. And I certainly don't want to be—" He halted.

"His infidelity has left its mark. Of course it has." She stated it plainly. Stephen wasn't the kind of man who beat around the bush or prevaricated. "He made a mistake,

Stephen. A big one, for sure, but he was human. It doesn't mean he wasn't a good father to you."

"It does mean he wasn't a good father to Anemone, though," Stephen added. "And I feel guilty about that."

"The guilt isn't yours. And have you said that to Anemone?"

He didn't answer, just reached for another biscuit. Esme smiled to herself. Stephen was so proud. She could imagine admitting such a thing would be difficult for him.

"And what happened with you, Stephen?" She picked up the lid of the tin and put it back on so neither of them could hide behind the sweet treats. "Your broken engagement. The wedding that wasn't."

He brushed his hands together. "I should probably get back."

He went to move but she grabbed his arm. "Not this time. Don't shut me out. Not talking about it isn't going to make it go away, you know." She paused before deciding to dive in. "What happened with Bridget? If you loved her, why did you break it off?" She knew from her mum that Stephen had done the breaking up.

He sat back down. "She wasn't who I thought she was. She…" He frowned, and his jaw took on a resolute set. "She was far more interested in what I could provide than in being with me. And maybe I should have expected it, but when I looked at my parents, who loved each other so much…" He stopped, then looked up at Esme. "Which sounds like a joke, right? Because how could someone love his wife so much and have an affair with someone else?"

Her heart went out to him. She'd never had to worry about her father falling off his pedestal; he'd never been up there to begin with. Her dad had died when she was little; she didn't even remember him. It was different for Stephen. He'd idolized his dad.

"Maybe I just expect too much from people," he said roughly.

"No, you don't." Esme scooted over a little, so she was sitting closer to him, and put her hand on his knee. "Stephen, expecting someone to honor their promises and expecting someone to love you for you and not your money and title is the *bare minimum*. But your faith has been shattered, and so now you don't trust anyone to keep their word. Am I close?"

His dark eyes held hers. "Closer than I'm comfortable with. But then, you've always been able to read me."

"Is there anyone you do trust? Because that's a pretty lonely place to be."

Stephen put his hand over hers, which was still on his knee. The grip was warm, firm, and encompassed her entire hand.

"I trust you, Esme. You've never let me down."

And then he leaned forward and touched his lips to hers.

Stephen wasn't sure what had prompted him to move that little bit forward and kiss her, but he couldn't find it in himself to regret it…not when she tasted so sweet.

Her breath came out in a sigh as she lifted her hand and cupped it softly around the curve of his neck. My God, this was Esme he was kissing. The girl he'd played with, skinned knees with, helped with history homework while she'd helped him with math.

But she wasn't that girl any longer. She was a woman—a beautiful, compassionate, alluring woman—and he'd been thinking about doing just this for three days.

He reached out and circled her waist with his hands, then pulled her onto his lap. The movement caused their mouths to break apart, and her startled emerald eyes met his, her lips plumped from kissing. "Stephen, I—"

He gave his head a small shake, halting her words, and then kissed her again, as if he couldn't possibly get enough of her to quench his thirst.

She pressed closer to him, welcoming his nearness, and he stopped thinking about everything except her—the feel and taste of her. She swamped his senses and he succumbed willingly, nipping at her lips, running his hand down her rib cage.

Another shift—hers, this time—and she'd straddled him, cupped his face in her hands, and had taken over.

Nothing could have surprised and pleased him more. He cupped his hands on her bottom and held her close. The desire to make love to her here was overwhelming. No one would find them. He imagined her fiery hair strewn over the rough wool blanket, her creamy skin, open to the air and his gaze…

He moved his hand over her breast and felt the tip with his thumb. Esme. This was his Esme. The need to truly make her his roared through his veins.

But he couldn't. It took all his willpower to put his hands on her arms and break the kisses that consumed them both, but he did it. "Esme. We can't. My God. I'm so sorry. I shouldn't have…" He didn't know what to say. Both of them were breathing hard.

But what surprised him most was when he looked in her eyes and saw them swimming with tears.

"Esme…what…?"

"It's okay. I shouldn't have either… I was foolish to think…" She scrambled off his lap, and he immediately felt the loss of her. He wanted her close again.

"Foolish to think what? That I could want you?"

She didn't answer, but the pink that climbed her cheeks and the way she avoided his gaze answered the question anyway.

How the hell could she think she was anything less than desirable? He reached out and put his hand along her face.

"I wasn't planning to kiss you. It was an impulse, but the spark…oh, there's more than a spark, there. Esme. Look at me."

She obeyed, her cheeks reddening further.

"I didn't expect it to be that hot. That instant. And I stopped because I don't have protection and if we'd kept going, that was where we would end up. With that choice to make."

She swallowed. "I practically jumped on you."

"Only because you beat me to it. I mean, I understand that it's weird. We're…friends. Though if I'm honest…"

He trailed off, thinking back to those days when he'd turned thirteen and she'd been twelve and sometimes the atmosphere between them had got awkward. Her breasts had just been budding but he'd noticed. And sometimes if they touched carelessly, he'd reacted in a new, exciting and frankly, uncomfortable way.

"If you're being honest, what?"

He lifted a shoulder and smiled at her a little. "If I hadn't gone away to school, things would have changed between us anyway. It was already starting to get awkward."

Her mouth dropped open. "For you, too?"

He nodded. "Maybe we shouldn't be so surprised that there's…chemistry."

He'd thought that the admission might ease something between them, but instead Esme seemed to pull away. Had he said something wrong?

"I should go back up to the house," she said, rising to her knees.

"Esme, wait. Don't go. If we don't talk about this it's going to be awkward. Please."

She hesitated.

"You pulled away when I said we had chemistry. Please tell me why."

She let out a long sigh. "This is a mistake. Thinking we were friends...we both know this can't go anywhere, and you're not just some random guy."

He held her gaze. "You mean I could hurt you."

She nodded slowly. "And it makes me feel very vulnerable to admit that."

She really had no idea that she also had the power to hurt him.

"We *are* friends," he asserted. He didn't care about their differences or that years had passed. "And I don't have many."

She snorted. "That's ridiculous. Look at you."

Annoyance flared at her careless words. "Why is it ridiculous? I have very few people in my life that I trust. That I feel aren't working some sort of angle because of who I am. You... I've known you since I was a child. I not only know you're not working an angle, I also think that my money and title actually put me at a disadvantage. I get the idea that this is not a life you'd want."

She looked at him steadily, then finally replied. "If that is the case, and it isn't what I want, then why would I sleep with you? It isn't something I do casually, Stephen. And especially not with people I value as friends. Why would I want to mess that up?"

"You tell me." He was unable to hold back his frustration. "You were the one on my lap."

She scrambled to her feet and out the door of the fort.

"Esme, wait. I didn't really mean that." He followed her out, straightening his shirt as he went.

She turned toward him.

"But you did. And we both know nothing can come of this. I'd be a liar to say I'm not attracted. That kissing you wasn't…" She huffed out a huge breath. "It was really good, okay? And hell yes, I've wondered what it would be like. But if we did more than that, we'd stop being friends. Or feelings would get involved and one of us would end up hurt." She took a few steps backward. "I'm not up for that, Stephen. I'm just not. Not again."

She turned and walked away, her feet crunching against twigs and stones leading to the path.

Stephen ran a hand through his hair, watched her go. She was right, of course. But what had she meant by "again?" If she meant her ex-husband, he really wanted to punch that guy in the face.

"I'm an idiot. Just a complete idiot."

Esme sat across from her best friend, Phoebe, and stared into her glass of beer. The whole afternoon she'd been playing the scene in the fort over and over in her mind until it nearly drove her mad. And this was not something she could talk over with her mum. There was no doubt that Mary Flanagan would have a lot to say about Esme letting personal feelings get in the way of work. Esme was in no mood for a lecture.

"You're not an idiot," Phoebe said, picking up her G&T and taking a sip. Phoebe arched a dark eyebrow as she stared at Esme. "I've seen pics of him in the tabloids. He's scrummy."

Esme snorted. Stephen would hate being described as *scrummy*. She caught Phoebe's smile and returned it, though rather reluctantly. Phoebe flipped her dark brown hair over her shoulder and lifted her chin in triumph. "You know you think so. I bet he smells good, too."

Oh, he did. The Aurora cosmetics department had a number of lovely scents, and Stephen smelled so delicious, like sandalwood and cedar and something clean and crisp. Particularly in the hollow of his neck, as the summer warmth amplified the intensity of the fragrance. He'd said he'd only stopped because he didn't have protection…he'd wanted to have sex with her. She still couldn't quite wrap her head around that.

"Look," Phoebe said, gesturing with the straw from her glass. "Your ex, who shall not be named, was an arse. We both know it. You cannot judge the Earl of Chatsworth by that crappy yardstick."

"I know that, intellectually," Esme retorted, poking her fork into the salad she'd ordered. "In practice it's a very different thing. And even if it weren't, as you say, he's the earl." Phoebe opened her mouth to say something, and Esme held up a hand, halting her. "That is not the life for me, and we both know it. Can you see me at one of their parties? Pheebs, I'm the woman who serves the canapes, not eats them."

"Canapes are overrated. And if you were Stephen Pemberton's wife, you could eat whatever you wanted."

"Wife? Okay, now you have lost the plot." Esme laughed, even as something wistful twisted inside her gut. Today, sitting in the fort together, kissing, touching him… for a brief moment it hadn't mattered that he was rich as Croesus and as handsome as the devil. He'd just been the person who *got* her like no one else ever had.

Phoebe took a bite of her dinner and then started gesturing with her fork, looking like she was conducting an invisible orchestra. "If I hear you say that you're not good enough for him, I'm going to have to stage an intervention."

"It's not even that." It was, a bit, but not in the way Phoebe was thinking. "Look, I know what the ex who shall not be named did. He chipped away at my self-esteem and made me doubt myself, and yeah, sometimes I have to really work to break out of those patterns. But it's not just his behavior that concerns me. It's my own. Why would I put myself in a position where I stood a very good chance of feeling overlooked and invisible? I've had to really work at overcoming that already. I can't put myself in a situation that risks me repeating that behavior. I've fought so hard to have my own life, my own agency. I'm so scared to lose myself again."

Phoebe's smile fell from her lips and she put down her fork. "Damn, Es. I can't actually argue with that. That's really self-aware of you."

"Stephen's a good man. He wouldn't mean to. But it's not about him. It's about me, and how I respond to things. It feels as if I'd be setting myself up for failure. I had messages for years about how I wasn't a good wife, how I needed to lose a stone or two, how I wasn't intellectually his equal. It would be very easy to go down that road again with a family as powerful as the Pembertons, especially considering the industry they're in." She let out a sigh. "Walking away from my marriage was the best thing I ever did, but I didn't do it without scars."

"I'd like to give him some scars," Phoebe muttered darkly, and Esme laughed.

She picked at her salad while Phoebe scarfed down her chicken alfredo.

"But Pheebs?"

"Yes, darling?"

"How do I go back to work there again? With it just being the two of us? How do I not jump his bones again? Because it was really, really good."

Phoebe burst out laughing, while Esme stared dolefully at her dinner. She started to push her plate away when Phoebe put her hand on Esme's wrist, halting the movement.

"You can't have any pudding unless you finish your meat," she said in an exaggerated voice, imitating Pink Floyd.

Esme shook her head and chuckled. "This is why you're my best friend. You are so totally random and wonderful."

"Of course I am. And so the advice I'm going to give you this evening—aren't you the lucky one—is threefold. One, stop worrying so much about one kiss from a guy who is only going to be in town for another week or two. You managed to go twenty years without crossing paths, and you wouldn't be now, either, except you're covering for your mum. Two, you could stand to have a bit of a fling, since by this time I'm a little concerned about the neglect your girly parts have suffered. This hasn't been just a dry spell, it's been the freaking desert."

Esme's cheeks heated, and she hoped no one at any of the nearby tables could hear Pheebs's life advice.

"Three," Phoebe said, ticking it off on her fingers, "you cannot leave this evening without getting whatever makes up the Death by Chocolate on the dessert menu. We can share."

As Esme dutifully ate her vegetables, she considered Phoebe's advice. It was true she hadn't been with anyone in a very long time. In fact, she'd only had sex once since her divorce, after she'd been out on exactly three dates with someone she met on a dating app, and she'd known immediately that it had been a mistake. She wasn't made for casual sex, couldn't shrug it off as simply a nice evening or attending to her needs. Both of those were true and perfectly fine, but the problem was it had left her feeling emptier rather than fulfilled...beyond the obvious, that was.

She supposed now that it was good the ex—she and Phoebe had a pact to not call him by name—was not her last. Not just because of how long it had been but because he'd always found her lacking in some way. At least Mr. Third Date had been...pleasurable.

But not fireworks. The whole thing hadn't been as incendiary as five minutes in Stephen's arms with all their clothes on.

She reached for her beer and took a long drink. Had the pub just got hotter? Or maybe it was her mind automatically straying to the thought of Stephen and fireworks and wondering what it would be like to have all that intensity focused on her.

But what was the point? With Stephen—if he even wanted to—it would still be casual because a relationship was out of the question.

And maybe if she kept saying it to herself, she'd believe it.

The chocolate torte came, complete with a scoop of ice cream and hot fudge sauce. Esme considered saying no, thinking of the extra few pounds she always felt she carried around, and then took a breath and pushed out the thought, replacing it with healthier ones. She was fine just the way she was. And she could surely share a dessert with her best friend on their weekly dinner dates.

When they'd finished the meal with the torte and coffee, Phoebe sat back and let out a happy sigh. "This was delicious. Next time we hit the Italian?"

"Sounds good to me." Esme smiled at her friend. Phoebe was a short, compact little package of sass, and had more self-confidence than Esme could ever dream of. "How do you do it, Pheebs? How do you stay so sure of yourself?"

Phoebe's eyes softened. "It's not always easy, you know. But if I don't love me, how can someone else? If I tear myself down, why shouldn't someone else? It sometimes takes some reminding, you know. But in the end... I treat myself the way I want others to treat me. With acceptance and love and a bit of a sense of humor."

"I wish I could manage that," Esme mourned, sitting back in her chair.

The waitress dropped off their checks and disappeared again, leaving a couple of mints behind. Esme grabbed one and popped it in her mouth.

"If I tell you my secret, you're sworn to silence," Phoebe answered, tucking her curtain of hair behind her ear.

"Duh," Esme replied.

"I write sticky notes to myself and put them on my bathroom mirror," she confessed. "And when I get up in the morning, I make myself say them out loud."

Esme considered that for a long moment. It didn't sound like the Phoebe she knew, but how could she ignore the proof that was right before her? Phoebe exuded confidence—not in a brash, arrogant way, but in an "I'm comfortable in my own skin" sort of way.

They paid their bills and parted ways after a quick hug on the sidewalk. Tomorrow she'd be back at Chatsworth Manor again, faced with Stephen. It was up to her to set the tone with him. She'd been the one to run away today. Before she went to sleep tonight, she had to decide exactly what she wanted from him and how she wanted to handle their relationship at the house.

By ten she was back in her own flat, listening to the silence that came from living alone. She hadn't wanted a roommate after the divorce, but now she wondered if she shouldn't ask the landlady if she could get a cat or something.

She flicked on the light to the bathroom and stared in the mirror. Big green eyes stared back at her, somber and perhaps a bit timid. She squared her shoulders and lifted her chin—better. She had no problem adopting this posture and attitude at work, but when it came to her own personal self-esteem… Esme frowned and put her hands on the edge of the vanity. Who was she kidding? Her self-esteem had been in the toilet for years.

There was a pad of sticky notes somewhere in a kitchen drawer. She marched to the kitchen and scrounged until she found them, slightly dusty, and a Sharpie marker. Then she stomped back to the bathroom, determination settling through her bones. She uncapped the marker and wrote on the first sticky "I am strong," then ripped it off the pad and stuck it to the mirror.

"I am strong," she said out loud. Huh.

On the next she wrote, "I am capable." Rip and stick. More stickies followed.

"I am smart."

"I have a good heart."

"I am the perfect size for me." That one was a hard one, but she wrote it and stuck it on the mirror anyway. On and on she went, scribbling and sticking until the multicolored notes covered the mirror except for an oval where her face remained.

She wrote one more. "I have great hair," she said, and found an empty spot to stick it.

Then she stepped back. She'd gone a little overboard, but she did feel…stronger. With more resolve. Was this… confidence?

She gave her reflection a nod, and then flipped off the light switch. Tomorrow was an early day.

CHAPTER EIGHT

STEPHEN HAD BARELY slept, waking before six and staring at the ceiling. It was a strange feeling, being all alone in the house. Esme would be here later, but there were no maids, no kitchen staff…and the house was so very large. Empty. This week he'd spent more time alone with his thoughts than he had in…maybe ever.

He got up, pulled on a pair of sleep pants and a T-shirt, and headed down two flights to the kitchen. By six thirty he had a steaming cup of Colombian in his hands, the aroma warm and soothing.

Esme had left yesterday afternoon without a word, and he'd been on his own for dinner. It hadn't been a totally satisfactory meal. He'd slapped together a grilled cheese sandwich and made a salad from the vegetables in the fridge, but it wasn't the same as Esme's cooking. It filled the hole, though, so that was something.

She would be here in a few hours, and he had to decide what he was going to say to her.

He shouldn't have kissed her. She'd responded and then it had spooked her, hadn't it? Hell, it had spooked him, but he wasn't the one who'd run away.

He owed her an apology. Somehow they had to put their friendship back on solid ground again. He'd meant what he said about not having an overabundance of friends. Maybe he and Esme hadn't seen each other in years, but they'd picked up as if it hadn't been any time at all. She got him better than anyone he knew. He'd be a fool to jeopardize that, wouldn't he?

He brewed a second cup of coffee and went to shower, then attempted to make his bed as tidy and perfect as the maids did. He pulled the covers up as neatly as possible, fluffed the pillows, and went back to the kitchen to eat something for breakfast.

When Esme finally arrived at eight fifteen, he was already in the library, laptop booted up, answering the emails that had been streaming in.

She found him there a few minutes later. "Good morning. Sorry I'm a little late. Did you want some breakfast?"

He looked up and made himself smile, trying to make it relaxed and warm. "I managed breakfast already, thank you."

Her face flattened. "Oh! Well, good." A smile flitted on her lips, but it seemed unsure. She was feeling just as off-kilter as he was.

"Esme, why don't you grab a coffee and come back up? We should talk."

"Well, I…" She looked even more uncertain. "I do have work to get to…"

"It won't take long." He met her gaze evenly. "We need to clear the air, don't you think?"

She nodded, and something flickered in her eyes that he couldn't quite decipher. Still, Stephen figured being direct was the best approach. He really didn't know how to be anything else, he realized. And that probably made him…intimidating.

She slipped out of the library and he sat back in his chair, tapping his finger on his lower lip. Why was he so blunt? Why wasn't he more easygoing, like William, or charming like his cousin, Christophe? He supposed it came with the weight of responsibility, but he rather suspected it might be something more.

He looked over at the photo of his parents on the corner of the desk. His dad, tall, strong, with William's steady temperament and enough charm to work a room and leave everyone feeling as if they were basking in his glow. His mother, regal, smart, and elegant, but with a hint of devilment around her lips and her unique rusty laugh. It was impossible to follow in either of their footsteps. Stephen had tried very hard to not be like either of his parents. To be someone different and yet still live up to all the expectations that came with being the eldest and heir.

"You know the only person putting those expectations on you is you," came a voice from in front of him.

Esme, cradling a steaming cup of coffee. She'd caught him staring at the photo, but how on earth had she been able to read his mind?

"I don't know what you mean," he said, picking up his own cup and taking a sip.

"You're a horrible liar. You try to be all nonchalant, but it backfires. It always did." She pulled up a chair and sat down. "So what's bothering you?"

He frowned. "Nothing." Except that if he wasn't like his father, or like his mother, and he'd been trying to be so different, who really was he? Did he even know?

"You're thinking way too hard for someone who says nothing," she said. "But that's your business." She took a breath. "I'm sorry I ran from you yesterday. It wasn't the right way to handle what happened."

Apparently he wasn't the only one who could be forthright. Granted, her cheeks were a little pink and he got the feeling she wasn't exactly comfortable with broaching the topic, but she was doing it anyway.

"I was out of line," he admitted. "I got caught up in the moment, that's all."

"We're not ten anymore," she said, giving a nod. "We had no business being in that fort in the first place." Then her cheeks flushed deeper. "Well, at least I didn't. Of course you can if you want. It's your fort."

His lips twitched. He was thirty-five and they were talking about a childhood fort. "We took a little time to rediscover our youth," he said, his voice a little warmer. "There's nothing terrible about that."

"Except you never kissed me in our youth."

His gaze snapped to hers. "You never kissed me, either."

Her lips dropped open a little at his quick reply. He hadn't been alone yesterday, and she'd definitely been a willing participant. The blame was mostly his, but not all of it.

"And now we're back where we started," she whispered.

He let out a sigh. "Esme… I'm sorry. It was wrong of me to kiss you. To get carried away. I'm only here for a short time and I'm honestly not looking for a relationship." He ignored the little voice in his head that reminded him how much he'd enjoyed their time at the pub and eating dinner here together two nights ago.

"I'm not either," she said. "Been there, done that. Have the divorce decree to prove it."

"That doesn't mean you shouldn't try again," Stephen reasoned, though he certainly didn't mean with him. Still, the thought of Esme alone for the rest of her life simply didn't fit. She had so much to offer the right man. Intelligence, beauty, a sharp sense of humor…

"Hello, Mr. Pot, meet Mr. Kettle." Esme lifted an eyebrow, then took a drink of her coffee.

Okay, so she had him there. "At least you actually made it through a ceremony," he groused, shaking his head.

She snorted.

Then her lush lips sobered. "Stephen, this...whatever happened yesterday, it's not real. I'm glad to see you again. I want to be your friend. But anything else is..."

"Is what?" He didn't necessarily disagree, but he wanted to hear her take on it.

"We're too different. And it's just... I don't know. Nostalgia, I guess."

"Different because I'm an earl and you're not."

"Different because one of your suits costs more than my wardrobe. One bottle of wine for you is my grocery budget for the month. You make business deals worth millions, and I am one step up from cleaning hotel rooms for a living." She lifted her chin. "Not that there is a thing wrong with good, honest work, and I like my job a lot. I always liked the feeling of a pristine room, ready to welcome someone inside and make their stay special."

"You're a nurturer, like your mother." He shrugged one shoulder. "I am not."

"That's what I'm saying. We're just...different."

It should have been the end of it. They were both in agreement that there could be nothing between them, so why did he feel the urge to ask about their attraction? Because their mouths were saying one thing and their eyes another. The eye contact put them right back on that blanket yesterday afternoon, in that charged moment when they'd hovered only inches apart, waiting for someone to make the first move.

She looked away first, and that was when he knew.

She was lying.

He wasn't sure what to say—whether to call her on it or let sleeping dogs lie. The first would be like lighting a match to paper, sparking their chemistry again. The second was the more prudent course. Keep everything platonic and professional and get through the next week.

He met her gaze. "I've been called back to Paris for a few days."

"Oh. I see."

She didn't, and probably thought he was running away from her, when nothing could be further from the truth. "There's a social thing, and someone in the family needs to attend. Gabi's come down with some sort of bug and Bella is already at another event that evening. And Annie... well, Annie hasn't really started representing the family at functions yet."

"So it's up to you."

"It's literally an overnight in Paris, maybe two, then back here for the gooseberry festival." He smiled a little. "My social engagements cover a broad range of activities."

"I see. So you're not just...avoiding me?"

He leaned forward. "No." Stephen normally kept his feelings under lock and key, but he found himself admitting, "I would rather spend the evening at the pub with you, if I'm honest."

Her green eyes held his, even as her teeth worried her lower lip. "What's the point, if this isn't going anywhere?"

He closed his eyes for a brief moment and pinched the bridge of his nose. "I know. Still doesn't stop me wanting to spend time with you." He opened his eyes again and looked over at her. "Es, something's changed in me since I came home. It's been difficult, but it's also been good. I think I need to see it through, whatever it is. And what I know for sure is that you're helping me somehow."

She made a funny, dismissive sound and started to roll her eyes, but he stopped her. "No, I mean it. I've told you more in the last few days than I've told anyone about the pressures I'm under. You can't know how important that's been." He folded his hands together on top of the desk to keep from reaching out to her. "Come with me to Paris. I need a plus-one anyway. Let me do something for you as a thank-you for all you've done for me."

Her face blanked with alarm. "Paris? With you? You're mad. Besides, all I've done is my job."

"We both know that's not strictly true." Her blush deepened, and he got up from his desk and went around to the front, resting his hips against it as he looked down at her. "Esme, I hate going to these things alone. And lately I've been paired up with my mother. Which is mostly fine but after a while…having your mother as your date for the evening is a bit…" He hesitated, unsure of what word he wanted.

"Sad?" He stared at her, and she laughed a little. "Sorry."

"No, you're right. Listen, it's only a few hours. I'll shake some hands and make small talk. There'll be some food and definitely champagne. The good stuff."

Esme stood and faced him. "You realize this is exactly the kind of thing that Evan would have asked of me. Dress appropriately, smile, shake hands, drink champagne."

Stephen pushed away from the desk. "Forget it, then."

"You don't have to pout about it."

He wanted to say, "I'm not," but he knew his voice had sounded decidedly petulant. "I wouldn't ask you to be someone you're not. I thought you might enjoy the getaway, and I could have company for the event that I actually enjoy. But not if you compare me to him."

"That's not what I meant—"

"Isn't it? I can't be less of who I am any more than you can, Esme. And if you think I would ask you to something and treat you as some sort of accessory, then you don't know me at all."

He went back around his desk and sat down again, his heart pounding against his ribs.

"I didn't say I wouldn't go," she whispered.

His gaze snapped back up to hers. She looked contrite, and a little scared, and perhaps even slightly defiant.

"I just said that this was something Evan would have asked me to do. No, not asked. Expected. And he would have made sure I understood I was not to embarrass him."

"The more I hear about your ex, the more I'd like to meet him," Stephen said darkly.

She went to him then, and rested against the desk beside his chair. "I know how to behave in social situations. I wouldn't embarrass you, and I know that. Any hesitation is because, well, I don't enjoy being under the microscope. It just invites comments that echo all my insecurities."

He couldn't assure her otherwise. He'd been in the spotlight his whole life and knew what it was like. "I understand," he replied.

She reached out and touched his arm. "Will there be press there?"

"Almost assuredly."

"And so my presence with you would open us up to speculation."

It wasn't that he didn't understand what she was getting at. It was more that he couldn't possibly live his entire life hiding from the paparazzi. She, however, could. "Look, Esme, it's fine if you don't want to go. I just thought it would be nice. I've done a million of these things before and survived."

He turned his attention back to his open laptop and touched his mouse to bring it back to life.

He was shutting her out.

Not that she blamed him. He'd invited her to Paris and

she'd immediately put up roadblocks. Legitimate ones, she supposed, but she didn't doubt his motives. She believed him when he expressed his appreciation for listening to him, and despite her misgivings, she was flattered that he would even consider taking her to some function as his plus-one.

"Where would I stay?" she asked softly.

His fingers paused over his keyboard. "Wherever you like. At a hotel, or there's a spare room at my flat. Wherever you'd be most comfortable."

A spare room. Not his room, then. She was both relieved and disappointed. Because she could repeat the word *friend* as often as possible in her mind, but it didn't wash away the beating of her heart when he looked into her eyes, or erase the taste of his lips against hers just yesterday.

Ugh, she was in so much trouble. She didn't do casual, he didn't do love, she'd never fit in his world, and yet her need for him was under her skin, like an itch she couldn't scratch. She wanted to go. Perhaps…just this once?

"I would need time to go shopping for a dress," she said. She couldn't believe she was actually considering this. Wasn't it exactly what she'd said she didn't want? And yet, the way he'd kissed her yesterday…what if this time it was different? What if she was letting something from her past ruin something that could be really great? It would be foolish to give what was done that sort of power, wouldn't it?

He turned and looked up at her. "You're certain?"

She nodded. "I can't hide away in this village forever, can I? And how often does one get invited to Paris?" She gave her head a shake. "I mean someone like me."

"Don't worry about a dress. What's the sense of working in fashion if I can't whip up a stylist at a moment's notice?"

A stylist? For her? She'd shopped at some nice stores

and been to some swanky dos, but she'd never had a stylist. Oh, she might be getting in over her head…

Just like that, her bubble burst. "I never thought. I'm not sure I can leave Mum."

"It's twenty-four, maybe forty-eight hours. I'm sure she'll be fine. Is there someone who can look in on her?"

"Her friend, Judy, I suppose."

"And it's Paris. If anything happens, I can have you back here in a couple of hours."

"What about…" Her face heated and she moved a finger between the two of them. "After yesterday…"

He got up from his desk slowly, and her breath caught as he stood mere inches away. She had to look up to see his face, and the moment she did, she had the urge to simply melt into his arms.

This would not do.

"Must we label it?" he asked, his low voice barely above a whisper. "Let's just be honest. I'm attracted to you, and if yesterday is any indication, you're attracted to me. Let's just see what happens. And if it gets to be too much, no hard feelings."

No hard feelings.

Her breath stuttered. He lifted his hand and slid it into her hair at the nape of her neck, then dropped his head and touched his lips to hers. Soft, gentle, seductive.

She was on fire.

Her reaction to him was like nothing she'd ever experienced. Never this burning need, the urge to dispense with clothes and feel his skin on hers, to be in his arms, become his lover. The urgency stole her breath, but she stood before him, barely moving, while the maelstrom of desire stormed within her.

She could stay in a hotel. Or in a room in his flat. What if she wanted to stay in his bed?

She was getting way ahead of herself. But she couldn't stop herself from responding to his kiss.

He stepped back, pressed his forehead to hers in a gesture that was surprisingly tender. "The event is tomorrow night. Can you be ready to leave in the morning?"

She nodded briefly, thinking she'd abandoned all sense and caution.

And then she slid out of his embrace and left the study, knowing she suddenly had a lot to do before she took the biggest risk of her life.

CHAPTER NINE

TELLING HER MUM she was off to Paris had been tricky. No matter how much Esme emphasized that she was going as a friend, Mary had that knowing look in her eye and a set to her lips that spoke of disapproval. It was almost as if she'd seen into Esme's brain and had known about the kisses she and Stephen had shared.

But they were both stubborn women, and Esme didn't change her mind, and Mary of course agreed that she could manage just fine for a few days without Esme's "hovering." Esme went home, packed a small bag for two nights, and met Stephen the next morning at the estate.

A driver took them to Gatwick, where a chartered plane zipped them off to Paris. Esme tried not to gawk. She'd been to some pretty upscale events as Evan's wife, but nothing like a hired jet to another country. Clearing customs was a whiz and before she knew it, she and Stephen were at his flat in the heart of the City of Light.

He smiled at her, opened the door, and swept his hand to the side, ushering her in.

Esme stood in the foyer, her eyes wide as she took in the sumptuous space. Stephen's apartment was spacious and modern, despite the building being old and venerable. She put down her bag and wandered in, admiring the crisp and clean décor. Off-white walls and large windows added to the open feel, and the kitchen, to her left, had state-of-the-art stainless-steel appliances and a wide counter for prepping meals. The kitchen led into a lovely dining room with a table that seated eight surrounded by plush chairs.

There was a big-screen television and a rich cream sofa for relaxing in the living room, with other wing chairs in vibrant fabrics adding a splash of color. There were also three bedrooms, each with their own bathroom. Stephen had made one of the bedrooms into an office, leaving a spare room and the main bedroom—his.

He had picked up her bag, and now placed it in the spare room. He truly wasn't making any assumptions, and she appreciated it. Now that she was here, nerves and doubts crowded into her heart and mind. Could she really do this? Could she be in this kind of world again, and still be… Esme?

Then she looked at Stephen and felt such a rush of emotion she knew she wanted to try.

Esme turned around, admiring it all. It was a different sort of opulence from the manor house, and unfamiliar. Still, it suited him somehow. It was restful, rather than sparse. She liked it a lot. She liked him a lot.

"Welcome to Paris," he said, and he pulled her close, kissing her long and slow.

"Mmm." Her heart hammered with pleasure at the gentle but seductive welcome. "Let me go out and come back in again. That was nice."

He chuckled against her lips. "I'm hoping if I kiss you long enough, you won't be nervous about this evening."

"I'm going to be nervous anyway, but kissing you isn't a hardship."

He stepped back, took her hands in his, and held her gaze. "You don't have to come. If it's too much, I understand."

She squeezed his fingers. "I think I have to try. But—"

She let go of his hands and sighed. "Can we talk first, before this stylist has a go at me? Because I think... I want you to understand where I'm coming from a little more." She swallowed tightly, afraid of her next words but knowing they were true. "I want to trust you with this."

He nodded. "Of course we can talk."

She didn't want to do this in her bedroom, so she skirted past him to the living room, where she could look out the wide windows at the city below. The view was stunning, and she took a deep breath, letting the view anchor her as she considered what she was going to share with him.

"It can't be that bad," he said, coming up behind her.

She turned to face him. The slight frown on his face was momentarily intimidating, but then she realized he wasn't frowning *at* her but rather *for* her and whatever unpleasant information she was about to share.

"It's not that bad," she said, trying to lighten things a little. "You already know a lot about my marriage to Evan... most of the important bits, anyway. This is more about what it did to me personally...on a self-esteem level, because going to this event with you tonight is more than not wanting to feel like arm candy. You see, when Evan had functions and dinners and whatnot, he always had opinions on what I wore, how I did my hair...if something was flattering, if I'd put on a few pounds, even what I was eating. I could order dessert or have it before me, but I could only have a few bites. He didn't like certain styles. I was never allowed to wear jeans. Those kinds of comments don't just go away when you sign your name on the divorce decree. I try to ignore them most of the time. But a night like tonight, where I'm going to be in a fancy dress and among beautiful people...it brings a lot of it back."

Instead of the frown disappearing, it deepened, and a

muscle ticked in his jaw. "So you're doing this to prove something to yourself?"

"In a way, I suppose I am."

He gave a brisk nod. "Good."

"Good?" She was surprised at his answer.

"Yes, absolutely. You've told me that I need to step out of my father's shadow, and I don't need to carry the weight of his actions. I realized that no one can do that but me, and no one can do this for you but you." His dark eyes were bright with resolve. "And if going to this thing tonight is helping you do that, I'm one hundred percent onboard."

Tears sprang into her eyes. Nothing had prepared her for his unqualified support. He wasn't trying to fix anything. He wasn't trying to tell her how wrong Evan had been. Instead, he'd validated every single one of her feelings and then basically said he'd be beside her while she dealt with them.

No one—not even her mother—had offered this kind of support. It was what the old Stephen would have done when they were kids. It was why she'd liked him. He'd always—with the exception of the day he said goodbye to her—treated her as an equal.

If he kept this up, she was going to fall for him—hard.

"Don't cry," he said, his voice gentle. "He's not worth crying over."

"That's not why." She sniffled. "You just…reminded me of the Stephen I used to know. I like that person a lot."

"He happens to like you a lot, too. But if I don't get you over to Aurora, you're going to be late for your appointment."

"I am?"

He nodded. "You are. And for the rest of today, you're not to worry about a thing."

From the outside, it looked like a simple cocktail party, with the usual wine, champagne and tiny but delectable finger foods. But Stephen knew that inside were some of the biggest players in European exports. The host was a well-known billionaire, and one did not turn down an invitation—not even if one was a Pemberton. Stephen slid his right hand into his pocket as he stood outside the small ballroom, waiting for Esme. She'd texted and said they were running a little behind, but that she would meet him here. It was now a half hour past the time on the invitation, making her fashionably late.

Normally this wouldn't faze him in the least. But it was Esme. And he was worried she'd got cold feet.

He cradled a glass of Scotch in his left hand, but he'd taken a single obligatory sip and that was it. He was too nervous and distracted. Just as he was ready to take out his mobile and send her a text, the elevator doors opened, and she stepped out.

His heart stopped for a second, then started beating again in a fast tattoo.

The dark green silk clung to her curves, dropping in a simple column over her hips to the floor. The V neckline and wide straps on her shoulders revealed the creamy, soft skin of her neck and arms, and the stylist had done the world a favor and left Esme's hair down, letting it fall in glorious copper waves and ripples that framed her face and whispered along her back.

This was the same Esme who donned plain black trousers and a button-down black shirt for work. Who pulled her hair back in a no-nonsense braid or bun as she managed the manor staff. She was utterly transformed, and yet exactly the same. She was, and always had been, magnificent.

"Wow. You… Esme. You take my breath away."

She smiled, her eyes lighting up. "You like it? Patrice said green is my color."

He figured any color would be her color, but he couldn't

deny the jewel tone suited her. "You're stunning." He swallowed against a surprising lump in his throat and tried a smile. "And in need of champagne, I think."

She looped her arm through his and they entered the ballroom. No expense had been spared; exotic flowers bloomed from every corner and at the center of each table. Candles sent flickering light through the opulent space. There was enough champagne flowing to fill a swimming pool, and glittering jewels sparkling at every throat. Every throat except Esme's, he realized. The stylist had picked the perfect Aurora couture gown and shoes, had ensured Esme's hair and makeup were flawless, but she was missing Aurora gems. He imagined her wearing one of Sophie's creations, something as unique and special as she was, perhaps in diamonds and emeralds. But it would have been foolish to make such a gesture for a single cocktail party, wouldn't it? When they were just friends?

Except they weren't just friends. The way they'd kissed earlier today had made that abundantly clear. Maybe he wasn't in the market for a relationship, but he suspected he was caught in the middle of one anyway. As Esme smiled and sipped her champagne from a gold-rimmed flute, the thought simultaneously terrified and thrilled him.

"Are you all right?" she asked, lowering her glass. "What's wrong?"

"Nothing," he replied, schooling his features. It wouldn't do for him to walk around with his emotions written all over his face. "Come, I'll introduce you to a few people."

They made their rounds and he shook the hands of all the people he knew he should. Champagne was drunk and refilled, but Esme turned down the offer of any food, and he thought he detected some strain around the edges of her smile. When she'd offered the seventh "Nice to meet you"—or was it eighth?—he swept her away from the crowd and onto the dance floor.

She felt so right in his arms, and as he made a small turn in time to the music, he felt her relax a little. "Sorry," he whispered near her ear. "I know it's a lot."

"It's fine. A little too familiar, perhaps." She leaned back a little and met his gaze. "I guess I...oh, never mind."

"You guess what? You can tell me."

She sighed, then looked up at him again. "I guess I just prefer a more genuine connection. I'm not one for show."

"And thank God for that," he said, as a new thought struck him. He kept his feet moving, guiding her in smooth, small steps, but he made sure to hold her gaze. "You wouldn't be you if you enjoyed the superficial. This is business tonight, but that's all. It's not...real. You understand that. Not everyone does. Some people think this is... I don't know. The goal."

"Like Bridget?"

He nodded, his throat tight. "I just didn't see it at first. This isn't me, Es. Oh, it's part of what I do. It goes with the position. But it's not me, in here." He let go of her hand and touched his heart, then took her fingers in his again. "You do know that, don't you?"

She bit down on her lip a little, then released it before she spoke again. "I do. You're so much more than this."

"And so are you," he murmured, his gaze dropping to her lips. He wouldn't kiss her here. He understood without her having to say so that she'd prefer to keep private things private. But he wanted to, and as he lifted his gaze, he saw by the flush in her cheeks that she understood.

"Thirty minutes," he said, his voice husky. "Give me thirty minutes to finish the duty rounds and we can be out of here."

She laughed softly. "I spent three hours getting ready for one hour and a few glasses of champagne?"

"I didn't say the night was over."

Her lips fell open as the song ended and he released her. From the moment she'd said yes to this trip, something had changed between them. Once they left the hotel, it would just be the two of them for the rest of the night. He couldn't think past that. For once, he was going to do as she suggested. He was going to lay down all his burdens. And in the morning, he'd decide which ones he would pick up again.

Esme had been nervous about the cocktail party, but that was nothing compared to how she felt now, after Stephen's last words.

The night wasn't over.

They sped through the Paris evening, the soft part of the day where the world seemed washed in pinks and violets. Stephen said nothing, but his fingers were twined with hers on the leather seat of the car's interior. Esme was so aware of him, of herself, that her breasts tingled against the silk of her dress and her stomach fluttered with nerves—anticipation, surely, as well as hesitation, because without saying so, she knew tonight her relationship with Stephen was going to change.

She wanted him. Wanted him so much she ached with it.

When they finally arrived at his building, he held out his hand and helped her out of the car, then let his palm rest on the hollow of her back, a warm, electric touch that skittered over her nerve endings and gave her goose bumps as the silk dress slid over her skin. The underwear Patrice had given her to wear—Aurora lingerie, naturally—was so tiny it was almost as if she weren't wearing any at all. The seductive slide of the fabric over her hypersensitive skin only added to her arousal—and Stephen hadn't even touched her yet. Not really.

But he was going to. She knew it as surely as she knew she was ready for him.

The flat was dark, and Stephen reached for a light switch, but she stayed his hand with her own. Twilight shimmered through the windows, lighting the flat intimately. Esme put down her clutch on a small table and turned to face him, shocked and thrilled by the naked yearning on his face.

She'd been dying to touch him for hours. The tension crackled, snapping between them like an arc of electricity. Attraction. Need. Desire. The fire in his eyes burned as brightly as hers, and in one breathtaking moment he gathered her in his arms and did what she'd been dying for all evening: kissed her silly.

The air between them had been thick like thunderclouds and opened up in a downpour of passion. After the first initial clash of lips and tongues he pulled away, but her hands yanked him back in. She followed his mouth with her own, nipping at his lower lip, and her hands went to his shirt, fumbling with the buttons.

They might be on the verge of making a huge mistake, but she was past caring. Not when her need for him was this sharp. And God, what a revelation. She felt so…alive. He made her feel so sexy and desirable, something that had been missing from her life for far too long.

His shirt gaped open and she ran her hands over his hard chest. He tangled his fingers in her hair and slid his hot mouth down the curve of her neck, making her gasp with pleasure. In one quick motion, he slid his hands down to cup her bottom, then lifted her and deposited her on the edge of the dining table.

"Esme," he growled, sliding his hands into her hair, holding her head steady as he kissed her again.

The slim column of her dress was restrictive, so she reached back to try to undo the zipper. Once Stephen realized what she was doing, he covered her fingers with his and slid the zipper to her waist. She shimmied out of the bodice of the gown, felt the cool air on her breasts as he flicked open the clasp on the tiny bra.

"I love your freckles," he whispered, sliding his mouth down her neck again, bending to her and tasting her sensitive skin. She could hardly breathe and leaned back, bracing herself on her hands as she opened for his touch.

But it wasn't enough. Only moments later he pulled her to her feet, and the emerald silk fell to the floor in a luxurious heap, leaving her standing in nothing but a barely-there thong and the stilettos Patrice had slipped onto her feet.

Stephen stared, and then he swore. The words were possibly the most erotic thing she'd heard in her life. She, Esme Flanagan, had reduced the great Stephen Pemberton to near speechlessness. The hunger in his eyes was so thrilling she thought she might melt from the heat of it.

They had to slow down. Make it good and not just fast. Especially if this was their one and only night. Nothing had changed. She just didn't care about the issues as much as she wanted him.

"Es," he whispered, more than a little awe in his voice. "Are you sure?"

She met his gaze with her own as she spoke her truth. "I've never been more sure of anything in my life."

"Es," he said again, the import of what she'd just admitted settling over them both.

"Don't think," she whispered, stepping toward him. "Don't talk if that's going to ruin what this is. Just let it be, if it's what you want." She swallowed. "If I'm what you want."

"I'm not the kind to make rash decisions. Every move I make is precisely thought out with cool calculation. But there's nothing cool between you and me, Es. It's a five-alarm fire burning out of control. But I want it. I want you."

"Just for tonight," she murmured, stepping closer to him. "I want to stop thinking, stop analyzing. I want to feel instead, and I want to feel you. I've waited so long, Stephen."

She reached for him, running her fingertips along his chest while his breath stalled. Her nails marked his skin lightly, and she was close enough now that her breasts rubbed against him, the feel of skin on skin so incredibly perfect. He caught her hand with his and kissed her fingers, then met her gaze. "Esme, I don't have protection. I can't…we can't…"

Esme traced her other hand over his face. "I'm on birth control."

Stephen swept her up into his arms and into his bedroom, where he laid her down on the soft duvet. She looked up, watched as he took off his tuxedo trousers and then his boxer briefs.

And when he joined her on the bed, she stopped thinking altogether, and gave herself over to the sensations of being his lover.

CHAPTER TEN

ESME ROLLED OVER in the bed and found the other side empty, but there was a dent in the pillow next to her. She'd slept here, in Stephen's bed. They'd made love again in the middle of the night, slower that time, and Esme had eventually fallen into a deep, satisfied sleep.

Water ran in the bathroom… Stephen's shower. For a moment she considered slipping beneath the hot spray with him, but in the light of day common sense…caution… reared its ugly head.

What on earth had they been thinking last night?

She needed to get up. Go back to her room, have a shower, and change her clothes. If she hurried, she could be dressed and ready for the day before he came out of his bathroom.

Except she didn't exactly want to run, even though she was afraid of what this meant for their…relationship. She didn't know how to feel. It had been the most amazing night of her life—and she included her wedding day in that assessment—but the fairy tale was over. Besides, if Stephen had wanted her to share his shower, he would have awakened her. He was probably just as anxious for her to be on her way as she was. They'd got caught up in the moment, that was all. Wasn't it?

Oh, God. This was going to be so awkward.

She scrambled out of bed, belatedly realizing she was stark naked. She moved quickly, trying to find her underwear. Nothing. Her dress and bra were probably still by the dining table. And her panties…

Stephen appeared at the door of the bathroom, where he stood wearing nothing but a thick, white towel. Her mouth literally watered at the sight of him, but she pushed the reaction aside.

A smile crawled up his cheek. "Looking for this?" he offered. The tiny string of the thong was looped over his finger.

She snatched up the sheet from the bed and held it over herself. Stephen burst out laughing, the sound so foreign and wonderful she couldn't stop the shy smile that curved her lips.

"You don't need to be embarrassed," he said gently, coming into the bedroom.

She avoided his gaze, wondering how to gracefully exit to her own room and the clothing that awaited there. "This is very new territory for me, that's all."

"I'm glad. For me, too."

She wondered if it was, really. He was a rich, handsome man. But then, she rather thought he meant it. The Stephen she knew wasn't the kind to indulge in random hookups. Instead he'd practically come right out and admitted he was lonely.

She couldn't seem to make herself go to the door, but she couldn't stand around in a sheet all day, either. "We, uh, might have got carried away last night."

He came closer. "Do you have regrets?"

She could say yes and this would all end now. One glorious night to tuck away in the memory banks. But the truth was, she didn't regret it. How could she when it had been perfect? The problem was it was so perfect it scared the daylights out of her. She had zero idea where to go from here.

"No," she whispered. "Do you?"

He shook his head. "I don't. I probably should. You and I...we go back too far for this to be a hookup. And if it's not a hookup..."

More panic cramped her lungs and made her head light. "What are you suggesting...that we start dating or something?"

She realized belatedly that she'd made it sound like a preposterous idea, which perhaps it was, but she didn't mean to sound so harsh. "Stephen, what I mean is—"

He went to a wardrobe, opened the door, and pulled out a shirt. "You know, this is very strange for me. All of my life, people have gotten close to me for what I could do for them. Sometimes it was just to be seen with me. Not just for the title—titles aren't as big a deal now as they were a century ago—but because of Aurora and all the money. But you don't want anything from me. Not even what I want to give you. I don't know if I should be insulted or relieved."

"Not insulted. Please, Stephen, don't think that." Ugh, they were going to have to have a whole discussion about it, weren't they? How could they not, after what had transpired last night? She'd been a willing participant...more than willing. There'd been a sense that they'd been heading in that direction all along. But now they had to deal with it. Just not right this minute.

"We need to talk," she admitted, shoving her hair back from her face. "But please...let me go for now. I need a shower, and clean clothes, and not to do this while dressed in...in a sheet."

He dropped the towel and gave her one delicious look at his backside before pulling on a pair of boxers.

The fact that his dark eyes now held what she interpreted as hurt made her feel guilty. But that was ridiculous, wasn't it? She couldn't possibly have the power to hurt him. She tried to relax a little. "I'll be back, okay? I just really need to clean up and get my bearings again. Last night was…" She trailed off, unsure of how to finish her sentence. Incredible? Absolutely. Unbelievable? In more ways than one. But it was really just a lot. She was feeling quite overwhelmed.

"Okay," he said, but she saw a muscle tick in his jaw. He wasn't as chill about this as the single word let on.

Esme slipped out of the room, leaving him behind, then shut the door as quietly as possible before hurrying across the hall. She swallowed against a lump in her throat. The morning after should have been lazy and sweet, with kisses before reluctantly tearing herself away from his arms. Instead, all she could see was expectation. Expectation to be someone she wasn't, to fit into his world if they took this beyond last night. And she had no idea how to explain it to him. She just knew she had to, because he deserved better.

Perhaps she needed to have a little faith in him. It was just hard when her faith and trust had been missing for years.

She took a quick shower, dressed and found Stephen in the kitchen, slicing fruit on a heavy cutting board.

"Hi," she said, feeling strangely shy. When she'd left he'd been in boxers, sitting on the bed where they'd been as intimate as two people could possibly be. It was quite different walking into a kitchen, seeing him dressed in trousers and a button-down, a knife in his hand and a pile of pineapple to one side.

"Feeling better?" he asked, looking over at her, a small smile on his face.

"Feeling more put together, anyway," she admitted, stepping closer.

"I made some breakfast for us. Sliced fruit, yogurt, and croissants. And coffee."

It looked delicious. "Sit down," he invited, leading her to the table. "Get some caffeine into you, and some food. You didn't even eat last night. You must be starving."

It was strange enough that the Earl of Chatsworth was waiting on one of the staff. But even if he hadn't had the title, being waited on was not something Esme had ever been familiar with. Evan had always just assumed that she would be the one to do those little things. He'd taken her nurturing side for granted, she realized, marveling as Stephen placed a steaming cup of coffee before her. As he went back to finish putting together their meal, she thought of how Evan had always been charming but somehow lacking in substance. Stephen, on the other hand, could be charming, could be a grouch, but he had layers that made him a complicated, caring man.

And she really had to stop comparing him to Evan. It was just that it was hard, because up until now, Evan had been her relationship yardstick.

"Breakfast is served," he said, bringing her a plate. There was a small bowl to one side with yogurt, artfully arranged fruit, and a flaky croissant. He returned with the butter dish and a jar of preserves.

"It looks wonderful," she said, still touched by his thoughtfulness. And he wasn't wrong. She was starving. Last night food had been the last thing on her mind.

She broke off a piece of pastry, buttered it, and added a dollop of jam. Flavor exploded on her tongue. A sip of the coffee proved to be hot and strong. Delicious. "You're spoiling me," she murmured. "And I don't deserve it."

"I disagree." He put down his cup and faced her. "Es, I understand morning-after jitters. Sex changes things. But I'm still me."

"Well, you're not exactly you. I mean, you've changed over the last week."

"How so?"

She popped another piece of croissant into her mouth. "Well, you've unclenched."

He laughed, the sound rich and happy. "I suppose. And I'll probably re-clench when I have to come back full-time and face all my responsibilities."

The reminder these few weeks were temporary deflated the mood, and Esme picked at her plate. "You don't have to, you know. Not if you've discovered some things that make you happier."

He reached across the table for her hand and twined his fingers with hers. "Like you, perhaps?"

Heat rushed up her face. "That's not what I meant—"

"But you are a big part of why I've relaxed. You know it's true."

"Yes, but I live and work back home. And you just pop in from time to time. Our lives are not even in the same country." Even as she said it, though, her hand stayed twined with his.

"Esme, last night…"

Here it comes. He was going to let her down easy, explain all the reasons why he cared for her, but they couldn't have a repeat of last night. She agreed with it all, so why did knowing what was coming cause a hollow pit in her stomach?

"Last night was…really good." He tightened his fingers, and when she looked into his eyes she was surprised to see a flicker of…could that be vulnerability? It seemed impossible. Stephen didn't do vulnerable. But there was an uncertainty there, an openness she hadn't expected. "I just mean…not just the sex, though that was pretty fantastic." His cheeks grew ruddy and she added embarrassment to her list of surprising emotions from Stephen. "But you… I don't trust many people in the world, but you've known me longer than almost anyone. That made it…special."

She gave a small laugh, and admitted, "I don't know what to say."

"I know. But you should know, Esme, that being with you…"

"For me, too," she whispered. "And it kind of scares me to death."

They'd both forgotten about the lovely meal he'd prepared as they stared at each other, linked by their joined hands. Uncertainty swam in Esme's belly. This couldn't go anywhere, couldn't end well, could it? So why hadn't she got up from the table and moved away? Why had she just admitted her feelings…or at least one of the many feelings rushing through her right now?

Because it was Stephen. And she trusted him, too. Regardless of money or status or expectation. He was just… different.

"You should know," she began softly, "that I haven't really dated much since my divorce. Leaving Evan was a big act of defiance for me, but that doesn't mean I don't have scars. I do. As hard as I try to overcome them, they never quite go away."

His dark gaze hardened. "He didn't treat you right." After a beat he asked, "Physically?"

"No," she answered, shaking her head. "No, he never hit me. But he put me down a lot. I never felt good enough.

I was always too fat, too thin, my hair was wrong, my clothes were wrong…or we never had enough money, or I didn't make him what he wanted to eat…"

Stephen swore.

She smiled. "Precisely. But I never stood up for myself, either. If he said I was overweight, I tried a new diet. If he didn't like dinner, I'd make something else."

"He could have made his own dinner," Stephen interrupted.

"Absolutely. But when your self-esteem is in the toilet, your brain doesn't work that way. I was not as strong as I should have been. But to everyone, we looked like the perfect couple. When I walked away, people kept telling me I was crazy." She sighed and looked up at him. "Even my mother. The only people who know what it was really like are my best friend, Phoebe, and now you. And I've only told you because you say you trust me and last night things changed between us."

"You don't think I…" He let the word hang.

"Of course not. At least, I don't think you'd mean to," she said gently, rubbing her thumb over his hand. "But if we started seeing each other… The world you live in, it's so visible. It's filled with beautiful people, and I would feel the burden of that expectation to be perfect. Maybe you wouldn't impose it, but you know perfectly well that I'd be under a microscope. I'm going to use the biggest cliché in the world, but it's really true. It's not you. Any woman would be lucky to be with you. It's me. I don't think I'm up to this."

Silence fell between them. Then Stephen spoke into the awkward pause.

"I'm so sorry that happened to you, Esme. You deserved so much better."

It was the last thing she expected him to say. She'd

expected him to say that it wouldn't be that way, all the empty reassurances and platitudes that changed nothing. Instead, he simply empathized with her, and the fact that he believed, cared, and acknowledged her issues meant so much.

She could fall for this Stephen very easily.

She pulled her hand away. "It is what it is, as Mum likes to say. I've worked really hard the last few years to overcome some of my issues. It wouldn't be smart to put myself in the kind of environment that would challenge all of that hard work."

"Of course not." He pulled his hand back, but his gaze never left hers. "And yet…there is something between us. Something more than childhood friends. Esme, I haven't had that kind of chemistry—"

She got up from the table abruptly. "Can we perhaps talk about this later? I'm still trying to sort it all out in my mind."

He nodded. "Don't go. Finish your breakfast." Then he crossed his heart. "I promise I won't bring up the fantastic sex we had last night."

She snorted out a laugh, she couldn't help it. He looked positively boyish. If only the paparazzi caught him like this, instead of always looking so severe…

But the thought sobered her quickly enough. She imagined dating him and being caught on camera. What would they say about her, where she came from, what she looked like? Just the thought of that kind of scrutiny made her chest cramp with anxiety. Oh, why couldn't he just be… normal?

She sat back down, stabbed a grape with her fork. "Only because I'm hungry."

Stephen smiled, but within seconds he was serious

again. "Es, would it really be so bad, being with me? You know me, you know my family. I'd at least like to give us a chance."

She swallowed the grape, her emotions a turmoil inside her. She wanted to…oh, how she wanted to. Last night with Stephen had been amazing. She'd laughed more this past week, felt more alive…but a few weeks in the summer was not the same as a serious relationship. "I don't think I'm ready for a relationship," she admitted softly. "Not even with you, Stephen. I like you. I trust you more than I trust any man, because I've known you longer. But a relationship… I'm not up to that. I'm sorry."

He nodded, disappointment etched on his features. "Me, too. And that's it for me, too, you know. I gave up on relationships. My trust level was near zero. But you… We have history together." He swallowed, his throat bobbing. "Thank you. For being honest. Even if the answer isn't what I wanted."

But had she been honest? Only partially. The other part of her wanted to ignore the past, ignore her problems. She'd had a crush on him as a boy but now that he was a man? She could see herself falling in love so easily—and could see herself getting her heart broken just as easily.

"You're a good man, Stephen."

"I'm not so sure."

"You are. Maybe you just need to give people a break." She met his gaze. "Stop expecting them to let you down like Bridget did." She leaned forward, peered into his eyes a little closer. "Like your dad did."

Stephen pushed his plate aside. "Yeah. I'm having trouble with the memorial in my mind. If my mother could forgive him, why can't I?"

"Because our childhood heroes are on pedestals," she

whispered. Little did he know that he was *her* childhood hero. And he was up on that pedestal, too. She refused to believe he would ever disappoint her, though. He had far too much integrity. "What your dad did hurt you, but you would never do what he did. That's why you can't understand it, and why it makes you angry."

He nodded. "And I can't change it. It certainly isn't Anemone's fault."

Stephen rose from the table and began collecting their dishes. "Now," he said, his voice a bit brighter, "let's leave all this heaviness behind. What would you like to do today?"

He was laying Paris at her feet. What would he say if she wanted to do the most stereotypical things possible? She'd been to the city a handful of times, but Evan had always insisted the touristy stuff was too "pedestrian."

"I'd like coffee at an outdoor café. I'd like to walk the Champs d'Elysées and see the Eiffel Tower."

He smiled at her. "Consider it done."

"You don't mind?"

He shrugged. "Why on earth would I mind?"

That was it. She really had to stop painting him with Evan's brush.

"You got breakfast. I'll tidy up and get ready, then. You're sure it's okay? You don't have to go into work today?"

"Work can wait," he answered, picking up his empty plate. "As someone told me recently, the world won't end if I don't handle everything myself."

She watched him put his plate in the sink and gave a little sigh. She'd told him she wasn't up for a relationship, but this certainly felt like the beginnings of one. Maybe they weren't spending the morning in bed, but they were going to roam through Paris together. It certainly felt...couple-y.

Tomorrow they'd be back in England. Would it be so bad to pretend for one more day?

CHAPTER ELEVEN

STEPHEN HAD NEVER really played tourist in Paris. He'd become acquainted with the city when he was a small child, and it had become a second home. But seeing it through Esme's eyes was something special.

She was something special. And it wasn't just the fireworks from last night, though they'd been spectacular. It was how he felt just being in the same space as her. Calmer. Happier. Definitely less stressed. The weight of the world wasn't quite so heavy when she smiled at him.

Now they'd stopped at a small café just as she'd wanted, sipping on small cups of espresso and nibbling on macarons and madeleines.

Esme let out a satisfied sigh and turned her face up to the early afternoon sunshine. "This has been the most perfect day."

"I'm glad." He popped the rest of a lemon and lavender macaron in his mouth, washing it down with a swallow of the strong coffee. "Though I can't believe you wanted to take the stairs at the tower."

She grinned at him, and it was like he was hit with a ray of sunshine. "You kept up. Well done."

And they'd walked along the Champs d'Elysées, just as she'd wanted. When he would have suggested a sensible lunch, she'd declared that it was dessert first day.

On the way back to the flat, he was going to take her shopping. She couldn't come to Paris and not shop a little.

Their coffees were refilled, and they were chatting about the memorial garden plans when his phone buzzed. A quick check showed it was from Maman. He scrolled through, his frown deepening. He was being summoned to a family dinner at Christophe and Sophie's. No excuses. Everyone was going to be there. Oh, and Esme was very welcome to join. It was a family dinner but casual.

Reading between the lines, there was something Maman wasn't saying. Tension settled across his brow. Could they not go a month without having some sort of family announcement?

"What is it? You look like you got bad news."

"Not bad news exactly. More of a summons." He shrugged. "Maman messaged to say the family is getting together at Christophe's tonight and attendance is mandatory."

Esme chuckled, and he sent her a dark look. "Okay," she relented, still chuckling. "I shouldn't laugh at you getting a summons from your mother."

He smiled reluctantly. "I might be the earl, but Maman is the head of the family. And it might seem like a summons, but the truth is, we'd all go to the ends of the earth for her."

"Like I would for my mum," she murmured.

"Exactly." Fondness for both their mothers flooded his heart. "I might not understand all her choices, but I love her."

"Of course you do. That's why it's so hard." She reached over and put her soft hand on top of his briefly, then slid it away. "Anyway, don't worry about me. I'll be fine this evening."

"The invitation is also extended to you."

"Oh." Her eyes widened. "Oh."

Going to a family dinner…would it seem as if they were a couple? Did he want them to be? Or would it be something more like catching up? Esme wasn't exactly a stranger, at least not to his siblings.

"I understand if you feel like it's walking into the lion's den. I can make your excuses."

She twisted a macaron, separating the top from the bottom. "I'm assuming they know I was your plus-one last night."

"Maman does. And the rest probably do by now as well. But guess what? We managed to avoid being in the papers or online, thanks to your fashionably late arrival." He smiled, hoping his words would relax her a little. Instead, her lips tightened, and she fiddled with her napkin. "Esme? What is it?"

"I don't know. It just feels like…well, sneaking around isn't any way to live. And it reminds me that last night was a onetime thing but going in separate cars and hiding away isn't really a strategy for managing the press."

She was right. And he truly understood her aversion to the public eye, especially after what she'd told him about her history. Which left them exactly where they were before last night's party, with one glaring exception: they'd made love. And it had rocked his world.

"Maybe," he said gently, reaching for her hand, "we can take this day by day. No commitments, no expectations."

She twined her fingers with his. "I'd like that," she whispered. "I'd like that very much."

Relief rushed through him. And while he wanted her to go with him tonight, he knew he couldn't push. His family was a lot. He and Es were at a tenuous place. "And if you don't want to go tonight, I understand. Truly."

To his surprise, Esme lifted her chin. "Well, if I'm to

go, I can't wear this." She looked down at her plain trousers and blouse. "I'll have to change."

"Let's do one better. Let's go shopping. We have time. Time for…lots of things."

She didn't miss his meaning as her gaze clung to his and her cheeks pinkened. If they were going to take things day by day, he'd have to make sure each day was something special.

Esme put the finishing touches to her hair and makeup and ran her hands over her new dress. The navy linen held its shape, narrowing in a V-necked bodice and then falling to the tops of her knees in flat but feminine ruffles that gave the conservative cut a hint of whimsy. Neutral heels cushioned her feet, and she'd kept her makeup light and fresh. She didn't want to be too obvious, but wanted to look nice. Like she fit in. Taking a final, deep breath, she stepped out of her room and went to find Stephen.

He was waiting in the living room, standing by the window and looking out over the city. At the sound of her heels, he turned. "Wow. You look gorgeous. I know better than to kiss you and ruin your lipstick, though."

"I'd rather have the kiss," she answered, her stomach trembling with nerves both about the dinner and about kissing him. "I can fix lipstick."

"And that is what I like about you," he replied, dropping a light kiss in her lips.

They hopped in a hired car and made the trip to Christophe and Sophie's home in the sixteenth arrondissement, which made Esme goggle when she first saw it. Real estate in this part of the city had to be astronomical, and they'd chosen a house with a garden. It was like a little bit of heaven right in the city, and Esme couldn't keep her head from moving to and fro, taking in the lush grass, shrubs, and flowers that offered a little haven of privacy around the venerable home.

"They picked here because of the children," Stephen explained as they made their way to the front door. "There's just the one, now, but they want a family."

"It's stunning."

The door was answered by Sophie herself, holding the baby in her arms, a tiny package dressed in a pink frilly dress. She was still awake and looking around at everyone with wide brown eyes.

Introductions were made and drinks offered in a gorgeous room that had French doors overlooking the back garden. Esme had just accepted a glass of wine when Charlotte and Jacob arrived. Charlotte was animated and chatty while Jacob held back and just set adoring eyes on his wife. Charlotte was a bit intimidating. Like Stephen, she seemed to be rather Type A. But when she looked at her husband, her face softened. Esme liked that about her.

Then came Bella and Burke. Bella was CEO of Aurora but brought a relaxed vibe with her, and Burke was utterly charming. He and Will had gone to school together and Burke was, in addition to being a top cardiac doctor, Viscount Downham. More wine was poured, Aurora showed up at the same time as Will and Gabi, and the noise level in the house rose.

"Your family is huge."

"Bigger now with all the partners. And children." Stephen smiled at her. "And there's still Annie and Phillipe. You'll meet them soon, I hope."

Bella approached with a bottle of wine. "You look like you need a top-up, Esme," she said, pouring a bit more into Esme's glass. "And I love your dress. It really suits you. That cut is fabulous, and the navy highlights your skin."

"This is my cue," Stephen said dryly. "I deal with dollars, not hemlines."

Bella waved him away, then turned to Esme. "I'm not going to mince words, Esme. We're all so pleased you're here."

Her mouth fell open. "You are?"

Bella laughed and nodded. "Are you kidding? Stephen has been a bear for the past few years. He was horrible to Gabi after she left him at the altar. Which is sort of understandable, really, but he's just been so…dour." She made a face. "He's always been the serious one, but after Bridget, he seemed to be more…brittle. But one look at him tonight…he's relaxed and smiling and not just going through the motions. If spending time with you is the cause, we're all indebted to you."

Esme took a sip of her wine, partly to cover her face which had to be blushing now. But she was also feeling rather defensive on Stephen's behalf. "Oh, well… I guess he's had a lot to deal with since your dad died. I'm sure he doesn't mean to be…"

"Crabby? Grouchy? Bossy?"

Esme wasn't sure how much she should say, but she remembered Evan always schooling her to be bland and polite. That just wasn't her. She spoke her mind. "It can't be easy becoming the head of the family overnight, with the estate and the company to worry about." She tempered her words with, "If he's more relaxed, then I'm so glad. He's a good man."

"Oh, you've got it bad," Bella said, a smile lighting her face.

"Not at all," Esme lied. "But we've been friends a long time. I care about him."

There was a pause as they both took a drink of their wine. Then Bella sighed and put a hand on Esme's arm.

"Would it be okay if I offered some advice? It can be hard being a part of this family, in the spotlight and knowing that strangers are going to delight in pointing out your flaws. Or taking something utterly normal and making it sound like a detriment." She pointed to her shoulders. "I stopped hiding my scars. I stopped giving away the power to own my own story. But I had Burke by my side. If you and Stephen do try to make a go of it, please remember that he'll be beside you. Don't let them own your story, Esme. Live it and let the others be damned." She gave a brisk nod.

"It's reassuring knowing you don't all hate me."

"How could we? We all knew you when we were little. You were always bright and fun. Stephen needs that in his life. And you're right, he's a good man. He'll be good to you, you know. He feels things very deeply, so if he says he loves you, you can believe it's true."

Esme's cheeks heated again. "Oh, there's nothing like that." Maybe there was for her, but she was certain Stephen wasn't in love with her. Care? For sure. And there was no denying their chemistry was off the charts. But love? Everything she knew about the Stephen of today was that he had closed himself off to that particular emotion.

"Hmm. Maybe. Now come on, Sophie was a smart new mum and had dinner catered. I think everything has arrived."

Esme followed Bella into the state-of-the-art kitchen and discovered Charlotte, Gabi, Sophie and Aurora all there, unpacking delicious-smelling containers. Sophie was dispatched to the dining room with plates and flatware, while Christophe fed the baby a bottle and the men took over uncorking and pouring wine. Before long they were all settled at the long table in the dining room, with scrumptious smells wafting up from the serving dishes.

Will stood up. "Attention, loud family!"

All the chatter ceased, and their eyes turned to Will.

"Sophie, do you have Annie on FaceTime?"

Sophie nodded and propped up her tablet. "Say hi, Annie!"

Annie and Phillipe waved from their home in Grasse.

Will cleared his throat. "Thank you to Sophie and Christophe for hosting tonight's dinner."

Christophe's eyes sparkled. "No problem. It saved me having to pack a massive diaper bag to cart to someone else's house, while inevitably forgetting some crucial item."

Everyone chuckled.

"And thank you all for coming. We haven't had a family dinner in such a long time, and with Stephen here this week, it felt like the perfect time. We're just missing Annie and Phillipe."

"We'll see you all in October at the wedding," Annie said, her voice tinny from the tablet speakers.

"Anyway, we really wanted you all here because we wanted to let you know that grandchild number three is on the way."

A chorus of congratulations rose from the table. Esme smiled, delighted that the family was so happy but feeling distinctly out of place, being included in something that was so personal.

"How're you feeling?" Charlotte asked.

Gabi shrugged. "Mostly good. A little morning sickness hanging on, but it's rare." She flashed a quick smile. "Will waits on me hand and foot."

"As he should," decreed Aurora. "Oh, congratulations, both of you." She went forward to kiss Gabi's cheek and then Will's. "I'm delighted."

"Now Bella and Burke just need to up their game," Christophe said.

Esme smiled at the banter, loving how normal the Pembertons were despite the opulent trappings of their lives. Thankfully, no one mentioned Stephen's single status. She wondered what it would be like to carry Stephen's child. Would he be a doting father? Practical? Happy? She'd wanted children with Evan, but he'd always wanted to wait. But wasn't this getting way ahead of herself? She and Stephen weren't even in a relationship. They'd spent one night together, that was all.

Aurora also passed by and put a hand on Esme's arm. "Esme, I missed you in the kitchen, but it's good to see you again. And to see Stephen so…unclenched."

Esme choked out a laugh and Aurora treated her to a sideways smile. "I do know my children," she said, giving Esme a wink.

"I told her the same thing, Maman." Bella laughed beside her.

So much laughter. And chatter. The food was delicious, the wine perfect, and for a few blissful minutes, she found herself with a sleeping baby in her arms. It awakened all the nesting urges she'd pushed down over the years, and she swallowed against a tightening in her throat. She still wanted children, and she was already thirty-four. She cuddled the blanketed bundle close, loving the baby smell that rose from the soft cap of curls so much like Christophe's.

By eleven they'd all departed, and Stephen and Esme were back in a cab on their way home. Well, Stephen's home. Not hers.

"Tonight wasn't too much, was it?"

It had been fine. More than fine. Not a single member of his family had expressed an issue with her presence. "Everyone seemed happy you were a little more chill than normal."

"See? I told you. Ogre. I must make a point to be grouchier. I have a reputation to uphold."

She laughed.

"Do you want to go out for a nightcap? Or head to the flat?"

"To the flat, I think," she replied. "I'm actually really tired. It's been a long day, with a lot going on."

They arrived at his building and got out of the cab and into the hush of the night. Her heels clacked on the pavement but soon they were inside and going up the elevator to his floor. When they reached his door, she let out a long sigh. She was reluctant for her magical time in Paris to end. But she needed sleep, too.

"Let me help you get off your feet." He swept her up in his arms, and she curled into his embrace.

"Stephen?"

"Hmm?" He kicked off his shoes, shut the door, and started walking toward the bedroom. Her heart fluttered. Was he taking her to her room, or his?

"Everyone keeps saying you were so grumpy before. That you didn't smile as much. And, I mean, I kind of saw that when you first came home."

He stopped in the doorway to his bedroom, then set her down. He took her hand and led her to the bed, sat, and patted the mattress beside him.

"Es," he began, "it's true. Sometimes I've been a jerk. Part of it was trying to protect the people I love from getting hurt like I was. But a lot of it came from me being unhappy and dissatisfied. It's not that you've changed me, really. It's that when I'm with you, I'm happy, so the other stuff fades away. I'm not proud of all my actions in the last two years. But you…you don't just make me happy. You make me want to do better."

"Oh," she said, trying not to cry at the sweet words.

"I know we're taking this a day at a time, and I know I'm not usually one to talk about my feelings, but I think you should know that."

She reached up and wrapped her arms around him. And as his arms tightened around her, she prayed she would be strong enough to never let him down. And yet she was so unsure about everything. Where did they go from here? Because as delightful as this forty-eight-hour interlude had been, tomorrow it was back to the real world, where he was the Earl of Chatsworth and she was plain Esme Flanagan. He didn't want love and she refused to settle. And there was only so long they could stick their heads in the sand and avoid dealing with all of it.

The return across the Channel seemed anticlimactic somehow. Stephen held Esme's bag as they made their way through customs and to the hired car, and they were both quiet on the drive from Gatwick. Reality was back with a slap. The festival was tomorrow, and Stephen only had a few days after that before he was scheduled to return to Paris. It would mean leaving Esme, just when things were developing between them. He would miss her. But then, if he really wanted to avoid an emotional entanglement, leaving was the best thing. But was that what he wanted?

He dropped her off at her flat, walking her to the door and carrying her overnight bag and the garment bag containing the emerald silk, which he'd insisted she keep. Her closed-off expression kept him from kissing her goodbye. Well, almost. He leaned in and dropped a kiss on the crest of her cheek. "I'll see you later?" he murmured.

She nodded. "Let me unpack and check on Mum. I'll come over later and…and catch up on work."

Right. Because she was the housekeeper, maid and cook, all in one. And he was lord of the manor. He wondered if she was reminding him as some sort of defense mechanism. She'd been reserved since this morning when they'd awakened in his bed.

She was likely as terrified as he was.

Back at the manor, Stephen stepped outside into the garden and took a look at the progress. It would be weeks before all the features and plants would be installed, but the shape of it was clear. It was an odd moment, two years after Cedric's death, to realize that his father was truly gone. But there was a heavy sense of finality in the pit of Stephen's stomach.

Cedric Pemberton was gone and with him, his mistakes and flaws. There was no need to carry them into the future, for they served no purpose. Stephen let out a massive sigh and rubbed his hand over his stinging eyes.

He would not let the good memories be tainted. Instead, he looked over the garden and fields beyond and let forgiveness into his heart. Who was he to blame his father for being…human? Lord knew Stephen had made his share of mistakes.

He went back inside and to the library, where he sat at the desk and pulled out the little box with the pocket watch again. He stared at it for long minutes, turning it over in his hand, the cool gold warming from his touch. For generations, the owner of the watch had sat in this very room, making decisions for the estate and for the Pemberton family. The gravity of that settled heavily on his shoulders, but it wasn't a burden, exactly. It was, he realized, the duty to simply do the right thing.

He picked up his phone and called the solicitor, giving him instructions to expedite settling the agreement the family had informally come to with regards to Anemone's inheritance. Christophe's old flat in Paris was family-owned and still vacant; it would become Anemone and

Phillipe's for when they were in Paris. There was a pearl and diamond choker that was Cedric's mother's, as well as a few other mementos that would also become hers. And the money. The five children had all agreed that Anemone should have an equal share. They would each sign over a portion of their inheritance.

Family was family, and that was that.

When his call finished, he sat back in his chair and let out a satisfied breath. And when Esme arrived at the door, carrying a tray of coffee and two cups, he sat forward with a smile.

This was all because of her. She'd been the one to help him start to heal. To help him begin to open his heart again. It was a damned miracle. And she didn't even know it. It occurred to him that it was because she'd always known his heart. And while they'd spent years apart, that heart-to-heart recognition hadn't disappeared.

He was falling in love with her and helpless to stop it. And he couldn't be bothered to try. Because this was Esme.

He trusted her.

"You're back." He got up from the desk and took the tray from her hands, noticing her cheeks turned pink. "Everything okay with your mum?"

Esme nodded. "I think so. The side effects from her last chemo are easing a bit. She's getting ready for her booth at the festival tomorrow."

He lifted his eyebrows as he put down the tray. "She is? Isn't that a lot of work?"

"Tell my mum that. She puts tarts and jam into the contest every year. Marjorie might be the cook here, but Mum can hold her own."

He shook his head. "Now I see where you get your stubbornness." But he smiled. He liked that she wasn't a pushover. Whatever her past with her ex-husband, she'd clearly moved into her own sense of independence. He looked at her closer. "Es, are we okay? You've been so quiet all day."

"Just in my head a bit." Her eyes shuttered a little, closing him out, but he wouldn't press. If she needed time to wrap her head around things, he understood. He'd been less than two weeks and in that time they'd reconnected, slept together, she'd met his family...again. Not as Mrs. Flanagan's daughter, but as his guest.

It was a lot.

"I understand." He poured coffee instead, handing her a cup fixed with a little milk and sugar, the way he'd discovered she liked.

"Things changed between us, Stephen. But I'm still the housekeeper... I think I'm just having difficulty sorting through the dynamics of everything."

"Give it time," he said quietly. "But don't shut me out, Esme. And for God's sake, don't lie to me."

Her gaze warmed a little. "I know that's a tough one for you, after Bridget and Gabi."

He nodded, his jaw tightening. "It is. I'd rather know the truth up-front, even if it isn't what I want to hear."

Esme put down her cup and went to him. "Oh, Stephen, I know that. I'm sorry. I really am in my head right now. Paris was...amazing. But it's all so new and overwhelming, and you're leaving again in a few days, and I guess I'm just trying to protect myself."

Which he also understood. And if she was overwhelmed, she definitely wasn't ready to hear the truth about his feelings.

"Let's just have a quiet dinner tonight and...maybe you can stay? But only if you want to."

She nodded, laying a cool hand on his cheek. "I would like that. I'd like that a lot. If we only have a few more days, I don't want to waste them."

He leaned down and kissed her, a soft, reassuring kiss that still managed to fire his blood and fuel his desire. A few days…yes. But the more time he spent with her, the more he was reconsidering whether being in Paris full-time was where he wanted to be. The first day he'd come back he'd felt the pull of home. Now, with Esme here, the pull was even stronger.

CHAPTER TWELVE

Esme tucked the vacuum away and wondered if Stephen was still in the library. This afternoon he'd put her mind at ease, at least a little. But she was still going back and forth in her head about what she wanted. She hadn't lied. Paris had been amazing, but fairy tales were not day-to-day living. That was done right here, at Chatsworth and in the village. Here, she and Stephen seemed to fit together like peas in a pod. In Paris, though, she was firmly reminded of the life she'd been glad to leave behind.

She wasn't going to let those thoughts ruin the last few days they had together, though, so she stuck her head into the library and said, "How about some dinner?"

"I could eat," Stephen said. "What's in the fridge?"

"I'm not sure. Let's investigate."

What she really wanted to do was pick up where they'd left off, in his arms and tasting his sweet kisses.

Once in the kitchen, she went to the refrigerator and stuck her head in the door. "There's some chicken, some salad greens… I can work with that."

"It's fine with me," he said. "After the feast last night, I could do with something lighter."

She set him about washing greens and cutting up veg for the salad while she sauteed the chicken. She added but-ter, herbs and white wine, whipping up a heavenly-smelling sauce. As it simmered, she made a simple vinaigrette with olive oil and balsamic vinegar, and before long they were sitting at the table, enjoying another meal together.

Stephen took his first bite and sighed. "Esme, this is delicious."

"I've picked up some things after so many years working in the service industry," she said, pouring them each a glass of wine. "There's nothing in the world that butter and a splash of wine can't make better."

He laughed.

They finished the meal and worked together to tidy the kitchen. It felt so natural to her, so right. She imagined what it would be like living together like a normal couple, standing together doing dishes in the evening. There was a rightness to it that settled in her heart. But that was foolish, wasn't it? Here at the manor, there were usually several staff on duty, and she remembered he'd told her he had someone come into his flat in Paris to clean and take on some cooking duties.

"You okay? You've been drying that plate for five minutes." He smiled at her with affection. "Or have you disappeared into your head again?"

"Something like that," she admitted.

He took the plate from her hands, put it away and returned to her. "I have a cure for that," he said.

She couldn't stop the smile that blossomed on her lips. "Oh, do you?"

"Mmm-hmm." He slid closer and clasped his hands at the base of her spine. "I have a few ways to take your mind off troubles. Care to hear them?"

"I'd rather you show me," she admitted.

They abandoned the rest of the dishes as Stephen took her hand and led her from the kitchen, anticipation simmering in her belly. Her footsteps were muffled on the carpet runner on the stairs, halting only when he paused to open the door to his room. Maybe they needed to talk about their relationship, but right now she wanted something more.

Once they were inside, she shut the door and reached for the buttons on his shirt. He held his breath, letting her undress him, his body growing rock-hard beneath her gentle touch. He lifted his hand and touched her hair—God, how she loved the way he looked at her—and reminded herself to be patient, that they had all night.

Once his shirt was off, she reached for her own, undoing the buttons and sliding it off, then slipping out of her bra. In the next breath, she was pressed up against his chest, skin to skin, in heaven.

It blew her mind how she could be so lucky to find the perfect lover in a best friend. But when they finally reached the bed and she fell apart in his arms, she knew she never wanted to let him go. And yet she'd have to, because after thinking all day, she still couldn't see a way to be a part of his world and still be herself.

The next morning the fair opened, and with it the local exhibits from artisans, cooks, and crafters. She asked for the morning off as Mary was determined to enter her wares in the gooseberry categories just as she had for the last twenty-odd years. It meant precious hours away from Stephen, though he'd ended up holing up in the library anyway, working on something or other.

They loaded up Esme's little Renault with boxes of jam, jellies, and tarts that Mary had baked the two days before. Some would be entered for judging, with the rest going on Mary's table to be sold. In addition to the gooseberry items, there were also various chutneys, strawberry preserves, raspberry jelly, pasties, and currant tea cakes. All recipes Mary insisted she'd learned from her mum, and Esme couldn't argue with their success. Every year someone new booked a table with fancy cupcake holders and tons of buttercream-topped goodies, but they came to Mary's table for home-cooked favorites.

No wonder her mum was exhausted.

They arrived at the fairgrounds and Esme looked over at Mary. Her color was still off. "Are you sure you're up to this, Mum?"

"I haven't missed the festival in over twenty years, and I'm not going to let cancer keep me from being here this year." Her mother's voice was firm, and Esme couldn't argue. That determination was so important for her mum's recovery.

"Well, will you let me look after setting up? Why don't you have a cup of tea with the WI ladies?"

"I might do." Mary looked at Esme. "Thank you, Es. You shouldn't have to look after your old mum."

"As if." Esme snorted, tamping down the emotion that swamped her chest. "Besides, you looked after me and I was no picnic."

Mary laughed. "I should help—"

"Don't give it a thought. You wander over in about thirty minutes and I'll have it all ready for you."

Mary nodded as they got out of the car, and with a small wave, headed in the direction of the WI tent and tea.

That concerned Esme more than anything. Her mother had capitulated too easily. It wasn't like her. Worry cascaded through her chest as she watched her mum walk away. What if the chemo wasn't working? What if the cancer came back worse than before?

She grabbed her phone and tapped out a quick text message.

Would it be all right if I took the whole day off? Worried about Mum. Going to set up for her but thought I might stay with her if possible.

The phone disappeared into her back pocket, and she grabbed the first bag of items needed for the table: her mum's "fair cloth" that was really just a cotton red-and-white-checked tablecloth, the stack of little card stock signs written up in her mum's writing with the item and ingredient list, and a little cashbox with a tiny float. She'd set up the table first and then bring up the other items.

She had just sorted the table, two chairs, and put on the tablecloth in the food items tent when a familiar figure came striding toward her, setting her pulse aflutter.

What on earth was Stephen doing here? He wasn't supposed to arrive until later this afternoon, for the judging.

"Hi," he greeted, looking rather delicious in what she supposed was his business casual dress of dark gray trousers, a fine dress shirt open at the throat and rolled to the elbows, and the Italian leather shoes he liked so much.

"Did you get my message?" she asked, unsure of what to say.

"I did. I thought I'd give you a hand. And perhaps…" He bent down and looked into her face. "Perhaps some moral support? Is Mary not doing well?"

She loved how he cared so much. "Maybe I'm worrying for nothing, but she seems so tired, and she's pale. She spent the last two days baking, and I probably should have been here to help her. When we got here I suggested she find a cup of tea and I'd set up and she didn't even argue."

Worry puckered Stephen's eyebrows, and she was relieved that it wasn't just her that was concerned about her mother's uncharacteristic behavior. "Well, let's get her set up."

She tried to ignore the warm feeling that went through her, knowing he'd dropped everything to come help this morning. Instead, she focused on loading his arms and hers with items from the car and carting them back to the table. Once there, Stephen suggested he do the rest of the lugging while she arranged the items. By the time he'd returned with the next load of jams and jellies, she had the table half-full of goodies, as well as the little sign her mum used that quaintly announced *Mrs. Flanagan's Fancies*.

They worked together, stocking the table and then stowing the extra stock beneath the skirting. When it was nearly finished, Mary came around the corner and stopped. "Oh, that looks lovely!"

She had a paper cup with steaming tea in her hand and Esme was glad to see she looked brighter than she had in the car. "It's all set up for you, Mum," she said, pulling out a chair. "You just tell me what you want taken to the contest and I'll deliver it."

Mary looked up at Stephen. "You came to help."

"Of course I did, Mrs. F." He went forward and enveloped her in a rare hug, which made Esme's eyes sting. "Though I haven't had breakfast so I would consider payment in the form of one of those pasties." He pulled back and treated her to a smile. Oh, how irresistible he was when he smiled and the hard edges of his face softened.

Her smile brightened and she tsked at him. "Of course you shall have one." She moved behind the table and made short work of putting a golden-brown pastry in a napkin and then into his hand. "There you go. Better than even Marjorie's, though she'll deny it." Mary sent him a wink.

Stephen took the obligatory bite. "Mmm. Delish, Mrs. F."

Esme watched as her mother blushed. Blushed! It was all she could do to hold back a chuckle.

"Are you all set now, Mum? I put the cash tin just to the side there, see?" Esme showed her where the little cash box was. "And I added the signs and ingredient cards."

"You're a wonder," Mary replied, settling into her chair.

"Oh, it feels good to be out and doing something. I'm not made for idleness."

Esme was going to protest, but Stephen stepped forward instead. "I'm sure," he said sympathetically. "But we all need you to get well, so rest is essential. Don't push yourself too hard, now."

"I won't."

"And I'm here to help, too," Esme said.

Mary looked up in alarm. "But you have to get back to work. I'm fine here, truly."

"Don't be silly," Stephen insisted. "I can manage on my own for a day. Besides, both of you should enjoy the fair." In another hour or so the midway would open up and there would be rides, too. All the vendors would be selling their wares and the good-natured but sometimes cutthroat competitions would begin.

"Shall I take the samples over for the judging?" Esme asked.

"That would be lovely, dear. Thank you."

"I'll help," Stephen offered.

Esme went to work packing the items Mary gave her in a shallow box. Mary hesitated with the last jar, making Esme look up at her.

"Are you sure you know what you're doing, darling?"

There was no sense pretending she didn't understand. "It's okay, Mum. I promise." She kept her voice low so Stephen couldn't hear, though he'd wandered down the aisle in the tent, looking at the other tables. "We're just friends."

"I'm not sure of that. I've never seen him look at anyone like he looks at you. He cares for you. He took you to Paris."

"I care for him, too." She chanced a look over at him to be sure they wouldn't be overheard. "But our friendship is more important. And our lives are too different." She took the final jar and tucked it into the box. "Mum, I know we don't talk about Evan, but he was so critical of me. I'm certain I couldn't handle Stephen's world, living under a microscope. My eyes are open, don't worry."

"I just want you to be happy."

At that, Esme smiled. "Well, I do too!" she said. "Love you. Now sit and enjoy the sunshine while we've got it."

"You two should enjoy the fair, too. You don't have to sit with me."

"What if we take in the events and come to check on you periodically?" That came from Stephen, who'd returned from his wander and caught the last of their conversation—and hopefully nothing earlier.

"I'd enjoy that. And if you happened to find yourself at a curry truck at lunchtime…" Mary's eyes twinkled, and Esme was happy to see it. Maybe she did just need to be out and doing something vital.

Mary took a currant cake and pressed it into Esme's hand. "You probably didn't have breakfast," she said, in a very mom-like way.

"I'm not going to eat all your profits."

"It's one cake. Go, have fun. Stephen, you probably haven't been to the fair in years."

"Not since the last time Esme and I were here, I don't think, Mrs. F. And things have changed a lot since we were kids."

"Indeed," Mary replied, packing a lot of subtext into that one word.

"All right then. Where to first, m'lord?" Esme looked up saucily and then took a bite of her tea cake.

"I think we should scout out the competition," he said, and reached down and took her hand.

Esme wasn't sure what to do. To hold his hand in pub-

lic…too much of a statement. To withdraw…awkward. In
the end she waited until they'd walked a half-dozen steps,
then extricated her hand from his grasp, despite how nice
it felt cushioned in his strong fingers.

Stephen didn't react, but she felt the difference between
them. And it wasn't that he shut her out or became cold.
Instead, the awareness between them ratcheted up to about
a zillion. Because not touching each other did absolutely
nothing to curb the fact that they wanted to.

Stephen couldn't remember when he'd last spent such a
day.

The village fair had changed in some ways, but in others remained the same country fair he remembered as a
child. The Women's Institute had their cakes for sale,
from gorgeous, layered concoctions swirled with icing
and adorned with fresh flowers to the requisite sponge
and the plain but no less delicious lemon drizzle. There
were still the craft tables, but they were augmented by
artisans with blown glass, paintings, and jewelry. There
were even workshops available for both children and
adults, which Esme tried to convince him to try but he
balked. At noon they bought chicken tikka at what Esme
decreed the best curry truck, and took a Styrofoam con-
tainer back to Mary, who was faring well at her table,
chatting and selling her goods at a brisk clip. Stephen and
Esme found a rare empty picnic table with an umbrella
and sat to eat their lunch together.

It was so…normal. So lovely. And he hadn't thought
about work or responsibility once.

Esme smiled up at him and his heart caught.

It was a strange moment to realize he wanted her in
his life forever, but he supposed there was never any real
rhyme or reason to it. One moment, a tantalizing bite of

curried chicken, then next, wham. His heart had pretty much left his body. And it was inconvenient as hell. Esme had made it clear that she wasn't up to an actual relationship. Wasn't that just his luck? He finally, finally found the right woman, but he wasn't the right man for her.

He understood what it was like to be burdened with the weight of expectation, of worrying he was never good enough. But he would never do that to Esme. He loved her just as she was. Could he make her understand that?

The fact remained, he'd gone and fallen in love for the first time since Bridget. And it was exhilarating and scary and so darned wonderful he wasn't sure what to do with it all.

He had no idea how to bridge the gap between them. To compromise. He couldn't change what he was. He was, and always would be, the Earl of Chatsworth as well as Aurora Germain's son. He was responsible for the estate as well as a good chunk of the Aurora, Inc. empire. He could no more walk away from his responsibilities than he could grow wings and fly. But how could he ask her to leave her life behind for him? That was hardly fair.

"You got awfully serious all of a sudden," Esme observed, dabbing her lips with a paper napkin. "Are you all right?"

He smiled. "I am. I was thinking that I spent the whole morning not thinking about work, or the estate, and just focused on relaxing and it was amazing."

She smiled back. "But then you started thinking about work?"

"Exactly," he lied, because she wasn't ready for the truth about his feelings. "Let's check out the rides," he suggested. "The last time I was here, there weren't any. Just Splat the Rat and the usual games."

Esme laughed. "It's changed some. The town's grown,

and for the last few years there's been a traveling funfair that sets up at the same time as our local event. It's brought in nice crowds."

Something else he'd missed in all the busyness of his life. "I'm game if you are."

"Let's check on Mum first, and then you're on."

Mary was managing fine, though Esme made sure to take her a fresh cup of tea. Stephen then led the way to the part of the fairgrounds that housed the small midway and games.

They bought a string of tickets and first headed to the Tilt-a-Whirl, sitting together on the padded seat and holding on as the car spun around in every direction, depending on the angle of the track. Esme made the car spin even faster by leaning into the curve, the sound of her laughter ringing in the air. When they were finished there, they hit The Scrambler, tame but fun, and then she got him into the bumper cars.

There was no sitting together and holding on for this ride. Instead Stephen found himself ensconced in a purple "car" while Esme was in a green one, and a handful of others were in other cars, each person for themselves. Stephen was hesitant until one boy who couldn't have been more than seventeen rammed the side of his car, and then all bets were off. He cranked the wheel and started off, focused on retribution when he was jolted from behind— Esme had snuck up and rear-ended him.

She was still laughing. God, it brought back memories. Back in the day there hadn't been rides, but they'd run through the fair and played games and ate candy floss until they were nearly sick. She'd laughed then, too. He remembered she was always laughing. Until the day he'd said he was going away to school.

That day she'd cried.

He understood the feeling now, because the thought of going back to Paris without her made him feel horribly empty.

"Come on, Stephen! Give it to him!" Esme was cheering him on, and he shook off his thoughts and got back into the game, laughing as everyone bumped everyone else with abandon.

When it was over, she got out of her little car, grabbed his hand and pulled him over to the candy floss stand. In moments he was holding the blue-and-pink spun sugar in his hands, feeling like he was about sixteen years old, running through the fair with the girl he had a crush on.

He took a bite and winced. "My God, that's sweet."

She wrinkled her nose and took a bite of her own. "You could use some sweetening up."

If they were alone he would snag her around the waist and kiss her teasing mouth, but since they were in public, he held back. "I probably could," he admitted. "But this… wow. Good thing I'm not diabetic."

She laughed again, and they started walking among the rides and games. "So, what's next?" she asked. "We still have a few tickets left."

"The Ferris wheel," he said, lifting his chin at the ride that towered over the others. "I know it's slow, but—you're going to think this sounds silly—this village, the estate… it's my home. And at the top of the wheel, I can see so far and feel…"

She stopped and looked up at him. "Your roots."

He nodded, a little choked up that she understood him so well. More and more he was questioning the need to spend so much time in Paris. What if he were here, at Chatsworth, more often?

"You can take the earl out of the county, but you can't take the county out of the earl," she said, jostling him with her shoulder. "Which is as it should be. You should have a connection here."

The connection was more than just geography. He was coming to realize that now. He'd been sent away to school and then to Paris and it had all been to make him a better steward—of the title, the land, and even the company his parents had built. The irony struck him. He'd had to go away to truly appreciate how very tied he was to the place he'd only visited in recent years.

He thought of the Paris flat. It was luxurious, exclusive, beautiful. It had everything he could want. But it wasn't home. And he wondered if that was part of the reason why he never seemed quite settled or content, and why others saw him as…a grump. That wasn't the man he wanted to be. But he was thirty-five. Pretty sure the die had been cast.

They were at the Ferris wheel now. They each handed over their last tickets and got into the seat, waiting while the security bar was locked around them. For a few minutes, they only moved by increments, as the person running the ride stopped to let on more people.

The wheel started to move smoothly, arcing over the top and descending to the ground again. Esme had gone quiet; something had changed between their conversation about home and getting on the ride together. It wasn't even a bad quiet; more like she was waiting, though he wasn't sure for what.

They went around the bottom, starting the incline again, until they got closer to the top. Stephen looked out over the valley and felt a pang in his chest. He loved it here. He always had. He'd been a carefree boy, laughing and smiling. When had all that changed? When he'd gone off to boarding school at thirteen? In university? Taking on increasing responsibility at Aurora? He had laughed more during this visit than he'd had in years.

Esme reached over and took his hand. "It's beautiful, isn't it?"

Beyond the village were green fields, broken by lines of trees and roads. The English countryside was beautiful.

"It is. It's home."

"I'm glad you realize that."

He faced her as they made another turn around. "What does that mean?"

"It means that you've been running. Ever since you left for school, the manor house has only been a place you visit, even if you call it home." She looked out over the fairground, over the fields beyond, and let out a replete sigh. "I'm connected to this place. It's part of me, no matter where I go. But I've stayed because my heart is here. Despite all the bad things."

"Bad things," Stephen echoed, unsure of what she was getting at.

"My dad dying. The bullying when I was older. My failed marriage. Mum's cancer." She shrugged. "There are reminders of the not great things here, certainly. But there are so many good memories, too. My childhood with you. My best friend, Phoebe, whom you've yet to meet. My mum. The way it feels to go into a pub and have them know your standing order. Shopping at the market where you chat with the cashier about whatever the town is buzzing about. Walking to work and smelling the geraniums, unless it's tipping down and you're under an umbrella. Things I would miss if I left. Things I wouldn't find anywhere else."

God, she was the purest, loveliest person he'd ever met. And her description of her life wasn't perfect, and yet somehow seemed idyllic in its simplicity and beauty.

Perhaps it was time to stop running. Stop avoiding what was right in front of him and start running to the life he craved.

He put his hand along her face, leaned over, and touched his lips to hers.

Esme knew she should stop the kiss, but she was helpless to. His lips felt so good on hers, so right. At age six, he'd been her everything. Now, at age thirty-four, he was rapidly moving into that role again, and as much as it terrified her, she couldn't make herself pull away.

Instead, she kissed him back.

He was capable of such tenderness. This kiss was different from their previous ones. Less fevered, less surprising, but with a connection that ran straight to her heart. It was generous, giving. Sweet and loving. And this simple kiss on a Ferris wheel was even more devastating than what had transpired between them in Paris and last night.

Their lovemaking had been fueled by passion. This, though…this was different. She felt herself falling and lacked the will to put on the brakes. Her heart was well and truly involved now.

The wheel stopped, halting them at the top, the seat swinging slightly. Esme finally broke the kiss, then rested her forehead against his. "Stephen," she whispered.

"Don't say it," he said. "Not if you're going to say we can't be together."

She sat back a little so she could meet his gaze. His dark eyes were wide and full of emotion, so much that it frightened her a little, even while deep down she rejoiced in it. It complicated everything, but this thing between them… it was real. Not just a quick tumble, getting each other out of their systems, or even simply satisfying a need.

"I'm falling for you, Esme. I didn't plan it. I know how you feel about my life. But I have to be honest about my feelings. I've spent my whole life not being honest. I've glossed over my emotions, camouflaged them with ambition and this…façade. I'm tired of being that man. I'm not that man with you. With you… I'm who I'm meant to be."

The attendant was letting people off; they moved another increment over the apex, toward the bottom.

"Oh, Stephen…" She thought about her life here, her safe, predictable life. She'd meant everything she'd said only minutes earlier about why she loved it and why it was home. But perhaps there was another way of running away. Perhaps she'd run away from a lot of possibilities, hiding behind her contentment.

She suddenly realized that if she walked away from Stephen now, without trying, she would always regret it.

"I'm scared," she admitted. "Scared of what it would mean to actually be with you. Not as the housekeeper's daughter. Not as an old friend…but *with* you."

"I know that. But we can take it slowly, can't we? There's no need to take out a page in the *Times* or anything."

She laughed. "You're right. Except…you're leaving soon." The knowledge washed over her, killing the flash of excitement she'd felt.

The wheel moved again, then stopped. There were only two seats left before they'd have to get off the ride. Somehow she didn't want to. She wanted to stay on here forever, where nothing could change, and it would just be the two of them.

Stephen held her hand tightly. "Maybe I can stretch things out a little longer, until we see how we feel. I know you have reservations and rightly so. But…what if we miss out on something really good? I have trust issues, Es. But I trust you. Doesn't that tell you something?"

They were nearly at the bottom now, and suddenly it seemed like a ticking clock, like something had to be decided before the wheel stopped turning and they had to get off. He was leaving it up to her. They could go in one direction, staying friends, staying safe and comfortable. Or they could take a different path, take a risk, see what happened. She thought about what life with Stephen would entail. Could she do it?

She didn't know. But just as surely, she knew she had to try. She would wonder *what if* forever if she didn't.

"I'd like you to stay," she said, looking into his eyes.

The moment the words were out of her mouth, it felt as if everything shifted. They were no longer dancing around desire and need but moving into relationship territory. It was heady and exciting, leaving a ball of nerves tangling around in her stomach that was both anticipation and trepidation. She was not a risk taker. But this...

This was Stephen. And she'd never been able to say no to him. Not really.

"Es," he whispered, just as their seat jolted to a halt at the bottom and the attendant reached for their safety latch.

They got out of the bucketed seat and went through the exit. Esme's heart seemed to be dancing a little jig right there in her chest, but they walked away as if nothing had changed. He didn't reach for her hand—it appeared being discreet was still a thing, and for that she was glad. She wasn't ready to go public with this. It was bad enough they'd kissed on the ride.

But then to her surprise he tugged her behind a canvas tent and pulled her into his arms, planting a kiss on her startled lips. "To tide us over until later," he said, gazing into her eyes.

This was the Stephen she remembered. Game to take a chance, laugh, have fun. The Stephen that had existed before boarding schools and universities and billion-dollar industries and titles. She loved this version of the man so much, but would that disappear once he was back in his usual world? She was enough now, but would she always be?

Enough with the negative talk, she told herself sternly. They'd agreed on one day at a time, and she wasn't going to indulge in a self-fulfilling prophecy. She stood on tiptoe instead and pressed her lips to his once more, a fleeting kiss that still echoed right down to her toes.

When she lowered her heels again, she sighed. "The hardest part is going to be pretending that nothing's changed," she said softly. "With Mum, mostly."

"But only until we're sure. We need a little time to be certain this is—"

"Exactly." Esme nodded, then changed the subject. "So what now, Lord Pemberton? More of the fair, or are you done for the day?"

He smiled at her. "More. We haven't even played Splat the Rat."

She burst out laughing. "Truly? That's what you want to do?"

"It is. Should we bet on it?"

"Only if we go to the Coconut Shy after."

"Done."

Esme couldn't remember the last time she'd had this much fun at the fair. They dissolved into laughter as she missed hitting the rat—more than once—and then Stephen nailed him on his first try with a definitive smack. At the Coconut Shy, she did better, hitting one of the three coconuts with her ball and winning a ridiculous stuffed monkey key chain. Stephen excelled here, too, hitting all three coconuts and winning a foot-tall Paddington Bear, complete with hat and little boots.

He handed it to her, looking as proud as if he'd given her a diamond necklace.

They passed a few other games, but it wasn't until Esme saw the balloon pop game that she knew she was in her element. She stepped up, paid her money, and took her darts. Different colored balloons were for different sized prizes, and she took aim at the rarest color. Stephen watched quietly as she let the dart go.

Pop.

Cheers sounded from behind her, and she smiled a little, but didn't lose her focus. She took the next dart and lined up.

Pop.

More cheers, and someone called out, "Go get 'em, Esme!" She gave a little laugh, but then took her last dart and focused again. The nights spent at the local pub with pals had a purpose after all.

There were only two purple balloons left. She pulled back her arm, kept her eye on the target, and threw the dart.

Pop.

"And the lady wins the prize!" Each of the balloons held a different prize, but she had the option to put all three together and get something huge. She did—she traded in all three of her prizes for a giant brown-and-white stuffed dog, which she then handed to Stephen. It was nearly as big as he was.

She was offered congratulations when she turned around and several pairs of eyes looked at Stephen speculatively. She merely threw him a saucy grin and they started off back toward Mary's tent, wordlessly agreeing they should check on her again. After that, Stephen would go to the tent for the judging.

Esme noticed her mother seemed tired; maybe it was the heat or all the commotion, but either way she didn't want her mum to overdo it. "Mum, why don't you let me finish here? I can pack everything back in my car at the end of the day. You don't need to be here for twelve full hours."

"Oh, I couldn't ask you to do that."

"Sure you can."

Stephen came around the corner, still holding the big, goofy-looking dog. "I can take you home after the judging, Mary. It's no trouble at all. And I can come back and help Esme pack up."

Esme caught his gaze. Ah, a plan to end the day together. Clever. And then what?

"Stephen, I…" Mary shook her head, emotion etched on her face. "Your family has already done so much for me."

He gave Esme the dog and went to the table, squatting down so he could look her in the face. "Mrs. F, you're family, too. Don't you know that?"

She flapped a hand, but Esme saw the tears in her eyes. Her mum had dedicated her life to working for the Pemberton family. It was only natural she got attached to its members.

"All right," she said, giving a nod. "Esme, you know the prices."

"I do. Don't you worry about a thing."

Stephen offered to escort Mary to the competition, but

before leaving he leaned toward Esme. "I'll be back," he said softly. "I won't be long."

Then the man she was falling in love with disappeared with her mother...the two people she cared for most in the world.

CHAPTER THIRTEEN

THE NEXT MORNING, Stephen dealt with the mess from their rushed breakfast while Esme headed back into the village to check on Mary. He knew she was worried her mum had overdone it the past few days, and Mary had seemed very tired last night, even though she'd been pleased as punch to take first place for her tarts and third for her jam.

He was finally ensconced in the study with a fresh cup of coffee while the landscape crew worked outside. The schedule for all the installations was planned, including the fountain and the planting of fall bulbs to ensure a bounty of color in the spring. He was due back at Aurora in a few more days. He had mixed feelings. He was ready to go back to work. But that also meant going back to Paris and leaving Esme. It was too soon. He wanted more time with her.

He was toying with the idea of working from Chatsworth for a while longer when the video call app rang. It was Bella, and he doubted this was a "catch up with my brother" call. He answered and turned up the volume. "*Bonjour*, Bella."

"Good morning, big brother." Bella's smile was warm. "How is your vacation?"

He raised an eyebrow. "I have been working, you know."

"Undoubtedly. But still finding time to take in local attractions?"

There was something in her voice that triggered some unease. "I suppose. I did go to the local fair yesterday to do the gooseberry judging." He laughed a little. "The burdens of being an earl. More gooseberry tarts than I could eat."

"Of course, I remember. You complained about it enough." Bella's easy tone slid into one a bit more guarded. "I meant more that you went on some rides. And not alone."

Cold sliced through his chest. "We were discreet."

"Apparently not. The *Mail* has a very large photo featuring the Ferris wheel, the Earl of Chatsworth, and Esme Flanagan."

Stephen dropped his head in his hands. "Can we never escape the damned press?"

"No, and more's the pity. A minor peer is one thing. COO of Aurora, Inc., however, is another story. A bigger one, apparently. Don't worry, big brother. We've all been there. Now it's your turn."

"You forget, I've already had my turn. Twice."

"Then you're a dab hand at it. Esme, however, isn't. Are you in love with her? Is she in love with you?" Bella didn't hold back. "It looked like things were heading in that direction this week when you brought her to dinner."

His stomach rolled over. "I can only speak for myself, Bel. I'm pretty sure this is the real thing." He lifted his head out of his hands and looked his sister in the face. She was sitting in her office in Paris, looking absolutely flawless, just as she always did. "She has reservations. And this is going to play right into them." Could he not catch a break? Less than twenty-four hours ago they'd agreed to take things slowly. Now they were in the papers.

"It's not easy loving a Pemberton," Bella acknowledged. "Anyway, listen, I wanted to talk to you to see if there was even any need for damage control. The piece isn't great, but you know as well as I do that we can't respond to every story that is simply out to sell papers. I don't think any of it is *not* true. Esme is our housekeeper's daughter. And she was married before. Those are facts."

Stephen sighed. "We thought we were discreet. No one ever bothers us when we're at the house or in the village. Dammit, Bel, we talked about taking it slowly, and now this just kicks it into high gear."

"I can have Charlotte call you. Come up with a strategy."

"No, don't. I'll see if I can find the article online. As if that'll be hard." He ran his fingers through his hair. "And then I'll decide. Chances are it'll be like most every other story. We ignore it. We both know we can't try to control what the press says about us. It's like a big game of Splat the Rat. Besides, Esme is lovely just as she is. I don't give a damn if she's the housekeeper's daughter or if she's been married before."

"You know the family is behind you. Especially if this is real. You deserve to be happy too, Stephen."

Did he? Maybe not. He hadn't been the best big brother lately. Or the best earl, either. But he was trying.

"Keep me posted," Bella was saying. "And take extra time if you need to."

"No, I'll be back next week. I've been away long enough. And by the way, you'll be receiving papers soon. You all will. I think we've finally got Anemone's inheritance sorted."

"Oh, that's lovely. I know it was a difficult thing for you."

"In the end, not so much. She's as much his child as we are. And we got to have him as our father. She missed out."

"You've changed your tune."

He shrugged and met her gaze. "I'm trying this new

thing called deciding what sort of earl I'd like to be. For the estate and for the family."

Bella's smile was soft and reminiscent of their father's. "Well, that sounds grand. Now, I've got to go, but reach out if you need help with the media storm."

They clicked off the call and Stephen sat back in his chair, swiping his hand through his hair.

He'd thought they'd have time before their relationship got out. Thought maybe they'd be lucky and slip under the paparazzi radar altogether, like they had at the Paris party. But that was a naïve hope, as it turned out. And now he somehow had to get to Esme and tell her first.

Esme had ensured her mum had a good breakfast and spent an hour tidying around the flat so Mary could get a little more rest after her busy days.

"Esme, I'm fine. I promise." Still, Mary looked a bit pale. Esme wasn't convinced but recognized that might be her own worry talking. These days she was the one who felt like the parent and found it difficult not to hover.

"Mary, you won't believe what—" Judy Brown came through the door, knocking as she entered, and halted suddenly as she saw Esme. "Oh, Esme. I…well."

"I won't believe what, Judy?" Judy was Mary's neighbor and Esme had known her for years.

"Oh, well, I…"

Esme noticed she had a newspaper in her hand—she was one of the few that still read the paper copy over digital. "What's happened, Judy?"

To Esme's surprise, Judy's face turned a bright scarlet. She cleared her throat and tried a smile. "Congratulations, Esme. I didn't realize you and Stephen Pemberton were involved. What a great catch!"

Esme stilled. What was Judy talking about?

"Esme?" Mary's voice now, and Esme added guilt to the list of feelings roiling around inside her.

"It's very new," she said quietly. "We weren't really planning on going public…yet." She added *yet* because obviously they would have had to at some point. "How did you hear, Judy?"

Judy's expression softened. "It's in the paper today, love."

In the paper. Esme's body went numb. "May I see it, please?"

Judy looked like she'd been caught shoplifting—positively scandalized. "Now, Esme, you remember that reporters go for whatever will cause a sensation. It's just fluff, that's what it is."

"Clearly it's caused a sensation with you. May I see, please? Otherwise I'll just go find it online." Her voice was steadier than she might have expected, considering her insides were quaking.

"You'd better give it to her, Judy." That from Mary.

Judy handed over the paper; it was already flipped to the correct page and folded over. Esme's heart sank to her toes as the picture took up a quarter of the page, with the ridiculous headline, *Upstairs, Downstairs…*

The picture was, of course, of them kissing on the Ferris wheel.

Not a difficult photo, she supposed, considering the paps used massive zoom lenses that would surely cause them cervical spine issues later in life. That intimate moment splashed all over the paper and presumably the internet.

But the worst was the article itself. "Red-haired beauty" she supposed was all right, but it went on to highlight her as "Esme Flanagan, hotel housekeeper and divorcée" as if they were flaws, and also that her mum was the housekeeper at the manor. It painted her as a nobody—well, not a nobody, but a "healthy, country girl" which she knew was a dig at her figure. It pointed out her jeans and plain top as firmly tongue-in-cheek "high street chic," not a compliment at all. The tone beneath it all was that she was far below Stephen and how the writers couldn't blame him for tasting the "local flavors."

Oh, that last line was disgusting.

As calmly as she could, she handed the paper back to Judy. "Mum, you'll be all right for a bit, yeah?"

"Of course, darling." Mary's tone was subdued, as if she knew Esme's temper was holding on by a very thin thread.

Then Esme left the flat and walked straight to her car. There was only one place to go—Chatsworth Manor. And when she got there, she had to do what she hadn't been strong enough, smart enough to do yesterday when he'd suggested they make their relationship into more.

She had to say goodbye to Stephen.

Stephen heard the front door slam and knew it was Esme. He took a breath and shut the cover of his laptop, but he already knew everything that had been said in that horrendous article. Honestly, didn't people get tired of being disgusting and invasive?

Not that he cared. It wasn't the first time he'd had half a page of coverage. But this was Esme's biggest fear. By the sound of the heavy oak door, she'd either seen or heard about it.

She appeared at the study door, hair falling out of its pins, cheeks flushed, eyes snapping.

"You've heard," he said, keeping his voice neutral. He didn't want to make it sound like a dire thing, but neither did he want to brush this off. The article hadn't exactly been complimentary.

"One of Mum's neighbors had a paper this morning. You?"

He hooked a thumb toward the laptop. "Video chat with Bella."

Esme made a sound of disgust. "Your family must be appalled."

"Appalled at what?"

She came further into the room. "Um, did you read it? Earl of Chatsworth *in flagrante* with the country bumpkin who changes sheets for a living."

Stephen could be a patient man, but he was also a man of strong opinions, and right now he was annoyed that the classist garbage in the paper was being repeated.

"First of all, I would hope you know my family better than that," he replied, standing in front of the desk. "When have I ever looked down on you because of your job? What about how the family welcomed you just a few nights ago? They're irritated at the press, not at you, and Bella wanted to know if we wanted any help with damage control. They, like me, do not care about what you do for a living. They care that whoever I'm with makes me happy. Full stop."

That set her back on her heels a bit, and he hoped she was taking a few moments to cool down and think things through.

"Moreover," he said, "I can't believe you just said the words *in flagrante*."

Her gaze met his, mellowed a little, and her lips curved the tiniest bit. "I might have been reading a few too many historical romances," she admitted. "But seriously...the Ferris wheel? What paper sends someone to cover a tiny village fair with a few rides and some gooseberry jam?"

Stephen sighed. "Honestly, it could have been any local journo with a decent zoom lens, on site to cover the event. Selling that photo to a paper is pure profit. Then a few online searches and bam! You have yourself a story."

Esme began to pace. "But it was so…so…" She halted, turned to face him. "It made me sound awful."

She started pacing again.

"I know, darling, and I know it is exactly what you were afraid of. The criticism, after all the hard work you've done since your divorce. Which is not a dirty word, like they made it sound. You left and made a healthy choice for you. Look, the papers and websites are after eyeballs. The more sensational, the better."

She stopped and looked at him again. "This isn't your first experience."

"No, but it's yours, and I remember how awful it was when Gabi left me at the altar. We actually ended up in full damage control mode. This time, though, it's easy. My answer will always be that I've fallen for the loveliest woman on the planet who makes me happy."

She was at a loss for words for a few moments, but then she shook her head and tears shone in her eyes. "I don't think I can do this, Stephen. It took our one day at a time thing and obliterated it. Now not only does the village know, but also the whole country."

He took a deep breath, wanting to stay calm rather than give in to the panic that was strangling his lungs. He didn't want to lose her, not when they were just getting started. "Es, the thing is, now that the story is out there, people are going to talk. They're going to do that whether you're with me or not. I'm so sorry this happened, and so soon, but the best thing is to ignore it. Get on with our lives. It'll blow over. It always does."

"That is easy to say when you're the hero of the story, and I'm the gold digger with a spotty romantic history and an empty bank account. When you're the handsome billionaire and I'm plain and…what was the word they used? Dowdy."

He moved toward her. "Esme Flanagan, you are not, have never been, and could never possibly be, dowdy."

"I've had those jeans for at least five years and the shirt was one from the bargain rack."

"So?" He frowned and reached out, holding her upper arms in his hands. "Why does it matter so much what one person thinks? Or even many people? We know the truth."

She pulled away and shook her head. "I can't. Today's story was me being dowdy and poor. If I stay with you, I'll be in the public eye more and more. How long before they comment on the size of my breasts or hips, the blemishes on my face, start picking apart my body?"

"You'd give away what we have, what we could have, because of the words of a few journalists? What we have... what I feel for you..."

"You don't understand." She took a breath and faced him, her eyes stormy. "Do you know how long it took me, how many therapy sessions, just to be able to have fish and chips on a Friday night at the Lizard? Two years. How long I went before I stopped analyzing everything I put in my mouth or stepping on the scale every day? Do you know how hard I've had to work to gain the upper hand over my insecurities?"

His mouth fell open.

"How often I went home from an event and laid awake most of the night replaying conversations and wondered if I sounded stupid, or talked too much, or embarrassed myself?" Her voice rose. "I was supposed to be perfect, you see. And no one is perfect, and I know that. But having some stranger point out all my sore spots...it just takes me right back there again, Stephen. I'm not strong enough to do this. I wanted to be, but I'm... I'm not."

Desperation clawed at his lungs. "Then let me be strong for you. Please, don't give up on us because of this. I have my wounds too, Es. Ones that terrify me. But I'm willing to step out there and trust you. Can't you trust me, too?"

Her lower lip trembled just a bit and her eyes glistened. "I'm scared, Stephen. I'm scared of everything that's not in the neat little corner I've made for myself."

He understood that, perhaps more than she realized. He'd had his life laid out for him for years. There was comfort and safety in it, but at some point he had to step out on a limb and take a chance.

"Esme, I love you. Please don't walk away."

She took a step back, momentarily stunned. Then he watched as she regained her composure and lifted her chin. "You told me yesterday that I needed to be honest and up-front with you. I'm doing that. It's not fair to let this drag on. I'll… I'll only hurt you worse."

She was leaving him.

After years of closing himself off, of swearing he was done with affairs of the heart, he finally fell in love. And what did he get for it? Not a damned thing. The kicker was that one woman had wanted him for all that he had but not for himself. And the woman standing before him wanted him but wanted nothing to do with his kind of life.

He closed his eyes. The ache in his chest to stop hollowed him out, stealing his hope and joy.

"You're right," he said, his voice tight. "I did say that."

He'd also told her he loved her. But she hadn't said it back. Other than staring at him for ten seconds, she hadn't said anything about it at all.

He turned away, devastated and determined not to show it.

"I should go. I… You're leaving in a few days anyway. I can call Lucinda and get her to come back a little early and she can look after whatever you need."

"Whatever you want," he said hollowly.

There was a pause, a quietness between them. He could tell she was still behind him, but if he looked at her he was going to lose it, and dammit, he would not fall apart again. Not like he had with Bridget.

"I'm sorry, Stephen. Desperately sorry. I thought I could do this, but when I saw that article this morning… I can't do a lifetime of this. It's better to end it now."

He took in a shaky breath. "Then go."

He felt her leave, felt her absence in the room once she was gone, and heard the front door close behind her. The house echoed, empty once more.

Then he sat down at the desk and pulled out the pocket watch from the drawer.

"Third time wasn't the charm, Dad," he whispered, turning it over in his hands. "But I promise to do this right. The estate will go on."

And maybe the promise seemed hollow at the moment, but it was all he had.

Esme couldn't face her mother until the next day. Instead Phoebe had showed up at her flat with two bottles of wine and a bag of dark chocolate truffles, and kept Esme's glass filled as she alternated between crying and resolving that she didn't need Stephen at all.

Now it was nearly noon, her head was still in the dull thud stage, and she couldn't imagine the thought of eating anything. Mary took one look at her and lifted an eyebrow.

"Would you like some tea? Or hair of the dog?" She gave a sniff. "Cabernet?"

"Pinot Noir," Esme said, wincing. "Peppermint tea, maybe?"

Mary went to put on the kettle.

"You look better today," Esme said. "You got some rest?"

"I did. Worried about you, but you're a big girl. I figured you'd sort it. You want to tell me what happened?"

Esme reached into the cupboard for a tea bag. "You were right, Mum. It was a stupid idea. We ignored all the problems and got involved anyway."

Mary was quiet for a long moment.

"Loving a man like Stephen is hard," Mary finally said. "There's just so…much. Yes, you two come from different worlds. That never really mattered before, but it's a big adjustment now. He's a public figure, therefore you will be, too. And the words will rarely be nice."

"Because nice doesn't sell papers or get website hits," Esme agreed. "Already, I'm painted as not being good enough for him."

Mary turned her head to stare at Esme, her eyes flashing. "That's codswallop."

Esme laughed, though it hurt her head. "Thank you for saying that, Mum."

"Esme, my love. This has nothing to do with whether you are good enough for Stephen or not. Of course you are."

"He said he loves me."

Another small silence, and then, "Oh. Well, that does change things, doesn't it?"

When Esme glanced over, Mary's eyes had softened.

Esme sighed. "He's so different from Evan. There's never a criticism. Never pointing out my flaws and using them against me."

"I never realized that about Evan, you know. He seemed so…lovely."

"He could be. But living with him… Mum, back then I chose the relationship I wanted rather than the one I had, if that makes sense. I didn't have one based on mutual affection and respect. It was…conditional. This isn't like that. But…" She dropped the tea bag into a mug. "But it changed how I saw myself. When I saw that article yesterday, I realized that I won't be able to withstand that sort of visibility and comment for the rest of my life. It doesn't matter if I love him. I would be unhappy, and I would make him unhappy."

Esme looked over and saw tears in her mother's eyes. "You know I had a wonderful relationship with your father. I wish we could have had so many more years together. And I've never remarried because I never met anyone who could live up to that. It's been lonely, Es. But I wouldn't trade those years with your dad for anything. If you love Stephen…don't be so quick to toss him away."

Esme's eyes filled with tears, and she swiped them away with a hand. "I thought you didn't want us involved. That it crossed the line."

"When it's love, it's different. Love just is." Mary folded Esme into a hug. "Sweetheart, if this is how Stephen makes you feel, you must at least try. You will regret it forever if you don't. And maybe it won't work, and you'll have to pick up the pieces, but pieces can always be picked up again. Second chances don't come around every day."

"Mum," she said, her voice thick with emotion. "I don't know if I'm strong enough."

"I don't want to see you get hurt, darling. But I also don't want to see you miss out on something wonderful. And Stephen's a good man. Not perfect, but a good man."

"I need time to think."

"Of course you do." The kettle whistled and Mary poured water into two mugs, the bright scent of peppermint filling the kitchen. "Let's forget all about it for a while and make some biscuits."

And so Esme dealt with her heartache the same way she had nearly twenty years ago: in the kitchen with Mary, rolling out biscuit dough and humming along to the radio. And when she went home that night, she got out her sticky note pad and wrote, "I am strong." She stuck one, then two, then six, then a dozen of them on the bathroom mirror until she could stand back and see them all, her face framed in the middle.

"I am strong," she repeated.

And if she said it enough, maybe she'd believe it.

CHAPTER FOURTEEN

A WEEK HAD PASSED, during which Stephen had made the decision to base more of his time out of the manor house and less in Paris. Maybe he was a sucker for punishment for staying close to Esme, but he didn't want to lose all the positive progress he'd made. He was still dedicated to taking the title and making it his own. And he still saw Chatsworth Manor as his home, even though now there were memories of Esme in every corner.

He was standing at the top of the memorial garden, wishing for his father's wisdom, when Aurora, here after a quick visit to see Charlotte, appeared at his side.

"Wish he were here," she said softly.

"Me too, Maman." He sighed and put his hands in his pockets. "I wish I could talk to him. Have him help me make sense of everything."

"Oh, *mon petit*, of course. What is that saying...? 'It is lonely at the top.' You are navigating this alone and trying so hard not to show any weakness. That is a heavy burden, Stephen."

He nodded, his throat tight.

"Maman, I know it wasn't always perfect between you. There was Anemone...you knew about her, but you and Dad...you made it through. And your love was real. We all felt it growing up."

Aurora sighed. "It took a lot of work to get past what had happened. There are mistakes and then there are mistakes, if you know what I mean. But we loved each other. We made the decision to make it work, and that took a lot of talking. A lot. The only way to heal wounds is to acknowledge they exist, and then work through them. When you're doing that with another person, that means communicating."

He nodded. "I screwed things up with Esme."

"We figured."

He laughed then, and a burden lifted off his shoulders. Maman never minced words, and he loved her for it. "Being a part of the Pembertons…it's a lot to ask. The money, the fame…it comes with a trade-off. One that, for her own reasons, she doesn't feel she can take on."

Aurora turned to face him, her face wise and beautiful, and put her hand on his cheek. "I'm sorry," she said. "I remember when I first started going to functions with your father. Do you know, his mother brought someone in to give me etiquette classes so I wouldn't embarrass myself?"

"That sounds horrid."

"Maybe, but it saved my pride more than once. Oh, your father didn't care. It was I who didn't want to look foolish and provincial. And back then there wasn't the internet and social media where things could go viral in half a second."

He considered that.

"Give her time, Stephen. Everything happened so quickly between you. In ordinary circumstances that's overwhelming. When it's our family, it's exponentially more complicated. If you love her, don't give up hope."

"I do love her," he admitted. "And the one thing I was most afraid of happened." He met his mother's wise eyes. "She left me. Like Bridget did."

"Bridget was a fool. Esme is smart. And she loves you. It was written all over her face. Patience, darling."

"Thank you, Maman."

"You deserve happiness. If it's with Esme, then you need to take the first step. And the whole family is behind you. Don't forget that, either."

"I love you, Maman. Dad was a lucky, lucky man."

"Yes," she said, "he was." She looped her arm through his. "Now, show me around the garden and tell me about all your plans."

The next Friday, Stephen found Esme at the pub, having her weekly night out with Phoebe. Phoebe noticed him first, and she reached over and tapped Esme on the arm.

Esme looked up. Their eyes met, and the jolt ran straight from his heart to the soles of his feet. God, she was beautiful. Her bright hair was pulled up in a messy bun, a halo of fire that he wanted to sink his fingers into. And her face…those moss-green eyes widened and then flickered with what he hoped was longing. He certainly felt that way.

"Esme," he said as he reached the table. He dragged his gaze away from her and looked down at her friend. "And you must be Phoebe."

"I am," Phoebe replied. "And I'm also finished. You can have my seat, Stephen."

"No, you don't have to—" Esme said, reaching for Phoebe.

"You two need to talk," Phoebe said, picking up her handbag. But she skirted around Stephen and went to Esme, giving her a kiss on the cheek. "Call me later," she said.

And then she was gone, leaving the two of them alone.

"May I?" Stephen asked, motioning toward the empty chair. Esme nodded.

The waitress came by and took Phoebe and Esme's plates, and Stephen ordered a Pimm's out of more of a courtesy than a need for a drink. When she left again, Stephen met Esme's gaze, and the first thing he said was, "I'm sorry, Esme."

Her throat bobbed as she swallowed. "What for?" she asked. "I'm the one who walked out on you."

Business was steady but not so loud that they couldn't have a conversation, though perhaps somewhere more private would have been better. His Pimm's arrived and he took a sip, but then put it down again. "For the article. For not being patient. For…well, that you had to go through any of that stuff at all."

"I reacted badly too, instead of sitting on my feelings for a bit. I got so mad, and then so scared. I couldn't see any other option."

Did that mean she wasn't quite as certain as she'd been that morning?

"I've been a wreck since you left," he admitted, holding her gaze, his heart pounding as he made himself utterly vulnerable to her for a second time. But the difference was he still trusted her. Esme was always straight with him. "You walking out poked me right in my sore spot. But Es, when we were together, I felt more alive, more myself, than I have in… I don't know how long. It was like someone came in and turned on a light, making everything bright and clear. That's something I didn't think was possible."

Esme reached for her water glass and took a drink, then put it back down, as if buying time to find the right words. "I honestly thought the part of me that wanted love and romance had dried up and died." She gave a little laugh. "Clearly it hadn't. You made me feel beautiful, and desired, and accepted."

"Because you are all of those things. And anyone who

doesn't think so isn't someone who matters." He reached over and took her hand that rested on the table. She twined her fingers with his, a tentative link. "Can we talk now? Do you want to go somewhere more private?"

She nodded, and he quickly turned and caught the eye of the waitress, motioning for the check. "I'll look after this," he said. "Then we can go wherever you like."

Esme gave a quick nod and gathered her purse, but he noticed her hands were shaking. He told himself not to get his hopes up, but as she turned her green eyes up to look at him, he couldn't help himself.

Esme had simply planned on a chill supper with Phoebe. She hadn't even known Stephen was back in town. But when he walked in, all her senses kicked into overdrive. Nothing had changed for her. Nothing. They needed to talk, but all she wanted to do was step into the strength of his embrace and forget it all ever happened.

He put his hand at her elbow, a purely solicitous move, but tingles ran up her arm at the casual touch. She had to face facts: she was far from being over Stephen Pemberton.

They left the pub and walked to a nearby park, where there was a little more privacy. A bench sat beneath a canopy of oaks, the late-day sun filtering through the leaves. "Shall we?" Stephen asked, and she nodded.

They sat. Esme turned toward Stephen, tucking her left leg under her right so she could face him. She reached out and took his hand—presumptuous, maybe, but she didn't want to go longer without touching him.

"When did you get back?" she asked.

He smiled. "I never left. Lucinda has been running the house. She's not you, though. Anyway, what you said was true. This is my home. Not just because I'm the earl but because it's in my heart. I'm changing things to spend more time here. I'll split things a little more evenly between here and Paris. It's an easy trip anyway."

He hadn't run off to Paris. He'd been here the whole time.

"That day at the fair," she began, her voice trembling just a little, "I could see my life changing, and I knew that our time together was coming to a close. I was already thinking about how we were going to try to make things work, living in two different countries most of the time. But when you said we could take it day by day, it seemed perfect."

"Until the paper."

She nodded. "Until then. And I'll be honest, Stephen, the thought of facing that kind of scrutiny still fills me with anxiety."

"There's an important difference, though," he said softly. "Evan was the person who should have cherished you and loved you unconditionally. He was the person who mattered, and he didn't value you. But Es, you have to realize that I'd be right there beside you. You don't have to prove anything to me or be anyone other than the wonderful woman you already are. The tabloids, the gossip rags... those people don't matter, and they don't know you. I do. I, and the entire family, would be right there with you."

She hadn't considered that before. She thought of Bella and her horrible scars from her accident. How Jacob had gone from being a private security guard to being Charlotte's husband. Surely he'd had some insecure moments as someone who hadn't grown up in the same world as the Pembertons.

But thinking about both couples during the family dinner made her think that perhaps the love Burke had for Bella, and Charlotte had for Jacob, had helped deal with their vulnerabilities while in the public eye.

Because the Pembertons knew how to do one thing brilliantly: support each other.

Her heart was hammering now. Did they actually still stand a chance? It seemed they might, because here they were, talking and listening. Really listening.

"I let fear take over." She lifted her gaze to his again, found herself lost in the dark depths. This was the man who'd kissed her in the fort, changing their relationship. Who had touched her with hands like fire in moments of passion, then worshiped her with gentleness. Who had cared for her mother and told her she was family. He was the man who made her laugh and made her heart sing again. "I wasn't strong enough."

"And I didn't fight for you," he replied. "You needed to be able to count on me, and instead I let you walk away because of my own hurt pride."

"We're both a hot mess," she admitted. But she smiled at him anyway. *I am strong,* she reminded herself. And he was here again. Maybe it wasn't really over…

"I was scared of being hurt, but do you know what scares me the most now?"

She could barely breathe. "What?"

"Thinking I might have lost you forever. Going through the rest of my life without you. I can't promise I won't make mistakes." He lowered his gaze and shook his head. "I've been trying to be perfect for too long." He lifted his head again. "But if you want to work this out, I'm in. I'm a hundred percent in, because I love you. I think I always have. I know I always will."

A tear slid from the corner of her eye and down her cheek, and she dashed it away. She wasn't a weeper! But what he'd said just now was so honest and true she couldn't help it. "I could say the exact same thing. You're not Evan. I knew that, but I used what happened as an excuse because everything was too perfect and it scared the hell out of me. But life is dreary without you in it now. I think... if you really mean it... I think I'd like to try. Because Stephen? I love you too. So much."

He closed his eyes for a moment, as if absorbing the words. "I mean it," he said, opening his eyes, and then leaned forward to kiss her.

His lips were soft and beguiling, familiar and yet new, because this was a new beginning. For once, she didn't care that they were in a public park, didn't care that someone might snap a picture and sell it to a paper or post it online. She loved him. And he loved her. Shutting out the critics would be a work in progress, but she would not let her hang-ups make her miss out on happiness. She was stronger than that. And when she wasn't, she'd learn to rely on the people who loved her.

"So we're going to do this?" he asked, pulling away a bit.

She nodded. "We are. And it won't always be easy. I think it happened so fast, and seemed so perfect, that when we hit a bump we both panicked. Let's not do that this time. Let's turn toward each other when we're scared, all right?"

"God, I love you, Esme," he said, pulling her into his embrace. "And I've been thinking. I can certainly change the balance of my time between Paris and here. I've already started. Charlotte does it, after all. That way you're close to your mum."

"And I don't have to work at the inn. I can find something else. But I do want something, Stephen. I'm not built to be arm candy."

He laughed then, a soft, full, happy laugh. "You can do whatever you like. I know you. No one is going to stop you from getting what you want."

She looked at him for a long moment, considering his

words. If she really wanted to embrace her future and leave her past behind, with all the criticism and gaslighting, there was one thing she could do to really reach out and grasp what her heart desired.

"In that case, Stephen…" She clung to his hand, her stomach trembling but her heart beating steady and strong. "Do you think you might marry me?"

CHAPTER FIFTEEN

THE WEDDING OF Stephen Pemberton, Earl of Chatsworth, and Esme Flanagan promised to be the event of the year. At least that was what the magazines and papers said as they scrambled to unearth details of the upcoming private nuptials.

The entire family had descended upon Chatsworth Manor for the November occasion. Mrs. Flanagan, recovered from her final two chemo treatments, was back part-time, helping Lucinda and the rest of the staff manage the house. Despite her daughter marrying the earl, she'd declared that being at Chatsworth Manor was where she belonged, and that's where she intended to stay. To Mary's relief, Stephen had agreed, though he'd told her that the moment she wanted to retire, she would have a house and be provided for. Esme had been delighted. And she rather suspected that retirement would come sooner rather than later, once she and Stephen started their family.

Which she hoped would be soon. But not too soon. They were still adjusting—and enjoying—their time alone.

As alone as one could be in a big family that all worked together. Except for her. Stephen had already gifted her with an early, perfect wedding present—the deed to a boutique hotel in Paris. Her dream of running her own inn was coming true. As soon as the honeymoon was over, she would install a new manager who would run things when she and Stephen were here at the estate.

The morning of the wedding she woke in a different bed—not Stephen's. They'd both agreed to sleep separately the night before the ceremony, not that she'd slept all that well. She was too nervous, too excited. Her dress hung in the wardrobe, her shoes, too…and in an hour the house would be a hive of activity as everyone got ready. The family section of the chapel would be fairly empty, because she and Stephen had agreed to having his brothers and sisters as bridesmaids and groomsmen, though Gabi, being nearly seven months pregnant, had suggested she sit with Aurora. Esme had asked Phoebe to be her maid of honor, and Will was Stephen's best man.

A knock came on the door. "Come in," she called, and to her surprise it was her mum, bringing her a breakfast tray.

"Hello, sweetheart," she said, smiling. "I couldn't resist. You'll find it hard to eat later, so I wanted you to have a good breakfast."

"Thanks, Mum. Sit with me?"

"Of course."

There was coffee and toast and beautifully scrambled eggs, just the way she liked, as well as a bowl of fresh strawberries. "I feel so spoiled."

"After today you're going to be Lady Pemberton. A countess. I think you might have to get used to it."

Esme laughed. "I don't think so. It's not really who I am, title or not."

"Do you have what you need? I think your hairdresser is due to arrive at nine."

"I'm going to take a nice lavender bath. Try to relax."

After breakfast Mary left, and after a luxurious soak,

Esme dressed in her undergarments and a silk robe. Phoebe arrived, followed by the hairdresser team—there were eight women requiring styling—and the makeup team, all from Aurora Paris. By noon, Esme was buffed and polished, dressed in an Aurora original gown—a gorgeous concoction with long, lace sleeves, appliques, and a cathedral-length veil that had made her sigh. She was about to become a countess, but she felt like a princess.

Phoebe was next to her, dressed in Esme's favorite emerald green. The bridesmaids' dresses were a clean and simple cut of the finest silk and rustled a little as Phoebe came to her with her bouquet, a stunning arrangement of white and cream flowers.

"You look… Oh, Es." Phoebe's eyes filled with tears. "Like a miracle. I'm so happy for you."

"I'm happy you're with me today." She looked around the suite. It was full of the women of her new family: Bella, Gabi, Sophie, Charlotte, Anemone, even Aurora, who'd stopped by with champagne once the clock ticked over twelve. There was chatter and laughter. Mary was there, too, sipping from a glass of champagne, talking to Aurora—for this one day she'd agreed to be a mother of the bride and not a housekeeper. Bella had insisted on taking Mary on a trip to find the perfect dress. Now her mum was dressed in a stunning navy gown, with a new wig framing her face until her hair came back in.

She was happy they all were there. And laughed when she caught Gabi's eye and the woman sent her a thumbs-up.

It seemed like no time at all that they were scheduled to leave for the chapel, and even though it was a short walk within the estate, they had cars lined up waiting as the weather had been showery all morning. She took a breath, clutched her bouquet, asked Phoebe for the tenth time if she had Stephen's wedding ring, then descended the stairs to begin the trip to the altar.

Stephen stood at the front of the chapel, his knee locking and unlocking. None of the usual platitudes eased his nerves. The last time he'd been in the family chapel, he'd been left at the altar. It was hard to forget that day, but he knew that Esme was entirely different. They were in love. God, so in love he didn't know what to do with it all. And soon…in a few moments…she'd be walking down the aisle to him, and they would take their vows.

Will stood beside him and leaned over with advice. "Don't pass out. Maman has just been ushered in."

Stephen looked over his shoulder at Aurora, who smiled at him. Then he caught a glimpse of Christophe escorting Mary to her seat and he knew it was time. The ushers joined Stephen and Will at the front of the chapel and the vicar stepped forward.

The music changed.

Behind him, Anemone, Sophie, Charlotte and Bella made their way to the front, and he saw Phoebe take her place to his left. She smiled up at him, and he smiled back—he quite liked Phoebe. And then the music changed again, and there was an audible gasp from the guests. His pulse hammered as he imagined her stepping to the door…

"Oh, my God." That was Will's voice, and it was full of awe. "Stephen, she's gorgeous."

Stephen turned around and there she was. A vision in white lace, her veil trailing behind her, her fiery curls shining beneath the sheer fabric. His throat tightened as he realized she was wearing Maman's wedding diamonds.

She was perfect. And she was walking toward him just this minute, a soft smile on her face, her green eyes alight with happiness and hope.

His miracle.

For the briefest moment, he was transported back nearly thirty years, waiting for her at the fort, happy when he saw her skipping along the path to meet him. They had come so far. Even then, she'd been the sunshine in his day. Now he'd have her for all of his days.

And as she reached the altar and he took her hand, he knew that his heart had finally come home.

* * * * *

COMING SOON!

We really hope you enjoyed reading this book. If you're looking for more romance, be sure to head to the shops when new books are available on

Thursday 1st September

To see which titles are coming soon, please visit

millsandboon.co.uk/nextmonth

MILLS & BOON®

Coming next month

CAPTURING THE CEO'S GUARDED HEART
Rebecca Winters

The Eiffel Tower stood 1063 feet tall on the Champ de Mars, not that far from the jewellery store. Anelise noticed the seven-thirty traffic moving toward it had grown heavier, but she couldn't take her eyes off the engagement ring and bracelet.

"It's hard to believe that some people can actually buy the kind of jewels I'm wearing. Tonight, a man put sparkling jewels on my finger, wrist and ears. I know I only get to wear them for a little while, but I've been granted an old wish. When you conceived the plan to expose the culprit, I never dreamed I'd have the time of my life doing it with you."

Nic had to stop for a light and looked at her. "If you want to know the truth, I've never had more fun and I find it astonishing that there's a woman alive this easy to work with, let alone please."

His words found their way inside her until they reached the parking area outside the famous monument. "It's a good thing I've already ordered dinner. From the look of the crowd gathering, we'll be lucky to make it before closing time."

"Except they wouldn't close knowing you're coming," she quipped. Together they made their way through people taking pictures and entered the exclusive elevator taking them directly to the restaurant. His strong arms went around her as they ascended, making her feel safe and cherished. Remember this isn't real, Anelise. Don't get carried away.

The maître d'hotel met them the second they stepped inside. He fell all over Nic after greeting him.

"Marcel? May I introduce my beautiful fiancée, Anelise Lavigny."

"It's my great pleasure to meet you, Mademoiselle Lavigny," the older man said with a twinkle in his eyes. He showed them to a table with lighted candles, centred at the window overlooking Paris. The other tables had been placed further away to give them privacy.

Nic reached for her left hand and massaged her palm. "So far we've aroused the insatiable curiosity of everyone in this room including undercover journalists. By the time we finish dinner and leave, it's possible the person responsible for bringing us together will be among the diners."

"Let's hope so."

The sommelier poured the vintage wine Nic had ordered. He raised his glass and clinked the one she was holding. "To the most successful adventure of our lives."

Anelise couldn't help but smile.

Continue reading
CAPTURING THE CEO'S GUARDED HEART
Rebecca Winters

Available next month
www.millsandboon.co.uk